...ers, the BBC and the *Financial Times*. She writes regularly for *Foreign Policy* magazine and the *Spectator*. She is the author of *In the Footsteps of Mr Kurtz*, a portrait of Mobutu's Congo and winner of the PEN James Sterne Prize for non-fiction, *I Didn't Do It for You*, which focuses on the African nation of Eritrea, and *It's Our Turn to Eat*, which tells the story of John Githongo, a Kenyan whistle-blower. *Borderlines* is her first novel.

Praise for *Borderlines*:

'Wrong's greatest achievement is Paula herself. Her voice crackles across the page, compelling and persuasive, witty and charming, sometimes acerbic ... It is a delight to discover Wrong's particular gifts as a novelist ... Sensory details are conveyed elegantly and briskly, and the prose is rich in physicality ... A good, old-fashioned legal thriller'

F. T. Kola, *Guardian*

'In its Graham Greene-like exploration of human failings, *Borderlines* discourses brilliantly on the politics of cartography ... Africa is rendered in vividly glowing prose ... Written with narrative verve and a reporter's eye for detail'

Ian Thomson, *Financial Times*

'No other writer I know of is capable of making Africa seem just as accessibly screwed up as our own messy political backyards. It helps to explain why refugees from the Horn are queuing for boats in Libya, and portrays the searing disappointment of fighting a liberation war for years only to be betrayed by your own side. That disappointment isn't African; it's universal'

Lionel Shriver, author of *We Need to Talk about Kevin*

'Beautifully ju... ...Wrong knows her subjects –

...ctator

thoughtful investigation o Western engagement ...
But Africa is no mere backdrop for Western angst, and
Michela Wrong brings the place and its characters to life in
a stylish novel'   Iain Pears, author of
An Instance of the Fingerpost

'I read *Borderlines* in a single sitting. Paula Shackleton is an
anti-heroine for our times: clever, spiky, complex and flawed.
Michela Wrong has gained a reputation as a fluid, perceptive
writer of non-fiction – now she has added a twist of imagination
to create a gripping novel'   Lindsey Hilsum,
author of *Sandstorm*

Also by Michela Wrong

NON-FICTION

It's Our Turn to Eat
I Didn't Do It for You
In the Footsteps of Mr Kurtz

MICHELA WRONG

BORDERLINES

4th Estate • *London*

4th Estate
An imprint of HarperCollins Publishers
1 London Bridge Street
London SE1 9GF
www.4thEstate.co.uk

First published in Great Britain by 4th Estate in 2015
This paperback edition first published in 2016

1

Typeset in Sabon by Palimpsest Book Production Ltd, Falkirk, Stirlingshire

Printed and bound in Great Britain by Clays Ltd, St Ives plc

MIX
Paper from
responsible sources
FSC
www.fsc.org   **FSC™ C007454**

For Jessica, who had to wait her turn

Nothing that mankind has accomplished to this date equals the replacement of war by court rulings, based on international law.

Andrew Carnegie,
US steel magnate and philanthropist,
August 1913

If you fly often, this may have happened to you. You're stuck in Economy, folded awkwardly against a window, legs twined like pipe-cleaners, half awake. It's dark outside, the window blind has been pulled down, and you're where you hate being: five miles high, defying the laws of gravity and plain common sense. The slight ache in your feet, which have been pressing upwards into the bottom of the seat in front (someone, after all, has to do the hard work of keeping this machine aloft), confirms this fact. You are bitterly aware that the atmosphere inside the plane has turned into one troubled communal fart. And then, quite suddenly, it happens. With no real warning – perhaps a brief bumpiness you assume to be high-altitude turbulence – *the plane makes impact*. For a moment, you know that you are dying, because this mid-air collision, so high above the Earth, will leave no survivors, no body parts even. You convulse in your seat. You gasp aloud and your neighbour gives you a worried glance. And then your brain executes a massive feat of intellectual recalibration. You flick up the blind with a trembling hand. That's the ground outside the window – zipping past you terrifyingly fast, it's true, but in a controlled and orderly manner. *This is a landing, you idiot.* Sleeping, you missed the change in engine tone, the dipping of the nose, the minutes of what feel like freefall, the clunk of landing gear descending.

Landing in mid-air. A sobering exercise in shattered assumptions, the shock realisation of ludicrously false premises. When I look back on my time in Lira, it often seems like a version of that heart-stopping mid-flight experience, extended over the space of a year. Well, what can I say? Some people are just a bit slow to catch on.

1

By two a.m. the glare was really beginning to bother me. African airports don't, on the whole, go in for soft lighting, and Lira International was no exception. I didn't need a mirror to know what I looked like in the greenish-white light given off by the fluorescent strip running the length of the ceiling: baggy-eyed, sallow, prematurely old.

I lay on the stiff acrylic carpet, my bag under one ear as a makeshift pillow, hands between my knees, pretending to ignore my guard. He was actually in the next room, but the door had been propped open, and since most of the wall separating the two rooms was glass, he could see me without leaving his desk, where he sat reading a newspaper, occasionally sipping a glass of dark tea.

Earlier, I had gone through the outrage, shocked innocence and I-demand-an-explanation routine that seems *de rigueur* when a young white woman is suddenly, mysteriously, diverted from a path leading to a boarding gate, the trundle across the tarmac in the warm night air and then, *aah*, the microcosm of Western civilisation that is the modern aircraft, a little bubble of agreed conventions and soothing yogic rituals. I'd declaimed at considerable length on my key role in the Legal Office of the President. I'd dropped my boss's name, demanded to speak to the presidential adviser and brandished my files, to emphasise how vital it was that I reach The Hague in time for the announcement of a historic ruling that would shape his country's future.

Green Eyes, as I had mentally tagged him – like any good lawyer, I'd asked for his name but he'd only grunted – hadn't turned a hair. The absence of reaction, in fact, was the most terrifying thing about the whole affair. An insincere apology, an attempt at intimidation, anything would have been better than the total lack of expression he'd shown as he had turned on me his light, limpid gaze – so disconcerting in this country of dark brown eyes – and said, 'No flight for you tonight.'

He had taken me to identify my luggage so it could be removed from the pile. He had led me to Immigration to have my passport's exit stamp crossed. He had walked me to the kiosk where I'd paid my airport tax to get the dollars returned. Each of these small transactions had been conducted in silence by the officials who had processed me twenty minutes earlier, this time without the friendly smiles. They knew now I was toxic, leprous. Then Green Eyes had brought me upstairs to this room, where the only furniture was a desk, pushed against the wall, and a plastic chair, and indicated I wait.

My first reaction had been to get out my mobile and start composing a text to Winston. I was just typing 'detained at' when Green Eyes held out his hand. I handed it over, unzipped my shoulder bag and took out my laptop as if to start it up. He held out his hand again, this time more brusquely, and I passed over my weathered Dell. 'No computer. No mobile,' said Green Eyes. 'All is forbidden.'

Over the next hour and a half, I'd watched through the glass as the other passengers on the flight went through the routine I, too, had been planning: the pointless trawl of the airport shop in search of suitable presents (biography of Julius Nyerere, anyone? Copy of the Ministry of Health's five-year plan?), a beer at the bar, cigarette on the terrace, the cluster at the boarding gate, a final cursory search before disappearing through the doors.

A few threw curious, embarrassed glances in my direction. Wasn't that the deputy director of UNHCR, the UN refugee agency? I'd certainly met that blond young man – Norwegian Embassy? Danish? One of the Scandies, in any case – at some party. But I did not call out. 'All is forbidden' had somehow done its work. I was already aware of a film between me and my fellow expatriates, the gelatinous membrane that separates the innocent from the compromised. A strange shame held me back, the conviction that they would have walked on past me as I mouthed my silent appeal.

'Come,' said Green Eyes. I followed his beckoning finger out of the room, past the café-bar, now closing, and across to the terrace, which looked out over one of the least-used runways in Africa. Green Eyes pointed to where the Alitalia flight was turning on the tarmac, testing its flaps. I knew exactly what the atmosphere would be like on board. Some destinations specialise in jolly flights, others come tinged with relief, a few drenched in heartbreak. Flights from Lira always seemed infused with a certain grim pragmatism. No one aboard would be ending a wonderful holiday or laden with souvenirs. The airport was not the chosen port of departure for fleeing locals: too visible, too monitored. The expatriates, banking generous salaries for what was judged a hardship posting, would be heading off for briefings back at Headquarters, short breaks with semi-estranged wives and children parked at boarding-school. They would be back all too soon.

The plane hurtled past the terminal building. Heading out across the plateau, it wheeled until its nose pointed north-west. I could almost hear the clink of the mini-bar bottles as the air stewards handed out the required anaesthetics, tucking a few extras into seatbacks. A few minutes later, it was no more than a winking light in the careless splatter of stars that was the

Lira night sky. Green Eyes savoured my expression, his point made. I was on my own.

'Come,' he said again. We walked back to my holding area, where my turquoise case crouched, like a giant scarab beetle. Funny how you can come to hate an inanimate object. In one of those side pockets nestled the passports, cash and academic certificates that I assumed lay at the root of this whole sorry affair. Someone, it was clear, had blabbed. I could guess who that might be.

For a while, I sat in the plastic chair. After an hour, buttocks numb, I moved to the floor, draping myself strategically over the case – a girl needs a pillow, no? I put my coat over my head to shield my eyes from the light and under that screen, my hands got working. At the very least, I needed to separate the money – an aromatic wodge of hundred-dollar bills – from the rest. I could claim personal ownership of the cash, even if that meant admitting to breaking currency regulations. The passports and certificates were another matter. Maybe there was somewhere in the airport I could dump the incriminating evidence. With infinite slowness, I opened the zipper into the bag's side-pocket, closed my hands on the documents and slipped them up the sleeve of my sweater.

When I removed the coat from my head, Green Eyes was staring at me. Had he noticed the wriggling? 'I need to go to the Ladies,' I said.

'Come.'

I followed him down the corridor. Three sinks, dripping taps, the smell of bleach, more bad lighting and a wall-to-wall mirror, which confirmed that, yes, I did indeed resemble a warmed-up corpse. Disconcertingly, Green Eyes did not make his excuses. I entered one of the cubicles, locked the door, sat down without dropping my trousers. Think! Where could I stow the documents? Down the drain? That would cause a flood. How about the cistern, Al Pacino-style? If Green Eyes had not followed me in, maybe. But he would certainly hear the scraping as I lifted the heavy porcelain lid. As for the *Papillon* solution, no orifice was going to accommodate two passports. I'd run out of ideas. I transferred the papers from my sleeve to my knickers and flushed the toilet. Then I walked past Green Eyes with my face set. Hollywood had failed me, as it tends to. If he wanted to find my cache, he would.

I resumed my previous position slouched over my bag. Green Eyes was playing it cool, so I would match him for insouciance. I would simply fall asleep from sheer boredom. But, of course, too many internal voices were clamouring to be heard. One was near-hysterical, something approaching a banshee shriek: 'Oh, how could you? How *could* you – how could you do this to your parents? And what about Winston? After all he's done? You stupid, stupid, *stupid* cunt.'

I began composing a speech, my last presentation. 'I fully realise the mortifying position I have placed you in, and I can only apologise for that,' it began. 'Not only do I expect you to disassociate yourself from me, I demand it. I betrayed you personally and put the case at risk, both unforgivable acts. I have surrendered any claim to professionalism. No one else should pay the price for my rashness.'

The other voice was quieter, grimly realistic: 'So, let's think this through. To anticipate is to be strengthened. This is a pretty serious offence. Winston will fight for you, you know that, whatever you tell him. The embassy might try to help, but that could just make things worse. The one thing going for you is your skin colour. No government wants the Amnesty International press releases, the Human Rights Watch reports that go with torturing or executing people like you. Even this government. So we're probably talking, *if* you're lucky, a few years in a container on the coast. Can you handle that? Hottest place on earth. No privacy. Malaria. Cholera.'

A girding of the loins. And the answer that came back was a slight surprise: 'Yes. Yes, I think I can.'

But then an image came to mind, of a rough sketch I'd

spotted on Winston's desk, drawn by a young man who had compensated for his limited artistic ability with a certain graphic brio. It showed someone lying on their stomach, back arched, knees bent, hands reaching behind to seize toes. In yoga, something similar is known as the Bow Pose, a good way of stretching the spine. In the enemy prisoner-of-war camp into which that youngster had had the misfortune to fall it was known as the 'helicopter position'. The accompanying text, written by a doctor from the Red Cross, helpfully explained that the same technique was used in Iran, where it was called 'the chicken kebab', and in Latin America, where it was dubbed 'the parrot's perch'. It became intensely painful after a few minutes, the doctor wrote, and, if sustained, could cause deformed bones, deep sores and, in a few recorded cases, pulmonary embolism.

The doctor's name, I remember, was Boronski. A Pole? I could remember the photos paper-clipped to the drawing, showing the welts and scars. The ugly Polaroids flashed across my mind's eye, like lurid prompt cards. If the other side used that technique, you could be sure our boys did, too. And how about rape? Maybe I could handle it once, but repeatedly? Day in, day out? What would that be like? I remembered a newspaper article about a hospital in eastern Congo that treated male soldiers raped so often they'd had to use sanitary pads. But, hang on, this wasn't Congo. What had Winston once said, explaining why it was important never to shout in the office? 'This is a society where nothing is seen as more shaming than a loss of self-control.' But now we were back to Winston again, and how he would react, my parents and their feelings, that tidal wave of mortification.

I briefly tried the line of argument that had powered me so effectively through the last few years. The one that ran: 'Without Jake, there is nothing left to lose. There is nothing at stake.' But despair no longer consoled. My anxiety scurried like a gerbil on a wheel. The passports had long ago shifted from pleasantly cool to clammily sticky against my skin. I tried some deep breathing, but my heart wouldn't stop pounding, and my mouth was so dry that my lips kept sticking to my gums. At intervals, I lowered the coat off my face to ask Green Eyes for water, and once in a while, he ordered a colleague to fetch me a plastic beaker.

At a certain point, though, the adrenalin runs out. And then you find the peace of acceptance, the passivity of the internee. By the time I noticed that dawn was about to break, golden shards of light piercing the long grasses at the far end of the runway, I felt Valium-calm and as ancient as the landscape. There was nothing they could do to me now that would frighten or surprise me. I had done their work for them. I had dismantled myself.

There came a changing of the guard. The morning shift arrived, a shorter, older official taking over from Green Eyes, who gave me a knowing, strangely intimate look as he headed out the door. There was a woman with him, small and busty in a tightly fitting uniform, carefully made-up. 'Hello, sister,' she said coldly, and gestured to me to follow. And in this country where, as I had once explained in an email to my British friend Sarah, no one ever allowed you to carry anything ('My arms are atrophying'), Whitey was this time left to lug her own bag. The new dispensation.

I knew what to expect now. I'd be led to a car so nondescript it could only belong to the secret police. I'd be taken to an equally anonymous room and there my luggage and clothing would finally be properly searched, the passports and cash immediately discovered. I would be professionally interrogated, my story picked over until, inevitably, it fell apart. And then I would be asked to sign something, and I would be taken to a real cell, with bars, cockroaches and an open toilet, not the soft-focus version of internment I'd been treated to up till now.

Instead, the two walked me out of the deserted airport to the taxi rank. I noticed a woman, swathed like a mummy in white cotton, sitting on the concrete kerb. A little boy lay across her lap, fast asleep, saliva crusting his lips. The female officer rapped on the window of the only cab waiting and what had looked like a bundle of linen stirred and straightened, morphing into a bleary old driver, who automatically pulled the seat forward and groped for his keys.

The male officer turned to me. 'You will pick up your passport from the Ministry of Immigration, Room 805.'

Oh, sweet Jesus, they were letting me go. Suddenly I rediscovered my lost outrage. 'What was this all about?'

'Room 805. Ministry of Immigration. This afternoon.' Indifferent, they turned and headed back towards the terminal.

Louder now. 'What's been going on here?'

The woman officer swivelled and looked back at me. She had a half-smile on her face, and I noticed that her eyebrows had been plucked entirely away, then redrawn in black pencil. 'We had an information about you.'

I scrabbled at the taxi's door handle, my hands suddenly shaking so violently I could hardly open it. I gabbled instructions and we headed downtown. Lira was beginning to stir. In a night-chilled courtyard, a first dog barked. The bark was taken up by the dog next door, and their joint yelping relayed from one neighbourhood to another, a widening chorus of syncopated alarm spreading to wake the reluctant, befuddled city.

I sat huddled in the corner of the taxi, trying to control a juddering that had now spread to my legs. One thought occurred. After all those months of velvet-glove treatment, I'd finally been paid the ultimate compliment. Paula Shackleton had been treated like a local.

2

'What's a girl like you doing in a place like this?'

That was the running gag of an unlikely friendship forged in a bar down an alley with the cabbagy reek of open drains, hidden away from the Horn of Africa's punishing highlands light. There's a long, meandering answer to the question, and then there's the one-paragraph executive summary, easier to digest but lacking in nuance. I'm opting for the former, and that means jumping back a bit.

The Chicago law firm I worked for in 2004, Grobart & Fitchum – or 'Grabhard and Fuckem' as I liked to think of them – was involved in a complicated negotiation between a Swiss department-store chain raising capital to expand into Eastern Europe and a banking client who was running the deal out of their Boston headquarters. The job involved a huge amount of conference calling, and since the Swiss were our overlords, they got to arrange the schedule around their bedtimes. Grobart & Fitchum had flown in a five-man team, and as the days went by, we began to resemble a group of sleep-deprived inmates from Guantanamo Bay, pale-faced and pouchy-eyed. The mood between us was wary: we had been at it long enough to grasp who could stay lucid and keep powering through without enough sleep and who was becoming so loopy their workload would soon have to be added to ours.

Luxury is the knee-jerk consolation prize in this business and Dan, my immediate boss, had automatically booked suites at the Langham, housed in a former Federal Reserve building. There's something uniquely depressing about being offered a range of services, from the however-many-metres swimming-pool to a range of 'Chuan scrubs and wraps' you know you will never get time to use, and the British puritan in me was disgusted by the extravagance. The carping refrain *No wonder they're all obese* ran through my head every time I surveyed the breakfast buffet with its mountains of pastries and steaming trays of bacon. The Langham was just like every other gilded cage I'd stayed in, a fitting setting for my botched, interrupted, pointless demi-life.

On the morning in question I was sitting over a plate with a single bread roll placed defiantly in the centre – none of that greasy crap for me, thank you – staring into the middle distance, when a blur in my blind spot crystallised into the shape of a small black man. Compact, neat, a clipped corona of greying curls framing a high, round forehead, he wore a crumpled linen suit in an unusual shade of lemon custard. He stopped as he reached my table and gave me a very direct look from a pair of long-lashed, honey-coloured eyes. I noticed a distinctive spattering of moles around his nose, as though someone had taken a coffee stirrer and flecked espresso in his face.

'It isn't mandatory.'

'I beg your pardon?'

'You look like someone trapped in Purgatory. Boredom and frustration aren't obligatory. You could try something more stimulating.'

For a moment I thought he might be a Jehovah's Witness and I was about to get the 'Have you been saved?' routine. My face assumed a rictus of polite refusal and I raised a palm in an instinctive fending-off motion.

He blinked those long lashes a couple of times, then gave

me a shy smile of enormous sweetness. 'You're the British lawyer, aren't you? Part of the Grobart & Fitchum crew?'

I nodded warily.

'Paula? I noticed you all earlier in the lobby. I'm Winston Peabody. Dan and I go way back. We both did time at the Justice Department.' We shook hands and he nodded at a signboard in the lobby. 'I'm here for the seminar on my favourite topic, corporate sleaze. But I'll also be giving a speech for the human-rights crowd. Can I tempt you? It'll make a change from your usual fare. And sometimes I have work for people like you.'

'People like me?'

He pursed his lips and gazed at me speculatively, like a tailor measuring his client for a suit. 'Oh, people with that questing look in their eyes. The Unrooted, I call them. Take it as a compliment. Complacency's not exactly attractive. Anyway, come along. I'm trying to rustle up an audience. Nothing more embarrassing than talking to an empty room.' He scribbled the venue and time on the back of a business card, placed it on my table and walked off.

That last bit was one of his little jokes, of course. Winston Peabody III, the first black partner at the Washington firm of Melville & Bart and a celebrity on the human-rights circuit, did not need to beg strangers in hotels to attend his talks. When seats ran out, people would stand. He was one of those speakers adored by the media and envied by academics, who could popularise without dumbing down, rendering dry specialisms so accessible that listeners who had never dreamed of opening a law book found themselves wondering whether they had missed their calling. There are men who seem to change shape, to grow in stature when they climb onto a public platform. Behind a desk, over the phone, Winston was always formidable. On a podium or presenting in court, he became positively sexy, acquiring a town-hall charisma, the spiky, sardonic edge and instinctive timing of the stand-up comedian who knows how to play an audience. Had he wished to at that moment, he could have tapped almost any woman – and a fair number of the men – on the shoulder and they would have considered fucking him a privilege. But in the seconds it took him to step off the stage, he visibly shrank, folding, like an empty Coke can in a weightlifter's fist, to become just a small, slightly paunchy man in a creased yellow suit whose salt-and-pepper halo of hair could not conceal advanced male-pattern baldness and a tendency to dandruff. Incredible Hulk to mild-mannered Bruce Banner in the blink of an eye.

I honestly can't remember the details of Winston's speech, hosted by a human-rights group that had hired a hall on Harvard's campus for the purpose. Sheer exhaustion had brought matters to a head on the Swiss deal. My skills were not required for the final session with Zurich, and I found myself with a free afternoon. He must have spoken about the hunger for justice in societies emerging from war, how ending the climate of impunity held the key to peace. He probably talked about the debt the West owed developing countries for the horrors of slavery and colonialism and the cynicism of the Cold War. I do recall that he gave some gory examples, anecdotes from visits to East Timor and Cambodia, work done in Colombia and Sierra Leone. Members of the audience gasped at references to stairwells daubed with blood, defence attorneys disembowelled in their offices, human-rights campaigners pulled over on remote country roads and beheaded in the spotlights of their killers' cars. I saw one girl, long brown hair falling to her waist, close her eyes and lean her head on the shoulder of her boyfriend, who put his arm round her in a manly gesture that signalled: it's OK, I'm here. What impressed me, though, was not the heartrending stuff, or that Winston spoke in meticulously punctuated sentences – you could actually *hear* the semi-colons, dashes and quotation marks and when he told his audience: 'I'll come back to that point later,' it wasn't just a phrase, he really did return, topping and tailing his thought processes like a chef preparing green beans – no, it was the surgical coolness of his eye. This was an impassioned, angry man, but one who never allowed his emotions to interrupt a methodical taking of notes. On his deathbed, as his nearest and dearest gathered to weep, Winston Peabody would be calling, 'Hush', the better to analyse the timbre, tone and length of his own death rattle.

At the end, I dutifully took my place in the throng of acolytes gathering around him. Don't ask me why. I think I wanted him to know I'd bothered. Waiting, I registered that I was a good decade older than the rest.

'Mr Peabody, I just feel, like, what's happening is just so awful. What can I *do*?' twittered a pigtailed blonde, her cheeks flushed with emotion. She was almost pogoing with enthusiasm, flashing glimpses of a toned stomach and pierced navel. I spotted the gleam of metal in her mouth. Dear God, she was actually wearing braces. This was not the place for me. I turned to leave, but at that moment Winston caught my eye. He reached forward, the human Red Sea somehow parted before him, and placed a restraining hand on my sleeve. 'Please. Don't go.'

Fifteen minutes later, the flock of groupies had dispersed and we were in the campus canteen drinking coffee.

He spoke as though picking up an interrupted conversation. 'So, since 1997 I've been working *pro bono* for the government of North Darrar, in the Horn of Africa. I don't expect you've heard of it?'

'Well, actually …'

His eyebrows shot up in query.

'I've heard of Darrar, that's all.'

'That's more than most people can say. Good. In many ways North Darrar encapsulates the problems faced by traumatised post-conflict nations. A breakaway state that has just come through the second of two wars with its neighbour and former occupier, and finds itself having to negotiate its border – prove

15

the country's right to exist, in essence – in The Hague. They're trying to build a democracy from scratch, but their best people were either killed or fled into exile during the independence struggle so the last thing they need is this kind of international court case. They weren't rich to start off with – the last war bankrupted them and there's only so much you can make exporting badly cured hides and potash to the Middle East – and the other side hires the best.'

'And?'

'Well, up till now I've been fighting this battle virtually single-handed, juggling the job with my paying clients. Melville & Bart help out on the practical side, preparing documents, making our evidence look halfway presentable. But that's just basic drudgery. We're reaching a crucial stage. This is complex, sophisticated stuff, and I simply can't do it alone. I need a deputy. Will you help?'

I blinked. I'd been wondering where the preamble was leading, but it hadn't occurred to me that this might be its destination. 'Look, I really don't understand why you think any of this is my business … Why don't you get one of your admirers to pitch in? I'm sure one of those kids would jump at the chance.'

He sighed. 'Sadly, experience proves that the eager intern is more hindrance than help. The first had an attack of the runs, decided he'd caught cholera and insisted on being medevaced out. The second went mountain biking, hit a camel and broke her wrist – no more typing. I can't play nanny – I'm temperamentally unsuited to it. I spend all my free time in Lira, but I need someone based there to keep the show on the road during my necessary absences. Are you interested?' He was spooning sugar into his cappuccino as though determined not to acknowledge my disbelieving eyes.

'This is nuts. We've barely met. You don't know anything about me.'

'Well, I know what I saw in your face the other day. I've

rarely seen a bleaker expression. And actually,' he took a slurp and shot me a look over the cup's rim, 'I know slightly more than you think. As I said, Dan and I go way back. He briefed me on your, er, personal circumstances over lunch a few months ago. I knew we'd bump into each other one of these days. Dan suggested Grobart & Fitchum was no longer the right place for you. Oh, he had nothing but praise for the quality of your work but he thinks you'd do better – be happier – elsewhere.'

I flushed. 'How very considerate of him.'

There was a pause. He took another slurp and said slowly, 'My own policy is to welcome kindness when I see it, however clumsy or awkward a form it takes. It's a rare commodity, especially in our profession.'

I looked away, my eyes pricking. 'I think I heard you use the phrase "*pro bono*". I need to eat. Grobart & Fitchum pay extremely well. My savings account looks pretty healthy these days.'

'Well,' he leaned forward to hold my gaze with those sorrowful, honey-coloured eyes, 'your savings account may look healthy, but you certainly don't. In any case, you'd get a decent salary. The North Darrar government can afford to pay one international lawyer's stipend – I've persuaded them they have to. It took some doing, believe me.'

I was beginning to feel cornered. I'd met this man only two days ago, and already he had arrogated a say over my future. It was absurd. 'You said this was a border case? That's totally out of my area of expertise. I do corporate law.'

'Nothing you can't handle, believe me. Dan assures me you're one of the smartest lawyers he's ever employed. I'll hold your hand, and they do say that I'm a born teacher. I notice you wrote your thesis on –' he took out a card '– "Challenges of peace: when former Latin American guerrilla organisations turn law-makers". So it seems you already have some interest in the developing world.'

Ah, yes, my thesis. An eccentric pimple on the bland epidermis of an otherwise unremarkable post-graduate degree. Fuelled by the sheer lust I'd harboured towards Gavin, the sole Caribbean student on our LSE course and the only one who brought books by Chomsky and Che Guevara into lectures. A sudden mental image. Gavin dashing into the sea one miraculously mild October weekend in Dorset. A dark Michelangelo's *David*, nipples erect in the chill, pulling off a pair of jeans as I watched from the shingle. I'd wanted to impress him, hence the thesis; its drafting had outlasted the relationship.

'Regard this as the equivalent of a further degree in international law, prepared under expert guidance,' Winston continued. 'I'll be expecting you to do some of the presentations, so you'll get priceless experience. I know lawyers in their mid-forties who are still waiting for their law firm to grant them permission to stand up in a courtroom and argue a case. They're not even halfway up a chain twenty links deep. Put in a few years and you'll come out of this with a whole new skill set. All courtesy of the North Darrar government. I'd call that a pretty attractive offer.'

I sat in silence, surprised I had allowed the conversation to go on as long as it had.

Winston picked up his briefcase and turned his head slowly from side to side, uncricking a stiff neck and carrying out a panoramic survey of the café, with its gaggles of chatting students, the odd loner hunched over a laptop and a muffin. He was considering what form to give his closing remarks. Had he chosen the bombastic – anything on the lines of 'doing something worthwhile with your life', or 'helping millions of poor Africans who never had your chances' – I would have slipped off his gleaming hook, like a sliver of jelly off a fork, consigning the whole episode to the surreal-encounter-best-ignored category as swiftly as I left campus.

'Look, Paula. One of the great satisfactions I've discovered, working in Africa, is being able to have a disproportionate impact per hour of effort put in. Call it big-fish-small-pond syndrome, call it stroking my own ego, whatever. I'm not, despite appearances, the world's brightest lawyer. But there is – and I'm not boasting here, just stating the facts – no one in that entire country who has my skills. They've been fighting for nearly three decades, they know how to repair Kalashnikovs and make a handful of lentils and a gourd of water last a week. They're confident they can build a socialist Utopia, but they can't do this. And I can. I cannot describe to you the professional satisfaction that brings. You may never experience it anywhere else ever again.'

It was a deft, manipulative appeal. But I was ready to be manipulated, pining to be told what to do. I was so tired of being master of my fate.

We met on the ice.

A woman on the cusp of thirty, with a muss of brown hair, sits on a bench by the side of the Rockefeller Center Ice Rink in New York in mid-February 1999. Having laced up her hired skates, she stands with wobbly care. It's been a long time since she had these on, but she is determined to see this through. Hitchens, the firm where she works as a transactional lawyer, crossing the legal t's and dotting the i's on bond deals, overlooks the sunken rink and she has been watching the skaters from her office window for weeks, envying their fluid grace.

These two, though, she does not envy. They are graceless and comic. A bearded, middle-aged man in grey jeans and a lumberjack shirt, flailing and juddering on his skates, and a ponytailed brunette, all white cleavage and heavy eye-liner, draped, giggling, on one arm. Her eyes skim over them – she assumes they're a couple. The buxom girl must be wife number two or three. Only she is not going to be allowed to ignore them. Because just as she ventures warily onto the ice the two career towards her. There is a loud scream, the girl falls, showing even more of that milky cleavage and still laughing, and the woman is knocked violently back. Her skates slide out from under her and she finds herself half lying, half sitting on the ice with the man sprawled on top. For a split-second, his eyes, grey-blue, are locked on hers. As, arms flailing, he attempts to right himself – 'God, I'm so sorry' – he briefly places a hand on her left breast.

'Straight for my tits. What a lech,' she will chide him later on. The episode is something they both enjoy examining, returning to.

'Only way of getting your attention,' he will reply, looking absurdly pleased with himself. And then he will usually kiss the top of her head as you might a child's.

'The custom, where I come from, is to shake hands,' is what she says at the time. On his second attempt to get up, the man is careful to place his hand on the ice for leverage. His hands are the most atypical thing about him, she will come to know. They are a peasant's hands, stubby-fingered and as wide as paddles.

'Oh, I believe in cutting to the chase,' he replies, then apologises again. And she later finds out that this is not a joke. Just as she has been watching the skaters, admiring their grace, he has been watching her, noting her daily routine, plucking up the courage to introduce himself. He works in the same building.

They both stand up – she will sport large bruises on her buttocks for weeks. Names are exchanged, the girl, slapping ice dust off her trousers, is introduced. She is Sophie, his younger daughter. So he is older than he looks. Her accent is remarked upon and she gives her usual trite explanation of how a junior British lawyer ends up on Wall Street. Then he gestures to where a figure wrapped in a cashmere scarf, fur hat and gloves stands on the far side of the rink, near the gilded statue of Prometheus, a chilled silhouette radiating

20

boredom. Two glossy pedigree dogs pull impatiently at their leads. 'My wife is waiting. And so are Laurel and Hardy. We'd better go. Till the next time.'

A wife, she notes. Why bother with 'till the next time'? But she will bump into him later, in the ground-floor café of their building. She will discover that he works for a respected firm of architects, then that he not only set up the firm but has a claim on the entire building in which she works. Jake Wentworth is, in a minor way, a local celebrity, the well-liked unpretentious scion of a WASP family that made its fortune hurling railroads across the United States. One day he will inherit the family fortune, but in the meantime he is doing the job he loves, juggling draughtsmanship with a regular arts column and the directorship of a charity for political asylum seekers, funded by Wentworth money. She will meet him on the ice again, alone this time, and neither will get any skating done. Instead, they will talk about politics, discuss the Coen brothers' latest film, and he will give her a witty-yet-not-unkind potted résumé of twenty years' New York high society gossip, for these are circles to which his name grants entry. They will both be surprised to find that it feels like a conversation between old friends after a long break, rather than a first exchange between strangers. And soon she will discover, thanks to a personal assistant's indiscretions, that the impatience she glimpsed in the female figure by the skating rink extends further than irritation at the cold: there are independent bank accounts, solo holidays, separate bedrooms. And the young woman will find herself hoovering up office tittle-tattle with unbecoming greed.

He has made contact. He has made her care.

3

I woke staring at an unfamiliar grey ceiling. A gecko was spread-eagled directly above my head, in unconscious imitation of my position. It skittered away as I reached for my mobile phone blinking on the bedside table: 6:00 a.m. I had slept only a couple of hours since my taxi had deposited me in darkness at the White Star Hotel in Lira but felt wide awake, my body still on US time. I staggered to the bathroom, rinsed my face in water, wrenched open doors giving onto a balcony and stepped out. The street lighting was so sparse that the only detail I retained from the drive in was a giant 'WELCOME TO LIRA INTERNATIONAL CAPITAL OF CULTURE AND SCIENCE' banner slung across the airport road. I wanted my first view of the city.

But there was to be no grandiose panorama. My room lay at the back of the hotel and I found myself gazing instead across a flat plateau fringed by a jagged mountain range over which the sun was rising, thawing the thin layer of frost crusting a russet and dun patchwork of ploughed fields. A gentle wind was ruffling the tawny savannah grass that lapped around the hotel, setting off the rhythmic chirruping of invisible crickets.

My nostrils crinkled as I caught an unfamiliar aroma – a mixture of chilli powder, cumin and ginger, I guessed, and the scent of roasting coffee. There were other, less appealing, elements: the acid tang of what might be mule manure and petrol fumes from badly maintained cars. So this, I thought, was the smell of Lira.

I craned across the balcony railing and looked north, registering that the escarpment lay above the cloud cover, which stretched across the horizon like a lumpy quilt, neatly tucked in at the corners. How high up were we, then? Two thousand metres? More? I spotted a hawk fluttering above the plains in the chill layer where a cerulean sky merged with the navy of deep space. There was a giddy feeling of gravity defied: both of us – woman and hawk – were suspended far beyond the reach of ordinary mortals.

Suddenly overwhelmed by nausea, I bowed my head, dry retching as the clot of grief and rage that had stoppered my throat since I'd lost Jake bubbled up. I spat once, took a deep breath and closed my eyes. The cold air was as invigorating as a lungful of alpine oxygen, the sun on my face a caress. Something about being so close to eternity was waking me up. After months of lethargy I felt a brisk sense of purpose. An unfamiliar sensation stirred inside: hope. Like generations of sinners, mavericks and reprobates before me, I'd joined the Foreign Legion, exiling myself from my own. And that self-banishment felt good. Winston was right. I should have done this sooner.

Extracting a shawl and two thick box files from my luggage, I arranged myself in a tangle of wool at the balcony table. I'd once prided myself on being a meticulously briefed lawyer, but if there was one lesson recent personal history had taught me – and we'll come to that – it was that you can never really prepare. While serving my notice period with Grobart & Fitchum, I had focused exclusively on mundane tasks: selling the car, notifying my landlord, settling utilities bills. When a package from Winston had arrived, containing a fold-up map, three chunky history books and several files of background information, I had not taken up the proffered invitation. I had a few hours, now, to get some overdue homework done.

'THE PLACE', someone – presumably Winston – had written in red felt tip on the first file. It began with a photocopied page of a 1999 Bradt guide to the region, one paragraph highlighted in yellow. 'Sanasa lies slap bang on the border between the tiny state of North Darrar, Africa's newest nation, and the giant Federal Republic of Darrar, which reluctantly conceded independence after a David-and-Goliath war of secession. There is nothing of any interest here to the ordinary tourist.'

The next document was a rather florid account by an English writer called Hugh Winterdale, who had toured the Red Sea coast in 2000 as part of a series of travel books baptised 'Forgotten Places':

The port of Sanasa, 550 kilometres north-east of the highland capital of Lira, is little more than a long curving jetty of giant coral bricks, stacked like pink sugar cubes to keep the sea at bay.

A sultan held sway here for a few hundred years, doing deals with Ottoman traders and Egyptian bureaucrats, and that period left behind crumbling coral ramparts and a few gracious town buildings, whose delicate wooden verandas now slump earthwards. The Italians left behind a delightful openness with strangers and a liking for pasta and strong coffee. As for the British, they only took away, removing anything in the port made of metal, to be used in other, more important, colonies.

East and west of here lie terminals with ship-to-shore mobile gantries and yards piled high with orange containers. As Africa enters the twenty-first century, these modern ports will come to play a vital role in the continent's revival. In contrast, Sanasa, which only exists because the coast here – with the help of a little excavation in the 1870s by a Swiss adventurer – forms the deepest harbour for 200 kilometres in any direction, boasts very little in terms of equipment. Things are done the old-fashioned way. Three rusty cranes loom over the harbour, and when a ship docks, they cluster above the vessels' innards, picking over the cargo like feeding storks. To a chorus of male shouts, hooks descend, cargo slings are attached, sacks of grain and cement are lifted and deposited on the harbour front, morsel by painstaking morsel. A brigade of whippet-thin stevedores then springs into action, T-shirts stained with sweat, loading the sacks by hand into the Isuzu trucks lined up in anticipation.

But such moments are becoming ever rarer. A well-used port makes for dark, polluted waters. Sanasa's are an inviting, translucent blue; zebra fish nibble and flit around greasy anchor ropes. Container vessels increasingly bypass Sanasa, leaving it to process the occasional, surreptitious dhow. Painted sky-blue, these tiered schooners waft in laden with sugar, cheap Chinese plastic sandals, the odd microwave oven and state-of-the-art 4x4. Not an inch of space is wasted. By the time they depart, the dhows have been transformed into smelly, bleating vessels of animal distress, loaded to the gunwales with goats and camels destined for the butcheries of Yemen and Saudi Arabia.

'*Wordy but helpful*', someone had scrawled in the margin.

Sanasa's remoteness, its very inefficiency, lends it a particular advantage. Rarely coming to the attention of officials in Lira, it is popular with smugglers, petty traders, who do their calculations in their heads, and livestock owners, who ignore frontiers as they follow routes established by nomadic forefathers. It makes for a rich mix of languages and faces, a polyglot blurring of nationalities and customs.

For most of the day, the town sits stunned into near-imbecility, paralysed by the joint assault of light and heat. Pock-marked mongrels lie by the whitewashed trunks of old neem trees, tongues out, stomachs pumping like pistons. The only sound comes from the cawing of the crows picking for forgotten fish scraps along the cement jetties, crunchy with salt crystals. It is in the evening that Sanasa stirs. Under the arcades, harbour workers sip cold Coke, relishing the bracing zing of ammonia from the sea and providing a running commentary on the comings and goings from the town's lone brothel. Urchins dragging adult-sized flip-flops trawl, half-hearted, for custom, carrying neon-coloured plastic basins of hot peanuts. They stand uncomplainingly, ignored, absorbing the gossip of the baritone-voiced adult world. As a velvet night descends, the spot-lit bars and restaurants, each with its dizzy halo of insects, become helpful landmarks for residents accustomed to manoeuvring the streets as much by feel as by sight.

I turned the page, expecting more, but the passage ended there. Winterdale's creative juices had clearly run dry.

Next came some photocopies of unclassified cables between a US deputy ambassador in Lira and the State Department, dating back to the early 1990s. One highlighted snippet read:

Sanasa is merely one of a handful of settlements whose proximity to a poorly defined colonial border is a potential source of strategic concern. Yet when Western diplomats raise the issue with officials in either capital, their concerns are laughed away … The line is that the governments established by the two former rebel movements now running Darrar and its progeny, North Darrar, are ideological soul-mates, with near-identical, progressive agendas. 'We're brothers!' officials will often tell embassy personnel. Families in the border areas, they say, are interconnected by marriage, friendship and commerce and barely know themselves where the frontier begins or ends. 'Who needs a border when there's trust on both sides?' is a refrain we often hear in these parts.

But, evidently, the picture was not quite as harmonious as it seemed. For on the night of 7 June 2001, something had happened on Sanasa's outskirts, and it was hard to believe that individual explosions of temper could have escalated quite so quickly had the incident not tapped into long-accumulated grudges.

I stretched, checking my watch, abandoning my shawl. It was eight a.m.: the heat was rising, hotel staff would be up. I rang room service to order breakfast and opened the second, fatter, file, marked 'THE INCIDENT'. This one was a mess. It contained a collection of transcripts from local-radio broadcasts picked up by BBC Monitoring, several editions of *Africa Confidential* and scores of press cuttings that contradicted one another in key details. The newspaper titles scrawled on the scraps meant nothing to me. I guessed they represented the contrasting views from the two neighbours' capitals.

One thing they agreed upon: that on the evening in question, fifty-five-year-old Ahmed Ibrahim had settled his bill at a restaurant on the Sanasa quayside, shouted farewell to the proprietor, and boarded his 7.5-tonne Isuzu. In the summer months, like most local drivers, he always waited till nightfall before moving. In daytime, the tarmac got so hot it could rip black fronds of rubber from tyres. He drove in darkness towards the border post on the edge of town.

What happened after that was murky. Some accounts claimed Ahmed was a hardened smuggler of cigarettes and cheap gin, accustomed to oiling his passage across the border with bribes. According to this version of events, his usual routine was sabotaged by an unexpected change of the Darrar guards: the two middle-aged regulars he had spent years befriending had been replaced by eager-to-impress youngsters, who insisted that he remove tarpaulins, unbuckle ropes and make his goods available for inspection.

A rival version painted a different picture. His truck laden with vital pharmaceutical supplies destined for a clinic across the frontier, Ahmed – a law-abiding, respectable father of six – had negotiated the North Darrar border crossing without a hitch, only to discover that Darrar's border post had shifted twenty metres closer to Sanasa since his previous trip. He had realised this a split-second after his truck had careered through the barricade, snapping it in half, bringing two Darrar guards piling out of a freshly painted hut, stuffing handfuls of pasta into their mouths, AK-47s at the ready.

Whichever version was true, a shouting match had broken out, which attracted the attention of the North Darrar guards on the other side of no man's land, who radioed a local militia for backup. A first rifle shot was heard – perhaps no more than the spasm of a nervous finger on a trigger – but the damage was done. Next came an answering fusillade, and someone, unbelievably, upped the ante by throwing a grenade, the explosion deafening everyone. When the noise and smoke subsided, Ahmed Ibrahim lay spread-eagled in the sand, breath bubbling from the granular pink mash that had been his face. Arterial blood was pumping from one border guard's thigh while another lay motionless, arms clasping a warm pile of entrails. Two more were writhing silently in the sand, squirming jumbles of bone and muscle.

The initial incident had not made the international news. On domestic television, it led the evening news broadcasts in both countries, but was consigned to a seven-line announcement read by carefully expressionless newsreaders. In the two capitals, emergency cabinet meetings were called, inquiries commissioned, generals summoned. Three days later, a motorcade of tanks, armoured personnel carriers and camouflage-painted trucks, dispatched by the government of North Darrar, trundled through Sanasa, heading for the blood-spattered checkpoint. A week later, Darrar's tanks reached the front line and the artillery opened fire. Both sides, the geeks from *Jane's Weekly* noted with interest, were using the same models of tank, the stolid T-55 bequeathed to the region by the Soviet Union during the Cold War era when the superpowers fought their battles by African proxy.

Leafing through the cuttings from *The Economist*, the *New York Times* and the *Financial Times*, it was clear that what had puzzled the Western journalists, diplomats and academics who had covered what followed was that Sanasa seemed so insignificant, the trigger incident so trivial, and both sides had so much to lose. Their articles smacked of exasperation: 'Why can't these people behave like adults?' they implied. It was not, I guessed, that these observers had forgotten the grotesque consequences of a single shot fired in Sarajevo, or the arbitrary connections made between the flattening of the Twin Towers and Baghdad's invasion. There was something more arrogant at play. In those cases, cause and effect might well seem disproportionate, historical justifications near-nonsensical but, dammit, they had occurred in places that *mattered*. The West could not tolerate a seeming absence of logic in a region so dry and hungry. Quixotic decision-making was a luxury denied countries this poor, as were the ingredients of most foreign policy: a leader's hunger for dignity, a community's craving for respect, destiny-defying pride. The domestic media showed no such bafflement. Their dispatches made knowing references to ancient kingdoms, nineteenth-century battles between feudal *rases*, long-running disputes over grazing rights, 'the perennial obsession with access to the sea', and 'the hot topic of national identity'.

Within weeks, Sanasa was nearly forgotten as the war spread like a virus, infecting three other border towns. As truckloads of fleeing villagers headed in one direction, mattresses and cooking pots piled high, live chickens clenched like feather dusters, military conscripts and the occasional flak-jacketed reporter headed in the other, towards what was now a 1,630-kilometre front line. Nothing went as expected, although it took a while for the two populations to make out the broad contours of the conflict. The front line juddered confusingly backwards and forwards, each jerk marked in corpses that twisted in the sterilising Red Sea sun to form green-and-brown strips of human leather, a grimacing spray of teeth at one end, bulbous black boots at the other; landmarks initially greeted with horrified respect but attracting growing scorn from fellow soldiers as positions on crags and knolls were won, lost and won again. Two and a half years later, though, it was clear which side had been pushed onto the back foot. 'We're like a bar drunk who knows he has lost but can't stop for dignity's sake,' the North Darrar minister of the interior confessed to an American diplomat one night over a ninth beer at Lira's Havana Bar, an insight duly relayed back to the State Department. 'One hand slapping our opponent in the face, the other leaning on him to avoid falling over.'

Across North Darrar's eastern, central and western sectors, more than 150,000 men and women had died. Darrar had gobbled up flood plains, seized valley settlements and captured hill forts, sending hundreds of thousands of villagers fleeing. The familiar flags of humanitarian agencies flapped over hastily built camps for the dispossessed. Sanasa had been occupied, then thoroughly looted. Bored Darrar artillerymen had laid bets to see who could rip through the jetty's slim rind, and the sea now poured through the Swiss engineer's 130-year-old stonework. Fishing boats had been burned, the mosque daubed with obscene graffiti and the port arcades mortared until their roofs acquired the consistency of ancient lace.

The light was now so bright I was squinting. I rose to fetch my sunglasses.

At this point, it seemed, the administration in Darrar had paused, suddenly aware that while sending the North Darrar government into exile was theoretically possible, the game might not be worth the candle. The two states agreed instead to send their presidents to Tunis for peace talks hosted by the African Union. A Cessation of Hostilities declaration was signed, catering for a buffer zone and a blue-helmeted force of UN peacekeepers, allowing both sides to pull back their forces without loss of face. The border must be demarcated, it was agreed, further bloodshed averted. Both leaders declared themselves ready to go to international arbitration.

The last item in the file was a news-agency photo of the two presidents embracing in front of the television cameras, Kofi Annan's hands resting on their shoulders in saintly benediction. I studied the image for a few minutes, wondering whether local viewers, while nodding in relief, had found themselves wondering how it was logically possible for both leaders – so certain of their own rectitude, so confident in the correctness of this method of solving disputes – to be simultaneously right.

4

I was sitting on the White Star Hotel's steps, watching a gang of sparrows quarrel in the oleander bushes and savouring my first cigarette of the day, when a bottle-green Toyota Land Cruiser pulled sharply into the compound, sending dustmotes dancing around me.

The man who unfolded from the driver's seat was tall – unusually tall for a local, I would come to realise – with a high, clear forehead. There was a touch of the 1970s dandy about him. He wore a soft, chocolate-coloured suede jacket, camel slip-ons, and his cheekbones were framed with a delicate suggestion of sideburns.

'Miss Paula Shackleton?' I reached up and we shook hands. There seemed to be no fat on his bones. 'I'm Abraham. Mr Peabody sent me. Welcome to Lira.'

His English was good – that was a relief. 'Thank you. I'm glad to be here.'

He shouldered one bag with ease and waved away my half-hearted attempt to take responsibility for the second. 'Hotel OK?'

'Perfect. I've settled up, as I was told to.'

'Mr Peabody thought it would be more comfortable to spend the first night here. It opened after Liberation – the owners are from the Canadian diaspora. But you will have your own villa, sharing with Sharmila, the other expatriate.'

'Really?' I felt a pang of dismay. I hadn't shared with anyone other than Jake since university. In my misanthropic state, solitude had become a Janus-faced friend, hated yet necessary. I made a mental note to discuss the arrangement with Winston.

He stowed my bags in the back of the Toyota and started the engine, throwing me a quick glance as he pulled away from the kerb. 'You smoke.'

'Is that a problem?' I looked around anxiously for the ashtray, my US instincts kicking in.

'No,' he said, letting go of the wheel to reach into his back pocket for his own pack, the Red Marlboro of the serious player rather than my half-hearted Marlboro Lights. 'It's good. Everyone smokes here.'

'Even the women?'

He raised an elegant eyebrow as he went through the gear changes, face expressionless. 'You're a woman? I thought you were our new lawyer.' I laughed, suddenly certain that I was going to enjoy working with Abraham.

We drove through bleached, single-storey suburbs whose flaking walls were draped with bougainvillaea, Abraham occasionally lifting one long index finger from the steering-wheel to point out a landmark. The headquarters of the UN peace-keeping force – a vast fleet of white SUVs behind barbed wire and cement bollards ('We could do with some of those') – the new 500-room Africa Hotel ('Lira's only swimming-pool'), the gate into the Imperial Botanical Gardens ('"Giardini", the Italians called them') behind which I caught a glimpse of cypress groves and gravel paths.

'Is it safe on the streets in the evening? I like to run.'

'Foreigners say it's the safest capital in Africa. I wouldn't know. No one will touch a hair of your head, I promise you, whatever time of day it is.'

We reached the centre of town and were bowling along a palm-fringed boulevard ('Liberation Avenue'), lined with imposing Modernist buildings, what looked like a theatre, a high court, ministries and a giant art-deco cinema plastered with posters of big-eyed Bollywood stars. I leaned eagerly out of the window, taking it all in. Jake would have loved this, I thought. He'd have known the architects' names, effortlessly identified the various styles, and could have explained the ideas and accidents behind the city's final layout. Without him, it was a meaningless agglomeration of buildings.

We branched to the right, up a street lined with shoe shops and grocers. I caught snatches of jangling metallic music from a café's open doorway. There was a driving, zesty quality to it, but the vocalist sounded closer to screaming than singing. Every now and then a garish mural flashed past, clearly a commissioned work of art. I craned my neck, but we were travelling too fast for anything more than a glimpse: a geyser of fire; khaki-clad fighters storming some citadel; a clenched male fist; prone bodies splotched with blood.

Abraham drew up next to a pollarded fig tree. 'That is the office,' he said, indicating a sober wooden door with a brass plaque next to it. 'And there on the corner is Ristorante Torino. Mr Peabody is waiting inside.'

There had been exchanges of emails while I'd been in the States, though not as many as my mother would have liked – 'Typical of you, Paula,' she'd wailed, 'moving to darkest Africa on the strength of a fax' – but I hadn't actually laid eyes on Winston since our Boston meeting. He seemed somehow larger, louder, a player in his element.

'So, first impressions?' he asked. Two beers magically appeared in stumpy unlabelled brown bottles. As the meal progressed, dishes kept materialising without orders being placed, and I realised he must eat at the Torino every day. Winston might be innovative and risk-taking inside the court-room, but out of it he was a creature not so much of habit but of obsessive routine.

'*Weeell* … the city isn't what I was expecting at all. I don't know what I thought an African capital would be like, but it feels more like a riviera resort, or a stretch of LA. The palm trees definitely bring Evelyn Waugh and F. Scott Fitzgerald to mind.'

He tilted his glass and carefully dribbled in some beer from the bottle. 'Most African capitals barely existed before colonialism, so the cities often still look as their colonial masters intended. Infrastructure that stands the test of time can be a mixed blessing. It's impossible to shake off.'

'It seems incredibly clean. I suppose I was expecting open sewers and tin-shack slums.'

'There are plenty of those, believe me, but not in this district. You're in what was once Lira's European quarter, which used to be off-limits to the "natives,"' he made inverted commas in the air, 'after the sun went down. It's still the most elegant part of town. All the embassies and most of the hotels are here.'

'And the climate …'

'The climate?'

'I realise I was a bit naïve, but I automatically assumed it would be hot and sweaty. I'm already wearing most of the clothes I packed.'

He looked nonplussed. 'Ah. Sorry about that. I should have asked Sharmila to brief you. We're very high up, so it gets pretty cold once the sun goes down. I'm afraid it didn't occur to me that would be an issue. My own wardrobe barely changes, irrespective of the season. You might be able to pick something up at the local market. Everything's made in China, of course.'

'Abraham mentioned I'll be living with Sharmila. I don't want to sound like a prima donna, but is there any chance I could have my own place, however small? I'm not used to sharing.'

He gave me a probing look, alert for potential trouble. 'Sorry, can't do. It's not penny-pinching, in case you're wondering. The government designates where expatriates on the payroll live. Getting us to share makes keeping tabs on us easier.'

'That sounds a bit paranoid. We're on their side, after all.'

'Not paranoid, just careful. The client's prerogative.'

He started elliptically, so much so that for the first fifteen minutes I wondered if he was meandering, a man who liked to talk for the sake of talking. But then I saw what he was doing. Like any good lawyer, he knew that context dictates meaning. He was painting in the background, sketching in the lines of perspective, ensuring that when he finally came to the story's core, it would be properly framed.

He ran through his curriculum vitae. A boy who had been parked for long hours in the library of the school in West Philadelphia, where his mother worked as a cleaner, who had grown to love the institution's smell of old leather, the hush of concentration and masculine gravitas, the atmosphere, he would later learn, of a gentleman's club. What would have been a tiresome ordeal for most boys his age providing him with a glimpse of a way out. A truck-driver father, whose absences were compensated for by a grandfather's loving attention: Winston Peabody I, despairing of his pool-hall-frequenting son, was self-taught, politically active, the kind of iconoclast who felt compelled to declare his atheism to all and sundry, had poured his frustrated aspirations into his grandson, who had soaked up the references to Orwell and Fanon, Garvey and Du Bois, safe harbours of thought and inspiration in the choppy seas of adversity.

The boy had fondly assumed that his grandfather – rarely seen without a pin-stripe waistcoat and half-moon glasses perched on the end of his nose – was a lawyer, possibly a judge. In fact, Winston Peabody I, the gifted child of railway labourers, had never spent more than two years in high school. When he left for work, battered briefcase in hand, he was headed for a legal aid office where the absence of a degree confined him to a clerk's desk but did not prevent him murmuring quietly authoritative advice to the poor mothers who sat in the waiting room, facing eviction and welfare cuts. The boy had repaid the attention – and the fund-raising support of his local evangelical church – by filling the blank space above his grandfather's desk where a framed law degree had always screamed to be. For the grandfather, it was a form of validation by proxy, the sins of the forefathers wiped out by the relentless determination of a legacy-conscious heir. The first and, to date, only member of his family to go to college, Winston Peabody III had gone one better, graduating from Cornell Law School first in his class. He was snapped up by the Justice Department's Criminal Division, eventually migrating to the Fraud Section. Then Watergate broke, and in its wake came Lockheed, Bananagate and a host of scandals whose revelations of slush funds, political skulduggery and sleaze had triggered a bout of national self-loathing that had given birth to the Foreign Corrupt Practices Act (FCPA). Winston had become a government sleuth, pursuing the kind of corporate misbehaviour deemed to bring the US into international disrepute.

And then he had walked through the revolving door, taking his forensic understanding of the new anti-bribery legislation to Melville & Bart, where he found himself advising exactly the kind of American corporations he had once sought to prosecute. I must have looked judgemental at this point because, for the first time, Winston became defensive: 'What people don't always realise,' he said, 'is that in a lot of companies, senior management often genuinely believes it is behaving ethically. The CEO's been kept in the dark by a regional manager who thinks buying the president's son a new Porsche is standard business practice. We show these guys how to clean up their act.' I nodded, as if in agreement. There was no disguising the fact that the gamekeeper had turned poacher, but it wasn't hard to guess why. As a senior partner at Melville

& Bart, Winston had probably pulled down in a month what he would have earned in a year at the Justice Department. Hard for a cleaner's son, raised in poverty, to resist.

A few years later, Winston had had an epiphany. A mining client had invited him to visit its project in Liberia. It was his first trip to the land of his forefathers and, strolling Monrovia's ramshackle streets, he was surprised by how at home he felt. He was also surprised, sitting on the terrace of his Mamba Point hotel, watching fruit bats stir in the palm trees, to overhear conversations that revealed his client was bankrolling both the government and the rebels in the civil war. 'I suppose it was pretty naïve,' he said, with a rueful smile, 'but I was shocked. When I came back, I called a partners' meeting. I told them I would no longer represent the client and urged Melville & Bart to withdraw. My colleagues refused. It got fairly unpleasant. I was on the verge of resigning. Instead we struck a deal. I'd continue reeling in corporate clients but they would make some room for me to do *pro bono* work in the developing world on the side. My way of salving my conscience. I can sleep at night, the firm's reputation gets a boost.'

Winston started wandering the world, and found there was no shortage of causes to champion. Once frozen hard by the Cold War, international borders had turned liquid and negotiable in the former Soviet Union, the Balkans and Africa. New nation states were emerging, in urgent need of constitutions and bills of rights. Relations between neighbouring countries were up for redefinition. It was work that few of those governments knew how to handle. It was work that Winston Peabody III seemed born to do.

There had been a long collaboration with Moldova's independence movement; he'd tried to establish an unbeatable case for the return of the Chagos Islands' deported residents; and had advised Afghanistan's *loya jirga* on a new constitution. Colleagues marvelled at his appetite for airlines blacklisted by US embassies, brothels masquerading as hotels, and his willingness to pop a

Lariam with his morning coffee at a stage when they had grown dependent on the five-star hotel, the chauffeured pick-up, the left aircraft swivel into business class.

I sipped my beer, silently noting the absence of any reference to 'my wife', 'my partner' or 'the kids'. No alimony, no pets. Gardening got a brief mention, but how far could that take a man? Was the law Winston's only passion?

The roundabout route had brought him to the Horn of Africa. Winston had led a team that had virtually written the constitution of still-unrecognised Somaliland. He had found himself drafting legislation on ancestral grazing rights for a young mayor in the Ethiopian highlands – the man had raved about his work at a regional conference. A job in South Sudan had followed, and finally the authorities in Lira had reached out.

'It was a bizarre experience. I boarded a bus in Juba, heading east. I thought this was going to be my only chance to see Lira – you know people rave about the 1930s architecture? – so I'd arranged a stopover. I couldn't remember telling anyone my plans. As I got off the bus two men in their fifties, both with that weathered, tough look about them you get here, stepped forward and said, quietly and politely, "Mr Peabody? Could we have a word?" They must have monitored me all the way from Sudan. This is one of only about three governments in Africa, I reckon, capable of running such an effective intelligence network. It comes of spending decades under enemy occupation, I suppose. You learn the tricks of the trade.'

They had virtually frogmarched him to a nearby café and explained that someone important wanted to see him. Then they had driven him to the old Italian governor's palace on the hill, through a single checkpoint – 'He doesn't do security, says if any member of the public wants to assassinate him he'll have outlived his usefulness anyway' – and ushered him straight into the president's office, where he had been relentlessly wooed. For what could have been better calculated to win round a

40

left-leaning maverick without a cause, a New World, African-American intellectual snob, than a brutally honest exposition of an African administration's lack of preparedness to meet the most testing legal challenge of its short existence, delivered in a gruff monotone by the Man Himself during a protocol-free tête-à-tête?

'For the first hour I wasn't offered so much as a glass of tea, which is incredibly rude in this culture,' he recalled, with a fond smile. 'The zero-charisma charm offensive, I like to call it, a Lira speciality.' And it had worked like a dream, I thought, noticing how uncharacteristically flustered Winston looked, like a lover voicing a girlfriend's name at the family table.

'He was just, well, extremely impressive.' Winston threw me a surreptitious glance. 'You'll meet him one of these days and see for yourself. I suppose it's partly that he appears to lack … wiles. What you see is what you get – that's half of the problem when he's operating in the international arena. No bowing and scraping from his staff, none of that "Your Excellency" nonsense. He was dressed very simply, an outfit I've now seen a hundred times. He was totally open, made no attempt to cover anything up. The machinery of government barely existed, he told me. They'd done their best in the bush during the war of independence, running clandestine schools, but literacy rates among the former fighters now in charge of the various departments were embarrassing. He had ministers, he said, who could barely read the newspapers, let alone master Microsoft Word. Wonderful military strategists, but they'd started out as goatherds. Even before the clash in Sanasa and the new war, most of the real work of government was being done by a few harried secretaries left over from the old regime whom no one really trusted. Shortages of printers, photocopiers, cartridges, even pens. The educated elite were taking their time returning from exile, and when they arrived they wanted to set up import-export outfits, not work in government. This was a state that could barely issue a driver's licence so contesting a border dispute in The Hague was simply beyond its capacities.'

'And you agreed to do it for them?'

He pursed his lips. 'That's not how I would phrase it. I see myself in a mentoring role. A facilitator, if you like. These guys may not have taken classes in international tort, but there's no shortage of brains. Part of your job here will be to pass on what you have learned, thanks to your privileged Western education, to the local staff. It's like water on a sponge – every drop gets soaked up. I won't tolerate any apartheid in the office. I can't stand that Western staff-versus-local-hire rivalry that so often develops. We all need one another's skills. They may not know the law but we don't know the local culture and don't speak the language. The ultimate aim of the Western staff – you, me, Sharmila and the interns – should be to put ourselves out of a job.'

'You'd better talk me through the case.'

'We're going to need to raise our blood sugar for that.' Winston made a vague gesture, and two slabs of vanilla ice-cream were placed before us. Vanilla ice-cream, I was to discover, was the only dessert that ever passed his lips. He would become agitated if any attempt was made – an oozing gash of raspberry ripple, a dollop of puréed fruit – to 'jazz it up'. 'It's perfect,' he claimed. 'Never tamper with perfection.' Carving cat-tongues from his magnolia ingot with a teaspoon, he laid it all out.

5

Most of us have watched so many police thrillers and legal dramas, we have a pretty accurate grasp of what form a criminal court case takes. International arbitration is different. It usually happens in private. It can take any form the parties decide. In this case, the two presidents had agreed to a two-stage process. First, the course of the contested border would be established by an independent Border Commission made up of lawyers and academics with pedigrees in international dispute settlement. Each government's legal team would plead its case before those veterans, who were both judge and jury. Once the border had been decided, the issue of who bore responsibility for starting such a wasteful scrap – *jus ad bellum*, as it was technically known – would be decided by a panel of inquiry to be set up in Addis Ababa by the African Union, which was keen to demonstrate its readiness to police the continent.

I was arriving late to the party. Both sides had already filed Memorials, opening salvoes in a contest that would climax with a ruling dubbed 'final and binding'. It was the experience of drafting the 'granddaddy of Memorials', as Winston referred to it, that had finally persuaded him he needed help. The Memorials summarised each side's arguments and were bursting with pertinent facts, set in historical context and backed up by legal argument and precedent. Winston had clearly found the task near overwhelming.

'It's a damn good piece of work, if I say so myself,' he said, scooping up his ice-cream with surprising speed. 'But, then, their side's isn't too bad either, as you'll see. I'd recommend that's all you do for the first few days here, just sit down and read the two Memorials. You're going to end up knowing them as well as a pulpit-thumping preacher knows his Bible. We have six weeks to prepare our counter-Memorials, demonstrating what fools and liars they've been. Then both sides swap those and prepare for the final showdown, the hearing.'

'What are we arguing?'

'We're going for a multi-strand approach. Hopefully each strand of the argument complements the others to form a nice thick rope of validation. First,' he said, ticking one stubby finger, 'we'll use nineteenth-century colonial treaties and the beautiful, beautiful maps that go with them.' Briefly he looked quite dreamy. Then his expression changed. 'Did you know that a map, without a treaty attached, carries almost no legal weight?'

'No, I didn't.'

'Any fool can draw an outline on a sheet of paper and claim it represents this stretch of land, that area of sea. Before aerial surveys and satellite photographs, maps were little more than explorers' imaginings. But maps have an emotional impact that all the written text running alongside them – which is what really matters in court – just can't match. Humans are very visual creatures. You can almost *hear* arbitrators heave a sigh of relief when they're presented with a map, however suspect: "Oh, *now* I understand."'

The prettier the map, he claimed, the greater the impact. 'I've built up a wonderful collection, which I'll probably end up donating to Lira's National Museum, once it exists. All thanks to our volunteers. We've got two youngsters sifting through the British National Archives in Kew, while Francesca de Mello, an Italian PhD student, is checking the Foreign Ministry's records in Rome. One of your duties, by the way, is to liaise with Francesca – sweet woman but needy, very needy. They've been sending me the treaties drawn up by Italian and British cartographers in the 1880s and 1890s, when the European powers were divvying up the region, anxious to avoid misunderstandings with the Negus of Darrar. A shame we didn't learn more from their example,' he said, pushing his empty bowl away.

'I thought the colonial powers were rather sloppy in that regard. The cuttings I read,' in the nick of time I stopped myself saying 'this morning', 'kept referring to "poorly delineated" colonial borders.'

'Well, imperial powers are like one's parents, aren't they? The satisfaction of criticising them just never wears off. It's true they don't go into quite as much detail as we would like. And there are some developments the colonial masters couldn't foresee. They used promontories, rivers and trees as reference points, and over a century rivers change course, trees die, coastlines dance around with shifting wind patterns. So it's difficult to build a case on treaties and maps alone, though I intend to have a damn good try.'

'What else, then, if you're worried that won't be enough?'

'Basically, a track record of administration, or "subsequent conduct of the party in question", as it's called. The other side, you see, is arguing that supposed "facts on the ground" made a mockery of cartography that was little more than colonial wishful thinking. Whatever the maps showed, Sanasa and other contested border areas were actually run by *their* officials, inhabitants voted in *their* elections, local businesses paid taxes to *their* capital. Just like the law, a treaty, especially one drawn up by foreigners who didn't speak the lingo, can be an ass, flying in the face of how residents actually behave. Or so the other side claims. We have to prove the opposite.'

I was suddenly aware of a strange sense of floating, the table seemed to be heaving. Jet-lag was kicking in. I frowned, forcing myself to focus. 'Presumably we also need to be planning Phase Two, the question of who started it.'

'Yes, and the outcome of that will pack enormous emotional and political punch. Just think of a teacher pulling apart two scrapping children. The first thing the kids shout is "He started it!"'

'But the teacher's response to that is always "I don't care. I just want some peace and quiet."'

'That's never true, though, is it? The kid that gets its bottom smacked is always the one fingered as the aggressor. An obsession with justice is a human universal, or you and I would be out of a job. And the issue of who initiated a fight is particularly important in macho societies where loss of face is seen as unacceptable.'

'They, presumably, are claiming North Darrar went first.'

'Went first and then deliberately escalated the conflict, rolling a column of tanks into their territory in an uncalled-for act of belligerence.'

'That rings a bell.'

'CNN ran the images of those T-55s pounding away on the eastern and central fronts for weeks. Which doesn't exactly help our case. There was a good tactical reason for that move, by the way. You can't defend an area by keeping your troops down on the plains. You need to take the high ground. That's what our army did.'

I registered that 'our'. 'So the African Union inquiry is key.'

'The international community's not very good at shades of grey. The press, the diplomats, the aid industry and foreign investors will expect the AU to tell them which country is a testosterone-charged bully, which one a blameless victim. The reverberations of that ruling will echo through the decades.'

I could see it all ahead: the nights in the office, the Styrofoam cups of cold coffee, the documents edited and re-edited until the English language seemed to lose its meaning.

Winston saw my expression and gave me an impish smile. 'Courage, my girl! Did you think you were coming on vacation?'

'Sorry – it just seems a bit daunting.'

'Relish the challenge, that's what I do. Having discovered early on that I was both good at and immensely bored by most of the jobs for which I was qualified, the search for something more testing began. It's no coincidence that all my *pro bono* clients have been involved in disputes in which the odds ran firmly against them. For an outsider who feels in his bones that he snuck into the legal establishment and could be ejected at any moment, the ultimate thrill will always be to pull off the seeming miracle. What *is* the appeal of representing Darrar, regional giant, friend of the West? I don't know how the other side's lawyers get up in the morning. Underdogs, that's my thing. Takes one to know one.'

He gestured to one of the waitresses, slouched against a wall, and made the air scribble that is recognised the world over.

6

And so I settled into my nest, like a dog turning round and round on a cushion, working the stuffing with its paws until it feels right.

My new home was an apricot-coloured villa, one of a dinky, pastel-coloured set of five built around a tennis-court-sized patch of dry grass on the edge of Lira's industrial district. It had been built so quickly that it was already falling apart, recently laid ceramic tiles cracking underfoot, light switches jiggling at the touch. I quailed inwardly as Abraham showed me around, registering the tiny bedrooms and a design scheme that had the kitchen opening directly onto the living room. The shelves in the bathroom were already crammed with lotions. There wasn't going to be much privacy.

My new housemate, Sharmila – owner of said beauty products – was a Sri Lankan-American using her time in Lira as the basis for a PhD. She was nominally in charge of three US student interns, the Braces-and-Barrette Set, as I mentally labelled them, who lived in the raspberry-painted villa next to ours. When we were introduced, Sharmila gave me a smile that showed perfect teeth but failed to reach her eyes. Her slim hands were smooth and manicured, making mine feel as rough as a butcher's. I sensed that she resented my prospective presence at the breakfast table.

'How are you finding it?' I asked, as she leaned against the door jamb, watching me unpack.

'OK, if backward shitholes are your thing.'

'Oh.' She'd succeeded in shocking me. We clearly applied different standards: I'd been struck by Lira's sophistication. 'What do people do here when they're not working?'

'I have a boyfriend, Steve, who works for the UN. We hang out. And you? Man on the scene?'

'Nope.' I pronounced the word very deliberately, accentuating the *p*.

'I suppose Lira could be fun,' she conceded, picking up a book from my case and giving it a careless once-over, 'if we weren't working for Winston. The other expatriates are mostly aid workers and they're up in arms about the government's human-rights record. So we get treated as pariahs. It's such a bore.'

'Don't you ever meet any locals?'

'I've tried, but it's pretty hard work. Not much in common, amazingly,' she said, with heavy sarcasm. 'I didn't spend twenty years fighting in a trench.'

On the first afternoon at the office, I grappled with the *faux*-leather chair, adjusting the back support and seat height, aware that these small adjustments marked the start of a new phase in my life. This was now my perch, a place where I was going to spend many future hours. I tipped the chair and swivelled it the full 360 degrees a few times, slowly taking in the view.

The Legal Office of the President of the State of North Darrar operated out of a former five-room apartment on the second floor of a colonial building. The main office, separated by a frosted-glass door that he always kept ajar – the better to oversee the rest of us – was for Winston. The rest was open-plan.

The local team included Barnabas, the office manager, and Abraham, driver, fixer, errand-runner. Winston loved referring to 'my two office prophets', occasionally adding, to no one in particular, 'If you ever meet an Isaiah, tell him he's got the job!' A quiet rivalry simmered between the two men, I came to realise, rooted – as the secretary Ribqa explained – in the fact that lean Abraham was an ex-Fighter (you could hear the respectful capital when she said it), while Barnabas was a trained civil servant, with an office worker's paunch, a man who had once dutifully served in what Abraham's comrades regarded as an alien administration, from which he expected to collect an eventual pension. That difference found expression in a strict division of tasks. Any problem arising inside the office – paperwork, form-filling, utilities bills, computers – was Barnabas's business. Anything involving the bracing, manly outdoors – the jeeps, fuel for the generator, field trips, picking up visitors – was Abraham's.

Then there were Yohannes and Ismael, two youngsters Winston had commandeered from the Ministry of Justice, talent-spotted while he was lecturing at the University of Lira's beleaguered Law Department. 'Very lucky boys,' Ribqa said to me, nodding towards them. 'If you work at the Legal Office of the President, no military service for you.' And, of course, there was Ribqa herself, whose attitude to all our goings-on could best be termed as one of tolerant contempt, our work something she indulged but did her best to ignore. Her interest was the food she brought to the office: home-made bread or almond cake, which she would invite us all to sample.

The apartment must once have been the home of affluent white settlers, an urban *pied-à-terre*, perhaps, for an Italian family running an up-country coffee estate who felt they needed injections of city culture if the youngsters were not to run wild on the farm. It was still cluttered with dark, heavy furniture – ponderously carved dressers and armoires with blue-veined marble tops and tilting mirrors patched with golden mildew. While I was helping Abraham to push one of these to a wall to make way for a flat-pack desk – 'It's OK, Paula this is no work for a woman' – we paused to marvel at a manufacturer's metal plaque on the back.

'1831! Wow,' said Abraham, 'really old.'

'Yes. And really ugly.'

There was a quiet poignancy about the apartment's lofty

ceilings, with their alabaster light fittings and plaster mouldings, the wide, superfluous corridors in which we perched our printers, shredders and photocopiers. The people who had built it had assumed they were in Africa for good, so why stint, when labour and materials were cheap? Be sure to leave enough space for the servants you will always depend upon and the grandchildren you are certain to have.

Mantelpieces meant for wedding photographs now held stacks of memory sticks and hard drives, staplers and cartons of paper-clips. In between the giant maps that covered the walls – courtesy of the UN Logistics Office and dotted with Post-it notes and coloured drawing pins – you could see the ghostly outlines left by auctioned oil paintings. The tiled floor was the kind an Italian grandmother would order to be waxed, then protect with polishing slippers: I could almost hear the shrieks of delight of the children sliding along it when her back was turned.

There was a large kitchen, where we brewed coffee when working late, and a bathroom with deep-bowled washbasin and bidet dating from an era when the 'quick shower' had yet to be invented. The tub was kept permanently full of water, with a red bucket alongside, and had acquired its own ecosystem, a floating population of drowned beetles, spiders and expiring mosquitoes.

'What's this for?' I asked Sharmila.

'Oh, you can never count on water supplies in Lira,' she said, with an airy wave of one beautiful hand. 'It's our do-it-yourself toilet-flushing system. Disgusting, eh? If my parents could see me now! They left Sri Lanka to get away from this kind of thing.'

'I think I can probably handle it.'

She gave me a hard look. 'Just wait till you get an upset stomach. Then you'll see just how much fun a non-flushing bathroom is.'

The ceilings were high enough to accommodate old-fashioned fans, whose steady *whump*s, on a good day, conjured up memories of Somerset Maugham, gin and bitters. But those *whump*s were intermittent because power, like the water, came and went, a constant source of office tension. 'Oh, Jesus, no, no, no,' an intern would wail as a long-awaited fax from Washington stalled in mid-flow or a half-written document vanished from a screen before being saved. It was amazing how quickly one moved from self-admonition ('This isn't the US, adjust') via frustrated panic ('How am I expected to work?') to sardonic fury ('This place is stuck in the Middle Ages'), the process culminating, in my case, in a swift exit to kick a wall and smoke a calming cigarette.

The metal shutters on the apartment's windows had long since rusted into immobility, so those of us who sat beneath them were always simultaneously surveying and under surveillance. I spent so many hours gazing meditatively down the quiet street that by the end I could have drawn it in my sleep. The pavement of dimpled ceramic tiles. A blue-overalled workman digging up a decayed sewer. Local boys kicking a stuffed sock tethered to a whitewashed fig tree. A tabby cat taking the sun on the wall between the houses opposite, squeezing its eyelids rhythmically in silent pleasure. And, at the periphery of my vision, the corner where the street met the main boulevard, two soldiers, AK-47s slung over skinny shoulders, all hip bones, jutting Adam's apples and oversized black boots, checking the papers of passing pedestrians.

One soft spring evening, they spot one another at the opening of a photography exhibition sponsored by Hitchens at a SoHo gallery. A Senegalese musician is picking at a kora and the chilled white wine is flowing. There are no canapés, so they are both slightly drunk by the time Jake offers to walk her home. Relief floods her when he makes clear that she should take his arm – finally, an excuse to touch – and once their arms are interlocked he places a proprietorial hand over hers, making disengagement impossible.

They toddle south like an elderly couple, disappointed that there are few excuses to stop, point and pass comment, eking out the moments before separation becomes inevitable. With slowing footsteps they reach the entrance to her Greenwich Village apartment block, her voice squeaky with anxiety because she does not know what is about to happen or what she wants.

He pulls open the accordion door of the old-fashioned elevator – the reason she originally chose this apartment – kisses her chastely on the brow, steps back and pulls the grill shut. Phew, something nearly happened, she thinks. She smiles a polite farewell, finger hovering over the button to the fourth floor. As she presses, she realises that she has taken the wrong fork in the road. Meeting his eyes, she sees that he knows it too. Appalled, she calls, 'Jake!' even as he shouts, 'Wait!' Then she sees him running up the stairs as the elevator rises through the shaft. She is frantically pressing buttons – the elevator bounces, stalls, restarts, stops, and he yanks back the accordion door. The next ten minutes – which feel like hours – are spent kissing inside the metal cage until someone above shouts down to ask if there's a problem. They stumble out, head for her apartment and go straight into the bedroom.

Quite soon after that, she will hear herself saying over the phone to Sarah – who draws a sharp breath at the words 'married man' – 'I know, I know. The ultimate cliché. I somehow thought – I don't know why – that I'd had the vaccination against this one.'

Ah, the careless, wasteful folly of it all. Looking back at my younger self going through the rambling, half-reluctant process of getting to know this older man, agreeing to meet at a cinema, then cancelling because of a last-minute assignment, scrupulously keeping options open via the occasional blind date, repeatedly applying the brakes through a mixture of caution and self-preservation, I want to give her a good shake. 'Get on with it, you idiot!' I want to shout. 'There's no time.'

Because on the day we met, Jake had just four years, seven months and five days to live.

7

I called Francesca de Mello in Rome the morning after Winston had briefed me. It took three attempts, with the receptionist twice cutting me off instead of putting me through.

'Signor Pibody, he is OK?' Her voice was low and husky, and she had a very strong Italian accent, placing the emphasis firmly on the second syllable of Winston's surname.

'He's fine. He just wanted me to say hello since we'll be working closely together. I gather you're due to send us some maps.'

'I have four to scan and send. I will do it tomorrow from the ministry.'

'Great. Winston also asked if you could resend the map you scanned last week. We think there's a problem with the resolution – not your fault, but the file is too big for Lira's slow internet connection. We only received half of it.'

'OK, but I cannot do that now.' She gave a heavy sigh. 'Here where I am staying is no internet. Even with the telephone, always problems.'

It sounded a strange sort of hotel. 'Where *are* you staying?'

And then it all came out, in a plaintive wail of hurt pride and nursed grievance. As she talked a picture of Francesca de Mello formed in my mind's eye: a big, blowsy woman, I guessed, who spilled over both emotionally and physically. She had been directed to the Santa Elena convent, she said, by a researcher friend, who had explained that EU health and safety legislation had forced hundreds of convents and monasteries in central Rome to close their schools. The chattering gaggles of pupils in the severe black aprons and white collars of yesteryear were gone, leaving abbots and mother superiors sitting on hundreds of square metres of prime real estate. Spotting a commercial opportunity, many had carved the communal dormitories up into single-windowed bedrooms available for rent. 'Imagine. You can stay in the city centre at a fraction of the cost of a hotel. Such a bargain,' Francesca had boasted to colleagues in Turin, and they had congratulated her on her foresight.

But the bargain, she had discovered, came at a price. At Santa Elena the service culture was an alien concept. The nuns radiated constant silent disapproval, with communications a prime area for passive-aggressive hostilities. From her tiny room, where the only decoration was a large crucifix on the wall, Francesca would hear the telephone repeatedly ringing in the downstairs hallway. On the few occasions a nun deigned to answer, she would bungle the simple manoeuvre required to put the call through. After a male friend had rung – I guessed this was a boyfriend – Francesca noticed that she had gone from being hailed as '*Signora*' to what felt like a near-contemptuous '*Signorina*'.

'*Non sono mica un adolescente!*' she expostulated. 'I'm a forty-year-old woman and I talk to whoever I like. I could buy a mobile phone, yes, but why should I, just to please these *vecchie zitelle?*' What was more, the nuns operated a virtual curfew, making clear that late-night returns would not be tolerated.

'Sounds awful. But, look, I'll keep trying. I can be very persistent.'

She heaved a doleful sigh. 'OK, we try.'

'Winston said you're working towards a PhD. What's the topic?'

'Ingegnere Enrico Agostini and the contribution Lira's sewerage system made to the history of nineteenth-century Italian colonialism.' Agostini was one of the founding fathers of modern Lira, she explained, her voice flat. In the 1890s his workmen had built water courses and laid sewage pipes, taming the rivers that meandered across the high plateau. 'I am in the fourth year now. The doctorate is nearly finished.' There was no discernible enthusiasm in her voice. I felt a bubble of hilarity rising in my chest and hung up, shaking my head in amusement.

Winston was watching me from across the room. 'Was that the lovely Francesca?'

'Yes. I see what you mean. She's a tad lugubrious, isn't she?'

'Indeed.'

'I got the firm impression she'd far rather speak to Signor Pibody than to me.'

'Ah, but that would defeat the point of the exercise. With time, I'm confident you two will bond. Now, would you mind going to see Dr Berhane? He has a report for us. Background stuff, but he also said he'd stumbled upon something we might find useful. His office is opposite the Methodist church, above the hairdresser's.'

'Who's he?'

'Berhane Mikael. The closest thing we've got to a local historian. They use first names on second reference here, by the way. He's the ruling party's favourite intellectual, lots of friends in high places. I've asked him to draft a few pages on the background to the conflict. Get Abraham to run you over.'

I jumped over the sheet of dirty water that a stocky woman in a headscarf was expertly guiding down a cascade of mottled marble steps with a broom. The sombre courtyard, stacked with white plastic chairs and pot plants was a once-grand entrance now well past its prime. But the first-floor office was a revelation. Not so much an office as a miniature library, lined with the kind of books you need two hands to lift off the shelf. Leather-bound in rust-brown, maroon and baize-green, the lettering picked out in gold, these were objects of beauty rather than study. *The Oxford Dictionary of National Biography* in twenty-two volumes. *An Illustrated Guide to the Flora and Fauna of East Africa*. Ten volumes of *Dizionario Letterario Bompiani*, a *History of Modern Thought*, *A Bibliography of the Negro Work*. And then there were the legal reference books, whose volumes took up an entire wall. The books possessed such presence that I almost missed the man himself, sitting behind an antique desk in the far corner. He was looking at me over the top of a pair of spectacles. 'Very impressive.'

'Yes,' he acknowledged, with a small smile of satisfaction.

'You must be Dr Berhane. I'm Paula, from the president's legal office. How did you manage to build up this collection? It's amazing.'

He rose from his desk and surveyed the shelves with the quiet pride of a headmaster at assembly. 'This country used to have a large expatriate community. They left in one panicky wave after another. Each time, the books remained behind. Too heavy to move. Many of those leaving were my friends and, knowing my predilections, they consigned their collections to me. Which accounts for the slightly eccentric range you see before you,' he said. 'I even own a five-volume encyclopaedia of equine diseases. A more rigorous archivist would cull a few topics, but I cannot bear destroying books. It feels like an atrocity. Look.' Extending one index finger, he levered out the first of eight plum-coloured volumes – Gibbon's *Decline and Fall of the Roman Empire* – and slowly ruffled its pages with his thumb. Each page had a thin gold rind; the layering leaves formed a block of iridescence. 'Just like a peacock ... Such beauty.'

'And they came through all the occupations and rebel attacks unscathed?'

'Oh, fighting men are greedy for many things – beer, women, pornography, pills. But the one thing they won't bother looting is a good read.'

He shouted instructions down the corridor and one of the cleaning ladies brought tea, served in glasses with a dissolving inch of sugar and a segment of green lemon no bigger than a baby's fingertip. As I sipped, I gazed around the room. The shelves behind him were crammed with neon-coloured files, tatty notebooks covered with Post-it notes and piles of black floppy disks, all carefully labelled.

'What do you do when you're not writing statements for our office, Dr Berhane? Winston told me you're a historian.'

'A historian by inclination, but with no formal education. I originally trained as a quantity surveyor, but there's not much call for such skills when your country is occupied. What you see here are my preparations for a post-colonial history of this country. I realised a few years ago that the men and women who had witnessed or, rather, masterminded my country's independence struggle were dying off. We do not live long here. Loss and hardship wear us out. So I set about recording what was left before it was too late. Those files and floppies contain interviews with scarred old fighters, fragile former politicians, Supreme Court judges. Bar girls who were once mistresses to generals – withered hags no man would want to touch now.' He barked with laughter. 'Snipers who assassinated colonels, active young men now anchored in wheelchairs. They are all captured there, in my notebooks and my disks. Some of them spoke to me when they were already on oxygen masks in hospital. I caught what were literally their dying words, snatched between breaths. They were so glad to tell their story before the last silence descended. For me, as a patriot, it was an honour.'

'It sounds an absolutely priceless resource.'

'It is. It would be in any society, but particularly this one. Correct me if I'm wrong but in your country, in all Western countries, there is a general agreement, a consensus as to what occurred, wouldn't you say?' He was looking at me with a whimsical expression, knowingly provocative.

'Er, well, I'm not sure about that.' He had caught me off-guard. I hadn't been expecting a discussion on truth and meaning. 'Isn't there always some academic spat going on over whether or not General Custer was a moron or Richard Nixon much misunderstood? Isn't history constantly being revised?'

He shook his head. 'Not in its grand lines, I would suggest. What you are describing is really froth on the surface, wrestling matches for the hyper-educated. I'm talking about the mass of the people. The mass of Britons, for example, agree they behaved superbly during the Blitz. The mass of Europe knows Nazism was an evil aberration, and the entire world today signs up to the American capitalist dream, which is why our own boys and girls keep drowning in the Mediterranean trying to reach it! Think of it as the kind of history you whisper in the ear of a seven-year-old when you are walking through a museum hand-in-hand. "Mummy, why is she crying?" the child asks, as you pass that famous photograph of the Vietnamese girl running naked from the napalm attack. And you mutter something about Communism and the domino theory. That's the kind of history I'm talking about. The broad lines of the narrative. And here, in this region, that has still to be written.'

He paused, tilted back in his chair and stared at the ceiling as he spun his spectacles around with one hand. He had given this speech before, I could tell. It was his way of reassuring himself, aloud, as to the purpose of his life.

'Why do you think that is?'

'Not enough intellectuals like me around!' He laughed again. 'No, that's not the reason. Partly it's because it's all too fresh. Our story still hurts. But it's also the nature of this society. We pride ourselves on our discretion. Blabbing and wallowing are not admired. The people now running this country created

60

a Trotskyite rebel movement in an occupied land, which depended on secrecy for its survival. The member of one operational cell might be best friends, share a house, or even be having sex with the member of another and never know it. Those instincts die hard. Even in today's free Lira, no one will ever tell you anything important on the phone. We got so used to being bugged, we internalised the police state. Former rebels have a mental block about writing their memoirs. So I will do it for them.'

'How much have you written?'

There was a long moment of stillness. Outside in the street I heard the jingle of a mule's bridle. I wondered if a cloud had crossed the sun, for the office suddenly seemed darker. He darted a sideways glance at me and waved a dismissive hand. 'Oh, I have not yet reached that stage. I am bringing in the sheaves, like any good harvester, stockpiling my grain, making sure conditions are nice and dry and there are no mites.

'The time for writing will come,' he continued. 'But that is why the award you and Mr Peabody will win for us in The Hague – because I have no doubt you will win – is so important. It will be one of the building blocks of the consensus I am talking about, a message written on school blackboards and explained in museum cabinets. You, too, are writing our history. So, here, my modest contribution.' He passed me a stapled wad of paper, covered with double-spaced text, then placed a floppy disk on the desk. 'And here's the digital version. Your system can still read these?'

'Yes.' I leafed swiftly through his statement, experiencing an unexpected rush of pleasure at the elegance of his prose. 'You write well, Dr Berhane,' I blurted out. 'Very well.'

He bowed his head in self-deprecation, but it was clear he was enormously pleased. 'The skill that validates my existence. We each have one, no?'

I wondered for a moment what mine was. Knowing how

to smoke in a US law firm's WC without setting off the fire alarm? It had taken years of practice.

'And, finally, what I discussed earlier with Mr Peabody. He will know what this is about.' It was a Moleskine exercise book, well thumbed and dog-eared, the paper so fine it was almost translucent.

Back at the office, I placed the package on Winston's desk. He picked up the exercise book and leafed carefully through the fragile pages.

'Aha. Captain Peter Lewisham's diary. Dr Berhane came across it when he was cataloguing some books. Looks authentic. Captain Lewisham – retired – worked here briefly after the Italians were defeated in the Second World War and the British grudgingly took over Mussolini's favourite colony. He was posted to Kakardi, which is up in the highlands about two hundred kilometres south-west of Sanasa, where he ran a police station. Berhane says he talks a lot about trouble with the *shiftas*.'

'*Shiftas?*'

'Bandits. Most of the local men recruited by the Italians to fight on Mussolini's side – the *askaris* – were demobilised, but some disappeared into the hills with their guns. I guess they were the forerunners of the rebels who eventually won independence. Anyway, there might be something in there. Think you can decipher it?'

The handwriting, in dark blue ink, was tiny, the words packed so tightly they struggled to breathe. But it was surprisingly clear. 'I think so.'

'Thank Heaven for all those lessons in copperplate our ancestors had to sweat through. That'll be your job, then. Go through it and transcribe anything in it of relevance to our case.'

'Such as?'

'Anything that shows where the British administrators believed the border to be in the 1940s and 1950s. Relevant evidence is like pornography, in my experience. As the Supreme Court's Justice Stewart said, "You know it when you see it."'

'Dr Berhane also said he'd appreciate any memory sticks or floppies we have to spare. Apparently the ones on sale here are three times what they cost in Dubai airport. Local retailers making a killing, I suppose.'

'Anything to help our resident myth-maker. I'll get Abraham to drop a box off.'

'Is that how you see him? He thinks he's working on the first draft of history.'

Winston sighed. 'Ah. Myth, history, fables, reportage ... Whatever I may claim in a hearing, my dear Paula, there are times,' he gestured at the paperwork on his desk, 'especially when I'm reading the conflicting accounts of what happened in Sanasa, when the distinction between the various genres seems to me as fluid and shifting as the sandbanks of the Red Sea.'

8

Captain Peter Lewisham's Diary
Kakardi, 1950, pages 60–65

20 December 1950 – Took Johnny, Derek and Danny down
to the border on the Great Fowl Hunt. A winding valley
running along the Abubed river. Just because we're in
Fuzzy-wuzzy Land, no reason to pass up a Christmas roast.
We staked out the valley. Tesfay and the boys agreed to be
beaters. Turned out a treat. We counted sixteen guinea fowl
by the end – ten hens, six cocks. Came back and I showed
the women in the canteen how to hang them. They giggled.
Apparently local men steer well clear of the kitchen.

Christmas Day 1950 – Slap-up meal with all the staff. Derek
and Danny decked the canteen with ribbons and invited
some girls over from the village: pretty young things, all big
eyes and whispers. We all agreed guinea fowl is actually
better than turkey. The cook did her best with the stuffing,
but it tasted strange: too many spices, Johnny reckoned. Still,
quite a feast. We sang carols and toasted the King with the
local whisky. God, it's nasty stuff. Tiny has promised to drive
over from Lira with some imported booze next time he's on
leave. Duncan got so drunk he fell asleep with his face in the

gravy. All in all, I've got lucky. We all rub along together well enough, and I'm largely left to my own devices by HQ. Still, I'm looking forward to Christmas with Flo in Lyme Regis next year.

3 January 1951 – The boys have been hitting the local gut-rot for a week now. So today I took them on a route march. Woke them at 5.00 a.m. and marched them up the escarpment, along the crest and then down to Sitat. About sixteen miles in all. Johnny fainted halfway through, and two of the native boys were sick behind a wall when we got back to base. The lads will rib them for days about that. It feels good to be back in harness. I've got fifteen years on these chaps but I can still march them into the ground.

14 January – Pretty quiet week. Tesfay asked me to intervene in a local dispute. A dead donkey. I laughed my head off, but it's serious stuff here, a big investment. I got Tesfay to summon the parties. We made it as official as we could. One farmer said he'd lent his donkey to his neighbour, who needed to pick up supplies from the market. Neighbour allowed the donkey to wander, it broke its leg and died. The farmer wanted compensation. The other chap said the donkey was sick when he took possession and collapsed on the way to market. 'He beat his animals too much.' King Solomon had nothing on me. I asked to see the body, which meant all of us piling into jeeps and heading off to Tentet. It stank to high Heaven – I almost lost my breakfast. No sign of a broken leg and the carcass was covered with whip marks, so I said there was no case to answer and ordered them to bury the body, chop, chop. I hate the way the locals treat animals. There's no call for it.

27 January – Johnny came into my office in a terrible state. He's only gone and got a village girl pregnant. Apparently

she's one of the ones who came to the Christmas bash. I tore a strip off him, asked him what he thought the johnnies Doc Sam gave him on arrival were for and did he plan to spend his life raising camels with a brood of café-au-lait urchins? He was in tears by the end. I've contacted HQ to request a transfer. What a bloody fool. We'll be the ones who have to clear up his mess. The family will expect compensation and it's not British government policy.

3 February – There's been a shifta attack, the first for a long time: near the Italian bridge over the Abubed. Truck driver beaten up, his goods – mostly beer and fertiliser – gone.

11 February – Tiny drove over from Lira. It took him all day and he lost his way three times, perhaps not surprising given that he was still squiffy on arrival. That boy's a miracle worker. Turkish champagne, French pastis, twelve bottles of sherry, twelve of gin, two crates of beer. Women's drink, a lot of it, but anything as long as it's not local is my motto nowadays. The party began forthwith, but we're going to have to ration ourselves or this stuff won't last till the weekend. Duncan's been given orders to keep the rest under lock and key. And absolutely no drinking in front of the natives.

9

A fortnight after my arrival, Winston dispatched me on my first evidence-gathering trip. 'This dispute is all about land so you'd better get to know what it looks like. God knows it's pretty dramatic.'

We hit the road at dawn, just as you're supposed to on African journeys. I ran out of the front door of the apricot-coloured villa, passing Amanuel the district night-watchman – wrapped up like Scott of the Antarctic and apparently dozing upright – and dived into the Land Cruiser, whose exhaust was snorting in warm white gasps. The street was quiet. Two middle-aged cleaners moved silently along the pavement, their heads hidden in the clinging white cotton shawls that always called to mind burial chambers and high-pitched wailing.

'Uph, really cold,' I said, breathing on my hands. 'I should have filled a Thermos.'

Abraham, freshly shaved and immaculate, smiled and turned up the fan heater as we bounced over the pot-holed back-streets. It made such a racket he was forced to shout. 'Ah, Paula, you foreigners don't know how to deal with our climate. On a morning like this in the highlands you need –' he thumped his chest '– *internal* heating. A shot of our local speciality.' A Baroque triton, he blew a white trumpet of vapour theatrically into the air.

'Oh, God. Are you actually saying I have a drunk driver? I think that comes into the don't-ask-don't-tell category.'

He laughed. 'Fasten your seatbelt, Paula.'

I reached for the buckle. 'How about you? Am I the only one who's going to wear one of these things?'

'A seatbelt? Oh, no.' He laughed. 'Those are only for you Westerners. If you knew our history, you'd understand that we locals have already died a hundred times. It's actually a ghost driving you, Paula.'

The prospect of a road trip had clearly put him in a good mood. 'Seriously,' he continued, 'it was my birthday last week. I am the only one from my primary-school class who reached forty. If it is my time now, I will go. Only God knows. A seatbelt will make no difference.'

'Well, if you do feel it's your time now, please let me know so I can get out first.'

We were crossing the industrial area, passing what had once been, according to the rusting signboards, a soap factory and a beer-bottling plant. Then came an obligatory stop at a check-point, where two young soldiers looked at Abraham's travel permit and insisted on inspecting our luggage. One gazed at me with frank curiosity and said something to Abraham with a grin.

'He wants to know if you are married,' he said, as he returned to the Toyota, pocketing his documents.

'Tell him I'm far too old for him.'

The road to the coast appeared to point straight off the edge of the plateau, into a measureless void. Abraham pressed hard on the accelerator, the Land Cruiser roared, and for a moment I wondered if we were about to do a Thelma and Louise. As I muffled an exclamation and instinctively grasped the seat, we breasted the hummock and the road unfolded harmlessly before us, hugging the escarpment. Abraham whooped in delight and gestured wide. 'See, my beautiful country!'

It was a salt-and-pepper landscape of ruthless privation, of unpitying absence. Rents in the cloud cover revealed, thousands of feet below, riverbeds winding through valleys like motorways of sand, but no glint of water. The acacia trees that followed those fitful courses were dark witches' brooms of hostile thorns. At intervals, the odd baobab gesticulated, a giant angry triffid. Flocks of white goats picked at the slopes on the side of the road, but it was hard to see what they could find worth eating on that stony scree. A sprinkle of wild olive saplings failed to conceal the bareness below. Behind the first range of mountains I could see a series of hills, their tops peeping through a sea of early-morning mist, which was dissipating as the heat began to take its toll.

I thought for a moment of the buttercup-strewn meadows and shadow-dappled orchards of Kent, where I'd spent my childhood holidays. The green promise of glades enticing you into darkness, the haze of bluebells and wild garlic under the trees. Before their marriage had turned sour, my parents used to rent a cottage on a trout-fishing stream, and I could still remember the thwack of cow parsley against the bonnet as Dad forced the car down the lane, and the soft humidity of midge-filled evenings when I was supposed to be asleep and they sat talking on the patio. That careless lushness had come to represent beauty for me, the only scenery that might conceivably be worth dying for. But *this?* So many had died fighting for *this?*

'Beautiful, yes,' I volunteered politely. 'But so bleak, Abraham.'

He looked sombre. 'It was not always like this. Once this was all trees. I give you my word. The invaders cut them for fuel. That's what armies do. They eat the land, like locusts. Our side was the same, always hungry for firewood. Our new government will replant, and then it will go back to the way it was before, our beautiful, fertile country.'

We were looping rhythmically now, one hairpin bend after

another as we worked our way methodically down the gradient. I silently thanked the Fates that I was not doing the driving. Abraham fed the steering-wheel expertly through his slim hands, manoeuvring around a broken-down lorry over whose overheated engine two men dangled, T-shirts black with oil and sweat. Another loop, and a controlled swerve to avoid a donkey rubbing its back into the warm tarmac, exposing a cream-coloured belly. Another turn, and we skirted a burned-out Soviet tank, its barrel twisted at an impossible angle. 'From the last war, not this one,' explained Abraham. Each loop brought us a few metres closer to sea level, and I peeled off my new fleece, feeling the temperature rising.

I opened a window, aware of a rising sense of nausea. 'How much more of this is there to go, Abraham?'

'Another thirty minutes, then the road begins to level out. Do you want me to stop? Many people vomit the first time.'

'No, I think I'll be OK.' I took a few deep breaths. Then, to distract myself, I riffled through my satchel, extracting the file Winston had given me the previous night.

'So, this is one of five camps for the internally displaced in the eastern sector and it contains up to twenty thousand people from Sanasa and its outlying villages. Have you been to the others, Abraham?'

'Yes. They are bigger than this one, closer to Lira, so we did them first.'

'Winston's given me the names of fifteen people he would like us to interview.' Most were men. 'It's not politically correct to say so,' Winston had explained in the office, 'but the fact is that a lot of women in this culture make terrible witnesses. They've been brought up to be respectfully silent in the presence of men, and they can go totally mute. "Blood from a stone" is perhaps the appropriate phrase.'

'What do you want me to find out?' I'd asked.

'There's a list of standard questions. They're all aimed at collecting testimony proving an unchallenged record of civilian administration by our government. Things like tax-paying, voter registration, utility bills, any interaction with the authorities. Land deeds would be wonderful, but IDPs almost never have those.'

'A lot of these witnesses seem to be in their sixties and seventies.'

'Lawyers are like biographers. We love old people. The further back we can go, the more legitimacy our claim acquires.'

Another few loops and Abraham applied the brakes so suddenly I lurched forward and we stalled. A trio of camels was undulating across the road, whipped on by a tousle-haired teenager in a white shift. He squinted at us, shielding his eyes from sunlight so harsh it bleached everything to black and white. 'A good sign,' commented Abraham. 'When you go from goats to camels, it means you've nearly conquered the mountain.'

I took the opportunity to crouch behind a fig cactus and pee. On my return, Abraham was stretching his legs. Getting back in, he pressed the cigarette lighter and lit a Marlboro. 'Tell me something, Paula. We call these people refugees, you call them IDPs, what is the difference?'

'Ha! I asked Winston exactly the same question last night. Apparently the UNHCR, the refugee agency, insists on sticking to legal terminology. You can only be a refugee if you cross an international border. Otherwise, you're internally displaced. Just a question of definition.'

But that wasn't quite true, I thought. Everyone knew who refugees were. They were those people we'd seen in black-and-white stills pushing carts across 1940s France in shabby coats, and the Hutu families who had trudged out of Rwanda, sleeping mats balanced on their heads. They shared the same expression of questing desperation. 'Internally displaced persons'? Who were they? The phrase conjured up some painless version of community musical chairs. Professional do-gooders and diplomats might wake at night fretting over the fate of IDPs, but the public at large reserved their sympathy for 'refugees'. They had been screwed by language, their plight leached of poignancy by UN officialese.

A deadening torpor descended as we hit the straight coastal road. At his request, I fed Abraham first cigarettes, then sticks of chewing gum: it's harder to fall asleep when your jaws are working.

We passed a giant tortoise, up-ended in the road like a salad bowl, stubby legs protruding. The plains sparkled in the early-morning sun, flashes of light bouncing off shards of quartz, fragments of gypsum, crumbs of pink marble, granite and all the other deposits, Abraham explained, that lay behind the 'mineral-rich' promise made in the government brochures once handed out to visiting investors.

A troupe of baboons galloped through the thorn bushes. The alpha male stopped to present an outraged scarlet face towards us, defiant and unafraid.

'This road is so quiet now,' commented Abraham. 'In the old days there were hundreds of commercial trucks heading to the coast and back again. The truckers always drove like idiots. I lost friends on this road. Now the other side refuses to use our ports and the only way you can have an accident is from boredom.'

But soon it stopped being boring, as the tarmac disintegrated and Abraham fought the road, swerving to avoid giant pot-holes carved by winter rains. At times, he lost patience and simply drove off piste, munching thorn bushes below the bonnet, bouncing off gravel banks and furrowing riverbeds whose sands were as soft as fudge. Yet whenever another vehicle appeared ahead – usually an army truck – I noticed that respectability returned, and two vehicles that had been plaiting wildly rebellious courses always observed the decorum of passing on the right.

For what seemed like hours, we stared at a red dot shimmering on the horizon, the only patch of colour in the drab landscape. Abraham slowed as we approached. A battered old Fiat was drawn up on the roadside, its hood up. I realised that there was human life in the shade of the thorn bush next to the car. An old woman was holding a toddler, waving flies away with a straw fan. Her wizened husband, swathed in white, sat half in the shade and half out of it, one brown hand holding out a giant gold kettle. His face was expressionless.

Abraham braked, reached into the back for a jerry-can of water and got out of the Land Cruiser. A few words were exchanged as he filled the old man's kettle. I was astonished when he returned to the Toyota and pulled away.

'Hey, wait, Abraham, not so fast! Shouldn't we give them a lift? Where are they heading?'

He looked at me in surprise. 'I don't know.'

'But they could die of thirst. This is the middle of nowhere. We should take them somewhere.'

'They were not asking for a lift, Paula. They were asking for water. I gave them what they asked for.' I stared anxiously into the Land Cruiser's side mirror as the red dot receded into the distance, but no one leaped from the bushes, hollering for our return.

By the time we reached Transit Camp, Eastern, No. 3, the air-conditioning was working as furiously as the heater had a few hours earlier. Abraham parked outside the gates, and as he switched off the ignition I realised that the metallic buzzing I'd assumed to be generated by the engine was part of the great outdoors: a cicada chorus. I took a slow breath, quietly dreading what lay ahead, then reluctantly opened the door. The heat was absurd. I laughed in disbelief, waited instinctively for the assault to pass, then realised it never would. The sweat glands in my armpits and groin began to prickle.

'Where first?'

'The camp administrator, Sammy. I remember him from the front – a funny man, good singer, so we called him Sammy Davis Junior. He will know everything.'

'Not UNHCR?' I asked, pointing to what was clearly the refugee agency's office, an air-conditioned container. A small mountain of empty water bottles had collected next to it. 'To be polite?'

Abraham grunted in scorn. 'Their job is to hand out tents. That's all they know how to do. And we do not need to be polite. If the UN had done its job in the first place, we would not be in this mess.'

'Winston said that, whatever happens, we should try to avoid accepting a meal. Ribqa gave me some packed lunches.' Winston's exact words had been: 'Personally, I find it mortifying to see a refugee family slaughtering their prized goat to fatten a well-fed Westerner.'

Abraham shrugged. 'We can try. We will fail. Hospitality is part of our culture. These people have nothing, but they will insist on sharing that nothing with us.'

The administrator's tent was at the camp's high point, the path to its door marked with whitewashed rocks and a row of lovingly watered oleanders planted in recycled cooking-oil tins. To the north we could glimpse the molten coast, a biscuit-coloured blur whose horizon shifted and melted in the heat, making it impossible to distinguish sea from sky. To the south stretched the IDP camp.

A blue haze of wood fire rose above a giant, pixelated canvas of blue and white rectangles, a gaudy mosaic whose tarpaulins surreally brought to mind funfairs and candy floss. It gave off a rich, steady murmur. It was the sound, I realised, that all cities would produce if traffic was removed, a complex, constant hum which contained within it the metallic clink of saucepans being washed, the comforting pock of wood being chopped, the bleat of goats, barking dogs, babies wailing, adult chat, bursts of laughter. I felt my tense, hunched shoulders relaxing. Of course. How melodramatic of me. An IDP camp was just another type of community.

'Your first refugee camp?' asked Abraham.

'Yes.'

'How does it seem?'

'I expected worse, to be honest. Squalor, wailing, that sort of thing.' I gave an embarrassed laugh.

'Losing your home doesn't mean you lose your dignity.'

'So I see. It seems very well organised. Big, though. Makes clear the disruption the war caused.'

'They have kept the original villages intact,' Abraham said, and my eyes followed his finger. This was an emergency city with distinct neighbourhoods, the tents arranged not in functional rows but in clusters. 'All the camps are like this. It's easier that way. Everyone knows who is who and what their role is. And it means when the word comes they are ready to go back.'

Go back? They would only go back if we won the case.

Inside the tent a small delegation was waiting, drinking tea and fanning themselves with UNHCR registration forms. Under the tarpaulin, the shade smelt of old rubber and was as hot as soup, but at least it was shade. Greetings were exchanged and introductions made, warm Fantas and Cokes extracted from a crate. Abraham and Sammy leaned in to one another, bumped shoulders, then patted and held one another in a comradely way that I guessed represented recognition of shared battlefield experience; the rest of us made do with respectful murmurs and rapid intakes of breath. I was trying to work out why my handshake with Sammy had felt slightly peculiar, when he reached to scratch an eyebrow. Two fingers were missing. He noticed my glance and held out a maimed hand, showing pink stubs. 'I was too slow throwing a grenade. Not this war, the last one. It's been a long time since I could blow my nose.' Hearty laughter from the men. The women in the group looked either uncomprehending or slightly awkward. But the joke had broken the ice, and everyone seemed to relax.

'Your colleague told us yesterday that you wanted to interview people from Sanasa,' said Sammy. 'Most of the IDPs come from there, so you will not be short of candidates.'

'In fact, you could talk to anyone here,' added a bearded young man in a blue and white checked shirt. He had introduced himself as George, the camp doctor. He was handsome, with the lean ranginess of youth and huge brown eyes. He spoke perfect English, but with a distinctive twang – Australian, South African? – that reminded me of someone.

'That's wonderful,' I said, quailing. I hadn't expected it to be so hot. Large damp crescents had formed under each arm, and as I reached for my Fanta I could feel wet flesh separate and glue itself back together. Abraham's upper lip was beaded with sweat, I noticed with some satisfaction. At least I wasn't the only wimp. 'Maybe we should start. I don't want to waste your time.'

Sammy shrugged. 'Oh, don't worry about that. The one thing IDPs have plenty of is time. Your visit is the most exciting thing to happen in the camp this week. Everyone has been looking forward to it.'

A gaggle of children had already gathered at the tent's door flap, mouths open in wonder. One tiny girl, a small finger exploring a nostril, was wearing what must once have been a Western housewife's cocktail dress, which dropped to her ankles and fell open at the side. The boys, whose heads had been shaved to leave a single central forelock, wore oversized shorts belted with packing twine. Sammy swirled and barked at them, mutilated hand raised, and they fled, squealing. Even as he turned to face me again, they were edging back into the frame, playing an undeclared game of Grandmother's Footsteps. Cocktail Girl, I noticed, was all skirt and no knickers. I suppressed a smile. Silence fell, and I realised that everyone in the tent was looking expectantly at me, waiting for the day's entertainment to start.

'We're going to have to talk to each person one-on-one, I'm afraid. We can't do group interviews.'

'No problem,' said Sammy. 'You will have all the privacy you need.' He began issuing orders, and soon plastic chairs were being unstacked, a folding table erected. 'I will go and check the catering arrangements. You will be staying for a meal, of course.'

I exchanged looks with Abraham, who raised an eyebrow, refusing to rescue me.

'Er ...' My mind raced. Brainwave. 'I'm afraid I don't eat meat.'

'You don't eat meat?' Sammy looked incredulous. 'That sounds very unhealthy. You will change your mind when you see how our women prepare it.'

A few minutes later, I heard a piteous bleating and caught a glimpse, through the tent flap, of a hobbled white kid being led to its fate.

10

A few hours later Abraham and I took a break, exiting the tent to light each other's cigarettes in the shade of a giant euphorbia cactus. We stood in silence, savouring a welcome moment of blankness after all the questions and answers, the names, dates, family trees and locations.

Down at the main entrance we spotted a white truck bearing the UNHCR logo manoeuvring laboriously in the dust, and George the doctor locked in intense conversation with two local soldiers.

'What's going on down there?' I asked idly. One of the soldiers was shouting, spittle spraying from his lips. I winced as George, neck muscles bunched, jabbed a finger aggressively in his face. Now the other soldier had snatched a handful of George's checked shirt, but he yanked himself free, pushed the first man back with a flat hand to the chest and stalked up the hill in long, emphatic strides. He was so overwrought he nearly careered into the two of us.

'What happened? Are you OK?'

He ignored me, unleashing a torrent of words at Abraham, who held out a placatory hand and said something soothing, to no avail. George stomped to the barbed-wire fence, where he stood cursing under his breath. Then he slowly returned to where we stood, staring with bitterness at the checkpoint, where a crowd was slowly gathering around the truck.

'Cigarette, please,' George said, reverting to English, gesturing at my pack. His hand quivered with adrenalin as he pulled one out.

'What is it?'

'The soldiers are conscripting the IDPs,' he said, with a grimace. 'That's twice this month. They come and round up the young men – some are no more than boys – and we never see them again. It's a violation of international law. IDP camps are places where people should be protected, not drafted. We are not here to supply the army with cannon fodder. Look, they even move them around in UNHCR trucks! And nobody does anything about it.'

'Why do they do it?'

'Ah, they talk about every youngster having to do his duty, that they are part of a great national project. As though carrying a gun is the only service you can provide. You know,' he said, looking at me, 'I left a houseman's position at Liverpool's best hospital to come here. That was a job a lot of my contemporaries wanted. I got it, and I gave it up for my country. And then you come back to what your parents always raised you to think was home and they treat you like – like shit, frankly, because you're "only a civilian" and because the government despises the diaspora.'

Now I realised whom his accent brought to mind: Ringo Starr. 'From Liverpool to Transit Camp Number Three. That's a hell of a journey.'

He laughed for a moment, his face relaxing, and he looked no more than a boy. 'Yeah, who needs drugs when you can take a trip like that, eh? Forget the LSD, just getting on and off the flight is enough to blow your mind. When I first came, I used to send weekly emails to my friends on the Wirral trying to explain what was going on. Then I stopped. I couldn't make the leap.'

'What's the Liverpool connection?'

He shrugged. 'My parents fled the first war, like so many of their generation. My dad was a maths professor, but no one recognised his qualifications. He ended up working as a bus conductor. He never complained, but he always drummed into me that I must come back some day, put my medical training to good use. So here I am.' He took a last drag on his cigarette and threw the butt away.

'My family originally came from Sanasa so this war feels pretty personal. It's *our* land that's in dispute. I don't regret coming, but what's going on is a lot more complicated than that generation wants to admit. OK, time to lodge my usual protest, for all the good it will do. In the UK, by the way, I'm a non-smoker. I can get quite preachy about it, in fact.'

He walked off in search of Sammy. Down below, the white truck's tail flap had been lowered and I could see bundles of possessions – jerry-cans and knotted flour sacks – being thrown aboard. Then the soldier who had grabbed George's shirt began calling out names and IDPs scrambled aboard.

'Looks like he's right,' I said to Abraham. 'It's a bit strange, isn't it? I thought both governments had agreed to demobilise, now that the war is over.'

Abraham arched one eyebrow. 'Is the war over?' He didn't seem to share George's anger. 'Maybe it never will be. And, you know, those boys, they want to go. They love their country. And it is very boring, being an IDP, just like the guy said. This gives them a purpose.'

We were on to Witness No. 5, and were both finding it hard to concentrate. The language issue meant that running through Winston's list of questions, which ranged from details of the IDPs' daily life in Sanasa to the precise circumstances of their flight, took three times longer than anticipated. George had helped with translation for the first few hours, but then he had been called away to deliver a baby, leaving Abraham holding the fort.

Sitting next to a boy she had identified as her grandson, Ali, Selam had given her age as fifty. I'd stared at her for a moment, struggling to believe that this aged crone, with her lined forehead and puckered mouth, was younger than my skin-toned, liposuctioned mother.

'Can that be right?' I'd whispered to Abraham. 'She looks a hell of a lot older.'

'Life wears the body out faster here.'

She certainly had the energy of a young woman, unburdening herself of her testimony in what sounded like one sustained scream. I wondered whether she always spoke like that, or whether, like the American abroad who assumes that everyone becomes an Anglophone given sufficient volume, she thought it the only way to hammer her message into a foreigner's brain. Communication by assault and battery. Abraham kept trying and failing to stem the shriek until, losing patience, he whipped up one hand in a not-to-be-denied stop gesture, like a policeman at a traffic junction, and we all paused for breath. He sighed, then began to translate as I typed the responses into the laptop.

'OK. She says that in the morning she was preparing to go to the market to buy some onions. A neighbour came knocking on the door and told her not to go down the road, the Darrar soldiers were coming. She says she looked out and could see that they were setting fire to the *tukuls*. There was smoke rising ...'

'A *tukul* is ...?'

'A hut. The villagers make them from mud and straw. Anyway, she could hear someone screaming and the soldiers were already in sight. She told her grandson, that one there,' Abraham pointed to Ali, watching in silence, 'to take the goat, then grabbed one of her three saucepans, and they ran. And she is very annoyed, because she only has one pan now to

84

cook the family's meals in and this was the second time it happened. She is very upset about the pans.' He was talking like an automaton, barely listening to his own words.

Noticing the thin layer of dust gathering on my laptop screen, I reached into my satchel for a tissue. My hand emerged blotched in sticky blue ink. A pen had exploded in the heat, emptying itself over the satchel's contents.

'Oh, God,' I muttered, wiping my fingers. 'Sorry, Abraham, the second time what happened?'

He put the question. A slightly shorter scream followed. The ink had got everywhere, I noticed, soaking into the clean T-shirt I'd packed. Feeling the onset of a dehydration headache, I kneaded my temples for a moment. There was a brief silence.

'You have ink all over your face now, Paula.'

'Never mind. Let's go on.'

'So, she says it was the second time the soldiers had driven her out of her house. It had happened to her once before.'

'When?'

'A year earlier. And that time she managed to take the pans and all her cutlery, but lost her stove. She is very into kitchen equipment, this woman.'

'Well, if it's all you own … But, look, maybe my brain has turned to porridge in the heat, but her story doesn't make sense, Abraham. How can you be pushed out twice from the same place? What did the soldiers do? Come in, burn everyone out, then make their excuses and leave?'

He stroked his cheekbone, tracking one sideburn with his middle finger. 'OK, I'll ask. I just wish she would talk normally, though. It's so tiring interviewing her like this.'

I sat poised, fingers over keyboard, as the long scream resumed.

'How was it?' It was ten o'clock the following night. The neighbourhood was deserted, the office corridors silent, but somehow I'd known that Winston would still be at his desk, the focused centre of an aura of light.

'First things first,' I said, heading straight for the office bathroom, where I filled the sink and washed off the patina of sweat and sand that had formed a greasy face mask. It felt fabulous. Returning, I made a faint-hearted attempt at smacking the rust-coloured dust off my stained satchel. Everything I was wearing and carrying looked five years older than it had when I'd left.

'Gruelling, to be honest. Very slow. But Abraham was a star. And we met a lovely doctor, who made all the difference. He became our *de facto* second translator.'

'It tends to go like that. You slept there?'

'Yeah. When we knew we weren't going to get it all done in one day, we borrowed a tent. Lot of those around, in an IDP camp. So glad we packed our bed rolls. Remind me never to go on a trip here without taking one along.'

It had not been the most comfortable night. I'd lain awake trying to ignore a rising sense of claustrophobia generated by the close, rubbery smell, while Abraham, who had gallantly positioned his mat outside the entrance to the tent – playing the part of both chaperone and security guard – had snored like a champion. At two o'clock I had slipped out in search of fresh air and, stepping over Abraham's body, found myself staring at eternity. The IDP camp gave out almost no ambient light, leaving the night sky to assert its ancient, inky dominion. I woke at dawn back inside the tent, eyes gummy, my face inches from the muzzles of two mongrels that had slipped under the tarpaulin to join me, forming a piebald mêlée of limbs and snouts, which gave off the odd beatific sigh.

'Anything useful?'

'I think we have most of what we need, though I have to write up my notes before I can be sure. But here's the thing.' I took up position in the chair before him, the better to capture his full attention. 'Abraham and I collected some evidence that puzzles me. Signed testimonies from at least three families. They all fled Sanasa in July 2001, yes, but they told us they'd already been moved once by then. They'd effectively been charity cases, camping with better-off relatives in the port, when the soldiers came the second time and they had to hit the road again.'

He peered at me intently over his bifocals. 'And the first evictions were …?'

'A year earlier, they all said. July 2000. I thought some of them might be getting their Julys mixed up, but no. One was most insistent, said he was absolutely certain, as his daughter had just been married and they'd had to leave her dowry behind. He said in one day they lost all their savings.'

'The key question, then: where were those IDPs from?'

'Neither Abraham nor I could find it. There's just not enough detail on the map you gave us. The village of Yala, they said. A hamlet of about twenty *tukuls*, near a small reservoir, on the side of a hill. We tried to get them to locate it, but that wasn't a huge success.'

The first witness had placed his finger with absolute confidence in the middle of the sea, the second had simply stared at the laminated paper for several minutes, his forehead furrowed, trying to match up a familiar landscape with the flattened version. Then he had turned the map slowly on the table, round and round, anxious to help, trying to find some mental access point. Watching his face, I'd grasped that it was the first time he had seen the local geography captured in two-dimensional form. And why should it make sense? If you had learned the heft of a hill by dint of herding your goats round it, why should a piece of paper hold any meaning?

'Yala, Yala …' Winston was on his feet now, examining the giant map that covered half of the office wall. 'Did you get any co-ordinates at all?'

'No. One guy said the village was fifty kilometres south-east of Sanasa, but another insisted it was eighty kilometres. When we asked for distinguishing features, they couldn't come up with much, apart from an abandoned railway station, which they said dated back to a mining project the British launched after Italy's surrender.'

'Ah! Now that's a great help.' He bent at a right angle, buttocks pointing in my direction. 'Here, I think I have it. Take a look.'

I leaned over. His finger slowly traced the winding course of a railway track, which extended from Sanasa towards the base of the mountain escarpment. I could read 'disused' and just below, in tiny, barely legible italics, 'Yaah Liah'.

'That's it. Found it.' He took a ruler from the desk and measured the distance, then compared it to the grid. 'Your villagers aren't too far off. Seventy-five kilometres, give or take, south-south-east of Sanasa. Absolutely fantastic. Well done, Paula. You just earned your entire year's salary. I've been waiting, hoping, for something exactly like this.'

'How do you mean?'

'There have been a few hints. North Darrar has always maintained that Sanasa was not an isolated incident, that there'd been a series of border violations by Darrar dating back at least a year. I've been trying to pin the reports down, but we haven't had any reliable witnesses up till now. It was all too vague.'

'And why is it important?'

'It doesn't make any difference to the border ruling but it could hold the key when it comes to deciding who started the war. If we can establish a pattern of encroachment, of army raids and evictions, show an escalating series of abuses, the other side's attempt to make us look like a regional psychopath begins to look suspect. There were reasons why our boys were primed for a fight. They saw this coming. Many of the ministers are convinced Darrar's end game is a whole new coastline.'

'Well, that's great,' I said. 'And now I really need a drink, a bite and a bath.'

Winston grunted, hands in pockets, still sizing up the wall map. 'We may need you to go back there to re-interview.' He caught my expression. 'Oh, not immediately, don't worry, you'll get a breather. Did the villagers say if anyone had been killed during the Yala raid?'

'No, just *tukuls* burned, goats snatched. I got the impression it was a community in which goats counted for a great deal.' I stowed my laptop and notebooks in a drawer and fastened my satchel. 'One question. Does this process of evidence-taking ever leave you feeling a little bit guilty?'

He looked astonished. 'Guilty? In what way?'

'Well, as Abraham and I were leaving the camp, the grandson of one of our witnesses ran up, asking when they could expect the money and land. It turned out all the witnesses thought the government had sent us to assess financial compensation for what they lost in the war.'

He pursed his lips. 'That's not what the camp administrator was told. And I hope it's not what he told them.'

'No, but that was what they assumed. That we were there to help. In practical, immediate terms.'

He shrugged. 'Console yourself with the thought that in the long term what you're doing for those IDPs, for every citizen of this country in fact, is far, far more helpful than momentary financial compensation.'

I said nothing. I remembered Ali's puzzlement as Abraham stumbled through a jargon-laden explanation of what we were doing, in which I'd heard, 'The Hague', 'arbitration' and 'international boundary'. Ali had nodded so energetically it was clear he had not understood a word. Laying a hand on his heart, he had bowed low and said, 'Thank you, Miss. God bless,' then positioned himself next to the main gate. I had gestured at him through the window as Abraham started the Toyota, trying to get him to stand back. He had stared uncomprehendingly, waving frantically as we pulled away, sending a cloud of beige desert grit billowing into his face, just as I'd known it would.

When I think of falling in love with Jake, my school biology lessons come to mind. Those silent shots, taken under the microscope, of a human cell dividing. You start with a jellied glob of fluid, its soup of cytoplasm swirling around a nucleus packed with dark rods of DNA. The nucleus bulges and spasms, its chromosomes clot as the enzymes get to work. Suddenly you notice that two identical mini-nuclei are forming and a translucent membrane appears, spreading across the cell. The squiggly organelles start migrating, forced to choose on which side of the new boundary to lie. The nuclei wrest themselves away from one another and there are now two globs of jelly, complete with dark eyelets, where before there was one.

With Jake, it was that process in reverse. Our cells bumped against one another, independent, self-contained, our respective nuclei safe behind bouncy membranes. But before we knew it, those divisions were dissolving. With every chat, every exchanged glance, a hole was torn in our respective membranes and through those tiny openings leaked our vital ingredients, cytoplasm and mitochondria moving where they had no place to be. We slopped carelessly into one another, DNA intermingling in confused promiscuity. It was effortless; it was largely unnoticed; it was incredibly foolish.

He told his wife, Olivia, none too soon for my liking, but earlier than my friends had expected. He claimed he had done it out of selfishness, not consideration, because he couldn't bear to keep me to himself. 'I want to tell everyone about you,' he said.

For a long time he lived like a student, moving around with a backpack, clothes permanently rumpled. He divided his nights between my place in Greenwich Village, the apartment on Upper East Side he had bought with Olivia and a studio in

Alphabet City, a restless shuttling designed, as far as I could make out, to reassure Sophie, Charlotte and Eric, all either at college or setting up in their own apartments, that they would always have a family home.

We spent much of our time in bed, trance-like sessions that cannibalised afternoons and ate into nights, folding and unfolding one another like human origami. I had thought of myself till then as a polite, considerate lay. Politeness and consideration were exactly the qualities missing with Jake, and with their departure went self-consciousness and embarrassment. The expression on my face the first time I sprawled like a sweaty starfish across his hairy chest, listening to his heart pounding as he stroked my sodden hair, must have been one of bemused surprise. How come this had never happened before?

We travelled, as far as our work schedules allowed. Jake's hobby was military history, so these were not, perhaps, your average romantic retreats. We celebrated the new millennium clinking beakers of Calvados on a hotel veranda in Normandy, where we were tracking the Allied landings. We spent another holiday in Monte Cassino, on a guided tour of the US 34th Division's historic assault on the Gustav Line. In Istanbul we visited the mosques and Orthodox churches, then drove to Gallipoli to re-imagine the battle of the Dardanelles. Sometimes Jake's children joined us, Daddy dangling air tickets under their noses, and over meals or walking recreated trenches, we began, warily, to declare peace. Sophie, the indulged baby of the family, showed me the way in. She was an instinctive mediator: social tension soured the mood in a way she would not tolerate. Her wide-eyed charm ensured we reluctantly fell in with her casual plan that we should All Just Get Along.

I suppose we were blissfully content. I think he knew it, but I, who had never experienced loss, knew only that I felt safe, at harbour. All my life, a sardonic, lonely voice had been sounding off inside my head, providing an ironic commentary on my own behaviour. In the silence it had grown shrill and exasperated. But now I'd found my ley lines, established my compass points. Jake had effortlessly taken up residence and that jabbering voice was calmed. In my favourite photo from those times Jake has me in a bear hug, and I have almost disappeared in the folds of his jacket. His eyes are closed in what is only partially spoof ecstasy. Mine are open. I'm looking in wonder at the camera and there's an artless smile on my face. 'The Happy Idiot' is my mental tag for that photo. I don't think I've smiled like that since.

11

I was typing up the field trip when Barnabas deposited a cream envelope on my desk. There was no stamp, and my name was scrawled in flowing black fountain pen. 'Hand delivered,' he said, raising a curious eyebrow.

I took out the thick cream card inside. 'I've been invited to lunch by Brett Harris, economic counsellor at the US Embassy,' I said aloud.

Winston looked up from his desk and exchanged a glance with Barnabas. 'So, no hanging about. Far be it for me to interfere, but that might be an invitation worth taking up. And I'd like to hear any impressions you're willing to share afterwards.'

I read the card again. 'Would I be correct in assuming from your reaction that this man is more than he seems?'

Winston shook his head in fake despair. 'Tsk, tsk. After all your training, Paula. Never assume. Work on the facts.'

'Well, is he CIA?'

'You should ask him what his degree is in.' This, quietly, from Barnabas, sorting the office mail.

'Sorry?'

'When I worked at the British Embassy, local staff always said the ones who had degrees in art history, music or media studies were MI6. In those subjects, you will always pass, even if you never turn up for a lecture. So they enrol, get a certificate a few years later, but all the time they're learning to be spies.'

Winston beamed. He enjoyed this kind of exchange. 'Let's take a more analytical approach. How many expatriates are there at the US Embassy, setting aside the marines?'

Barnabas ticked them off on his fingers. 'The ambassador, the deputy chief of mission, the political officer, the economic counsellor, the military attaché and his deputy, the cultural attaché and that fat secretary at Reception who sweats a lot.'

'In a posting like this, there certainly has to be at least one CIA operative,' said Winston. 'It's not going to be the ambassador or the deputy. Or the military attaché or the fat secretary. How smart is the political officer?'

Barnabas was politely silent. Commenting on the intellectual abilities – or absence of them – of members of the expatriate community was clearly not something he saw as part of his job description.

'OK, does the cultural attaché actually do anything? Cultural, I mean.'

'A short-story competition on the radio. Opening a new library wing. And he often invites famous American DJs to run training workshops.'

'So, that leaves the political officer and the economics counsellor. Which one does the most travelling around the country? Who has the best SUV?'

'Mr Harris, definitely.' said Barnabas.

'I would guess, then, Paula, that you're going to have an interesting lunch.'

'A BA in music. I wrote my thesis on Gregorian chants. Why do you ask?'

I stared at Brett, slightly shocked that everything could fall into place quite so simply, Barnabas's half-jesting prediction so swiftly confirmed. 'Oh, I just find it amusing to compare the careers people end up following with the degrees they took. Usually, there's barely any correlation ...' I blithered on for a bit to cover my tracks, but he wasn't really listening.

He was as handsome as a shop-window mannequin. Grey eyes, square jaw. Better in profile than head-on, admittedly, but he could have sprung from the glossy pages of the *New Yorker*, leaning tweed-clad on a golf club in an advert for overpriced watches. I tried imagining him breaking into a sweat, but it was like imagining Barbie's Ken with pubic hair. Rip open his shirt and you would surely discover a latex chest. The only human things about Brett were his shaver's rash and his voice, which came, disconcertingly, in two different registers, as though competing personalities were struggling for control. For much of the time he sounded like a CNN anchorman, oaky, resonant – I suspected professional voice coaching – but when he got excited or cracked a joke, his voice shot upwards, turning into a peevish East Coast whine. Which was the real Brett? I wondered. Golden Timbre or Nasal Whiner?

He had booked a table at the Italian Club, just off Liberation Avenue, in an alcove where we could watch the waiters, who sported bow-ties, white shirts and maroon waistcoats, crunch in swift relays across the gravel. Clearly a cut above the Ristorante Torino, it boasted an international menu and a range of local dishes, which Brett encouraged me to try.

'What's this one, then?' I asked him, pointing to the first item.

'A kind of stew. Beef, I think.'

'How about this?'

'Also stew. But different.'

I put my finger on the third item. 'This one's stew, too, isn't it? Never mind, I'll just have the first.'

He hailed a waiter. 'In case you were wondering about this lunch, I thought it would be a good idea for us to get to know one another. Not many expatriates here in Lira, you'll find, so any new arrival creates a bit of a buzz. Especially when you're virtually one of us. You're a US resident, right?' He gave a broad, insincere smile.

A bit of a touchy subject, actually. 'Right.'

'We're eager to maintain cordial relations with your office. I haven't met Mr Peabody, but I hope to rectify that very soon. It's been hard to catch him between his trips to The Hague and Washington. A man with a lot on his plate. I wouldn't want to distract him. As far as the embassy is concerned, you guys are on the side of the angels.'

I didn't bother to hide my surprise. 'Really? I thought the Americans had distinctly mixed feelings about international justice. After all, the US has never ratified the statute setting up the International Criminal Court, has it? You didn't want your soldiers facing trial in Iraq or Afghanistan, right?'

A spasm of irritation flickered across his face. His voice shot from baritone to adenoidal, 'A superpower's entire foreign policy is not dictated by one Bible-thumping reactionary.'

I looked at him blankly.

'I'm referring to Jesse Helms, former head of the Senate Foreign Relations Committee, a man who almost single-handedly ensured the US kept out of the ICC. Never mind. That remark was out of line. The point is that, as a nation, we're bigger than that. Our vision extends further than a trigger-happy Republican administration tangled up in the fallout from 9/11. Administrations may come and go, American values will endure.'

I blinked and nodded in vague, hypocritical encouragement.

'Look at the grand sweep of history and you'll find no country has contributed more to the drive for universal justice that followed the First World War than the US, including hammering out the international criminal law that led to the ICC's establishment. If it weren't for Teddy Roosevelt, Andrew White and Andrew Carnegie, The Hague would be just another boring North Sea resort. We supported it until we sensed it was being hijacked by nations bent on settling scores with the US. But I can see your eyes are glazing over. Let me show you something.'

He opened his case and fished out a stapled report just as the waiter deposited our dishes on the table. A rich mix of herbs and spices – that smell of Lira – wafted up and I took a deep, appreciative breath.

'Seen this? It's the Human Security Report, put out by the University of British Columbia. First of its kind.'

'Actually, until recently the only reading on Africa I'd done was *Tarzan of the Apes* and that was when I was thirteen.' He probably thought I was joking.

Brett flipped through the pages, too fast for me to take in anything but a series of graphs and charts. 'The centre has carried out a global tally of armed conflict. The long-term statistical trends are very exciting, and they include Africa.'

'Oh, yes?'

'Look.' He put his index finger on one highlighted sentence and read it aloud in his newscaster's voice. '"In 1992, more than fifty armed conflicts involving a government were being waged worldwide; by 2003 that number had dropped to twenty-nine. Battle deaths have declined even more steeply." Despite all the stories of genocide, gang-rape and child soldiers, violent deaths in the developing world are actually plummeting. The general public may not have noticed – we've the media to thank for that – but Africa is an increasingly safe, ever more peaceful place to live.'

He had genuinely surprised me. 'I must admit that wasn't my impression.'

'It took its time but the end of the Cold War has finally worked its magic. Twenty years ago any pissy little rebel movement with a gripe and a halfway charismatic leader could count on funding and weapons deliveries from us, if only to ensure he didn't go begging to Moscow. Don't know about you, but I'm pretty ashamed of my country's track record in the region.'

I looked at him with suspicion, wondering whether this was an attempt to draw me out. But there was no hint of irony in his face.

He leaned forward, slipping into his upper register. 'Was there any sick, corrupt psychopath we weren't willing to fund? Have you driven past the stockpile of old tanks and weapons on the outskirts of Lira? They call it Tank Graveyard.'

'Not yet.'

'Well, you should. It's a chilling indictment of superpower policy. But those days are over. Everyone recognises now that peace doesn't come from the barrel of a gun. If you want settlements to stick, they have to be based on mutual agreement. The strategists of the Kissinger variety, with all their cynical realpolitik, are making way for seasoned mediators, UN peace-keeping forces and experts who apply international law.' His finger was jabbing the table; his voice had jumped half an octave. Who was he trying to convince? Himself or me?

'Like me and Winston.'

'Exactly. In the future, parties with gripes won't go to war, they'll fight it out in the courtroom. International arbitration backed by global powers, so any rogue government thinking of walking away knows it *has* to respect the eventual award. Leaders have behaved like delinquent children for long enough. Final and binding agreements, the grown-up way of solving disputes.' He paused.

I had finished my stew, he'd been so busy talking that his plate was virtually untouched.

'In theory, yes,' I said cautiously. His enthusiasm for my job was unnerving.

'And in practice, too. It's working, Paula, and as long as we can keep the Islamic extremists in check, Africa's peace dividend will be immense. Have you been following the arbitration between the Sudanese government and SPLA in Abyei?'

'Not as such.' He really had no idea how little preparation I had done. Perhaps the notion of caring so little had simply never occurred to someone as ambitious as Brett.

'And then there's Cameroon and Nigeria. They've agreed to go to arbitration over the Bakassi peninsula. With any luck that's two wars avoided. Your case is part of a very promising trend my government wants to encourage.'

He seemed to have paused, so I excused myself and headed for the toilet. As the door to the Ladies swung open, I caught a reflection of him in its glass panel. He was gazing after me with the casually speculative look of a man deciding whether or not to make a pass. Inside, I peered into the mirror and saw myself briefly as he probably did: no great beauty, but definitely presentable, about the right age, shame about the hair. In another life, another Paula might have taken up the challenge. I grimaced at my reflection. He had no bloody idea.

When I returned to the table, Brett was busying himself with the bill. I sat down with a feeling of relief. It was nearly over. 'And what role is your embassy going to play as the hearing approaches?'

'Well, of course we can't take sides.' He looked, for a moment, ridiculously prim, as though I had suggested having sex under the table. 'We value our relationship with both governments. Our overriding concern is that we want this legal process to work. So – strictly between ourselves – if there's anything, practically speaking, we can do to help, just say the word. If your office needs a new photocopier, gas for the office car – we're expecting the government to introduce rationing, by the way – a few additional computer screens, the odd technological gizmo ...' He shot me a sideways glance and paused. 'God knows, even getting hold of a memory stick can be quite a challenge here at times ... Think of it this way: it's going to cost us a lot less, in the greater scheme of things, to help you with the practicalities now than to spend years smuggling arms to a doomed rebel movement in the hope it might eventually bring peace to the region.'

We walked out of the restaurant courtyard and I stopped dead, so abruptly Brett careered into my back. He exclaimed, then went quiet. He had felt it too. Liberation Avenue was still dotted with pedestrians, but a wave of invisible unease seemed to be rippling along it, freezing everyone into position as it rolled towards us. The music jangling in the nearby bar was stilled. Traffic halted. Even the swifts that swooped around the mock-Renaissance cathedral seemed stopped in flight. The only objects that continued moving were a grey sedan followed by a dark blue Land Cruiser. Every head turned to watch as they purred along the avenue. The drivers and passengers were all male. Some were moustachioed, one was bearded, all wore sunglasses. They looked neither left nor right. The shimmer of tension snaked through and past us, like a nail drawn across water. And then, as though a magician had snapped his fingers, people were walking and talking once again, a taxi gingerly pulled out from the pavement, and a mustard-coloured dog swallowed and yawned.

Brett smiled. 'Your first glimpse of the Prez?'

'Yes.' I was speechless for a moment. 'Only two cars? No armed police outriders, no wailing sirens? No backed-up traffic for miles around?' But that's not it, I thought, not the point of what just happened. There had been nothing laid back or approachable about that motorcade.

He shrugged. 'They do things differently here.'

'I've noticed there are no photographs of him around town. I thought African presidents went in for portraits behind every shop counter.'

'So last century, Paula,' he teased me. 'Way too crude for these guys. You don't need a magic cane and a leopard-skin hat to be the Man.' He put one finger to his temple and nodded to where two of the waistcoated waiters who had served us were still standing, eyes warily following the disappearing convoy. 'It's what goes on inside people's heads that matters. And, believe me, these guys have got that nailed.'

When I got back to the office, Winston shot me a quizzical look over the top of his screen. 'So?'

'The Americans love us, positively adore us and everything we do. If you ever need any help, photocopiers, transport, technical support, just say the word.'

He snorted. 'Ever study any Latin? No? What *do* they teach youngsters, these days? *"Timeo Danaos et dona ferentes."* Virgil's *Aeneid*. A weasel use of the word *"et"*,' he mused, showing off. '"I fear Greeks *even*" – or perhaps "especially" in the case of your American friend – "when they bear gifts." Did he go so far as to ask you to copy all our files for their perusal?'

'Not in so many words. But I felt in my bones the offer was on the table.'

'Well, I'd have been disappointed if he hadn't tried. Whenever you find yourself feeling well disposed to our – or, rather, my – brethren in that monstrosity of an embassy, remind yourself that their counterparts across the border are being just as pally towards the other side's legal team. Equal-opportunity schmoozing.'

'Good point.'

I typed solidly for the next few hours, trying to recoup lost time. There was an email from Francesca, which began discussing maps but ended up reading like a diary entry, confessing her fears for the relationship with her boyfriend. 'If he leaves, I don't know what I will do. I am too tired, Paula – *troppo stanca* – to start again.'

The office slowly grew quiet as, one by one, staffers switched off their laptops, locked their drawers, and Ribqa did some final shredding. I gave my papers to Barnabas to stow in the office safe, and signalled to Abraham, who was patiently perusing a newspaper in the corridor, that I was ready to go.

Winston looked up. 'Off home? Good idea.' He yawned like a cat, then looked at me meditatively. 'You know, there isn't an embassy in this shockingly diplomatically under-represented town that wouldn't like to know what goes on here. We're under very close scrutiny. I'm sure you're going to partake in Lira's famous nightlife, but I would confine your conversation to the banal. This is a small and very nosy town. Half the residents are related to each other and the other half fought alongside one another during the liberation struggle. They loathe or love each other, often simultaneously. Best not make any close friends while you're here.'

Well, I thought, that really shouldn't be a problem.

'One last piece of fatherly advice. In conversation, I've learned never to source anything.'

'As in?'

'Never relay to one Lira resident the views of another. It just feeds the general paranoia. If you learn something you need to double-check, never, ever say where you heard it or who told you. You'll find the phrases "I gather that", "I understand that", or "We know" all come in very useful in Lira. Keep it nice and vague.'

12

So, of course, I ignored Winston's advice. I didn't deliberately set out to defy him, I somehow slipped sideways into it.

Sumbi's Café was not the nearest bar to the office, or the most salubrious: a leaden miasma permeated the alley outside. My natural destination would have been either Ristorante Torino or the Italian Club, where I'd met Brett. But Ristorante Torino meant eating with the same man I spent eight hours a day working alongside and the Italian Club proved to be the favoured watering-hole for Lira's diplomats, NGO staff and UN officials. On my second visit there, the Israeli ambassador hovered at my table making idle chit-chat and the UN's press officer invited himself over for coffee. On my third, I found my path to the toilets ostentatiously blocked by the Concern representative and a woman from Save the Children, who had been holding a whispered conversation while casting glances in my direction. When I finally tapped Concern Man on the shoulder, he looked at me in hostile silence, moving the requisite inch.

After that I set off in the opposite direction. Sumbi's was hidden between a cobbler's and a fruit shop, its entrance screened by a curtain of jangling plastic beads. I'd order an espresso at the ancient Gaggia coffee-machine, settle myself on a chocolate-brown sofa that sighed as I sat down, light a cigarette – invariably remembering how Jake hated me smoking indoors – and read another excerpt from Captain Lewisham's diary.

I was sprawled there when a customer tapped me on the shoulder. I looked up, flushing with irritation.

'Excuse me. You're new here, aren't you? This is going to sound rude, but what you are doing right now is considered very offensive.'

He was certainly someone you noticed. An acrylic Jimi Hendrix shirt that screamed Oxfam, top buttons undone to expose a jangle of metal: one CND pendant, one skull and crossbones, a silver Playboy bunny – peace, death, love. Like many of the local men, he was surprisingly petite. He had a messily tailored beard that strayed high on his cheekbones, doleful spaniel eyes, and a Medusa nest of hair. His hair, I was to discover, was always an indicator of mood. When it was clipped and combed, things were going well. It was when he resembled a Don King that you had to watch your step: it was a sure sign that he was somehow off-kilter, disordered.

He was gesturing towards my crossed feet, which I'd propped on a stool; the soles, caked with Lira's fine white dust, were pointing at Sumbi's entrance. 'To show someone your feet like that. In my culture, you are disrespecting every man who comes into this bar.'

My heels hit the floor, a little harder than I'd intended, and I flinched. 'I'm sorry. A misunderstanding. In my culture, this position means I'm a slob, but not intentionally rude. Point taken.' I inclined my head, gave him a fake smile and lifted the newspaper as shield. He'd won, I'd ceded, and now I wanted this censorious prick never to talk to me again.

He didn't move. 'To make up for my own rudeness, can I now buy you a coffee?'

'Oh, no, that won't be necessary.' Big smile again.

He looked at the barman, who was watching the exchange impassively, summoned a second espresso with a raised eyebrow, then sat not far from where my feet had been a moment ago, leaning forward with his hands spread on his thighs.

'You work for the government's legal office up the road, yes? You're the new hot-shot American lawyer who will represent us in The Hague, yes? Mr Peabody's right-hand woman. We were expecting a man, originally.'

'British, not American. It seems everyone knows my business.'

'Lira is a small town. In a few weeks' time everyone here will know what you feed your cat and which pizza topping you prefer.' He took out a cigarette packet, lit up, then studied the glowing tip. 'And that,' he said, with slow, careful articulation, 'is what I hate about this place.'

That was how my relationship with Dawit began. Looking back, I'm not sure exactly why we hit it off. He was chippy, resentful and as petulant as a grounded teenager. He could rarely resist trying to get a rise out of me with some staggeringly offensive sexist remark; he drank and smoked far too much and frequently smelt. None of that mattered. I think I was drawn by a bone-deep cynicism, an apocalyptic acceptance of adversity tinged with a hint of hysteria that matched my own. His negativity made me feel safe. And he possessed another quality I was beginning to value in a city where everyone seemed to feel the need to explain, expound and tell me what to think about Africa. He rarely lectured.

He was a regular at Sumbi's, which he had nicknamed Zombie Café because, he joked, 'It's full of the living dead, just flesh walking', smoking, picking over a bowl of peanuts (to the barman's increasing annoyance) and nursing cappuccinos till they turned stone-cold. 'It's not about the money,' he assured me. 'The flavour is stronger.'

After that first meeting, he always seemed to be there. Lunchtime, mid-afternoon or late at night ('I suffer from amnesia,' he explained, so categorically I didn't dare correct him. 'I cannot sleep at all'). Sometimes he'd be arguing with another regular, but usually his head would be bowed low over the newspaper. He'd look up, catch my eye and point at a headline, a tobacco-stained, gap-toothed grin spreading across his face. 'Such bullshit, Paula,' he'd say (he always pronounced it 'boulesheeet'). 'Total, first-class boulesheeet!' Only *The Economist* was not boulesheeet. He got it third hand, from the cousin of a friend, and not a paragraph went to waste. He read it from cover to cover, including adverts and economic indicators, squeezing every morsel of text until it had given up its intellectual juice. 'This is why we fought in the Struggle,' he said. 'For the freedom to be intelligent. One day, I will go to your country, shake hands with Mr Bill Emmott and say, "Thank you for fighting the boulesheeet. And he will look around him and say,' he rocked with laughter, '"Call security! Who is this hairy little man?"'

Sumbi's was never full, so we did as we pleased. Whenever I couldn't face the awkwardness of a meal at the villa with Sharmila, I'd stay and play chess with him on a board fished from behind the bar. We tried to humiliate one another at bar football, screaming and cursing as we spun the heavy handles. He taught me Italian card games, whose rules appeared to change with every session, until I refused to play and we returned to chess. Occasionally, he'd offer an impromptu seminar on 1960s rock, reggae and soul – Jimi Hendrix, James Brown, Prince Buster – artists whose cassettes, he claimed, had taken so long to reach Lira they were still considered cutting edge. When I looked sceptical, he slapped the table and exclaimed, 'Anyways, they will always be super-best!' His favourite, though, was Frank Zappa – 'My moustache is my tribute' – and sometimes he would freeze, cock his head to one side and quote the master: 'What's a girl like you doing in a place like this?' then chuckle in delight when I played along, narrowing my eyes, hardening my face and muttering: 'I'm in it for the money, baby, only the money.'

Initially I was puzzled by Dawit's seemingly endless free time. He showed neither resentment nor unease when a military patrol descended on Sumbi's for a spot check of ID cards and leave permits, taken as a signal by other customers to hit the road. 'Oh, that guy has nothing to worry about from the patrols,' Abraham explained, when I asked him. 'He's seen more military service than a T-55, and everyone in Lira knows it.'

'How come? He can't be much more than, what, thirty-five?'

'Take it from me, Dawit's older than he looks. In any case, he was recruited into the Movement as a child, one of our famous Revolutionary Cubs. We used to joke that their mothers were always losing them out in the field because they were born wearing camouflage. Ask him to show you his scars. And, Paula, be careful. Dawit seems very interested in what happens in this office. Too much so. He could be a spy.'

'A spy for whom?'

'Who knows? The other side, the UN, the Americans, the Europeans, the Chinese, the government itself … Lots and lots of nosy people in Lira.'

'So you don't trust him?'

'I fought with him at the front. I would trust him with my sister's honour and my life,' Abraham said implacably. 'That doesn't mean he can't be a spy.'

'I have an expedition planned this weekend,' Jake announced one Friday. 'I think it's time you met my aunt Julia.'

'That sounds like a test.'

'Sure is. She's the closest thing I've had to a mother most of my life. If she doesn't meet with your approval, I don't know what I'll do.'

I laughed. 'You know that's not what I meant. I'd be honoured.'

'OK. Dress code is what you Brits would call "smart casual".

You be smart, I'll be casual. It works best that way. And ... well, there's a property I'd like to inspect while we're over there.'

'Over there' was the famous Wentworth estate, in Orange County. A ninety-minute trip along the turnpike, followed by twenty minutes on a winding rural road fringed with thick forest. He drove saying very little. He was one of those men who become instinctively more cheerful when driving and this was a route he could have traced blindfolded. I watched his hands on the steering-wheel with a kind of lecherous wonder. They were the hands of a man built for physical labour, to wield a pickaxe and dig ditches. Or perhaps to scoop out a cave from the rock and mud, like some troll-like Tolkienesque creature. 'I always advise interns to recognise their competitive edge and capitalise on it,' he once joked. 'My competitive edge is that I can open any jar I choose. I'm just not too sure where to go with that.'

'Here we are,' he muttered, drawing up outside a bottle-green, wrought-iron gate. We were buzzed in and crunched up a looping gravel drive for a couple of kilometres, Jake taking the bends with laborious, exaggerated care, laughing when I nudged him impatiently in the ribs, building up the anticipation. The estate gradually opened before us, as it had been designed to do: carefully mown terraces, layered flowerbeds dotted with lichen-covered urns, pollarded fruit orchards, a lily-pond, all a visual appetiser for the main course – Griffin House. He braked well short of the entrance, watching my face, enjoying my incredulity.

'Holy cow. This is a bit *Citizen Kane*, isn't it? I knew you were a poor little rich boy but I never thought you were in this league.'

He laughed. 'Well, you know Americans, we never do anything halfway. Actually, as my aunt could tell you, it's a bitch to heat, the hot water only works occasionally and the bathrooms in the west wing probably haven't flushed for fifty years.'

'Who built it?'

'A rifle manufacturer, one of our first tycoons, who made a fortune selling the US Army weapons to clear the Indians off the plains. He then lost his fortune during a card game and shot himself, leaving behind a young, very pretty wife called Betty. It went up for auction and my great-grandfather bought it and married the grieving widow. All very neat.'

'I'm guessing your aunt employs a small army of staff.'

'Yeah, this place needs them. But Julia's never been exactly short of cash. She does a lot of the gardening herself, though. It seems to have become a growing obsession with the passing years.'

From the driver's seat, he picked out individual features with a stubby forefinger. 'The gatekeeper's lodge – a house in itself – the coach house, sleeps four, the gardener's cottage, very modest, up on that little knoll, the dovecote. No dove has ever roosted there, but my ancestors were obsessed with all things English and liked to pretend they were living in an ancient country manor. Around the back are the tennis courts and the croquet lawn. Over there you find Lake Lacombe and Betty's Forest, christened after the famous widow. Quite a few deer, raccoons and woodpeckers in there, some wild turkey, too, and there was a time when we bred pheasants, and local grandees were invited on the Wentworth shoots. The whole estate was once thirty thousand acres, but my family have been donating tranches of it to the county for decades. There are only about three thousand left now.'

'Only ...'

'You can imagine what it was like growing up here. Tennis, skinny-dipping in the lake, ponies to ride, learning to shoot, canoeing, camping on the estate. Paradise on earth, really. We were out in the open most of the time, and I think having all that space meant we just didn't mind as much that my father was drinking and my mother hysterical with rage. The first sign of tension, and us kids would head out the door. I think

*the relationships we forged with the gardeners, the gamekeeper
and estate manager filled the hole left by a dysfunctional family.
I love it here, and I know my sister feels the same way.'*

He parked the Jetta, rang the bell and a dark-haired, olive-
skinned young man opened it. He wore a white linen shirt and
dark trousers. No tie or jacket, but somehow it was obvious
that he was in uniform. 'Mr Jake. Very good to see you. Your
aunt is having a drink on the terrace. Would you care to join
her? Let me take the bags to your rooms. I put you and Ms
Shackleton in the east wing. Good afternoon, Ms Shackleton,
I'm Miguel.'

'Rooms', plural. So we were observing the social niceties
that weekend.

Julia had her back to us, as we walked onto the terrace,
gazing out. It was certainly a view worth savouring: the lawn
unfurled before us, a green tongue fringed with dark teeth.
The woodlands behind stretched to the valley below, where a
grey ribbon of highway, glinting with the flash of passing cars,
could just be glimpsed.

'Julia, this is Paula. Paula, my aunt.'

You could tell she had once been extraordinarily beautiful.
Now she was drained of vigour and bleached of colour, the
once-blonde hair almost white, the skin papery, but the essence
preserved. She wore her hair in a chignon, emphasising a stem-
like neck and ivory clavicles. Her cheekbones were high and
she spoke with the clipped, peremptory tones of the elderly
Katharine Hepburn. 'Paula, how delightful to meet you. Jake
has told me so much. I've been looking forward to spending
the evening with someone who speaks with a proper English
accent, for once.'

We had drinks – I was passed a gin and tonic without being
asked – as Julia pointed out various local landmarks. Then
she gave an exaggerated shiver, a signal for us to move to the
black marble mantelpiece, where a fire burned. Above it loomed
a gilt-framed portrait of Senator William Wentworth, posed

tweed-clad in a gunroom, framed by gleaming weaponry and loyal retrievers.

'My handsome father,' said Julia. 'He loved hunting, riding, he was a world-class skier and an avid surfer – one of the first. He was the ambassador's right-hand man in London, liaising between Roosevelt and Churchill, at one stage during the war. But,' she said, with a small smile, 'one always felt those activities were never much more than hobbies. Sport was what he really loved.'

'And women, right, Julia?' Jake chimed in. 'Those were the days when a man could have the most outrageous affairs – a mother and her daughter at the same time, wasn't it? – and none of it ended up in the press. Ah, happy days, happy days.' Ignoring Julia's look of reproof, he guided us into the dining room, where a woman I took to be the Filipina cook was putting the finishing touches to the table.

I sat largely silent as they ran through family news and estate gossip. In New York that summer, conversation was dominated by the Concorde crash and the sinking of a Russian submarine, but foreign policy seemed a long way from Griffin House. Julia fretted over an upcoming charity ball she was throwing, and they chatted about acquaintances met on Caribbean cruises and the chance of re-election of the incumbent senator, a family friend. I had a glimpse of a life punctuated by black-tie evenings, golden summers in Martha's Vineyard, casual church attendance and afternoons spent on charity boards. Occasionally I was politely asked a question about 'the situation in your country', before the conversation was whipped away. 'Actually,' I interrupted, the third time this happened, 'I really don't know the answer to that because it's been four years since I lived in the UK.'

'Really?' Julia said. 'So you are something of a rootless person, are you? How curious.'

'Well, I never loved Britain so much that I felt I couldn't live anywhere else.'

111

'Oh, I'm quite the opposite,' she said, picking at her salad. 'For mē, roots have become paramount. As you get older you realise that when everything else goes, they are what remain, spanning the generations. Roots and land,' she said, gesturing towards the windows overlooking the estate. 'The eternal nature of the landscape.'

After supper, as the staff silently cleared the plates, Jake and Julia settled on a large leather sofa and set about examining the estate accounts, his salt-and-pepper confusion of curls and her smooth pale head bowed together over the books, brandies at their sides. I wandered back to the terrace, where Julia eventually found me, smoking.

'Oh.' She looked affronted. 'I didn't realise you smoked. Miguel,' she called, 'an ashtray, please.'

I'd been intending to stub the thing out on the gravel. 'Bad habit,' I said politely, offering up the ritual smoker's acknowledgement that they are committing a sin. Not one I'm likely to give up just to please you, though.

'It does so permeate the clothes,' she said, wrinkling her nose in distaste.

We watched the sun descending over the trees together for a few minutes. Jake was still leafing through the accounts, no doubt tactfully granting us this moment's privacy to 'bond'.

'What are you thinking, my dear?'

'Well ...' I hesitated, wondering how direct I should be. 'As a Brit, I come from a country where we're all very aware of class, of where everyone stands in the pecking order: working class, lower middle, professional middle, upper middle, impoverished aristocracy. And we constantly tell ourselves that this is all very feudal and rather embarrassing. And we hear the propaganda telling us that in the US, in contrast, reinvention is always possible, meritocracy the name of the game. So it's very naïve of me, especially given that I've been here a while now, but I'm always surprised when I'm confronted with evidence of an American class system. This house, your history, it seems a million miles away from the America I know and work in.'

She looked at me and I noticed how the lapis-lazuli necklace around her meringue-white throat accentuated the blue-grey of her eyes, the same colour as Jake's. I wondered if she would take offence, or simply deny my rather crude assertion of her privilege.

Instead, she said, 'Oh, I'm glad you noticed that.'

Inclining her head, she spoke gently, as you might to a child. I wondered if she was keeping her voice low to ensure Jake could not hear. 'There are frontiers, invisible lines that can be sensed but not seen in the US, just as in Britain. The difference is that because we have all been taught that you can do or be whatever you want to be, no American is inclined to recognise that reality. I suspect your countrymen have a far more mature and clear-eyed understanding of the true state of affairs. The lines are there. And it's usually a mistake to try to cross them, in my experience.' She gave me a pearly smile. Her teeth were perfect. 'Even when someone as lovable as my nephew invites you to do so.'

I flushed. I had set myself up for it, but her directness still shocked me.

'I'm not exactly trailer trash,' I said, stammering.

'Oh, I realised that,' she said. Her voice was dry. 'But that's not really what I'm talking about. It's about feeling comfortable. The French have a phrase for it: "bien dans sa peau" – "comfortable in your skin".' She pronounced it carefully, like someone eating fruit. 'In the end, when sex has faded – and it always does – good manners reassert themselves, the years stretch into decades and people often find that what matters is feeling at ease in a place and community. Don't you agree?' Her gaze travelled the room, embracing the oil paintings and gilt-edged mirrors, the horsy bronze statuettes and imported European antiques, and the unreadable Miguel, who was closing the heavy velvet curtains.

13

Captain Peter Lewisham's Diary
Kakardi, 1951, pages 85–9

25 February – Busy couple of weeks. On Tuesday shiftas shot at an Italian farmer and his wife driving on the Tentet–Sherano road, killing the wife. I suspect it was an accident, but the Italian has been hollering that this was a part of an anti-colonial uprising, we Brits are in league with the shiftas, etc. We drove to his farm, found him arming his workers, swearing revenge. I calmed him down – poor chap was genuinely heartbroken – and arranged for the body to be crated up and sent to Lira. It'll be shipped back to the mother country. Five days later the same bunch of shiftas attacked a bus twenty kilometres further east. No one killed this time, just money and grain stolen, but I sent six men down to take statements, show we were taking it seriously. I've asked Tesfay to put out feelers and find out who's involved. The locals are bound to know.

2 March – Received a letter from Flo today. All well back at home, she says, only the dog has had a litter of puppies and she doesn't know what to do with them. Doesn't want to drown any. Always good to hear from the old girl.

13 March – HQ have been in touch about the shiftas. They're sending an intelligence officer down from Lira to discuss strategy. That's going to be interesting. Johnny's transfer to Neraye has come through. He'll be off on Monday. I'll miss the boy. A cheeky lad, but always has a cheery word for everyone. He keeps morale up. I asked Tesfay to arrange a surprise party.

21 March – Some of the villagers came up to the post to complain about a local jackal that has got very bold, breaking into compounds and slaughtering chickens. I promised I'd organise a night stake-out, give us a chance to practise our marksmanship.

30 March – On my instructions, the cook prepared a slap-up meal to mark Johnny's departure. Two lambs stuffed with rosemary, roast potatoes, stewed cabbage, all washed down with the last of Tiny's beer. I gave a formal speech, then the lads piled in, making various comments on Johnny's inability to keep it in his trousers. We all ended up quite tearful, with Johnny saying – shortly before the lads carried him to bed – this had been the best year of his life.

3 April – Intelligence officer arrived today. Bit of a dry stick, he told me over supper that HQ have commissioned a report on what's behind the rise in shifta attacks. Seems it's not just eastern sector, it's all over the country. They want to know whether they're being instigated by Darrar, to show the world this country will be ungovernable unless it's amalgamated, or whether it's banditry pure and simple. I said, 'Good luck with that,' but he then revealed he wants to meet one of these bandits. Here in Kakardi. Not my idea of fun, but I said I'd see what could be done.

8 April – Rupert, the intelligence officer, has come and gone. We ended up hitting it off. Turns out his family live in

Dorset, and he's a fanatical angler, knows every twist and turn of the Tess. We talked rods and flies well into the night. Made a change to have some civilised conversation. Tesfay is going to see if he can set up a parley with the shifta chief, who, he says, is a one-eyed former sergeant recruited by the Italians. Narrowly survived the battle of Derden against our boys in 1941, bit of a war hero by all accounts. So I'm guessing there's not much love lost for Brits there.

12 April – Villagers keep complaining about jackal raids, so we pegged out a couple of dead chickens in the headman's compound and took up position. Three rifles in all. It was almost too easy. At 23.10 hrs precisely, a little vixen slipped under the fence and made for the bait, rippling across the ground like a ginger ribbon. I landed a bullseye: she flipped into a somersault, dead before she hit the ground. Job done. I'm going to see if I can get her stuffed. Plucky little thing.

17 April – Tesfay says he thinks he can arrange a tete-a-tete with old One Eye. On his territory – a cave up on the escarpment – and we'd have to agree to be disarmed first by One Eye's men. Not an arrangement to my liking, but HQ seem dead set on it. So I am now waiting for Rupert. Bit of a showdown at the office this afternoon. Three old geezers turned up, all wrapped up in turbans and shawls. Turns out one of them is the father of the girl Johnny knocked up. They'd just heard about his transfer. The father slammed his cane on my desk, saying Johnny was a coward, had a responsibility to his daughter. Bloody cheek. He was lucky I didn't order the lads to give him a good thrashing. We threw the three out. Told Tesfay to offer him compensation after tempers have cooled. HQ won't hear of it, but I reckon we can organise a whip-round here and pay the old boy off. It's the decent thing to do.

14

We flew to The Hague in mid-December to file the counter-Memorials.

'Strictly speaking, this could be done by email, post or fax,' Winston had said the night before, rhythmically smoothing and pleating his shirts as I perched on his bed. Watching a man pack is a strangely intimate experience, but I was beginning to register that there is an element of governess – nursemaid, even – to the relationship between a younger female employee and an older male boss. Nursemaids get to see the underwear.

'But commissioners have old-fashioned ways of doing things and I have no objection. You should regard it as an opportunity to get to know the lie of the land, familiarise yourself with the facilities ahead of the hearing, when we'll barely have a moment to think. Anything we're likely to need, hard drives, paper supplies, ink cartridges, mobile phones ... Let's get it all now and store it at the embassy. I don't want to be bothered with trivia, come the main event. You're to be my scout, adjutant and quartermaster on this one. Understood, Paula?'

'Understood.'

'There's another reason for trooping all the way to The Hague,' he said, selecting two silk ties off a hanger. 'I want the commissioners to get to know your face. Make eye contact, look friendly, if not,' he chuckled, 'actually beseeching. Say what you like about the bloodless neutrality of universal justice, the commissioners are human beings, and we all find it difficult to be disobliging to people we feel we know. That's why hostages are told to strike up conversation with their kidnappers. I don't know what's going on with the other side, but they keep changing their legal teams. Such a blunder. We've always made an effort to present the commissioners with the same panel of battered faces. By the time we reach the award, a certain degree of unacknowledged empathy will have built up, while the other side will remain strangers. It's a lot easier to rule against strangers.'

'I think Sharmila rather minds that she hasn't been asked along.'

'Does she?' The possibility clearly hadn't occurred to him. 'We need her here. Someone who can email us anything we forget and fob off government enquiries with a certain authority. Abraham comes – that man is worth his weight in gold – she stays. It's a tribute to her effectiveness, in fact.'

'Well, maybe you should make that clear to her.'

'Noted … I'm missing a shirt.' He looked around in exasperation. 'My God, Paula, you're sitting on it!' He was clearly appalled.

'Sorry, I didn't think you'd be taking it. It's very frayed at the cuffs. Why don't you leave it here and we'll pick up a batch of new ones when we're in The Hague?'

He shook his head. 'We can't.'

'Why not?'

'Because these may look like ordinary white shirts to your uninitiated eye, my dear, but in fact they come from Boothes & Harker on Jermyn Street, London, and are hand-stitched from Sea Island cotton, which is as close to silk as cotton can get. They have as much in common with your off-the-rack Walmart shirt, which is clearly what you'd like me to purchase, as a Rolls-Royce has with a Trabant.'

'Well,' I said, handing over the treasured item, 'you need some new ones, whatever they are.'

'The shop went out of business two years ago.'

I gave a scornful guffaw. 'So what are you going to do? Keep wearing the Last of the Mohicans till they turn into very elegant rags?'

'No, I will not wear them until they turn to rags.' His voice was suddenly very clipped. I caught a glint of real anger. 'I have done what any logical, forward-thinking person would do in the circumstances. I have put out feelers via US retailers boasting connections to UK menswear outlets and made clear that if a Boothes & Harker shirt size with a 14.5-inch neck ever crosses their desks, I am willing to pay a premium. I have written to the administrators of Boothes & Harker and asked them for their suppliers' contact details, with a view to placing a bespoke order – a correspondence that is finally showing signs of paying dividends. I have been advised to try eBay, an avenue I'm considering pursuing. And in the meantime I will wear beautifully tailored, scrupulously stitched shirts with increasingly frayed cuffs and I'd prefer them not to be indented by your posterior. Is that acceptable?'

I held up my hands in surrender. 'I promise not to raise the subject again. Fools rush in, clearly ... I'd better go. I've got some drip-dry blouses to fold.'

He stopped me on my way out. 'On the question of clothes ... It's good this came up, actually. After the counter-Memorials have been handed over, the UN's throwing a cocktail party at the Peace Palace. The two presidents, their foreign ministers, a host of diplomats and UN top brass will be there, along with the commissioners, of course. The idea is to foster goodwill. Not much chance of that, I'm afraid, but it might be an interesting occasion. You'll need something to wear. Now, um, what would that be?'

'A tracksuit, perhaps? A Lurex leotard?' He looked anxious. 'I'm joking, Winston. I'm guessing something black, in silk, perhaps with a bit of ruffle.'

'Just the ticket! Formal but chic? Do you happen to own anything like that? If not, Sharmila might be able to help.'

'Don't worry, Winston. There was a time when I virtually collected those kinds of outfits. A lot ended up in charity shops, but a hard core remains. Leave it to me.' He smiled, and returned to his hypnotic smoothing and pleating, like an anxious mother soothing a fractious infant.

The Royal Delft Hotel (marketing logo: 'Never Less Than Welcome') in The Hague was a modest establishment. Not in its first youth, the hotel had clearly received a partial makeover a few years before we became regular guests. But the scuffed linoleum on the stairs, the dirt ground into the carpet and the colour scheme on the upper floors – a wince-inducing 1970s combination of orange walls, maroon carpet and purple doors – along with the lift's tendency to swing from side to side as it rose through the building, gave the game away.

With the exception of the size of the bathrooms, nothing erred on the side of generous. Staffing was always kept to a minimum, with the receptionist usually doubling as bartender, baggage-handler and head waiter, much to customers' exasperation. But Winston had not picked the Royal Delft for its décor, or its service. He'd picked it because, if you showed due respect for the cyclists gliding silently along the pink asphalt strip running alongside the pavement – a charming local peculiarity he tended to forget – it was just a fifteen-minute walk from North Darrar's embassy, and about the same distance from the Peace Palace.

Winston claimed one room, I another. Between us was the spare. He immediately unlocked and propped open the connecting door: for Winston, there was never any division between work and private life. This became our *de facto* office. Chairs were piled onto armchairs to clear as much space as possible. Abraham drove off to the embassy to pick up photocopiers and back-up laptops, along with all the relevant documentation, carefully catalogued at the end of the team's previous visit. Soon, every wall socket sprouted multiple adaptors, extension cables snaked across the floor, and the computers and printers – cranky after months of inactivity – were booting reluctantly into life. The double bed, window ledges and bathroom shelves became our filing cabinets, covered with binders and laptops. The cleaner was told her services would be unwelcome for the duration of our stay, news she greeted with undisguised cheerfulness. And the first of many raids was made on the mini-bar's store of chocolate and cashews. One of my jobs, I discovered, was to keep it stocked so that Winston, who was wont to wander fretfully in and out of his own room and 'the office' in the early hours, could snack at will. I, in contrast, quietly worked my way through its mini-ature bottles of vodka, gin and Scotch. We lived, for the most part, on trays of *steak frites* delivered with increasing resentment by room service, the dirty plates gradually stacking up in piles under the bed, until, giving in to some atavistic feminine impulse to keep house, I'd transfer them in a whirl of exasperation to the hotel corridor. By the end of the trip we'd be bloated, constipated, hyped on caffeine and nicotine, gripped by insomnia yet exhausted.

'So who designed this, then?'

I frowned as Abraham pulled up at the main gate, showing our permit to the armed policeman on the barricade. The Peace Palace loomed above us, framed by fussy flowerbeds and what from a distance resembled Astroturf but was presumably lawn. Part neo-Gothic cathedral, part turreted Disney castle, part red-brick municipal library, it looked like the outcome of an architectural game of Consequences. Around the gate eddied a coachload of elderly tourists, posing for photographs and ignoring the policeman's shooing gestures.

Winston barely bothered to glance up from his mobile phone, which he was trying to fit with a new Dutch SIM card. 'Couldn't tell you, I'm afraid. I do know that it was built with American money – the industrialist Andrew Carnegie, robber-baron-turned-philanthropist, put up the funds. I didn't know you were interested in architecture, Paula.'

'Oh, I'm not. It's just that the architectural style is rather familiar to me, for reasons I won't bore you with. Not my taste.'

'It's not meant to be beautiful. It's supposed to impress upon people that what happens here is important. "This stuff matters. These decisions will last," it's telling the world. And so it is, and so they do. This is where the principle that international law made war unnecessary was enshrined in bricks and mortar. Interestingly,' said Winston, still struggling to remove the back of his mobile, 'Tsar Nicholas the Second was the international peace movement's main driver. Maybe he had a premonition. The Peace Palace was finished just in time for the First World War, and a few years later, poor old Nicholas and his family were murdered by the Bolsheviks.'

'Why did they pick The Hague? Wouldn't New York have made better sense, next to the United Nations?'

'Tut, tut, Paula. I see your grasp of history is as shaky as that of my countrymen,' Winston scolded. 'This was four decades earlier. The UN wasn't even a twinkle in the eyes of its creators. Why The Hague? Apparently the Dutch and Russian royal families got on famously. I think you'd better do this,' he said, handing me the segments of his dismantled phone. 'Too fiddly for my old fingers.'

We drove into the car park hidden at the side of the palace. 'Let Abraham handle those,' Winston said, with an airy wave towards the files stacked in the boot. 'I want to show you around. The whirlwind Peabody Tour available at a knock-down price, one day only.'

He lowered his voice as we walked into the foyer. The marble floor acted as a megaphone. 'This way.' I trotted behind him as he tip-tapped his way purposefully past the ticket booth, gift shop and cloakroom and, placing a finger to his lips, carefully pulled open the vast wooden door on the right side of the hall.

He poked his head in cautiously. 'Coast clear, come on in.' With its stained-glass arched windows and ornate wooden panelling, there was something distinctly cathedral-like about the Great Hall of Justice. The raised dais towards which all the shiny brown leather seats were turned, though, was designed not for priests but for men of law, and carvings of Veritas and Justitia, rather than saints, looked down impassively on the table that ran its length. A vast wall fresco showed three Biblical figures in flowing robes, dispensing wisdom, framed in celestial light.

'This is where the International Court of Justice has been meeting since 1945,' whispered Winston. 'Fifteen judges, all in black robes and white bibs, ruling on cases that UN member states bring against one another. This was the court that decided the Reagan administration was violating international law in Nicaragua by supporting the Contras – caused one hell of a stink. I sat in on quite a few of those sessions, fascinating times. The cases can drag on for years, so most of the judges set up home in The Hague. Rather them than me. Pleasant enough city, I suppose, but dull, dull, dull.'

He took my elbow and steered me back the way we had come, to an antechamber on the left of the entrance dominated by a giant black vase, garlanded with a two-headed golden eagle. 'Gift from the doomed tsar – he hadn't got long to go.' Winston traced a Latin motto on the wall. '"Peace will extinguish the flames of war!" Ha. Interior decorators with a sense of historic irony. And this – this is us.'

The Small Hall of Justice was cosier and warmer, but decorated in the same style. With its oak panelling, dovetail wooden ceiling and rows of brown leather thrones, it could almost have been a London members' club. A painting wriggling with winged angels and dragons rampant dominated the room.

'Headquarters of the Permanent Court of Arbitration. Small but perfectly formed, I like to think. You don't have to be a nation state to use this. It's the court Joe Public has never heard of because the arbitration that takes place here is kept private nine times out of ten. Which, in my view, is one of its major failings.'

'Why?'

'Because once you leave it to the parties involved to decide the rules of engagement and you remove public scrutiny and any right of appeal – all these findings are "final and binding" – bizarre things happen. It's amazing just how eccentric apparently sober members of the judiciary can turn when they know the nitty-gritty of their findings won't be picked over by their peers or denounced in the newspapers. Remember the old principle that "Justice should not only be done, but be *seen* to be done"? Here the detail isn't seen, so it's often not done. Well, that's the game we've signed up for, and this is where our commission will meet. The commissioners will sit there –' he pointed to a long main desk, lined with red baize '– 'our legal teams will be on either side, any observers we agree to allow perch at the back and those booths are for the interpreters. Proceedings are recorded and a transcript is usually ready within hours. The typists are incredibly fast.'

I ran my hand along the red baize. Compared to the grandiose main hall, the room felt like an afterthought. Whatever took place here would certainly attract far less attention. I felt both disappointed and relieved. 'This is going to be fine,' I said, more to myself than Winston.

Jake collected me from the breakfast room, where I had been brooding on my encounter with Aunt Julia. We drove down a bumpy dirt track until we reached a glade that looked out onto Lake Lacombe. Griffin House had disappeared from view and in its place rose a simple whitewashed boathouse. Behind it, mist rose from the water.

'Voilà. Lake Cottage. This is what I really wanted you to see.'

He fished out a large iron key, opened the door and led me round. Someone had been there very recently. The timbered rooms had all been freshly painted in white. The wooden banisters had been polished, and there was a smell of solvents in the air. The furnishings were basic: some faded Turkish kilims, a collection of stones and bleached tree trunks.

On the mantelpiece sat a single framed photograph. I peered at the sepia image. It showed a handsome man with a handlebar moustache, thumbs buried in his waistcoat, standing on a saddle-shaped rock. His sturdy boots were coated with dust, and gypsy locks tumbled over his ears. Chest out, he grinned defiantly at the camera, eyes rimmed with grime. He appeared to be standing on the edge of a precipice. Behind him rolled waves of mountain, each layer stacked like millefeuille. 'Edward, Darrar, 1868,' someone had scrawled in pencil on the cardboard mount.

'Who's he? A pirate?'

'Looks like one, doesn't he? The black sheep of the family, my great-great-uncle.'

'Where was it taken?'

'Edward ran off to Africa, hoping to make his fortune. He started building a railway up a mountain for the Italians but the funding collapsed. He died not long after that photograph was taken, probably of malaria. Maybe I imagine it, but I think you can see the fever in his eyes. We should go there one day, see if we can find his grave. We keep the photograph here as Lake Cottage was originally his idea. He couldn't stand the main house.'

'I share his taste, I think. This is much nicer.'

'None of that Griffin House pomposity, eh? It's very simple, not much decoration.'

'You don't need any – you have the lake on three sides. I feel as though I'm on a yacht, sailing out to sea.'

'Look,' Jake ran his fingers through his hair, 'I asked Miguel to get the cottage cleaned up because I wanted to know how you would feel about moving in. I can't keep shuttling between my wife's apartment, my studio and your place indefinitely. Nowhere has ever felt more like home, and for the last few months I've been fantasising about sharing it with you.'

He had taken me by surprise. 'Give me a minute.'

I gazed across the blue expanse. Three ducks chose that moment to land, slamming on the brakes as they hit the water. 'What about your wife?'

'She's started seeing someone, I gather, a stockbroker. As long as we can maintain the public fiction of a happy marriage, trooping out the family at weddings and the like, she may be satisfied. This arrangement may suit her quite well, in fact. Officially, I'm on the family estate, spending time with my increasingly frail aunt. Laurel and Hardy would love it here, too – they'd finally get the exercise they need.'

I hesitated. 'There's another side of things to think about. I'm pretty sure Julia hates my guts, Jake. Sorry, but we didn't really hit it off.'

He flopped down on a wicker sofa and eyed the room, probably working out where he would set up his laptop and desk. 'Really? I didn't notice. I suppose it makes sense. She adores Olivia. Her enthusiasm, looking back, was one of the reasons we married in the first place. She'd so disliked all my previous girlfriends, I was relieved there was one she warmed to.'

'I'm beginning to feel a bit like the narrator in Rebecca, *battling the ghost of an ex-wife in the mansion on the hill. Or maybe that should be* Jane Eyre.'

'Well, I'm done with all of that, Paula. I'm too old to care. Julia's not the woman in my life, you are, and if you're worried about rubbing up against her, I can reassure you that she spends six months a year on her cruises, where she dances with millionaires and plays bridge with her razor-thin widow friends. Hang on to your apartment in Greenwich Village for a bit, if you like. If it all falls apart you can run back there. But I'm really tired of commuting. I can feel time ticking away. Life's short, and I want to spend more of it with you.'

He walked over and captured both my hands in his. 'Want to live in sin, Paula? I honestly don't know what I'll do if you don't say yes.'

15

The commission was a three-man team. Practical, democratic, compact. One commissioner picked by our side, one by theirs, and a chairman both sides endorsed, making a voting stalemate impossible. Despite its determination to modernise, the commission had failed to challenge stereotypes in several predictable areas. 'All white, all male, all in their sixties and seventies,' Winston had commented, as he'd handed me over the commissioners' CVs. 'Typical of our hide-bound profession. If I'd been on board when they were picking 'em, you can be sure the line-up would have been more interesting. But our African employers were after credibility, above all else, and thought assembling a panel of doughy-faced members of the establishment with letters after their names was the way to win it. Who knows? Maybe they were right.'

Our side had chosen Professor François Rainier, a cadaverous-looking academic with eyebrows so luxurious they appeared to possess a life of their own ('French. Expert on maritime law. Don't ask me'). Theirs had gone for Eddie Connors, who bore a passing resemblance to Santa Claus ('American, set up Darrar's Human Rights Commission, married a local, one of those more-Catholic-than-the-Pope types').

The chairman was His Excellency Judge Ulrich Mautner, the son of a German lawyer who had fled the Nazis and settled in Buenos Aires, assimilating with the speed of the truly terrified. With forty years of international law under his belt, Judge Mautner had won his spurs representing the grieving families of Argentina's 'disappeared' and now sat on the boards of a spray of refugee organisations. He was beaky, rake thin, and must once have stood well over six feet tall, but age had curved him. He had a habit of putting his hands into his pockets and jangling coins stored there, hiking his trouser hems to reveal a pair of startling scarlet socks and raw-looking ankles. 'Those socks, those socks,' Winston mused. 'There's hope for a man who wears red socks in court. We may be dealing with a closet iconoclast in the person of Judge Ulrich Mautner.'

I had expected them to be wearing black gowns and white lawyer's kerchiefs, but it seemed any dressing-up was reserved for the International Court of Justice. For the filing of the counter-Memorials, they were in what counted as civvies: blazers and ties. They had swivelled the microphones to one side and, using their hands as screens, were whispering to one another, exchanging meaningful glances. It was impossible, somehow, not to feel slighted by this matey complicity. This is a contest, I thought. You're not supposed to become best pals.

There was a cascade of footsteps in the hall outside, and the door opened. The opposition had arrived, a team of seven to our modest three. There was a great deal of kerfuffle as the younger members of the delegation – a pair of willowy girls with their hair neatly pigtailed and a crew-cut youngster – wheeled two trolley-loads of documents to the front table. A giant tadpole of a man, the resemblance underlined by his plain black suit, settled on the other side of the strip of carpet that formed our invisible border. Head, neck and shoulders sloped into a broad seat – if he'd been a woman you'd have said he had child-bearing hips; his feet, in comparison, looked strangely tiny. I had a sudden memory of Jake in bed, trowel feet sticking out from under the duvet, admiring the flexibility of his toes as he solemnly announced, 'One thing life has taught me, Paula. Never trust a man with small feet.'

'Must be their new chief counsel, Henry Alexander,' said Winston, with a barely perceptible nod.

Next to Alexander sat a mottle-complexioned giant, who kept adjusting his spectacles with big, long-fingered hands. His hair, cut in a style disturbingly reminiscent of Richard Clayderman's, was making an uncertain transition from sandy to white.

'Breast Boy,' muttered Winston. 'Reginald Watts. Washington lawyer. Pretty average. Lacks the killer instinct. Was here last time. Blushes a lot.'

'*Breast Boy?*'

'You'll see,' he said.

The bustle around the front table was gradually subsiding. The youngsters, their unloading complete, retired to the back of the room. The two counter-Memorials were now sat stacked side by side. I found my hand had risen to my mouth in an instinctive movement of alarm, and lowered it as imperceptibly as I could. Our counter-Memorial was one volume, five inches thick. They were presenting ten wads of documentation, each at least as thick as our entire counter-Memorial. A chair creaked as Alexander, taking in the difference, folded his arms over his paunch, raised one eyebrow and gave us a Cheshire-cat smile. 'No contest,' his expression said.

Judge Mautner surveyed the room, waiting for silence to fall. 'Good afternoon, ladies and gentlemen. I would like to thank all of you for being here today. I know many of you have had to travel a very long way and I hope you are well rested. We have gathered to witness the submission of the counter-Memorials. Thanks to modern technology, all this evidence and argumentation could in theory be presented digitally, which would have saved you many hours in airports and railway stations. But the world is watching us, bearing witness. However laborious for the individuals concerned, physical attendance possesses, in the commissioners' view, a value in itself, underlining the absolute necessity to respect their eventual findings. So I am grateful for your indulgence.'

Winston and Alexander nodded in a noncommittal manner.

Judge Mautner continued: 'Mr van Straaten, could you please check that both counter-Memorials are present and correct?'

There was a pause while the clerk checked the submitted documents against a list, then nodded. 'All present.'

'Many thanks. In that case,' said Judge Mautner, 'I thank both sides for the work. The commissioners will give them all the attention they deserve. Your two nations, and the Horn of Africa, deserve no less. The submission stage of these proceedings is now at an end. No fresh evidence can be presented before the hearing. To underline the importance of this stage, we invite both delegations to join us at tonight's cocktail party in the Japanese Room. We see this event as helping to create a climate of mutual goodwill ahead of what we trust will be a constructive legal process. I look forward to seeing you there.'

He banged his gavel and the room rose.

Winston gestured Abraham over and pointed towards the other side's counter-Memorial. 'We're going to need a few of those plastic tubs from the back of the car.'

Henry Alexander sauntered up to the table, picked up our single stack, weighed it in one hand and flapped it casually in our faces, highlighting its lack of substance. 'Light on your feet, eh?' He chuckled, shaking his head like a mother who has caught out a mischievous boy. 'Bit of a rush job, Peabody? Or perhaps you're short-staffed. I hear funds are tight.'

Winston looked at him impassively. 'I think it was Niccolò Macchiavelli who said, "A wise man does at once what the fool does finally." We thought we'd spare you the verbiage right from the start.'

* * *

132

The first person I met on entering the Japanese Room with my patent-leather clutch in hand was Brett Harris, dapper in black tuxedo and bow-tie.

'I hadn't expected to see you,' I said.

'Oh, everyone's here tonight. It's like the bar scene in *Star Wars* down there.' He gave my black chiffon Valentino – a legacy from the Jake era – a critical once-over. It seemed to win approval but he pursed his lips. 'You're late.'

'Some last-minute emailing.'

'Well, everyone's three drinks in. No bad thing as it means they've finally hit the tipping point where they stop talking crap and say what they *really* think.'

Including you, I thought, registering the slight sway and undiplomatic language.

If the Grand Hall of Justice was portentous and the Small Hall of Justice functional, the Japanese Room was simply lavish. Its walls were hung with six huge silk tapestries whose designs – delicate cherry trees, blood-scarlet blossoms and preening peacocks – clashed unashamedly with the swirling Turkish carpet. Maintaining the Oriental theme, two giant Chinese vases sat on either side of the vast doors. In the light from the gilt-edged chandeliers, every gilded, embroidered, brocaded and over-decorated surface seemed to glow.

Leaning closer than was necessary, Brett talked me through the guest list, his voice as camp as a gossiping hairdresser's. 'That's our host, the Malawian head of the UN force and his Guatemalan general,' he said, nodding to where a tall, handsome man was slapping a moustachioed Latin American in full military regalia on the back. Winston looked on, smiling politely. 'Over there, my boss the ambassador, talking to the German and Israeli envoys.' Familiar faces from the Italian Club, they looked thoroughly bored: no doubt all three met regularly in Lira and had nothing new to say to one another.

'You haven't met the Prez yet, have you? Now's your chance.' He tipped his head, but the gesture was unnecessary. The same shimmer of nervous excitement I'd seen travel the length of Liberation Avenue now formed a flurried halo around the two presidents deep in conversation with Kofi Annan. Commissioners awkwardly hovered around the holy trio, not daring to interrupt a conversation that might conceivably make their presence in The Hague superfluous. I was suddenly reminded of the shoals of fish – so tiny they are no more than eyes and black ticks of spine – that swarm just under the surface of shallow waters. Were Big Men born that way, I wondered, with the capacity to draw all eyes, or was the magnetism acquired with age, tribute to a series of brave or dreadful acts they had proved ready to commit? It must be the latter, I thought, remembering the hush that would fall on the secretaries in Grobart & Fitchum's offices when Dan arrived in the morning. Dan was the most sweet-tempered of employers, yet his staff had wanted to feel the titillating thrill of fear around him. Charismatic leaders were created by subjects who needed to worship at the altar of someone more magnificent than themselves.

'I wonder when those two last got to chew the fat,' said Brett. 'What I wouldn't give to eavesdrop on that one.'

Abraham had told me that the two heads of state had once fought alongside one another, sharing rations, cartridges and even women in the gullies of the Grameen Mountains. They had gone their separate ways now, and the contrast was striking. Rotund and balding, Darrar's president was wearing what looked like a very expensive tuxedo. Above the startling white of his shirt, his face was sleek and full. He looked well tended, a man whose days in the bush were far behind him, more at ease, now, in the world of canapés and national toasts. Our president was the only person in the room who had made no attempt to smarten up for tonight's occasion. He had on the same short-sleeved safari jacket he famously wore to work every day, the outfit in which he had posed for his official photograph, pen poised over the affairs of state. From the look of it, he had not bothered combing his hair, and his beard could have done with a trim, yet he looked by far the more relaxed of the two. Perhaps that languid ease had something to do with the fact that he towered over his former comrade-in-arms by a good foot and a half. How mortifying it must be, I thought, to be forced to look up to the man you have come to hate.

'Now, how would you summarise the subliminal messages of those sartorial choices?' asked Brett, arching one eyebrow. 'I believe our man is actually wearing open-toed sandals.'

'Er ... their side's would be "I have successfully made the transition from rebel to world statesman and now take my rightful place among the luminaries of Africa. I can afford to buy my suits on the rue Saint-Honoré."'

'Yeah,' snickered Brett, 'our guy's is simpler. "Fuck this shit. You may be the regional power everyone sucks up to, but I'm twice your size and I still know how to head-butt."'

Henry Alexander, Reginald Watts and the youth brigade clustered behind the hovering commissioners. The youngsters seemed the only ones having a genuinely good time. One of the girls was bent double, champagne sloshing out of a flute, laughing at some witticism from the boy with the crew-cut. This was going to be the first stop of the evening, I guessed: later there would be a bar, a nightclub, and one of the girls would end up, slightly unprofessionally, in Crew-cut's bed.

'Now she,' Brett indicated a portly woman standing near a column, 'is the US deputy secretary of state for African affairs and she shouldn't be left on her own like that. So, if you'll excuse me, duty calls ... Great dress, by the way. You've got a cuter ass than I expected.' He timed the last so carefully that my wince of irritation was wasted on the back of his neck.

I wavered. At moments like this, facing a room of strangers, I missed Jake with fierce intensity. No shield, no ally. How glorious it would be to turn on my heel, retrieve my coat, run through the vast doors of the Peace Palace and out into the cool of the night, staggering in my unfamiliar heels down the drive to the safety of the main gate and beckoning taxi rank. 'Unprofessional,' I admonished myself. And suddenly there was a bald pate, so shiny it reflected the ceiling light, and a friendly face smiling quietly at me. 'Dr Berhane! No one told me you'd be here. How lovely to see you.'

'My friend Paula. You are quite right, I do not belong. You need only to look at my clothes,' he gestured at a worn tweed jacket, 'to see that. But I was in The Hague and the North Darrar ambassador, an old friend, ordered me to make up numbers. You, in contrast, look magnificent.'

He laid an avuncular hand on my arm. 'You need a drink. Here, this lovely girl has what we need.' He led me to a dark-haired waitress in a smart white jacket holding a silver tray with a selection of drinks. I took a glass of white wine.

'You can tell that beautiful Mariam is one of us, can't you?' said Dr Berhane, as the waitress smiled. I realised he was right. I saw young women with her honey-coloured skin and painfully slender wrists and ankles every day on Liberation Avenue. 'Second-generation immigrant. Her parents fled to the Netherlands during the 1970s,' elaborated Dr Berhane. 'A typical hardworking member of the diaspora. The only question is, which diaspora? Theirs or ours? It is impossible to tell, you know, whatever the maps say, because physically and linguistically we are so similar. I have been badgering her all evening but she will not say. She is very stubborn.'

Mariam flushed and lowered her eyes. 'It is better not to talk politics, these days. Excuse me, there are guests without drinks.' And she escaped into the crowd.

Dr Berhane gazed after her with a kind of mournful longing. 'Her parents are probably a mixed couple. That's almost certainly why she is so careful. Those are the people who have been the worst hit by this new war. Their children find themselves rejected by everyone. It's hard. Very hard.' He shook his head with slow, exaggerated emphasis.

'Are you OK, Dr Berhane?'

'Yes, but my sheets are in the wind, as they say. I must apologise for that. An empty stomach, an open bar and an impoverished African academic – a fatal combination. I will go back to the ambassador's residence soon. But I wanted to see for myself a little segment of history in the making. It's what I do, after all. And I did learn something by coming tonight.'

'What was that, Dr Berhane?'

His lips were against my ear. 'Look around you. Tell me what you see.'

I scanned the room. 'Presidents, foreign ministers, ambassadors, judges and lawyers, some UN officials, a few military men ... and all the catering staff, of course. What's your point?'

'Tell me, how many of those faces are African? And how many Western? And which outnumber which? Screw up your eyes. That way you won't focus on the detail and just see the colour. Tell me the ratio of brown to pinko-grey, as your Orwell called it.'

I didn't need to screw up my eyes. Kofi Annan had only managed to keep the two presidents talking for a few minutes. Like magnets forced briefly together, they had bounced off one another and hurtled to opposite sides of the room, forming the nodal points of two African clusters. Isolated brown poles in an overwhelming sea of white.

Dr Berhane whispered, 'No outsider, passing this room, would ever think an African process was taking place inside these walls, now, would they?'

'I'm not sure that's fair,' I protested. 'Most of the Westerners here are essentially technical advisers, like me. The decision-makers are all African. None of us would be here if we hadn't been invited by your two governments.'

'Ah, yes, but the invitations were the product of a system of universal justice hammered out in Washington, Paris and London, rooted in the deep scars left by your wars, wars of no relevance to Africa, a vision that our young governments felt obliged to endorse, assuming that was what all civilised nations did, only to discover their new partners were too old and wise to fall into that trap themselves.'

'But what's the alternative? It's not perfect but surely it has to be an improvement on what came before.'

'Oh, there is none now. It is too late to explore alternative methods of reconciliation and forgiveness. We are all singing off the page written by Amnesty International, Human Rights Watch and George Clooney. All toothpaste tastes the same wherever you go in the world. The few intellectuals who disagree end up sounding like collaborators with dictatorships, apologists for genocide. And, let's be honest, often that's exactly what they are. Still, I do not think this is healthy. I can recall too many wood-panelled rooms that looked exactly like this: chandeliers, tapestries, waiters in white jackets, a few token Africans being watched like hawks by powerful white men. The Berlin conference in 1884, Sykes-Picot in 1915, Laval-Mussolini in 1935.'

It was Winston who came to my rescue. 'There you are, Paula. Greetings, Dr Berhane. I hope you won't mind if I borrow your companion. I'd like to introduce her to the man who pays her salary.' He grabbed my elbow and steered me purposefully to one of the two nodes we had been surveying. I had never learned how to cut in at cocktails, but Winston simply tapped the man in front of him on the shoulder, forcing him to interrupt an ongoing conversation. 'Foreign Minister, you must meet Paula Shackleton, the woman who will be holding my hand as we go into battle. Paula, this is His Excellency Simon Gebreyesus, also known as Kennedy.'

Stocky, grizzled, the foreign minister had a bug-eyed look. I found my gaze shifting from one of his eyes to the other, trying to work out which he was using.

'And this,' said Winston, turning to the man Kennedy had been addressing, 'is Buster, presidential assistant and government spokesman.'

'"Buster"?'

'As in Buster Keaton,' said the presidential spokesman. 'Fighters are simple people. They like nicknames. In my case, I was famous at the front for never smiling.' He was not smiling now.

'I see.'

'So you are our new legal champion. You seem very young, Miss Shackleton, but Mr Peabody tells me you are tough.'

Then, as I was automatically muttering, 'He flatters me,' Buster introduced me to the president.

'Sir, the young woman you were asking about.'

The president took his time. I suppose you can do that when you're the boss, decide how long to stretch a pause while denying eye contact. I stood there awkwardly, wondering if he had heard. Mariam the waitress was at his elbow, holding a tray with the usual selection. He took a glass automatically, then stared at it with the incredulous disgust one might reserve for a bucket of elephant's urine. 'What is this shit?'

Mariam winced as though she'd been slapped. In the sudden silence, I heard a tinkling chorus: her hands, holding the tray of glasses, were shaking. 'Pinot Grigio,' she said, her face pale. 'It is an Italian wine.'

He returned it to the tray. 'I know what Pinot Grigio is. Get me a man's drink. Johnnie Walker.' He made a pinching gesture with his thumb and forefinger, indicating how much he wanted, a generous two inches. 'This much. No ice, no water.'

Then he finally deigned to look at me and smiled. It was the smile of a man in a mood for public jousting. 'Ah, our female Perry Mason. Our *very expensive* female Perry Mason. I had my doubts when Mr Peabody suggested hiring a woman, but he tells me in the US now they are just as good, if not better, than the men. So, tell me, why did you choose the law?'

'I have a mathematical mind. I enjoy solving puzzles.'

'So justice is a puzzle, then, like Sudoku? Not a noble pursuit, a guarantor of inalienable human rights? What do you say to that, Mr Peabody? I think your young colleague is older and more cynical than you.'

Mariam was back at his elbow. He took the tumbler of amber liquid off her tray and swallowed an inch with the smooth ease of a heavy drinker.

'It can be both,' said Winston, diplomatically. 'A mathematical puzzle and something deeper.'

The president ignored him. 'Did you know that I studied law at the University of Darrar, Miss Shackleton?'

'No,' I said, surprised. 'I had no idea.'

'As a youngster I, too, liked solving puzzles. And it seemed to me, as a nationalist, that many of my people's problems could be solved if only our occupiers at the time, the government of Darrar, were forced to apply the letter of the law. That was certainly what our lecturers seemed to imply. Then came the first-year exams. I did very badly. All of the students from what was then called Northern Province did. It was quite shocking how stupid we turned out to be. Has that ever happened to you, learning to your amazement that you are a lazy idiot?'

'No,' I said.

'So we broke into the dean's office one night. We opened his filing cabinets, we found our real marks – we had done well, distinctions in many cases – and the letter from the Negus telling the dean it was important the students from up north be kept in their place. So we went to the dean's house. We got him out of his bed, we stripped him naked, glued our exam papers to his body, and whipped him through the campus in front of the staff and students. Then, before the police had time to arrive, we left for the bush. We had completed our education. We exchanged our pens for AK-47s. We had understood that they would never let us compete on equal terms. We had to bring the whole thing tumbling down.' He smiled at the memory. 'Do you know the Malcolm X quote – "Nobody can give you equality or justice. If you're a man, you take it"?'

It was not, perhaps, the most appropriate anecdote to tell a lawyer, whose job was to assure the world your country will uphold its legal commitments, at a cocktail party thrown to emphasise the seriousness of an unfolding judicial process. Reading my mind, he smiled again. 'Don't worry, Miss Shackleton. Even at our most hot-headed, the Movement always upheld international law. Our record on the treatment of prisoners of war has been much praised. Just ask Mr Peabody – no African country puts international rulings into effect more swiftly than we do.'

Judge Mautner was approaching, a man with a mission. The president nodded in closure: my moment in the sun was over. But before moving away he turned and murmured quietly, 'Don't spend too long in Sumbi's Café, Miss Shackleton. Lira has better bars than that.'

Then the node and its shoal of hangers-on moved away, sucking Winston and Buster in its wake but leaving the foreign minister behind. I realised my mouth was half open and closed it.

'What is it?' Kennedy asked, noticing my expression.

'I'm impressed that the president knows which café I patronise.'

'It's a small town, Lira. Everyone knows everything.'

'So I keep being told.'

My mind was racing. Was I being watched? If so, who was the spy and how detailed was the monitoring? Were they listening to my telephone conversations, reading my emails, or just tracking my movements?

Suddenly, sanity returned. It didn't take much surveillance to establish that I hung out in Sumbi's. By dropping that one detail into the conversation, the president had created the impression of an all-seeing, all-knowing state. The intention was to rattle me. A classic technique, it had been entirely successful.

The foreign minister yawned and rubbed one eye, so vigorously that I realised it must be glass – another war injury? Hence the wandering focus.

'Tired?'

'When he is like this, he can go all night,' he confided. 'And so we, too, must go all night. I will rest when I get back to Lira,' he said, more to himself than me. 'Let us just hope that the pretty waitress obliges.'

'The waitress?' I was disconcerted. 'Mariam?'

'Didn't you see him flirting with her?'

'That was flirting?'

'Oh, yes. He will want to follow up. Let us hope she says yes. Then we can all get some rest. Do you know which nationality she is, though? Our side or theirs?'

'I have no idea.' The image of what might await Mariam left me dismayed and flustered on her behalf. I looked around the room, hoping fiercely and suddenly that her shift ended soon.

On the other side of the hall, Judge Mautner was ushering his VIPs towards the exit, where limousines were clearly waiting to whisk them away to a private dinner. The foreign minister paused a moment before joining them.

'You know, there is one thing all you Westerners here tonight must remember.'

'Which is?'

'For our side, all this is really just a game. As you said, a puzzle. A big puzzle being staged to please the West. We know we are in the right and it is time the world acknowledged that. So we will jump through its hoops, because a country without clear borders is like a woman without panties – anyone can enter. But we can always go back.' He gestured at the décor with contempt. 'We wouldn't miss any of this – this *decadence*. We know in our hearts that we can always go back to the trenches, the caves. That life does not alarm us. Just look at the enemy.' He grimaced. 'Their hand-made shoes and linen shirts. You know that my counterpart's daughters go skiing in Switzerland? His son is at Yale, he owns a villa on Lake Geneva. They have swallowed it all. Me, I still live in my mother's house in Lira, I don't own a car and my children took their degrees with the Open University. We will win because we can bear hardship and they cannot. The side that is ready to suffer most always wins.'

Identifying turning points matters in law. The precise moment a clump of cells becomes a foetus capable of sustaining life. The moment a squatter wins rights to a property. The millimetre at which no man's land becomes alien territory. But pinpointing transitions is hard to do in real life. I have no clear answer to the question of when things started going wrong between Jake and me. It was a messy accumulation of fractious experiences, each negligible in isolation, which knitted together to form a mat of miscommunication and sustained grudges, like the lint-laden pelt you dig out of a clogged vacuum cleaner. In that musty weave a few incidents hold prominence.

9/11 was one. Like every other New Yorker, I spent that strange morning in a state of febrile anxiety. Hitchens had assigned me to work on a bond issue and the team had pulled an all-nighter. The first plane hit as I was preparing to leave the office to catch up on my sleep. I spent the next hour trying, and failing, to call friends in Lower Manhattan, moving from the knot of employees gathering in front of the office television to the plate-glass windows, where we could see plumes of smoke rising from the Twin Towers and hear the first sirens swell to a wailing chorus of dismay. Uncertain what to do, Hitchens's partners eventually ordered an evacuation. Upstairs, Jake was doing the same with his team, and we joined the throngs of panicky workers walking home along surreally deserted streets, me to Greenwich Village, Jake to reassure a hysterical Olivia in the Upper East Side apartment, each of us wondering, as we kissed a rushed goodbye, whether we were heading in the right direction or would see each other again.

For weeks afterwards, the wounded city was united, its

citizens gentler to one another than was their custom, allaying the horror with unexpected gestures of selflessness, small daily acts of kindness. We were in bruised lockdown and I felt very much part of that state of siege. But as the months went by and the testosterone-charged Bush backlash began, I became aware of a growing sense of distance. The ubiquitous Stars and Stripes, evidence of the new in-your-face patriotism, began to grate. Overhearing office conversations, I realised I did not share the general sense of amazement. Outrage and anger, yes, but no surprise. And as soon as I heard Donald Rumsfeld use the phrase 'Old Europe', I knew why. I belonged to that despised category. My conviction that no individual can expect to be indefinitely spared acts of random violence was rooted in a scarred continent's long experience of war. I was out of kilter with my time and place, while Jake felt no such unease. I bit my tongue, watched what I said, but 9/11 left me with a new understanding. The US might be my base, but it was not yet my home. Perhaps that was why my immigration status began to prey on my mind.

The second incident was an interview with a prematurely pot-bellied young man wearing a brown pin-stripe suit in an office in the Bronx. He was rooting around in a pile of yellow files when I put my head round his door. It was a lawyer's office of the old-school variety, its walls lined with grey filing cabinets. On the top shelf of a library heavy with legal reference books, trios of brown cardboard boxes had been marked in thick red felt tip: 'REJECTED', 'PENDING', 'ACCEPTED', 'REJECTED', 'PENDING', 'ACCEPTED'.

'Larry Goldman?'

'Ah, yes ... You must be Ms Shackleton?'

'That's me.'

'Take a seat. Just a moment ...' He riffled through a few stacks of documents. 'Aha, here we are!' He extracted a yellow file with a flourish. 'So, yes, let me just refresh my memory ...' He sat and leaned back in his swivel chair, propping his feet on the corner of his desk. 'You know, Ms Shackleton, it really wasn't necessary for you to come in,' he murmured, scanning the pages. 'This office processes about five hundred visa applications a year, and I can count the clients I meet in person on the fingers of one hand. We usually find emails and faxes are quite adequate.'

'Well, I was in the area, so it seemed to make sense. Plus my office is open-plan and we all end up eavesdropping on each other's conversations. It can be awkward.'

'No problem, no problem, entirely up to you.' There was a brief silence as he read on, slurping coffee from a Starbucks paper cup. Finally, he closed the file and gave a conspiratorial smile.

'So. You've been with your current firm, Hitchens, on extended secondment from its London office, for three years. One of the City of London's prestigious Magic Circle law firms, right?'

'Yes.'

'Nice. You must be one of their rising stars,' he commented. 'And you're here on an intra-company transfer visa – the L1B. Which expires in four months.'

'That's right. I wanted to know what my options were, given that I'd like to continue working here in the States.'

'Not anxious to go home, eh?'

'I'm not sure where home is any more.'

'Well, the obvious option is simply to apply for an extension.'

'Ye-es. That's really what I wanted to talk to you about. The L1B locks me into a relationship with my employer, doesn't it? I mean, if Hitchens shift their operations to Texas, I'd have to move or go back to the UK, wouldn't I?'

'Yes, I'm afraid so.'

'And I can't jump ship, either, and take a job with a rival?'

'That's correct. You belong to Hitchens, in a way.'

'The point is that there have been rumours circulating for a while that Hitchens could be about to merge with a rival.

Heads always roll after mergers and, as I'm one of the younger employees, the principle of last in, first out would probably apply. I didn't take it too seriously at first, but I now have an American boyfriend' – I squirmed at that inadequate description of Jake – *'and I don't want to have to leave at short notice.'*

'In that case, I'd recommend applying for the H1B, the specialty-occupation visa. It allows you to change employers without having to repatriate. And after five years on that, you automatically qualify for the coveted green card, permanent residence.'

'How easy are they to get?'

'Well …' He tapped his teeth with his pen. 'Not that easy, to be honest. Not since 9/11. We've become a very paranoid nation, and it's made my working life a hundred times more complicated. Everyone's kinda twitchy and the US isn't exactly short of lawyers.'

It had been a mistake to come here, I thought. He was right. Just seeing this office, crammed with evidence of thousands of other questing hopefuls, made me feel vulnerable and insignificant, a morsel of plankton about to be sieved through the great maw of US bureaucracy. Best keep it to emails and faxes in future. Then I straightened my back. Don't be a wimp, I told myself, all bureaucracies are like this. Just understand the system, then work it.

'It's worth trying, at least?'

'Of course, of course. Quotas or no quotas, my job is to make sure you get what you need. Your employers' references are glowing, which helps. Right, you may as well sign the papers while you're here and we'll get that H1B application in the works.'

He was positively jocular as he reached for a final handshake. 'Don't worry, Ms Shackleton. We'll get there in the end. I say to my clients, "Unless you're going to go for the Depardieu option, you simply have to become a little bit Zen."'

'The "Depardieu option"?'

'Oh, my little joke. Gérard Depardieu and Andie MacDowell. Didn't you see the movie? She's the earnest American, he's a French composer. They stage a marriage of convenience to get him a green card, only they get caught. Yes,' he said, with a fond chuckle, 'marriage can be a fast track to permanent residence. But if you've seen the movie, you'll know why we recommend that our clients only pursue that option when there's a genuine relationship.'

16

Back in Lira, everything fell into a Spartan routine. I'd wake at what, by northern-hemisphere standards, would have counted as an obscenely early hour but there felt entirely natural, so insistent was the highlands light. Breakfast was a mug of espresso and a slice of toast, eaten standing, overlooking our back yard. Sharmila usually sat neatly at the dining-table, picking at a bowl of fruit. Increasingly she was joined by Steve, the UN peacekeeper, a ginger-bearded Australian giant. The UN had eighty rooms permanently booked at the five-star Africa Hotel, which boasted both swimming-pool and modern gym – luxuries regularly commented upon in the local newspapers – but Steve appeared to feel little fondness for his billet.

'He says the water pressure is better here,' Sharmila explained. 'Better showers.'

'And who said romance is dead?'

As Steve snorted and tromboned in the bathroom, Abraham would arrive to pick us up. On the way he would drop me off at Winston's villa, just off Liberation Avenue. By eight a.m. we would be hard at work.

Winston had divided Darrar's enormous counter-Memorial into bite-sized chunks for the team to analyse. The biggest chunk he had assigned to the two of us. He had asked if I minded working from his house, as he found it easier to focus when surrounded by plants. I could feel Sharmila's resentment at what she clearly regarded as gross favouritism burning into my back every time I scrambled out of the Land Cruiser, leaving her to continue on to the office. Winston would unlock the metal door that opened from the street onto a jasmine-draped courtyard lined with terracotta pots bursting with agapanthus, camellia and hibiscus, and I would take my place at the white plastic table, topped by a gaudy blue-and-white parasol.

'There!' he said on the first morning, depositing the wads of documentation on the table. 'Our homework for the next few months.'

'So, what's in it?'

'Everything bar the kitchen sink, by the look of it. Nineteenth-century correspondence between the Negus of Darrar and the Italians, between his successor and the Brits, then a whole load of letters from when Darrar swallowed North Darrar in the 1950s and labelled it their new Northern Province. Hundreds of military cables during and after the Sanasa attack. Prisoner-of-war testimony and compensation claims from thousands of farmers and traders who say they suffered grievous losses because of the war.'

I measured the blocks' depth with index finger and thumb. 'Would I be correct in detecting an element of machismo about their decision to submit quite so much?'

'It's a fairly classic technique. Drown the opposition in sheer volume. Swamp them in a tsunami of detail. Makes you look good in the eyes of the court – "See how open we are, we have no secrets" – and hope the quantity will bludgeon the other side into silence. A form of bluff. They assume that we'll be too lazy to actually read the material, so they get kudos points while losing nothing.' He rolled up his sleeves, cracked his knuckles and shook his head pityingly. 'The poor fools clearly have no idea who they're dealing with.'

'Oh?'

'I won't be going into that hearing without understanding

the meaning of every piece of evidence in these files. Hard work is not something that has ever intimidated Winston Peabody the Third. They've actually played straight into our hands.'

'How so?'

'Oh, I know exactly the process that will have been involved in producing this heap of verbosity. Everything has to be submitted in English. The one thing the other side have no shortage of is manpower. They'll have assigned a dozen government translators to work their way methodically through the documents. Junior officials in the Ministry of Foreign Affairs, the odd student on contract, perhaps. Those civil servants may be loyal patriots, but they have no grasp of the strategic issues at stake. Might as well use a robot army. They're trained to focus on minutiae, not to develop ideas above their pay grade. So they'll churn out cable after cable, letter after letter, never understanding what they mean when taken as a whole, and their bosses, who started off their careers as automatons, too, will assume that someone else, someone above them, is doing the filtering and analysis. That's how sclerotic bureaucracies work. Everyone passes the buck until it finally gets dropped and rolls away. Something important will have been missed. And you and I will find it.'

I pulled the first pile of paper towards me, suppressing a sigh. I couldn't help wondering if the counter-Memorial was just sound, comprehensive evidence. 'OK, so what are we looking for?'

'I can't tell you, exactly. But I have enough confidence in your intellect to believe you'll spot the great bow wave as the whale comes up for air.'

And so the days passed, the piles of checked documents by our respective elbows growing higher and higher. Occasionally we would break for coffee – it was somehow always understood that, although it was Winston's kitchen, I was responsible for refreshments – and to compare notes on possible discoveries.

At twelve thirty precisely, Winston would remove his spectacles, put down his pen and we would walk to the Ristorante Torino, where he would order his usual: macaroni cheese followed by vanilla ice cream. By one forty we would be back at work.

'Hmm,' Winston said quietly to himself one morning. 'I wonder.'

'What?'

He puckered his lips into a *moue*, then released them, gazing at a couple of pages of thin blue paper. 'A letter they've forgotten to translate.' He turned them over, then, finding nothing of interest, held the signature so it was only a couple of inches from his eyes. 'Can you read that?'

'Just about.'

'Does that name look familiar? I have a feeling I've seen it before. Somewhere else in the paperwork.'

'Really?' I was not going to admit it, but I was having difficulty distinguishing one local name from another. 'What's it part of?'

'A stack of correspondence from regional officials and police chiefs intended to establish a record of administration over a cluster of villages in the western sector. It could be nothing. But let's get Dr Berhane to translate it, shall we? How are you getting on with Captain Lewisham, by the way?'

'Oh, he's coming to feel like an old friend, the kind of favourite uncle who embarrasses you in company by telling politically incorrect jokes but is a pretty astute observer of human nature underneath.'

Towards mid-afternoon Winston would sometimes show signs of restlessness, getting to his feet, fussing over the plants with a watering-can, scrunching dried blossoms in his hands, squirting leaves with water mist. Other days, he'd seem to run out of energy, slumping in his chair. I'd raid the plastic bottles lined up on his bathroom shelf until I located what he described as 'one of my pep pills', wondering in passing why the container had no label. At five thirty precisely he would lean back in his chair and announce, 'Right, that's it, enough, you've done your duty Ms Shackleton!' just as Abraham sounded the horn outside.

Back at the villa, I would change into shorts and go running, tagged by a posse of mongrels and some laughing urchins who never seemed to tire of the spectacle. My route took me out of the suburbs and onto the plains, where the goatherds were starting the slow process of corralling flocks for the night. The air would be warm on my skin when I began, jiggling my shoulders to release the tension of the day, the descending sun's rays dousing the fields of sorghum and chickpea in a soft orange wash. I'd turn back once it sank below the horizon, silhouetting the indigo hills against the sky. By the time I was wiggling my key in the front-door lock I could feel a deadly blue chill reaching across that vast plateau to claim Lira, as the first stars blinked from the darkness.

Sometimes, when he sensed we were falling behind some unarticulated schedule, Winston would call to ask if I minded putting in a couple of hours' overtime. I was pathetically grateful for those summonses, which saved me from evenings brooding in my bedroom. If the call didn't come, I'd escape the demons by heading off for Sumbi's, where I'd usually bump into Dawit.

Occasionally, George called from Transit Camp No. 3. The first time he did this, he found some work pretext, but after that he just called to chat, about Liverpool, a DVD someone had sent him or, of all things, the decline of the National Health Service. I sensed it was my Britishness that appealed, a touchstone of familiarity.

'Nights are the hardest here,' he acknowledged, and I recalled the vast velvet sky that had stretched outside the tent on my visit with Abraham. 'You never get silence like this in the UK. It's what I remember from my visits to Sanasa in my childhood. The terrifying quiet.'

'What's Sanasa like, George?'

'What *was* it like. Most of it has been destroyed.'

'OK, so what was it like? I spend my entire time discussing what happened there, but I've never clapped eyes on it.'

'Oh, it was like all those Red Sea ports. As a boy I hated it, of course. It was so hot in the daytime, I couldn't really speak the language and the local kids made terrible fun of me. But in the evening, when it began to cool, the light turned everything gold, the whitewashed buildings went pink and suddenly this scruffy little port looked ...'

'Beautiful?'

He laughed. 'Almost. All the men would muster outside the mosque after prayers, lots of gossip and jokes, handholding – the men do that here, it doesn't mean they're gay. Then the shops opened and, to a kid, those kiosks lined with glittering packets of coffee, spices and chewing gum – all the merchandise here comes wrapped in silver and gold foil – looked like magic grottoes. There'd be women selling pastries at little stalls down the alleyways and the restaurants on the main square served up fish caught that morning, smeared with spices and roasted over an open grill. It was always a competition whether you could finish yours before one of the moth-eaten cats jumped onto the table.'

'It sounds idyllic.'

'Yes.' He paused and his voice changed: 'But I'm learning not to trust those memories, you know. The places diasporas care about don't actually exist. We reinvent them, then expect "our boys" to fight for our fantasies. At the end of the day, none of us in the diaspora would want to spend more than an afternoon in a place like Sanasa. You have to remind yourself of that.'

When I returned to Winston's villa in the mornings, I almost always discovered that he had been working quietly at the pile of documents in the night, drilling as methodically as a woodpecker attacking a redwood. It was a punishing routine, as repetitive as that of any detained felon, but I had no complaints.

I found it all deeply soothing. The harder I worked, the easier it was to keep thoughts of Jake at bay.

'What's with the nicknames, Dawit?'

We were sitting in Sumbi's, both of us nursing a third beer, flushed with alcohol and the adrenalin of a table football match that I, for once, had won. My question had been triggered by Dawit's introductions to a group of middle-aged men heading out of the bar. 'My friend, we call him Mule, his brother, known as Beanstalk, their cousin, Sinatra.'

'The nicknames. Everyone here seems to have one.'

'Correction. Every *former fighter* has one.'

'Well, same question. What's wrong with their real names?'

He waved his cigarette in the air, threatening to put my eye out with it. 'Oh, here, you know, there are only about six traditional names. They get used and reused. We ran out of combinations about a thousand years ago. So if that was all anyone used we would never know who we were dealing with. It just makes things easier.' He clicked his fingers. 'Snappy, to the point.'

'But you said it was only the former fighters.'

'Well … You're making me think, Paula. This is what I like about you.' He twiddled a forefinger in mini windmills around his temple. 'You ask such stupid questions,' he said, with a smile. 'They force the nails in my brain to go round.'

I laughed. 'Cogs, not nails. They're not stupid. Deceptively simple, maybe, yet insanely intelligent, I think you'll find.'

'Perhaps. So what you have to realise is that the Movement was, above all, a national organisation. Our commanders always told us it didn't matter what God we worshipped, what sex we were, which province we came from because we were all born equal, one people, fighting together. Over here you can usually tell from people's names where they come from. Really, you know everything about someone from his name, because it tells you who his father was, his grandfather, which village he comes from, whether it is highlands, coast, lowlands, whether he's Muslim or Christian. So a nickname is neutral. You are just a man, facing another man, it carries no – what do you guys say? – no luggage.'

'Baggage. I guess that makes sense.'

The question had triggered some train of thought. He stared into the distance, smoking, then began to play with his cardboard beer mat, frowning slightly as he drew its edge through a splash of spilled beer.

'Maybe there is something else, too, Paula. Something not so nice.'

'Like what?'

'You have to become someone different to kill people. If you stayed Dawit, or Paula, and your commander told you to take this AK-47, go and sit on that hill all afternoon, wait for the sun to go down, and when you see an old man coming over the crest, back from the fields with his goats, very calm and contented, you must take aim and put a bullet through his forehead – an old man who has never done you any wrong but whom the Movement thinks just *might* be a spy – well, then, you would go mad, wouldn't you, during the long hours of waiting?'

I stared at him, imagining the cold dread of that long stake-out. No wonder he found it hard to sleep.

'But,' he continued, 'if you are Rambo or Tarzan or Cobra when they ask you to do that, it is not so hard. You can do it, and live with yourself afterwards. Because it is not really you doing that terrible thing, it is someone else. And that is how you can tell that the guys we bump into at the Zombie Café, the Restaurant Torino and the Café Oriana are not yet ready for civilian life. They are still those other people. Buster, Kennedy, they will never be anything different. Abraham, maybe he will change back.'

'Abraham? Our Abraham? I thought that was his real name.'

'We baptised him Abraham at the front because he was such a good driver. We knew he'd get us to the Promised Land, like Abraham in the Bible. Me, I dropped my nickname when I came in from the field. I forced all my friends and family to stop using it. They did not want to at first, but I would not listen when they used it. These guys should do the same. We're not in the field now.'

'So what was your nickname, then?'

He cackled nastily. Lips curled, he gazed at me over the rim of his glass. 'Me? Bingo. I was a sniper. I never missed.' He took aim with an imaginary rifle, looked over the sights at me and made the sound of a bullet splatting against a target. 'Bingo!' he said again, with sarcastic relish, and downed the rest of his beer. 'Another one? Your turn.'

'I need the loo first.' When I returned, he was rooting ostentatiously through my handbag, impatient at the delay. 'Come on, woman, get on with it.' Too late, I made a lunge for repossession. He leaned back, out of reach, brandishing a photograph.

'Aha. What's this? A photo? I love photos! But it's of … two dogs.'

'Yes.'

He slapped himself on the thigh with delight and gave me one of his Hallowe'en-pumpkin grins. 'Wonderful, wonderful. What kind of dogs?'

'None of your business.'

'They look special. Expensive. Are they – what you call it? – pedigree?'

'A Hungarian Vizsla and a Weimaraner.'

'And what is the name of these special snob dogs?'

'This isn't particularly funny, Dawit.'

'But it is extremely funny to me, Paula. What is their name? Let me guess. Rex and Lassie? Charlie and Roger?'

He flipped the photo over. 'Laurel and Hardy. Very witty. You know, this tells me a great deal about you, Paula.'

'Like what, exactly?'

'Ah, you Anglo-Saxons, so sentimental, but always about the wrong things. A Spanish, a Frenchie, a Russian would have a picture of his kids in his wallet. Or a mistress. But you lot give your hearts to dumb animals that can't answer back. Maybe that is why you love Africa so.' He slapped the table in delight, choking on cheap cigarette smoke and his own wit.

17

Captain Peter Lewisham's Diary
Kakardi, 1951, pages 91–7

22 April – The last of Tiny's booze has run out. Danny says we
should start on the local beer, which looks like muddy water.
He says it doesn't taste too bad, but I'm not keen. I've got my
eye on these fig cacti. Come summer, I reckon we might be able
to set up a still and use the pears. Cactus cocktail, anyone?

27 April – The day of the Great Parley. Drove in two jeeps to
the foot of the escarpment. These guys know how to disappear
when they want to. I could have sworn there was no one there,
then suddenly there was a shifta on every rock. Skinny chaps
wearing bits and bobs of Italian uniform. We agreed that four
of them would stay behind as hostages. Rupert, Derek, Tesfay
and I then made a bit of a show of disarming – I wasn't going
to let a shifta run his dirty fingers all over me, told them the
word of a former British officer would have to do. Then we
followed a guide up onto the ridge. We were sweating like pigs
after the first five minutes, but they climbed like goats. The
path snaked through some giant limestone rocks. Marvellous
views. We came across a chain of shallow caves, full of
droppings: Derek said bats, Rupert said goats, I reckoned

baboons. In the third cave we found old One Eye waiting for us, sitting as they do here, knees around his ears, Lee Enfield at his side, taking snuff from a little liquorice tin. He offered us a drink, gestured to one of his men to bring us some of their looted beers, which he handed over with a twinkle in his eye. Cheeky bugger, but it had been a hot climb so we drank them. One Eye only spoke Italian, so we got Tesfay to translate. Rupert very politely (called him 'sir', which struck me as over-doing it) asked One Eye what his intentions were and why he 'felt compelled to take up arms'. One Eye looked a bit surprised at that. I'm guessing he thought several truckloads of grain, fuel and a sizeable stash of ready cash were pretty compelling, but he muttered something about 'foreigners' and 'occupation', which Rupert wrote down. Then Rupert asked him which nationality he felt he was, given all the talk in the newspapers of independence, union and federation. One Eye thought for a moment, smiled, then said, 'My loyalty is to the flag which leaves me alone.' Which seemed clear enough to me, but Rupert looked a bit nonplussed. I then took over the parley. Told him the British government was offering an amnesty and a plot of land to any shifta who put down his weapon and swore loyalty to the King, but that the offer expired in thirty days. He nodded, we shook hands and scrambled down to the valley, where the lads had been getting impatient.

30 April – Another letter from Flo, accompanied by some tea and Gentleman's Relish. All very welcome. She says they hear almost no news from these parts on the BBC, so to keep the letters coming.

6 May – Bad news from HQ. It seems Johnny was shot dead on patrol yesterday, hit in the chest by a sniper. Died very quickly, his last words for 'Mum'. Only twenty-two. Not clear why or who was involved, probably someone who just likes taking pot-shots at British coppers. It's happened before.

Everyone at the station is in mourning. I found the cook in tears, even Tesfay very downcast. 'He was just a boy, just a silly boy,' he said. I took the photo of Johnny grinning with the rest of us at our Christmas feast down from the noticeboard and will send it to his mother and tell her what a sport he was.

17 May – News from HQ. Word in Neraye is that Johnny was shot by the father of the girl he got pregnant. HQ say they've collected a few witness statements and I'm to arrest him. We piled into a jeep and drove down to the compound, only to discover the old man hadn't been seen since he set off with his son and two rifles last month. He leased his plot before he left and the villagers reckoned he'd settled on the other side of the border. So it was all prepared. I asked Tesfay what happened to the money we'd collected as compensation and he said he'd never got round to paying it. I think Tesfay hoped we'd forget about compensation and he could pocket the proceeds. I tore a strip off him in front of the lads, told him we'd be sending it to Johnny's mother back in Blighty along with three months' worth of Tesfay's docked wages, as what he'd done might have cost Johnny his life.

25 May – HQ say to prepare for imminent locust invasion. There's a swarm heading our way, best warn the farmers. So we hooked up our loudspeakers and toured the whole of the eastern sector from Sanasa all the way down to Gurah, taking in Tentet, Buleb and the settlements along the Abubed. Took us three days. In the end, a few crushed grasshoppers were found on the main road and that was it. HQ later say the winds changed and the swarm missed us. We all felt a bit silly.

30 May – Tesfay came to me, eyes big with excitement. Said he'd heard where Johnny's murderer was holed up. So we drove down to the border at Gurah, stopped the jeep and

Tesfay pointed to a whitewashed house on the Darrar side. 'That's where the old man lives now,' he said.

'He might as well be in India,' I said, pointing to the militiamen at the border post.

'We could sneak across tonight,' said Tesfay, 'take the goat trails, arrest him and bring him across. No one will know we were there.' Trying to make amends, I suppose. 'You bloody fool,' I told him. 'HQ wouldn't thank me for triggering a diplomatic incident.' On the way back we spotted Johnny's girl washing clothes at the back of the father's old compound, big as a house. No husband, no father, not much future. After all that fuss over her honour, she'll probably end up a prostitute.

2 June – Woke up last night in a sweat. It was something Flo said in her last letter. 'The village girl must have been showing very early.' Got me thinking. The dates just don't add up. So either Johnny was walking out with the girl a lot earlier than he said or some local boy was involved. We'll never know now. A bloody awful episode, when all's said and done.

5 June – Another early-morning shifta attack on a truck on the Tentet–Sherano route. No one killed, but they took the supplies, removed the tyres, the tools, even siphoned off the fuel. The driver was beaten, tied up and had a note stuffed in his mouth. It read: 'No thank.' Rupert tells me the amnesty has shown results in Central and Western Province, with 135 shifta handing in their weapons. One Eye isn't going to be among them. Tough old bird. I've got a sneaking respect for him.

18

The year's end was approaching. 'Darling, I'm going to miss you *dreadfully*,' my mother lamented on the phone. 'I hate the thought of you there on your own.'

'Well, I can't think of anywhere I'd rather be.'

Winston announced that a Christmas office party would be good for morale, while somehow making clear that it was up to us to put the idea into effect. So, Sharmila and I spent the day tidying up the villa, Ribqa installed herself in the kitchen and Yohannes and the one American intern who had decided not to fly home for the festivities draped tinsel around a plastic tree. On my short-wave radio, the King's College choir was singing carols. The references to holly and snow felt pleasingly surreal: there wasn't a cloud in the sky and we were all in T-shirts.

As the first guests started to arrive, I ventured into the tussocky back yard, where Steve was eyeing six chicken wings and a few lamb chops sizzling on a metal grill with an expression of acute suspicion.

'Things OK?'

He had the proportions of a Greek hero, but not of the lissom, androgynous variety. No David or Hermes he. This was the other male type glorified in classical sculpture: the heavy-set Atlas who could effortlessly hoist the globe on his shoulders in his prime but who would in middle age undoubtedly run to fat. He had blond eyelashes – the kind any woman would immediately coat in mascara – wore his hair shaved down to a russet fuzz, and had a milky complexion ill-suited to the Lira climate. I'd spotted a bottle of factor 50 in our bathroom cabinet.

'Well, we Aussies pride ourselves on being able to start a barbie just about anywhere, but this one nearly had me beat.'

'What's the problem?'

'The matches suck, the charcoal's damp and I have my doubts about the whole grill design. Apart from that, it's fine.' He showed me the can of lighter fuel he was holding. 'In my book, this counts as cheating.'

'I won't tell anyone.'

It was our first proper conversation, and felt like progress of a sort. We chatted cautiously about the weather, career paths in the UN, and rival diplomatic definitions of the term 'hardship post'. But then his eyes travelled to the kitchen window, where Sharmila was waving at him, and he seemed to recollect himself.

'You like it here?' he asked abruptly, turning a chop with his tongs.

'Yes, but I'm still settling in.'

'Whaddaya think of Winston?'

Before I could say anything, he gave me the answer: 'Bit of a weirdo. Sharmila says he's got no family, no kids – think he's gay?'

'No. Asexual, maybe.' I immediately regretted the indiscretion.

He snorted. 'What does that even mean? Anyway, what I do know is that he sucks when it comes to management.'

'Why do you say that?'

'Well, he should never have put you and Sharms in the same villa.' I wasn't sure I wanted to hear any more. The conversation had gone from friendly to confrontational with startling speed. It seemed Steve had played with the idea of some kind of entente, only to think better of it. 'You know that Sharms applied for your post?' he continued. 'How would you feel if you had to live with the person who whipped your job from under your nose?'

'I didn't know that. But thanks for telling me. It explains a lot.'

'Yeah, well, rather you than me,' he called, with fake cheerfulness, as I walked back into the kitchen. There I found Ribqa, craning over the sink, watching Steve through the window.

'Why is that man making a barbecue when your cooker works?' she hissed. 'I was going to prepare everything here in the kitchen. Doesn't he know it's illegal?'

'Illegal?'

'That charcoal. He must have bought it by the road. Our government has banned the sale of charcoal. How can we reforest our country if people keep chopping down the trees? Doesn't he *know* that?'

I could see Abraham drawing up outside the villa in the Land Cruiser. He discharged Winston, then helped out three old men, draped in white cotton shawls. They moved gingerly towards us, using their silver-topped canes to test the ground, gossiping all the while among themselves.

'Paula! Look!' exclaimed Winston, holding out his arms. 'I've brought the Three Wise Men. These gentlemen come from the village of Shanti in the central sector. They popped into the office today to say hello. I thought we should include them in our Christmas party.'

The oldest of the trio staggered across the lintel, clawing at my forearm with such vigour that I knew I would have bruises the following day. He was a head and a half shorter than me. His face had shrunk down to cheekbone, forehead and teeth, but the eyes, despite their white-rimmed irises, were full of mischief.

'Let me introduce you to Paula and Sharmila, my colleagues,' said Winston. The three old men made a great show of surveying us, looking from us to Winston, exchanged a few comments among themselves and started to giggle. The smallest of them laughed so hard that the others had to hold him up.

'Those are three very naughty old men,' said Ribqa, who had emerged from the kitchen, hand on hips. 'I will not translate what they just said.'

Then, his face suddenly serious, the group leader raised his cane to command silence. As the group gathered round, he clicked his fingers at Yohannes, commanding him to translate.

'He apologises for joking,' said Yohannes. 'He says, "We are old men, we will die soon, we laugh while we can. But we came to Lira for something serious. We heard about the work you are doing and want to say: 'Keep going.'" He says ...' Yohannes slowed here, careful to get the words right '... that Shanti's residents know who they are. He is ninety-two now, and since the day he was a baby on his mother's knee, he has known that the people across the river, cattle raiders and thieves, are foreigners,' the old man was making brushing motions with one hand, 'and this place,' the old man struck his cane's metal tip repeatedly on the ground, 'was home! "We need a proper border," he says. "A border means respect. You white folk must win that respect in that court across the sea in Holland, say what we cannot say because we are only simple peasants."'

Winston gave a little bow, graciously accepting his rough-and-ready categorisation. He was beaming with pleasure. 'Please thank all of them on our behalf, Yohannes. Tell him their fight is our fight. We will not let them down.'

The villa and back yard filled quickly after that, and when a full moon emerged, we discovered there was something to be said for an open-air barbecue, however illegal. As I stood warming my hands over the coals, clutching my shawl around me and shivering, Abraham strolled over. 'Merry Christmas,' I said, holding up my beer bottle.

'Merry Christmas.' He clinked his against mine, judiciously eyeing our ridiculous plastic tree and tinsel decorations. 'Of course, for us, Christmas is in January, not December.'

I choked, spilling beer down my front. 'What? We did all this on the wrong day? This evening is becoming a magnificent tribute to cultural misunderstanding.'

He laughed. 'Oh, don't worry, Paula. You may not know our customs but we know yours. But for Orthodox Christians, this is not the day, and for Muslims on the coast, of course, it's irrelevant. If you're in the Movement it's all superstitious nonsense anyway. The only God it recognises is Marx.'

The evening wore on. At midnight, Winston, slightly flushed and unsteady, clambered onto a plastic chair with the help of the three elders. He raised his beer bottle to the moon, a small, custard-suited Statue of Liberty outlined against the stars, and declaimed: 'To the finest international presidential legal team in the country!' and we cheered ironically, toasting what was, after all, an indisputable assertion.

I gazed across the faces. A few neighbours had strolled across to join us. Amanuel the night-watchman had been persuaded to put down his AK-47 and was wolfing some lamb chops. Barnabas was cradling the sleeping body of his youngest daughter, while Riqba gossiped with the intern. Suddenly my eyes were watering. On this remote plateau, among strangers, I had found some sort of haven. Numbed to the point of arrogance, I had come to believe I could never be touched again. But these were my people now, my team. I felt the warmth of a forgotten sensation and put one hand cautiously to my face to check. I was smiling. It almost hurt.

'I can't get married,' Jake said quietly. 'It would be bigamy.'

Demonstrating an entirely uncharacteristic level of self-control, I had managed to hold off the conversation about my immigration status until the weekend. We were lying naked

in bed, my head on his chest, Jake stroking my hair, one lazy
Sunday morning. After the scratching at the door became
unbearable, we had let Laurel and Hardy into the room, but
fended off their attempts to clamber onto the bed. Jake's tone
was soft and wondering. I laughed, but I could tell from how
still the bedroom had become that we both knew the impor-
tance of this conversation. I sat up and looked him in the
eyes.

'I've never wanted to get married. You believe that, right?
I've never nursed some fantasy about wedding dresses and
bouquets. The thought of being addressed as "Mrs" gives me
the chills, and "my husband" would sound, well, weird. But
I have to ask you now, for all sorts of horrible practical reasons,
whether you see the current arrangement as permanent.'

He stroked my upper arms, gazing into the near distance
with a frown. 'This is going to sound pathetic, but ...'

'What?'

'I just don't know. I haven't thought that far. I hate saying
that, because it makes me sound like some sixteen-year-old
who's just got laid for the first time. But it's true. Being with
you has been so amazing that getting married simply never
occurred to me. Living together seemed enough. Fate giving
me a second chance I didn't deserve.'

'I understand that. And I hate, I really, really hate, having
this conversation. But there's more and more gossip circulating
at Hitchens. If this merger goes ahead, if our New York office
gets amalgamated, I might have to return to the UK. The
immigration lawyer is going to apply for an H1B, but my
qualifications may not be enough to do the trick. It would
help if I knew whether the whole marriage thing was ever
going to become a possibility.'

He shut his eyes and sighed. 'It's difficult,' he said finally.

Suddenly I felt nauseous. I looked around for my clothes,
lying in clumps around the bed, trying to locate knickers, shirt,
jeans. I needed to get out of that bedroom, away from Lake

Cottage, and be on my own. I started prising his fingers from my arms, working my way out of his grip. 'OK, fair enough.'

'Paula, no. Listen, Paula, this is important.'

'You don't have to tell me that,' I said, detaching one hand and pulling at his other wrist. He would not let go.

'Stop. You have to listen.' He gave me a light shake, forced me to make eye contact. 'I love you,' he said. 'I really love you. I can't believe I've gotten so lucky, after having fucked up in so many ways. But Olivia is the mother of my children. She's Catholic. No one in her family has ever been divorced. Her parents just celebrated their fiftieth wedding anniversary. Social appearances matter enormously to her. The golf club, the church, the home-made cookies – even if Juanita actually bakes them – the family's occasional mentions in the newspaper, the lighting of the Christmas tree, the clan. Her obsession with what the neighbours might say is one of the reasons we drifted apart in the first place.'

'God, that's so banal. You have to stay married to save face? Isn't that the definition of bourgeois hypocrisy?'

'Maybe, but it's the way she is. And I have to respect those values. I owe at least that to my oldest friend. The last few years haven't been easy for her – they've challenged everything she thought important. I need to give her time to adjust to the new status quo. The kids seem to be taking it incredibly well, but their social standing, their entire self-image, isn't at stake. Hers are.'

'They're adults and I'd expect them to react as such. They knew your marriage was on the rocks and they want you to be happy.'

'So far it's gone better than I expected, but Olivia has a capacity for the melodramatic gesture that has taken me by surprise in the past. Look,' he ran his hand through his hair, 'there was one weekend, which I prefer not to remember, when she took all her pills, drank a bottle of whisky, and I spent the night in hospital while she had her stomach pumped. I'm secretly hoping Ted will step in and stake a claim. Then her focus will shift away from me, and all the terrible things I've done, to him and their future together.'

'So you're a husband praying to be cuckolded.'

'Pretty much. The point is that our lives have been entangled for two decades, Paula. They can't be untangled overnight, not without a bloodletting that I desperately hope to avoid. So I'm begging you, please give me a bit more time. Let me ease us into this. I promise you, we'll get there in the end.'

I got slowly out of bed – this time he let me – and started to get dressed. I was no longer angry. To understand all is to forgive all, but the resulting knowledge also serves to paralyse and atrophy. The conversation should never have taken place. It had shifted things between us, nudged the pattern of our relationship out of its groove. Before, our jigsaw pieces had slotted neatly and miraculously into one another, forming a tight seal. But now jagged white gaps had opened between them. Our age of innocence was over and there was nothing I could do to retrieve it.

'OK, Jake. You win. But you should be aware that "easing into this", if you leave it too long, could end up with me being eased onto a plane by the US Immigration Service.'

19

Winston left Lira in mid-January. An oil company he'd advised in the past had heard that its Indian subsidiary might have been violating US anti-bribery law – his speciality – and had asked him to investigate. 'Frustrating,' he said, 'but this legal porridge is what makes my time in Lira possible, so it has to be done.' At the airport, I dutifully filled in his immigration cards and currency declaration forms as he fussed over his hand luggage.

'So when will we see each other next, Winston?'

'I'll try to come back in April, but I'll need to assess the mood back at base. It's important the partners at Melville & Bart feel I'm bringing in my share of revenue. If I can't make it, we'll meet in The Hague in May for the hearing. But you'll hardly notice I've gone. We'll be in constant contact. An email or phone call from you *twice* a day, Paula.' Then he handed me a list of duties so detailed it might have mortally offended a more ambitious deputy.

'Ever heard of micromanagement?' I said. 'It's not usually meant as a compliment.'

He laughed, squeezed my shoulder and said, 'We make a pretty good team,' then walked through the scanner to reclaim his suit jacket.

Once he was gone, I must admit that I felt a certain loosening, a sudden headiness. Teacher had left the classroom.

And, it may be coincidence, but it was at about this time that things began to go ever so slightly wrong.

A phone call to Sammy in Transit Camp, Eastern, No. 3. Some of the IDPs from the camp were on our list of possible witnesses for the hearing, and I needed to discuss paperwork and travel arrangements. We ran through practicalities and then, as I was about to ring off, Sammy cleared his throat awkwardly. 'Paula, there is something you should know. That doctor you and Abraham spoke to when you were here …'

An image of George's handsome, bearded face. 'George?'

'Yes, George. I think you liked him.'

'What's happened?'

'Well … He was arrested. They took him away last night.'

'"They"?'

'The soldiers took him. A military arrest. The army can do that. It is because of the fuss he made about IDP conscription. We tried to argue with them but they would not listen.'

'What are they charging him with?'

'What do you mean?'

'You know, what legal charge? They should specify when they're arresting someone.'

There was a thoughtful pause. 'That's not what happens here.'

'Do you know where he has been taken?'

'Ah …' Sammy sounded tired and a bit bored. 'That kind of thing can take a long time to find out.'

'Well, could you ask, Sammy, make a formal request? *Habeas corpus* – "Show me the body" – is the most basic human right.'

His voice dropped very low. 'So he is dead, then? There is a body?'

'No, no!' I almost shrieked, flustered by the misunderstanding. 'It's Latin. "*Habeas corpus*" means the authorities are obliged to show us where they're holding someone. If we know where George is being held, this office can make representations. That might make a difference to how he's treated. We have a little bit of influence here so let's use it. And he's a British citizen, isn't he? The embassy should be told.'

Sammy sounded puzzled. 'But George was not part of your case, no? You were not going to call him as a witness?'

'No, but I like him. And he's right. They shouldn't be drafting the IDPs.'

'Well, OK. I will find out what I can. But that young man …' I knew he was shrugging his shoulders. 'He was just too outspoken. You can always tell the ones who have been educated abroad. Here our youngsters learn not to blurt out whatever is in their mind. George should have understood that. He was not stupid.'

It was chilling, I thought, as I put the receiver down, how quickly Sammy had started using the past tense in relation to George.

'Well, your young doctor has my sympathies,' Winston, in Washington, said on the phone, 'but, as Sammy said, these are really culture clashes. We may have a more pertinent problem, though, in regard to Transit Camp Number Three.'

'What would that be?'

'You may be aware that this government doesn't make it particularly easy for its citizens to leave the country. Buster tells me they're tightening the rules and it's about to be announced as official policy. No one leaves North Darrar in future without an exit permit.'

'Isn't that a bit weird? Most governments want to stop people arriving – they don't usually give a fig if they leave. One less headache.'

'Yes, but few governments are quite such control freaks as this one.'

'What's the rationale?'

'National solidarity. This is no time to abandon ship. In the post-war era, every citizen is needed to build the roads, bridges and dams. Which is all well and good, but it may cause us problems when it comes to presenting IDP testimony. I know what hoops I have to go through to get witnesses Dutch *entry* visas. Whether North Darrar will issue me with *exit* visas is less clear.'

'But we're arguing the government's case, for goodness' sake!'

'I'm putting pressure on Buster. But flexibility isn't a quality highly prized by these guys.'

'And how much damage will it do us, if we can't call witnesses in The Hague?'

'Well, an articulate witness can be an absolute bombshell. Human empathy triumphs, and commissioners forget hours of logical argument and remember one emotive detail. But witnesses can also be unpredictable. They lie, you can never be sure what they'll say on the stand. They suddenly choose to reveal something never mentioned during weeks of preparation. And increasingly, for us, there's the danger they might seize the opportunity of a trip to Europe to take off. So it's six of one, half a dozen of the other.'

I put down the phone and turned my attention to Ismael, who had been hovering uncertainly in front of my desk for the last ten minutes.

'What is it?'

He looked shyly at his feet, scuffing the tip of his trainer on the floor. 'Mr Peabody, when he came to speak to us at the university, he said always to keep the eyes open, yes?'

'Yes.'

'Even small things?'

'Yup, absolutely. Law can be about very tiny things.'

He had been photocopying the counter-Memorial on Winston's instructions, Ismael explained, when he had noticed a detail that intrigued him. 'Look, I show you.'

It was an 1899 letter between Heriu Tekle, the Negus's secretary, and the Italian Foreign Ministry; it came with a map. This was a key part of Darrar's evidence, I knew: Winston had often referred to it as 'the other side's mother-of-all-maps'.

'See, here, when I was photocopying I noticed these spots.' Ismael was pointing at a row of tiny dots running alongside the right-hand margin.

'Gosh, you've got good eyesight. I completely missed those. I see what you mean. Three, no, four dots. Just specks, really, but all in a neat vertical row.' I held the sheet of paper close to my face, then at arm's length. It didn't help. 'Now what might those be?'

'A watermark?'

'Too dark. They look like ink. What I wouldn't do for a microscope right now. OK, thanks, Ismael, it may be nothing, it may be something. I'll certainly draw it to Winston's attention.'

When I next met up with Dawit at Sumbi's, his head was buried in a newspaper.

'Hey, Paula, have you read about this sex scandal?' Dawit was looking unusually neat, I thought. His hair was short and had definitely been combed – no sign of incipient dreadlocks today – and he was wearing a white cotton shirt, for once, rather than one of his swirling Jim Morrison specials. The collar made him look like a choirboy, uncharacteristically innocent.

'"UN FORCE IN SEX RING SCANDAL",' I read aloud.

'Looks like our pure local girls are being *despoiled*' – he pronounced the word with sibilant, lip-curling relish – 'by our UN guests, who have been behaving like piggish swine. No orifice has been spared, Paula. Not one!' He smacked his knee in delight. 'Oh, boy, I love stories like this.'

I swivelled the newspaper round. It was a tabloid scoop of

a sort I'd never seen in Lira, with pictures and quotes from the four under-age girls who had, according to a government official, been accosted in a pizzeria by a group of UN officers, cajoled with promises of duty-free perfume and designer jeans, and later, drunk or drugged, video-taped taking part in a three-day orgy at one of the officers' villas. As is the way with all good secrets, the footage had been passed from laptop to laptop, email to memory stick, viewed in so many departments and offices that the UN had been forced to launch an internal inquiry to discover exactly which of its personnel had committed the original crime. The local journalist had pulled off the difficult feat of being both elliptical and salacious when it came to speculating on the exact nature of the sex performed.

'Oh, God.'

'Yes,' said Dawit, cheerfully. 'What's interesting is the government has clearly known about this for ages. These orgies were months ago. But they waited until now to publicise them. I'm guessing they're pissed off with the UN's failure to stand up to Darrar over its occupation of the border area and are getting their own back. Smart, eh?'

'How terrible for the girls.'

'Oh,' he said, 'they might as well commit suicide right now. Their lives are over.' He pointed gleefully at the last paragraph and snickered. 'Look, Paula, it says the UN is trying to work out who was involved. All they need to do is line every UN peacekeeper up, pull down their pants and compare their ... What's the word?'

'Pricks. Dicks. Schlongs.'

'Yup, compare them to the video. But,' he said, tilting his head to one side, 'I see you are not as amused as me. What's wrong?'

'Oh, some bad news at the office.' I had become the mistress of vagueness, thanks to Winston's warnings. 'You, in contrast, seem to be in a horribly good mood. And so smart. I didn't know you could look like this.'

'A business deal I've been working on for a while. It seems to be coming through. I feel like celebrating. Tomorrow is Sunday – let me take you on a picnic. To my favourite place in the world. You need to get out more! You're looking tired, these days, almost as though you were working.'

20

Dawit picked me up at the villa in a battered black jeep, borrowed from a friend. 'Sorry, but we have to go via my place first. I forgot my tape measure.'

'Why do we need a tape measure for a picnic?'

'You'll find out.'

We drove down Liberation Avenue, ignoring traffic lights and heedless of pedestrian crossings, plunged into the geometric maze behind the main mosque and parked outside what, by Lira's modest standards, counted as a supermarket. I followed Dawit up a narrow flight of stairs to a peeling central landing, where he fished out a pair of keys and opened a metal door. I hovered at the entrance, anxious not to trespass.

'Come, it's OK.' Dawit beckoned me in. 'I have no secrets.'

The room was the size of a prison cell. There was just space in it for a single bed, whose greying sheets were unmade. A sink and a rickety wardrobe were jammed between it and the window. No chair, so nowhere for visitors to sit. But, then, Dawit socialised at Sumbi's. The whiff of stale urine indicated a shared hallway WC. It should have been grim, but wasn't, because he had covered the ceiling with cuttings from magazines. Photos of gallery sculptures, ultra-chic furniture, modern architecture, vistas of the sky at night, close-ups of swirling shells, reproductions of art works by Andy Warhol and Jeff Koons, he had crammed as much colour and modernity into his eyeline as the space would hold, a mind-expanding panorama to gaze at as he fell asleep.

Dawit was watching me, craving approval.

'Goodness. You've really made it your own.'

The walls, in contrast, were bare, with the exception of a row of black-and-white photographs, about a dozen in all, separated by gold stars, the kind a primary-school teacher sticks approvingly into a child's exercise book. He waited in silence, willing me to examine each one. Some of the photos were clearly graduation pictures: they showed youngsters – all male – stiffly posed, holding scrolled certificates, men-to-be with wide brows and open, trusting faces. A few had been taken in photo booths and those faces seemed older, unreadable. They were framed by the wide lapels and corduroy caps of the 1970s. One brandished a pistol. There were no smiles. Whatever they were doing at that moment in their lives had felt too serious for that.

When I got to the end of the row, I asked, 'Who are they?'

'My friends. You see, most of the people I know are dead.'

My throat felt thick. 'I suppose, strictly speaking, you should say, "Most of the people I *knew* are dead."'

'No, most of the people I *know*. They are more real to me than the people I meet now. No offence, but even you. They keep me good company.'

I reached out an index finger to smooth down the corner of one of the gold stars, which was lifting off the wall, and tried to smile but managed only a grimace. 'It's OK, Dawit. I understand. I really do.'

There was a long pause in which we sized one another up, two battered, guilt-ridden survivors sharing a moment of complicity. He broke the spell. 'Anyways, I found my tape measure.' It dangled from one hand. 'So we can go.'

We drove through the suburbs and down the mountain road

I'd taken with Abraham. A rather different experience, this time. Within ten minutes, I was sitting with my hand over my eyes, moaning softly.

He laughed. 'What is it, Paula? Nervous?'

'Where did you learn to drive?'

'At the front, of course. Where else?'

'Did no one ever tell you that if you overtake on a blind corner on a mountain road you're quite likely to go off the edge?'

'Pah! There is hardly any traffic on this road. It's a calculated risk, a question of mathematical probabilities.'

'I think you and I went to different maths classes.'

Just as I was wondering if we were headed for a weekend at the coast, we braked on a tiny lay-by, fringed with thickets of juniper. I followed Dawit as he scampered along a stony goat's trail. We squeezed between two boulders, then stopped: a dramatic opening-up of perspective had reduced us to ants clinging to the side of a geographical basin so vast I felt dizzy and afraid. The last time I'd gazed across that landscape it had been early morning and the eiderdown of cloud had been retreating across the valleys. Now it was midday and the sun had burned the vapour off the terraced slopes, highlighting every rock for what felt like hundreds of miles. A few clouds floated free and high, throwing giant ink blotches of shade onto the plains below. The mountain ranges, giant rucks in a fawn carpet, stretched to the far horizon.

'Wow.' I was overwhelmed by a baffling sense of *déjà vu*.

Dawit hugged me in delight. 'You love it too, right? I bought this land five years ago. I couldn't believe they were selling it so cheap, this plot with the best view in the world. They must have been mad. Now the white man, he knew its value. See that line?' He traced a semi-obscured trail through the scrub. 'That's where an Italian company laid a railway, back when North Darrar was a colony. They planned to put the station here. Me, I look across at that,' he gestured across the valley,

'I breathe this air, and my heart is uplifted. This, Paula, is a place where a man can talk to his God.'

He jumped onto a flat, saddle-shaped rock, and at that moment I remembered exactly why the landscape felt so familiar. I'd gazed across it a thousand times. Dawit was standing where the doomed Edward Wentworth had posed more than a century earlier in the black-and-white photograph that had sat on Jake's mantelpiece. It was, I belatedly registered, an image that had played a subliminal role in my decision to take up Winston's job offer. His mention of 'Darrar' had set a little bell of intellectual curiosity pinging: it had been the dog-whistle slyly drawing me here. I gave a half-snort, half-gasp.

'What is it?'

'Nothing.' A superstitious person might have detected some fateful message in all this. The simpler truth, I told myself, was that the longer I lived in Lira, the more inevitable my encounter with this view had become. 'It's absolutely stunning, Dawit.'

'And this is where I'm going to build my cybernet café.'

I noticed now that I was standing inside a low breezeblock rectangle of walls in the making.

'I have it all laid out. It's taken me years to reach this stage. There are three of us former fighters in this together. You've met the others, Mule and Beanstalk. We've been slowly collecting the materials, using our demob money. A bag of cement here, some bricks there, timber donated by a friend, a little bit bought every time one of us makes some money. Now, very nearly, I have enough. Last week, I finally ordered the satellite dish from Dubai.'

He scampered from side to side, sketching out his vision with his hands. 'So the bar will be here. Popcorn, milkshakes, beer, Coke, tea, coffee, the basics to start off with, but then we will start doing cocktails, maybe food. We will play hip-hop, jazz, Motown, Lingala, customers can bring their own CDs.

The walls are going to be shocking pink, green, yellow, Day-glo colours – it must look young, radical. My art-college friend wants to stick a collage all over the insides of the toilets, something a bit edgy. He also says he can build us a pool table. We will have a jamming session every weekend, anyone who plays an instrument welcome. The computer screens will be set up along here.' He crouched and stretched out both arms. 'We will have the quickest connection in Lira and no government agents looking over your shoulder. I'm thinking of running computer courses for children – I will do that myself. When I can afford it, we will buy a plasma screen to watch music videos. And there will be a big basket of newspapers here, *The Economist*, the *International Herald Tribune*, to be read and shared. It's time Lira joined the twenty-first century. We're going to call it Panorissima. What do you think of that as a name?'

'Fabulous. I suppose the only issue is whether people will come this far.'

'The bus to the coast stops where we parked. Before the war, every family with a car would drive here on a Sunday to watch the sun go down. The bike riders stop here already, but up till now there's been nothing for them, just a tree to pee behind. If you make it the funkiest place to hang out in Lira, where youngsters can get away from their parents and plug into the world's conversation, they will come. It is what a developer would call a prime site.'

His face was glowing with excitement, I had never seen him so animated. 'I hadn't realised you were a budding entrepreneur, Dawit.'

'Oh, I've been planning this for a long time. You know, I'm not like all these youngsters. They fight because they have to. There is no enthusiasm. I fought for a reason – no one made me do it. I wanted to be a citizen of an independent sovereign nation. That dream kept me going. And now I live in that independent country, and it's not perfect, I know that better than anyone, and I will say it to whoever listens. I hate those fuckers in the Movement. I could kill them for all their petty betrayals, the comfortable lives they have built on the bones of my friends. But I lost a metre of intestines and several litres of blood for this country, and I'm not giving up on it. As long as I have my cybernet café and this view, as long as those guys leave me in peace, I'll be happy.' Then he set about the site with his tape measure, muttering numbers to himself.

That night he insisted on taking me to the Cinema Napoli, one of Lira's Modernist temples to the cult of Cinecittà. 'Pure escapism,' Dawit promised me. 'Better than getting drunk, or shooting heroin, not that I would know, ha-ha. It will put you in a good mood for a week, guarantee.'

'But the dialogue will be incomprehensible.'

'Oh, these films anyone can understand. The language they speak is universal, anyways. Because it is the language ...' Dawit thrust out both hands at ear level to form a human teapot and jerked his head from one shoulder to the other, eyes darting from side to side '... of ROMANCE!'

We teetered on stools at the bar, waiting for the previous screening to end. The mirrored drinks display must originally have been a jewelled mosaic of glowing elixirs and potions: Campari and crème de menthe, Fernet Branca and Curaçao, Cointreau and rum, a choice of grappas, tequilas and brandies waiting to be combined with a squeeze of lime or a splash of Angostura bitters by a slick barista showing off his cocktail-shaker routine. The mirror was smudged with fingerprints now, the only equipment wielded by the barman a bottle-opener, and there were only two beverages on offer: Coke or beer. I chose beer. 'So what's with you and Bollywood, Dawit?'

'I just take what's available. Not much choice in this town.'

'OK, then, what is it with Lira and Bollywood? Why does every cinema here specialise in Hindi films?'

184

'Maybe it was the Indian teachers the government recruited after liberation to teach us all bad English. They brought stacks of DVDs and would show them when they ran out of things to say. We got the taste. And they're dirty cheap.' He shielded his mouth with his hand to produce a hoarse stage whisper. 'In fact, when you use a pirated copy, they're not just cheap, they're free.'

The doors to the foyer were kicked open, a fug of cigarette smoke and hormones billowing out to engulf us along with the all-male audience. The auditorium, when we entered, had the fermenting warmth of a stable – a farmer could have raised seedlings on the nutrients in the air.

We settled in our seats, three rows back from the screen and squarely in the middle, at Dawit's insistence. But as the trailers began, I heard him curse. 'Shit. We should have waited. I usually skip this part.'

We had arrived early enough for 'Coming Attractions', which appeared to be a locally made war film. Tanks blasted at one another, the images so grainy I suspected this was genuine footage from the recent conflict. A moustachioed actor wearing what I now recognised as Darrar's national uniform screamed at a cowering prisoner, then slapped him. Cut to a close-up of a beautiful young girl weeping. Cut to a young hero, in our side's uniform, striding into the hills, AK-47 on his shoulder. The voice-over was hectoring and urgent. I could hear a low murmur from Dawit.

Then we were on to the second trailer. This time a patrol of enemy soldiers was setting fire to a hut as women ululated. One opened fire on an old woman begging for her life. A frantic voice summarised the plot. Cut to the face of the fatigues-clad hero, clearly being tortured, blood trickling down one side of his face. Dawit's muttering was now so loud that heads were swivelling on either side of us. The corners of his mouth were curved in a gargoyle grimace.

'Shush, Dawit. You'll get us chucked out.'

'Just sick, sick, sick, sick, sick of this *boulesheeet* – they just never stop, these guys, they never fucking stop.'

The screen went blank, a welcome reprieve. Then, suddenly, a still image. I giggled. It was the shot that appears when you feed a DVD into a player, complete with prompts for 'play', 'scenes', 'subtitles' and 'songs'. The projectionist clicked 'play' and we were off. A swirl of pink petals, we were drowning in coconut ice. Doves tumbled, golden curtains billowed, glossy saris twirled, even glossier lips stretched in perfect smiles. Some schematic subtitling had been provided, but Dawit was right. You didn't need to speak Hindi to understand the plot, a basic poor-girl-meets-rich-boy-parents-disapprove-but-come-round-in-the-end scenario. As the first dance number started up, I was aware of Dawit letting go next to me. His mouth had softened and his shoulders were no longer pulled up around his ears. He began humming the first number, and I realised he had seen the film before, probably several times. At the start of the third dance routine, his hand – so small compared to Jake's – crept across the seats to take mine. And I, who had always disliked that form of contact above all others, sat there with my eyes closed, allowing the nasal siren voices, singing so confidently of eternal love, to swamp me, a thirty-five-year-old woman recalling, for a moment, what it felt like to be touched with tenderness by a man.

We would never be so intimate again.

The visa business left a stain on us. A nugget of resentment I could take out and prod, testing for consistency and depth, then roll back to its position at the secret core of our relationship. My lone voice had returned, and now it was all poison. Doesn't love you enough to recognise you, it whispered, when a letter addressed to Mr and Mrs Jake Wentworth arrived. Naïve sucker, it hissed, when a New England rag reported that Jake was planning to run for Congress with Olivia at his side, an article he laughingly dismissed. And when a mix-up over dates occurred, the voice was always ready to highlight the discrepancy. Lying gets to be a habit, it murmured. He'll do to you what he did to her.

It was the keystone niggle on which I could build my arching insecurity. This, even though my fears – and Larry Goldman's warnings – proved entirely unfounded. Not only did Hitchens abandon the flirtation with its closest rival in a flurry of recrimination, I was granted an H1B in almost record time. And thank goodness I was: work suddenly took off and there would have been no spare hours in which to sort out my status after that.

I had originally arrived in New York on a one-year second-ment Hitchens had subtly presented as a favour to me and a burden to the firm. The expectation that I would treat this as a glamorous extended junket had always irked me, and I had set out to make myself indispensable by working harder than anyone else. Before I had met Jake, that had been easy. When the time arrived for me to return to London, the managing partner had asked if I would stay on. After that, no one both-ered discussing my return. I was officially a New York associate on partnership track.

I was now reaping the reward for that early effort. Juggling several deals at a time, always adding more, everything I touched seemed to turn to gold. The all-nighters multiplied – watching dawn rise over the New York skyline with a team high on coffee and junk food no longer felt novel. I was exhausted, but also very excited. The gods of Wall Street smiled upon me, and as the ugly 'deal toys' – trophies generated by a series of successfully closed bond offerings, the occasional merger or acquisition – accumulated on my shelves, I began to appreciate that my nationality wasn't necessarily a handicap. It served as a novelty factor, edging my profile a helpful inch above the competition. The generosity of Hitchens's bonus that year made my eyes pop. The boss took me aside at the office

Christmas party, made a joke about my Limey accent I'd heard thirty times before and told me, as Bing Crosby boomed across the hired hall, that it was probably time to run deals on my own.

Jake rejoiced. He took me shopping for ludicrously expensive designer suits – 'You need to give those dull grey men a tantalising hint of your inner slut' – and bought me a sleek maroon Gucci briefcase that was almost too beautiful to desecrate with my professional bread-and-butter: drafts of dry-as-dust memoranda designed to reassure securities regulators that our clients weren't defrauding investors.

That summer we decided to stay put at Lake Cottage. I already had a desk drawer of unused plane tickets, each testimony to a weekend break cancelled after a last-minute summons from the partners and, increasingly, the clients. Staying close to the office was a way of limiting the damage. Jake and I swam and read, Laurel and Hardy curled contentedly before us, half pets, half glossy footrests. It should have been relaxing, but we were both acutely aware of my mobile phone, sitting like unexploded ordnance on the table between us, ready to go off at any moment.

As my ego swelled, Jake watched, waiting for it all to pass. 'What you have to remember, Paula, is that I'm sixteen years older than you,' he told me, when I climbed into bed, bubbling with work chatter after a two a.m. conference call with a bank in Paris and an engineering firm in Delhi. 'I don't begrudge you any of this and I do understand the thrill of feeling like a Master of the Universe. You're quite a macho girl, you know. But I went through my equivalent of all this a decade ago.'

'You're not going to tell me,' I mocked, 'that when I'm your age I'll realise it's all a charade and wonder why I didn't opt for babies.'

'Stop trying to make me feel old, you female chauvinist pig,' he said, pulling me into the warm spoon of his curved body, 'and go to sleep.'

21

Winston rang me in the early hours, two weeks before the hearing in The Hague. The call shrilled through the villa, and on the other side of the thin wall I could hear Sharmila and Steve waking. On Washington time, Winston was all brisk efficiency. 'Paula, I've been thinking, and I'd like you to go to Rome. I need to know what those dots are. The dots on the letter attached to the mother-of-all-maps, the ones Ismael noticed. We need to see the original.'

'Rome? Are you serious?' I was muzzy with sleep.

'I am indeed.'

'But we're within days of the hearing. And what's the point? Neither side can submit new evidence now.'

'We can't add, no, but we could eliminate, if any of their evidence turns out to be suspect. I'm probably fussing, but that map is one of the foundation stones of their case. If there's anything wrong with it, I have to ferret it out. Fly to Rome, check it out, then go straight from there to The Hague.'

'Can't Francesca do it?'

'To be honest – and you must never tell her this – I don't trust her. It's got to be a quick in-out visit, and I need someone I won't have to coach every step of the way.'

'Well, I'm flattered, Winston, but you've got a bigger appetite for brinkmanship than I realised.'

I could tell from his voice he was smiling. 'Keeps me young. This is the best bit of the game, when everything's thrown into the air and you're forced to think on your feet, to start dancing.'

A few days later I checked into the Santa Elena convent off the Piazza Navona, after emailing a request for access to the Italian Foreign Ministry archives in Rome.

When I walked through the doors Francesca was waiting in the lobby. It was uncanny how accurately she matched my mental picture. Tinkling with silver jewellery, wide-hipped in a flowing gypsy skirt, she was the kind of woman who applied kohl eyeliner in the morning with a heavy hand, then left it to form smudged bruises as the day wore on. 'Paula, *final-mente*!' she exclaimed, pronouncing my name the Italian way. Wrapping her arms around me, she bundled me towards the exit, hissing, 'Ignore the witches,' as the nun at Reception looked on.

'I'm sorry to descend on you like this,' I said, when we were tucking into pasta at a restaurant round the corner. 'You must have assumed you were done with us. If you can just help me find what I need at the Foreign Ministry, I'll leave you in peace.'

'Oh, it's no problem.' She sighed. 'Any distraction is good.'

'Not enjoying your research?'

'Ah, that Ingegnere Agostini. A man of vision, but as a writer, oh, *Dio*! The letters, all they talk about is sacks of cement, the width of walls, the number of employees and what he paid them, down to the last lira. It's like a robot. This year, finally, I accept: Ingegnere Agostini, he was very, very' – *vairy, vairy* – 'boring. *Un uomo noiosissimo, in fatti*. This is my misfortune.'

'It must make it hard to keep going.'

She gave a low, rueful laugh. 'Some colleagues, they love the research so much they would do it for ever. Me, I used to

190

be like that, but no more. If I had my choice now, I would sit in the sun all day and eat ice-cream. I am only finishing this doctorate because I need it for my next job. Once I have financial security, Massimo can join me in Turin. But in the meantime, *uffa, che barba*. So helping Signor Pibody and my new friend Paula, I don't mind. Also,' she said, 'it makes Professore Tadesse very nervous. And that I like.'

I laughed. 'Who's he?'

'Tadesse? He is the Francesca for the other side. You didn't know? Darrar, they also pay someone to go through the files.' She explained that Professor Tadesse Zeleke, exiled patriot, had managed, even as Darrar's Negus was toppled by a military regime that led to a Communist dictatorship – itself replaced by a rebel movement that ushered in a socialist democracy – to keep churning out research papers that had won the approval of each successive administration.

'Funny thing,' she said, with heavy irony. 'Darrar politics change so much, but he always change too, at just the right instant.'

'In my country we'd call him a Vicar of Bray.'

'A man without principle. Massimo says Italy was full of Tadesses under Fascism. We never speak, but he watches me, and I watch him.'

The following morning we settled ourselves in the scoop seats of the bus Francesca used for her daily commute. I surveyed the rush-hour bustle outside, glad of the air-conditioning. Tanned businessmen wove through the traffic on Vespas, expertly avoiding groups of Catholic pilgrims, clustered around anxious guides. Those hot and bothered-looking hitch-hikers could only be American, I thought. No other race would think shorts and skimpy T-shirts appropriate for a series of visits to Renaissance churches and Roman temples.

Being in Italy felt strange. My peace of mind was premised on keeping the pre-Jake and post-Jake periods of my life as far apart as possible, but here they met. On my last visit to

Rome, I'd been with him, bound for the monastery of Monte Cassino. We'd flown out of New York a few days after Christmas and had spent the afternoon wandering through a Piazza Navona bathed in thin winter light, my cold hand buried in one of his pockets. A gaggle had formed around a pig-tailed blonde artist offering three-minute caricatures. We'd joined it and ended up sitting for her, laughing at ourselves. 'My love for you is as big as this piazza,' Jake had scrawled on the back of his sketch, then handed it to me, only to reclaim it over dinner when he crossed out the *a*, turning 'piazza' into 'pizza'. Walking to the bus stop with Francesca that morning I'd spotted the blonde artist setting up her easel and begun to tremble. Her life had probably barely changed in the last three years; mine, in contrast, had entered a parallel universe.

The bus lurched through the Centro Storico and across the Tiber, heading north. As the stops passed and the crowd of rush-hour passengers thinned, Francesca discreetly pointed out a few familiar faces. 'Dottore Corrado, expert on Cyrenaica in the twenties, Dottoressa Barzini, the colonisation of Somalia. As you can see,' she whispered, 'scholarship and glamour do not go together. We are a shabby lot.' When a lean, bearded gentleman in a tweed jacket boarded, her face froze in careful non-recognition. As he walked past she raised her eyebrows and silently mouthed at me, 'Tadesse.'

When the bus stopped near Mussolini's Olympic Stadium, the group alighted and formed what looked like a well-established straggle, some of the scholars teaming up in companionable twos and threes, others strolling alone, acknowledging their peers with polite nods. Our crocodile walked past the stadium's preening statues of wrestlers and athletes, breathing in the comforting medicinal scent under the umbrella pines, picking up speed as the Fascistic bulk of the Ministero degli Affari Esteri – the Farnesina – hove into view. By the time the side door opened, on the dot of nine a.m., many had reached an ungainly trot, with a luxuriantly moustachioed professor from Taranto the undeclared winner of the day's race.

'The archive section closes at two,' Francesca said, as we queued. 'So, five hours of work a day, maximum. Requests take a day to process and you can order no more than two box files at once. So you see why everyone arrives early.'

'Christ, how inefficient.'

She grimaced. 'Ah, when I started my doctorate, I went through that stage, as everyone does, of complaining at the laziness of Italy's civil service, the inefficiency of our historical research system – the US and British national archives are marvels, you know. Now I have learned to accept. I think you say in English, "It is what it is", yes? Every second is precious.'

Indeed she was divesting herself of coat, wallet and valuables at lightning speed, showing me where to stow mine in a locker, checking that I held only pencils, not pens, as stipulated by the regulations.

'Come and meet Beppe. He is a pervert, of course.'

I was digesting this unexpected remark as she led me to the main desk, where a middle-aged man, dandruff-flecked and balding, stood reading his request list while gently caressing his stomach, like a marsupial minding its young. She introduced me in Italian and I noticed that I had been elevated to Dottoressa Shackleton, presumably in a bid to win better service. 'Signor Beppe Scalfaro, the deputy archivist,' she said to me. 'Beppe speaks some English.'

'*Buon giorno*, Signor Scalfaro,' I said, offering my hand. His was soft and moist and, having fluttered upwards for a split-second to make contact, his eyes descended to the level where they clearly felt most comfortable.

'Oh, only very little,' he said modestly, gazing at my breasts.

At my request, Francesca had ordered the file containing the Heriu Tekle letter, with the attached map, the day before. We bore the box to the table, carefully choosing a spot that would require Tadesse, already bent over a pile of documents, to swivel an awkward 180 degrees to see what we were up to. Francesca and I slowly leafed through the contents. It didn't take long. It contained correspondence between Italy's Foreign Ministry and the Negus of Darrar in the first three months of 1899. None came with a map. My heart began to pound.

'It's not here,' I whispered. 'Have we got the right file?'

'The file numbers are correct.' Francesca checked the box label against her notebook.

We made ourselves go through the letters once again, more slowly. Nothing. What was I going to tell Winston? '*Shit*.'

The sibilants must have carried in the hushed room: Tadesse turned slowly in his seat, his gleaming dark eyes taking in the two of us, hunched conspiratorially over the box file. He looked down at it, up at our dismayed faces, and then he smiled.

Francesca straightened in her chair. 'Toilet, Paula, *now*.'

She marched us to the Ladies, where she checked each cubicle, then leaned against one of the basins with her arms folded, her back to the wall-length mirror.

'Tadesse did it. He stole the letter. You saw how he smiled?' She was shaking her head in disbelief. '*Vigliacco, vigliacco!*'

'Which suggests there's something in it worth hiding.'

'Maybe, but we will never find it now. I can't believe it!'

'How would he steal a document, though? Don't they search your bags before you leave each day?'

'Yes, but they are not always so careful. He could fold it up, put it in a pocket. His socks, his underwear. You hear stories.'

'But that's a big risk for a respectable professor to take, isn't it? If he were caught, his reputation would be destroyed. And this guy, from what you say, wants to stay in academia.'

'OK, so maybe the bastard hid it here, in the building,' she said. Her eyes were swimming with tears, her ample mouth curved in a bitter bow of resignation. Being beaten by a despised colleague, I suspected, was not a new experience.

'Don't get upset, Francesca. We don't know for sure Tadesse did anything.'

'I know in my heart he did,' she said. A tear trickled down her cheek. She wiped it angrily away, then ran the cold tap and splashed water on her face. 'All my life, all my life' – a sob – 'I have seen men like Tadesse win and decent people lose.'

'Let's not give up just yet. Help me to think this through. Are people allowed to use the lockers as deposit boxes?'

'No.' She blew her nose and checked her make-up in the mirror. 'You have to hand the key back every day.'

'So there would be no obvious place to hide a document once he'd removed it from the file.'

'No. But maybe he burned it.'

'Archives have smoke alarms everywhere, though, and library staff are hysterical about fire.' I thought for a moment. 'Why don't we ask Beppe? He must know all the tricks.'

She gave an incredulous laugh. 'We can't accuse a colleague without proof. They'd have to open an inquiry and Tadesse would destroy me.'

'Oh, come on, Francesca, no names necessary. We can hint. When you said Beppe was a pervert, what did you mean?'

'Didn't you see how he looks at you? Always, always the breasts.'

'Well, at least that suggests he likes women. So a bit of outrageous flirting might work wonders.'

'I don't think I can do this, Paula. He give me the creep. And I have to use this archive in future, for many more months.'

'Will you let me try, then?'

'Of course. I see now,' she said, with a rueful laugh, 'why Signor Pibody sent you. Paula the Unstoppable, eh?'

So we redeployed. Francesca returned to the table, from which she nervously kept watch on both me and Tadesse. I approached the desk warily, file in hand. Underneath Beppe's white cotton shirt, I noted, he was wearing a string vest. A good mamma's boy. Temperatures might rise to the nineties in midsummer, but Italy's army of civil servants would still wrap up warm each morning. 'Signor Scalfaro?'

He turned, giving my nipples his full attention. I leaned obligingly across the counter, eyes as wide as an ingénue's. Cop a look at that. 'I've been having problems locating some documents that should be in this box. I've checked the catalogue numbers, but neither Dottoressa de Mello nor I can find it.'

'Well, sometime documents they go missing. *Niente da fare*,' he said, with a shrug. Nothing to be done.

'Oh dear. This is terrible.' I ran my hand through my hair a couple of times, doing my best to look distraught. 'It's a vital document, you see, and we just can't work out where it might have got to. We were even wondering whether someone might have *taken* it. Francesca says you are the best archivist here,' I cooed. 'If you can't find something, she says, no one can.' I put one hand on his wrist, and kept it there.

I had his full attention now. Our faces were inches apart. His irises were the colour of stone, and one eyelid fluttered, out of control. Could this be the reason for his failure to meet women's gaze – self-consciousness over a disfiguring twitch – rather than an obsession with breasts? Then I took in the close-bitten nails, the careful comb-over. No, Francesca was probably right.

He cleared his throat nervously a few times. 'Let me see who last used that file.' Fingers a-tremor, he fussed over the records. '*Vediamo, vediamo* ...' Suddenly he stood stock still. He lifted his head to look across the room to where Tadesse sat. '*Chiaro*,' I thought I heard him say. Of course.

'If there has been any misbehaviour by a researcher, I am not aware. But you know the phrase "*nascondere in piena vista*"? "Hiding in full sight".' He enunciated with slow, exaggerated care. 'An archive is a very good place to hide a piece of paper, no?'

I stared at him, baffled. Then the penny dropped. 'The best

place to lose a document is in the files,' I said aloud. Tadesse hadn't needed to smuggle out or burn any documents, nothing so crude. Just misfile them. Call up an unrelated box and slip the letter from one into the other.

I stood there for a moment as Beppe busied himself with researchers' request forms, unsure how to pursue this insight.

'Might it be possible … to know which files enjoy the greatest popularity among your users?' I asked, trying to be elliptical.

'Every researcher's request is handled in strictest confidence,' he said primly.

'Of course.' It seemed we had reached the end of the line. I couldn't search the entire archive. Crushed, I was turning to go when I felt a sudden pain in my right hip. As Beppe bowed over his forms, lips pursed in a silent whistle, his left elbow was surreptitiously jabbing a fat clipboard into my side. I looked down. It was the chronological list of processed readers' requests: date, researcher and catalogue number. He was handing me the keys to the safe.

'Oh, Beppe.' I reached out and squeezed his hand. He blushed, a rose tide travelling up from beneath the rim of his vest until it reached his hair, turning him for an instant from creepy stalker to bashful Romeo. Then I took out my notebook and started scribbling down the catalogue numbers of every box Tadesse had called up in the last six months.

'We've found it.' My mobile phone call caught Winston scouring the morning papers at his desk in Washington. In the gathering dusk, Francesca and I were sitting at one of those overpriced cafés in Piazza Navona the guidebooks tell you to avoid, celebratory glasses of chilled white wine before us. It had taken two days. The letter and attached map had fallen out of a file dedicated to a 1927 survey of Tripoli port, which Tadesse had called up the previous November. 'And you were right. There is something dodgy about it.'

22

'Good morning, and welcome to these magnificent surround-ings,' intoned Judge Mautner. 'I am delighted to welcome the representatives of the parties to the opening session of our five-day boundary hearing on this fine May morning. I know everyone present has been keenly awaiting this moment, and I also know that each party fully appreciates the gravity of what will take place between these four walls.'

'Oh, do get on with it,' Winston muttered, so quietly only I could hear.

I had on what I thought of as one of my Jake outfits. Tight, black, androgynous, and probably twice as expensive as anything anyone else in the room was wearing. A hangover from my previous life, a legacy of the Paula who once was. Putting into practice a habit acquired at law school, where dressing up was the prescribed way of dealing with performance anxiety, I had gone through the ritual of light foundation, mascara, eyeliner and a wisp of eye-shadow in the Peace Palace bathroom.

Winston hadn't noticed until we'd got under the bright lights of the Small Hall of Justice, when he'd looked shocked. 'You've *done* something,' said the man who hated change. He was in the ubiquitous lemon sherbet suit; he must have had ten versions of it.

'War paint.'

'It makes you look … um … different. Harder.'

'Mission accomplished, then.'

Judge Mautner droned through the introductions, dutifully listing everyone present for the record. We had won the toss on which side got to go first and I was quivering with adrenalin, my heels soundlessly drumming on the floor. Yohannes, officially in charge of PowerPoint, was similarly hyped. Winston's eyes were hooded, his posture so ostentatiously relaxed he looked as though he might slip off his chair. Across the way, Alexander was studying his nails, while Watts gazed at the ceiling.

'So, without further ado, let me invite the agent from Lira to begin his presentation.'

Judge Mautner turned towards us, his eyebrows beckoned suggestively, and Kennedy, the foreign minister, sprang to his feet. This was scheduled to be his only speech and he was intent on making the most of it, slowly pivoting on his heels as he surveyed the room. He cleared his throat with unnecessary emphasis.

'Mr Chairman, commissioners, Your Excellency, my esteemed colleagues and counterparts, ladies and gentlemen…' he began.

Judge Mautner looked alarmed and switched on his microphone. 'Perhaps, Your Excellency, we should dispense with the honorifics, given that we have all, to a certain extent, got to know one another over the last few months.'

The minister looked crestfallen. 'Very well. Er … As I was about to say. Yes. Indeed.' Then he was off. 'My country may be one of Africa's smallest, but there is nothing modest about its instinct for justice or its proud tradition of independence, as ancient as the mountains themselves. We not only threw off the shackles of Western colonialism, we triumphed over the horrors of occupation. Our people have always shown themselves ready to make the ultimate sacrifice to defend the most fundamental of all human rights: the right to exist as a nation state …'

I became aware of the gentlest of raspings. I glanced at Winston and realised, to my horror, that his eyes were firmly closed. He was snoring. I leaned to one side as though consulting my papers, moved an elbow surreptitiously until it touched him. Then, slipping a hand beneath it, I gave his arm a sharp pinch.

He arched one eyebrow without opening his eyes. 'Just a bit of jet-lag,' he murmured, adjusting his bifocals. 'Not to worry.'

And then it was his turn.

I once worked as a waitress in a seafood restaurant in Brighton, a brief summer job. The black-and-white-tiled venue, close enough to the sea to hear the pebbles' roar, was modest but its owners nursed big ambitions. Alongside Carmen, the flirtatious Spanish meeter-and-greeter, Carlos, the morose Mexican barman, Angelo, his deputy, and a bevy of waitresses, I ferried squid ink and pumpkin risotto, fresh scallops in lime and coriander coulis, and miso cod with pickled ginger to the tables, a small cog in a humming machine. We never won any stars, and the reviews came too late to stop the place closing. But we knew. At two a.m., when the chefs were cleaning the Japanese knives and the last dishwasher load was churning, there would be, in the exchange of satisfied glances, the quiet acknowledgement that together we had pulled off something miraculous. All the staff bitched about their colleagues, none of us liked one another enough to socialise after hours, yet we felt a grudging affection. Rising above our individual failings, we had achieved magnificence for a moment, and we were grateful for the chance.

Working with Winston was like that. Even today, even after everything, I feel retrospectively privileged to have played a small part in a performance all the more poignant for remaining effectively unrecorded – the transcripts, which omit timing, expression and emphasis, give a flavourless hint of a proceeding whose flamboyant virtuosity was doomed to be unappreciated by clients who just wanted the job done, never mind the flourishes.

The other side worked through every argument with the dogged application of a prisoner breaking rocks on Robben Island. Correct pronunciation of local names, towns and geographical features was not a courtesy they extended to either government. If a point could be made once, they saw no reason not to make it four times, and even the commissioners – men with a high tolerance for legal stodge – sometimes rolled their eyes in exasperation. They stuck to bullet points; we used as many visual aids as we could legally justify. Winston would have sneaked a musical soundtrack in if he could have got away with it. He cracked jokes; they never cracked a smile. It was like watching a mastodon chomping through the undergrowth, small eyes unblinking as the great jaws worked stolidly away. Where they lumbered, Winston pirouetted. When they droned, he chirruped. 'The trial lawyer's first duty is to entertain,' Winston would intone, when we analysed the day's proceedings back at the Royal Delft. 'Bore your audience – and let us never forget that they *are* an audience – and you've already lost half the argument.'

And I don't think I'm imagining that when it was our turn to present the commissioners perked up, sat a little straighter in their leather-covered thrones; a hint of amusement appeared on previously stony faces and the atmosphere in the Small Hall of Justice subtly changed. Winston prepared meticulously in advance, but the order, links, illustrations and framing of his arguments were often done on the hoof. Nothing, he knew, was more appetising than the zing of freshness.

At a nod from Winston, Yohannes tapped his keyboard and a black-and-white photograph appeared on the large screen set up on one side of the room. It showed a nineteenth-century dandy in vaguely military regalia, one hand languidly resting on a ceremonial sword. A huge moustache curled like a double question mark around a frankly mischievous mouth.

'Count Lorenzo Camillo Fittipaldi was an emotionally incontinent man,' Winston began. 'It would be fair to say he lived life to the full. He eloped with his governess when still in his teens, fathered fourteen children – five out of wedlock.'

Judge Mautner was staring at Winston with incredulity. 'What exactly are you playing at?' hovered on his lips. Registering the rising gavel, Winston picked up speed. 'He was married three times, and spent much of his life as an adventurer and mercenary, surviving adventures that seem to have come straight from the pages of *Sinbad the Sailor*.'

He took a deep breath and paused. 'But, of course, we are concerned here with the professional man. And the professional man was a nit-picker. A stickler for accuracy, a skilled mathematician and an amateur engineer, he revelled in detail. He was a draughtsman so skilled his back-of-the-envelope sketches could be used as templates by architects. And it is to that count and his work that I ask you to look now, for it was he who provided us with the authoritative definition of the border drawn between Italy and Darrar back in July 1890 when, dispatched on assignment from Rome, he carried out the first complete survey of the area, moving from settlement to settlement in a long caravan of mules, camels and soldiers.

'My team has provided each of you with a full transcript of his report and a copy of the map he sketched, the outcome of an official fact-finding mission funded by the Italian Foreign Ministry. Next slide, if you please, Yohannes.'

Winston practically stroked the documents in front of him. As well he might. It had taken the office, with Dr Berhane's help, weeks to locate a photocopier in Lira that could properly capture the fading colours of the original and retain the full legibility of Fittipaldi's spidery copperplate.

'I would ask the commissioners to look at the overall shape of Fittipaldi's border. We have provided you with blow-ups of the eastern, central and western sector. Taking the eastern sector, where the port of Sanasa lies, you will note this distinctive diagonal. The slope is produced by running a straight line from the ancient clifftop monastery of Tolandino until it hits the junction between the Shishay and Abubed rivers. The Shishay subsequently serves as the frontier as far as the sea, and the river's mouth lies south-east of Sanasa. You will see – here, we have measured it for you – that the diagonal is exactly fifteen degrees to the horizontal. For the skiers among us, this is the gentlest of green runs. Now let me direct you to the hundred and twenty other diagrams we have submitted, also in your folders.'

Yohannes clicked on cue through the images, as Winston read out the dates and names of the surveyors: 'This map is the work of Sicilian cartographer Antonio di Perri, sent to the Horn of Africa by Rome in 1895. This one was drafted later that same year by British merchant Thomas Cullin. Here are two produced in 1902 by Portuguese railway contractor Pedro da Souza, exploring the possibility of a narrow-gauge railway … In summary, each of these documents demonstrates this identical diagonal, with this same fifteen-degree angle.'

I remembered Winston's words back in the Ristorante Torino: 'Did you know that a map carries almost no legal weight?' As promised, he wasn't letting that inconvenient fact stand in his way. A hundred and twenty maps, I thought. Not bad, surely.

He took questions from the commissioners, flicking backwards and forwards through the various maps until it was clear they had run out of comments.

'Let me conclude with my prize exhibit,' said Winston. 'This is a photograph taken just outside the Interior Ministry in Darrar, sent to me by a loyal customer of the premises in question. Some of his friends might say he is rather *too* loyal a customer, if his expanding waistline is anything to go by. This is one of the cardboard boxes in which the popular Red Sea restaurant on Revolution Square delivers its pizzas.'

'SLICES ... OF SHEER DELIGHT!' ran the slogan on the box, superimposed on a map of the region and a grinning customer's face. 'As you can see, that diagonal, with its fifteen-degree angle, is so uncontested in the region that even carry-out restaurants in Darrar use it in their marketing.'

A sudden snort of surprise from Yohannes. I looked at him with curiosity. He had spent weeks on this PowerPoint presentation but had clearly never fully digested what he was preparing. His hand was over his mouth now, stifling laughter. Eddie Connors gave an appreciative chuckle. François Rainier pursed his lips but could not prevent a quiet smile. The pizza-box shot was irrelevant, legally speaking, but it had amused the commissioners and, crucially, they were unlikely to forget it. We had imprinted our map of the border onto their subconscious minds without them even noticing the sleight of hand.

I shot a look at the opposition. Winston's presentation had pushed eccentricity as far as it could go without losing all claim to seriousness. The lawyers' faces were blandly unreadable, but their foreign minister's was as tight as a punching fist. He was staring at Winston with an expression of undiluted loathing.

That evening, the team gathered in our headquarters at the Royal Delft to mull over the day's events. 'We could just buy a proper bottle of whisky, you know,' I said, extracting a clutch of miniatures from the mini bar.

'Ah, but these are so very *dinky*,' said Winston, as I collected glasses from the adjoining bathrooms, ejecting toothbrushes as I went. We cracked open the bottles with a flourish and toasted ourselves.

'Day one!' said Winston. 'Four to go.'

'Day one!' murmured Abraham and Yohannes, and we all took a gulp.

'What is this?' spluttered Abraham.

'Oops, sorry, Abraham, looks like you got the Malibu. Here, swap it with my Bell's.'

He grimaced in manly disgust, downed my whisky as though cleansing his palate of an abomination, then left to watch football in the bar. Yohannes retired to a corner to check the following morning's PowerPoint, leaving Winston and me to study the room-service menu.

'Steak and chips or steak and chips, Winston?'

'Oh, steak and chips, I think. Medium rare. And Dijon, not Coleman's.' I picked up the phone and placed the order, then lolled back on the double bed, savouring the moment of free time before we got back to work.

'Impressions so far?' asked Winston, polishing his glasses.

'Fun, but frightening. As you've remarked a million times, it's just very different from a court case, isn't it? The commissioners got stuck in more than I expected.'

'Yes. From our perspective, that's all to the good. The more questions they put, the clearer a picture we can form of their foibles and idiosyncrasies. Knowledge that allows us to work our eventual crafty magic.'

'You're not implying, are you, that they're anything other than coldly logical decision-making machines?'

'Ah ...' Winston sipped his whisky, 'When I was young and credulous I worked on that assumption – this tastes a bit of toothpaste, you know – but now I know better.'

'How so?'

'When I started out I assumed law was like math. Here was this universe of beautifully limpid rules. A problem arises. You formulate an argument. If the premises are agreed, a certain verdict becomes inevitable. Axiom, deduction, proof. A bit like a Bach cantata. But the law isn't like that. One of the major revelations of my working life has been the realisation that judges, commissioners, arbitrators don't give a shit about rationality.'

'I'm not used to you swearing, Winston.'

'Blame it on your whisky-flavoured mouthwash. Believe me, the principle of one plus two equals three counts for nothing. I'm not saying these men and women aren't smart enough to recognise logical sequiturs when they see them. They just view them as potted plants on a ballroom floor, there to be nimbly waltzed around.'

'Are you saying it's all actually politics?'

'Not politics in the classic sense – I'm not suggesting the commissioners are covert Republicans or taking sides in some geostrategic power play, although I wouldn't rule that out, either. I'm talking about the politics of competing world visions, the type of politics you – we – can influence rather than the sort we can't.'

'I'm not sure I understand what you mean, Winston.'

'Law students go into law for all the wrong reasons, wanting to believe in a world of structure and process. But that would mean missing all the fun. What we're doing here is so much more creative than formulating a dry mathematical proof.'

The person he was describing, I reflected, had been me. I had plunged into law in the search of intellectual rigour, a steadiness I'd been unable to find at home amid the shouting matches between my divorcing parents.

'So what *are* we doing, then?'

'Operating in a world of fluctuating passions and subjective emotion, in which power lies with a group of people who fondly believe they possess all the merciless objectivity of a computer. So, to be effective, we need to imagine ourselves into their heads and turn those prejudices and quirks to our advantage, persuading them they always wanted what our side just happens to want.'

'How do we do that with these commissioners?'

'We vacuum up the tiniest hint of how they view the world and adjust our arguments accordingly. For example, it's clear to me that Eddie Connors harbours certain romantic notions about nationalist stirrings in the region during pre-colonial times. If he'd bothered reading Peter Lewisham's account of his parley with old One Eye, he might have grasped that patriotism is a nuanced, qualified sentiment, but I'm happy to pander to his adolescent view of history if it makes it a smidgeon more likely he'll find in our favour.'

Room service's arrival interrupted his flow. 'Maybe students prefer the maths analogy because it feels pure, virtuous,' I said, signing the chit. 'Some might find your approach rather cynical.'

He looked up from the task in hand, surprised. He had started smearing a molecule-thin layer of Dijon mustard across the surface of his steak, just as he always did. 'Cynical? *Moi*? You won't find a bigger idealist in The Hague, dear Paula.'

'You take a lot longer to undress these days.'

Jake, lying in bed with a book, is watching me dither around the room, preparing my outfit for the following day. My 'executive look': cream silk blouse, Oscar de la Renta skirt and matching jacket, patent-leather high heels. Getting to the meeting from Lake Cottage will involve a painfully early start and a trip standing in a crammed commuter train. It would have been a lot easier, I reflect, to spend the night in Greenwich Village, take my time over breakfast, and stroll to the venue. But it's been a while since we saw one another.

'Do I?' I say absently, not really listening. I'm looking for a pair of fresh tights.

'It was one of the things I always loved about you, the speed with which you got naked. I never met a woman who could strip as fast. No fake modesty, no coyness, it was incredibly erotic. Now it's more like an airline pilot running through checks before take-off.'

I should, at that moment, have stopped rooting around at the back of a drawer and said, 'Don't use the past tense.' I should have climbed like some needy baby monkey onto his furred chest. I should have said, 'Let's go away on holiday and dawdle in bed until Housekeeping knocks at the door.'

Instead I shrug my shoulders. 'That was when I had nothing better to do with my time.' And then, because the remark about undressing has hurt: 'You didn't really think the sex thing would last for ever, did you?'

When I remember that exchange, I get a lurid mental close-up, an image of my mouth as it enunciates the nastiness. Bright red Cruella de Vil lips curling in slow motion to wring the full quota of sarcasm from my put-down. 'YOOOOU-DIDN'T-THINK-THE-SEEEEX-THIIING-WOULD-LAAAST FOR-EEEEVER, DID YOU?'

And Jake, being Jake, looks at me over the top of his book and says, 'With you, actually, yes, I did. And still do.'

23

'Coffee is in order,' said Winston, when we arrived at the Peace Palace the following morning.

In the dim light of the Refectorium, he looked uncharacteristically washed out. There was a tinge of grey to his complexion, a hint of mortality peeping from behind the bravado. The pallor made the scatter of freckles on his nose stand out. I resisted a silly urge to lean forward and wipe them away. Maybe, I thought, presenting took more out of him than at first appeared. 'You look tired, Winston.'

'I am,' he said, shaking a pill into his hand and downing it. 'But I knew I would be, and that's why you're scheduled to take up the baton today. Gives me a breather.'

Fifteen minutes later, I was rising to my feet, heart pounding, as silence settled on the Small Hall of Justice and all eyes turned to me. 'Easy as pie,' muttered Winston.

'Commissioners,' I began, 'by examining the legal treaties, diplomatic evidence and the many maps history has left behind, we have conclusively demonstrated where the original border between these two countries lies.' Brazen, but so be it.

'We will now turn to the issue of subsequent conduct and

show how the relevant governments, in their everyday administrative behaviour, demonstrated their unquestioning acceptance of this line through the decades.'

My first piece of evidence was a 1940 report on a DDT-spraying campaign staged by the Italian authorities just before the colony was occupied by Allied forces. Malaria, I explained, traditionally claimed tens of thousands of lives each year. Despite the imminence of war, the Italian governor had decided to take action; DDT was seen as the miracle product of the day.

'Roberto Petrucci, the governor of North Darrar, ordered a country-wide eradication campaign. This involved spraying the internal walls of every house, *tukul*, stable and barn to prevent the malarial mosquito from settling. This image shows a photograph of the notice posted on tree trunks, walls and lamp-posts, warning locals to tether their livestock in the open air and vacate their premises during spraying. They also leafleted every household.

'In their survey, the Italians carefully listed the villages, towns, hamlets and isolated farms to be targeted. Let us see where those all lie.' I nodded to Yohannes, who called up a borderless map of the region. A series of green dots appeared, which coagulated to yield a shape bearing a rough resemblance to the modern state of North Darrar. Over them, we imposed the black outline of a 1998 Michelin map, which, until recently, had been in standard use.

'As you can see' – I used my laser pointer to highlight a series of gaps – 'this DDT outline does not match up exactly with a border that was, until the recent outbreak of hostilities, regarded as uncontested. The Italian authorities saw no point in spraying mountain areas so high and cold that no mosquito stood a chance of survival. But here in the west, south and east, the modern map's outlines are confirmed and validated.'

The commissioners sat with necks craned, staring intently at the screen, murmuring to one another. I steamed on, slowly laying a series of transfers on top of the existing map. Red, orange, blue: the places where electricity pylons stood, polio vaccinations were distributed, municipal taxes collected. With each layer, more white gaps disappeared, until the multi-coloured blob not only filled the Michelin map's black silhouette, it slopped over the line.

'I …' I had been about to say 'I think,' but stopped myself just in time. 'You don't think, you *know*,' I remembered an LSE lecturer intoning, slamming his hand down on a textbook. 'Never suggest uncertainty. You *know*, you *know*, you *know*.'

Winston shot me an anxious glance, but I had recovered. 'So it's clear where the Italian colony's uncontested limit lay, fifty years after its creation. Let us address whether anything changed after Mussolini's Fascist army was defeated at Derden in 1941 and the colony fell into British hands.'

On the screen, the commissioners were presented with a photograph of the first page of Captain Peter Lewisham's diary, with my typed transcript running alongside.

'We don't really need the captain, do we?' I had asked Winston in the run-up to the hearing. 'We're submitting all the sit reps. They're pretty conclusive.' The British administration's situation reports were a month-by-month record of events across the captured colony. Unearthed in the public archives in Kew, they had yielded a satisfying quantity of place names and landmarks.

'The sit reps are plenty, but they're sterile stuff. Our captain is a card. Go to town on him.'

So I talked the commissioners through the Great Guinea Fowl Shoot, Inquest on a Donkey and Lewisham and Co.'s sorties – drunk and sober – while omitting what was, for our purposes, a frustratingly inconclusive parley with the *shifta* chief. Amused smiles were playing around the commissioners' lips – like children at bedtime they were enjoying having a story read to them – to be replaced by bleak expressions when Johnny was shot. Judge Mautner leaned forward.

'This is fascinating detail, Miss Shackleton. But time is ticking by and perhaps you had better explain its relevance.'

'What Captain Lewisham doesn't say, nine-tenths of the time, is as important as what he does, Mr Chairman. When his jeep gets stuck in the mud on the road between Sherano and Buleb – a road that the other side would have you believe has always been in Darrar's jurisdiction – he doesn't behave like a sly trespasser, he makes as much noise as he can to get rescued. Because he knows he's on the right side of the line. When he drives into Mederatu looking for spare parts, or to Acle to scout for game, he encounters no checkpoints. As he patrols the countryside, he never once receives a polite but firm visit from a Darrar mayor or policeman pointing out his error. His bluff confidence – the confidence perhaps only a British officer of his era enjoyed – is rooted in a certainty so solid he never bothers articulating it: he's on home turf. And when he is presented with an opportunity to arrest a colleague's murderer, he does us the favour of spelling this out. Johnny's killer has moved across the border into Darrar, he tells his junior officer, beyond his reach. So, you see, every relevant regional authority in the fifties knew exactly where the border lay. There was no debate then. There should be none now.'

I sat down, dizzy with excitement, longing to continue. 'Thank you, Captain,' I whispered to myself. Quietly, Winston placed a hand over my own, both congratulatory and restraining.

One evening, I called Jake from my flat in Greenwich Village to explain that I'd had drinks after work and felt too tired to go up to Lake Cottage that evening. It was the third such conversation that month.

His voice was quiet. 'That's a shame. I was looking forward to seeing you.'

'Believe me,' I slurred, 'you're not missing anything. I'm

too *pissed* to make much sense. I mean that in the British sense.' There was a long silence. 'Jake, are you still there?'

When he spoke next his voice sounded strange, uneven. 'I'm lonely, Paula.'

Suddenly I no longer felt drunk. 'I'm sorry.'

'I never thought I'd ask you this,' he said, with a terrible weariness, 'but are you having an affair? Have you met someone you want to be with instead of me? Please just say so if that's the case.'

'No! Of course not! How could you think that? Why would I bother hiding something like that from you? I'd just tell you.'

'I no longer feel like I have your full attention.'

'I'm just tired – you know how hard we're working. God, this is awful, Jake, we sound like such a cliché.'

'Well, that's relationships for you. Nothing new under the sun. Every line I just said to you, my wife said to me at some point in the past. Fate teaching me a lesson, I suppose.' His voice became brisk, matter-of-fact. 'OK, well, drink lots of water, take half an aspirin so you don't get a hangover, and we'll talk tomorrow.'

A few months later, we had what I shall always think of as the Last Supper. It's the scene whose rewrite I keep imagining, the evening whose memory makes me shrivel, like a slug sprinkled with salt.

I was already in a sulk when I arrived at Lake Cottage. I had worked through lunch, and an afternoon's worth of caffeine and low blood-sugar had left me ratty and attenuated. I had driven up to the cottage in the Jetta to spend the Friday night with Jake, only to discover he planned to leave early the following morning. He had booked a week-long trip. He would visit Sophie at college, then head off hiking in the woods with an old college friend.

'What? I wouldn't have bothered coming if I'd thought you

weren't going to be here tomorrow. I've got a ton of work to do. You know how I feel about staying in the cottage when you're not around.'

He sighed. 'I booked this trip two months ago, if you remember, after asking if you were interested in coming along.'

'Well, forgive me if the detail escaped me. My diary is so crammed at the moment I can barely read the entries. A few verbal reminders would have been helpful.'

He shrugged, doling out two servings of stew. We were a very modern household: Jake did the cooking and I complained about my day at the office.

'I can't change it now. Why don't you take the opportunity to drop in and see Julia while I'm away? She's back from Grenada and was asking after you.'

'That will certainly be an unalloyed pleasure.'

'Please be polite at least, Paula.'

We ate without speaking. Laurel and Hardy lay at our feet, watching our lips with doleful expressions, pleading for scraps. The sound of our cutlery seemed unnaturally loud. He cleared the plates while I leafed through a mark-up of a purchase agreement. When I looked up some time later, he was sitting gazing at me. There was something in his eyes at that moment, a hard, cool reckoning, which frightened me.

'Paula ...'

'What?'

'Can I warn you against a tendency I've noticed in a lot of people? To be more precise, a tendency I've noticed in most of the women I've had relationships with. I suspect it's not a specifically female thing, but it does seem to have been a characteristic of the frighteningly smart, driven women I tend to be attracted to.'

He had my attention now.

'Which is?'

'I think women like you see relationships, men, as puzzles to be deciphered. You're intrigued, challenged at the start. You

216

hold them up to the light, like crystals, looking for their fatal flaws, trying to work out how the various molecules slot together. And then, having found the weak spot, the crack, you apply pressure. You work at it and work at it until the thing breaks, and then you look at the shards in your hands and throw them away. Nothing stands up to that kind of relentless scrutiny. Nothing. Look hard enough and you'll always find that fatal flaw.'

Jake had a way of doing this. Removing all the anger from potential arguments and replacing it with sorrow, terrible regret and shame.

I'll have to think about this later, I told myself, work out if he's right. Dear God, let him not be, because if he is, I'm doomed. 'I hope that's not true,' I whispered.

'And what I'm left wondering is whether there's something fundamentally wrong with our relationship, some imbalance that can be addressed, in which case we can both work at that, or whether you just can't help picking this apart because that's who you are, and that you'd be pecking and pecking at it, however wonderful the relationship, whatever I did.'

I dropped the purchase agreement on the table and hid my face in my hands, unable to look at him. 'I don't know, Jake.'

He walked to the windows and looked out at the lake, then bowed his head and leaned his brow against the glass. He hadn't intended to go this far, I guessed, but we were launched now. There was no stopping us as we toppled over our cliff, arms wrapped around one another in a throttling embrace.

'This is beginning to feel a lot like my marriage. And I hate feeling that way with you. I can't bear the idea of things just getting more and more petty and acrimonious between us. It's so demeaning. I don't know what's happened, but some kind of rot seems to have set in. I think you should move out for a bit, back to your own place. You don't seem to enjoy being here any more. Maybe you should examine that impulse, your need to get away from me. I think some time apart might be

217

good for both of us. Maybe you should take the opportunity while I'm hiking to work out what you really want.'

He spent that night on the couch and the following morning, after he'd driven off, I wandered the cottage, white-faced and weeping, making desultory, half-hearted efforts to pack my turquoise suitcase. Then I went outside and paced the lake's circumference, three, four, five times. When I came back, I picked up the case, hurled it into the storeroom, and slammed the door. Not now. Not yet.

I tried calling Jake's mobile, but it went straight to voicemail. He had not left an itinerary. So I did what I knew how to do. As the wind rose outside, whipping scuds across the lake's surface, I sat at the computer and worked the phones, researching my client, micro-analysing possible scenarios, building a prospectus. Trawling through the previous month's searches on his computer, I began to piece together his proposed hiking route, identifying the hotels he had probably booked. I knew his tastes, his foibles: I would track him down. And then I would go and meet him. I had made a colossal, stupid mistake, but there was still time.

24

On day three it was the other side's turn. They started, like us, with a speech from the foreign minister. If ours had chosen to emphasise North Darrar's dogged struggle for self-determination and its peace-loving nature, theirs dwelt on the greatness of an empire stretching back into the mists of time, sanctified by mosque and Orthodox Church alike. Then His Excellency threw us a venomous glance.

'We stand before you as innocent victims of an unprovoked attack launched on the night of June the seventh on the outskirts of the port of Sanasa. The timing of this attack, which led to tens of thousands of unnecessary deaths, woundings and mutilations, tells you all you need to know about the character of the belligerent sitting opposite. It was designed to catch our army by surprise and cause maximum damage, and that is exactly what it did.'

Kennedy was scribbling furiously on a notepad, tapping Winston's shoulder as he did so. But Winston was already on his feet. 'Mr Chairman!'

'Mr Peabody, as you know, the commission functions as a trier of fact and law. Objections have little role, if any, to play. It is considered impolite.'

'I'm well aware of that, Mr Chairman, and I must apologise for violating procedure. However, this speech is prejudicial and extraordinarily inappropriate. A condition of the Comprehensive Peace Agreement signed in Tunis was that the origins of the conflict were to be excluded from this commission's jurisdiction. If the other side brings in by a back door what it agreed not to bring through the front, the peace process is undermined. The issue of how this conflict began, and who bears ultimate responsibility, is to be decided by a commission to be appointed by the African Union. It has no place here.'

'Thank you for your intervention, Mr Peabody. You are correct, of course, but I must make clear that I do not intend to encourage a habit of interjection, so please consider this an exceptional case. Your Excellency,' he said, 'please try to confine your remarks to matters properly before us.'

Darrar's foreign minister inclined his head ever so slightly. 'It is difficult, Mr Chairman, because we feel so strongly.'

Winston snorted softly to himself.

The foreign minister talked the commissioners through a potted history so basic it could have come from a Baedeker tourist guide, then slipped the stiletto in once again: 'Through the millennia, my country has aimed to live in peace with its neighbours. Whenever its army has gone into action, it has only ever acted in self-defence. And that is what happened when our loyal army fell prey to a premeditated assault by North Darrar's troops, carefully timed to coincide with a head of state's visit abroad.'

Winston put his hands on the desk, jutted his elbows and raised his eyebrows, staring at Judge Mautner. 'I'm about to stand and object again,' the gesture clearly said.

Judge Mautner looked tetchy. It seemed he had lost patience. With the wrong side. To Winston, he said: 'As both teams are well aware, there is no jury to impress here, no public gallery. The commissioners are all legal experts with huge experience, fully cognisant of both the extent and limits of their official briefs, and no amount of grandstanding will sway us. Please continue, Your Excellency.'

I was careful not to turn my head as Kennedy pushed back his chair and slipped away, walking swiftly to the exit. Winston wrote slowly on his notebook and slid the pad towards me. 'NOTIFYING THE BOSS'. Then he carefully closed it.

'We cannot let this continue!' Kennedy exclaimed, fumbling in his overcoat for a packet of Marlboro. 'They are massacring us, *massacring* us in there, and we are not even *trying* to defend ourselves.'

It was the coffee break. The three of us had walked out across the car park and into the formal garden, halting only when there was a tacit consensus that we were out of both ear- and eyeshot. We were in a gravelled rotunda, surrounded by shin-high privet hedges caging prissy arrangements of yellow primulas.

'You heard the chairman,' said Winston, calmly. 'This isn't a court case. If we keep interrupting we risk losing the commissioners' sympathy.'

'But we cannot just let them keep telling these terrible lies.' Kennedy drew jerkily on his cigarette. 'We can prove who started the war, but we have chosen not to. Because we believed you, YOU,' he said, jabbing a finger at Winston, 'when you told us that the question was irrelevant and would only be decided by the AU.'

'And that is still true. The other side's protestations are so much hot air.'

'But we are letting their version go by default. You are not even interrupting any more. I may not be a lawyer, but I know military strategy. And what I learned in the field is that you do not let your enemy notch up easy wins because, in the end, you find yourself surrounded.'

'If you notice, Your Excellency, I was starting to annoy the chairman. And your military experience must also have told you that the long game is the one that counts and that the pain of small surrenders is wiped out by overall victory. This rhetorical posturing will come to grate on the commissioners' nerves, believe me. They will appreciate our side's focus, economy and professionalism. We will go for the jugular in Addis, where we will present the AU with Paula's evidence establishing a steady pattern of encroachment, I promise you. But not here, not now. This debate about the border's course is essentially a technical issue, and we should not allow ourselves to be distracted.'

The minister paced fretfully up and down the privet, finishing his cigarette, muttering under his breath. After a few beats, Winston said: 'You spoke to Him.' More a statement than a question.

'Yes.'

'What does He say?'

'"When you hire a water diviner, do not try to be his stick." It's a proverb in my country. It means …'

'If you keep a dog, don't bark,' I suggested.

'Something like that.'

'So,' Winston said quietly. 'We are your dogs. Let us bark. We're good at it.'

Reginald Watts was next. I immediately understood the reason for Winston's 'Breast Boy' nickname. He was over six feet tall, with large feet that tended to splay. I suspect that at some stage he had taken lessons in public speaking. His tutor must have told him to use his hands. He had done his best but had come up with just a single gesture, a circling motion that made him appear to be cupping two giant breasts in mid-air.

I camouflaged a giggle with a snuffle. 'I wish you hadn't told me that,' I whispered to Winston.

'Once you notice, it's hard to see anything else, isn't it?'

But the humour died fast. Watts threw us a probing look, then unveiled his Exocet.

'Mr Chairman, venerable commissioners, the other side spent most of the first day showing us the many, many treaties and maps they say bear out their border claim. They focused in particular on the diagonal, which supposedly establishes Sanasa's location on their side of the line. We have submitted a great deal of paperwork, but we intend, in this instance, to focus on just one written document and accompanying map.'

'Here we go,' murmured Winston.

'I will draw your attention to an 1899 letter written – as a matter of urgency – by the Negus's secretary, Heriu Tekle, to the Italian Foreign Ministry. The Negus, who took power after his father's suicide, had been on the Darrar throne only a few years and was anxious to shore up his empire. The letter is currently stored in Rome.'

Watts's assistant tapped her laptop and Tadesse's letter appeared on the screen. Time had rendered the mundane beautiful. The paper was the colour of Winston's vanilla ice-cream, the sloping copperplate as delicate as Arabic calligraphy. Ismael's dots were visible only if you knew what to look for.

'It is written in formal Italian and was triggered by an incident three months earlier, in which the Negus's troops were pursuing a band of *shiftas* – bandits – who had raided a village in the north-east and stolen livestock.' His hands caressed the air, lending emphasis where none was needed.

'The Negus's men pursued this gang on horseback until they rounded a hill and encountered an armed militia from the Italian colony, which claimed they had crossed the border. The militia attempted, unsuccessfully, to arrest them as trespassers. Shots were exchanged, no one – luckily – was hurt, and the Negus's men withdrew. The incident was clearly considered serious enough to prompt this exchange of correspondence.

'Let me read out the relevant section, which we have translated into English.' In the new PowerPoint image on the screen, the words had been helpfully highlighted in luminous green.

'Tekle states as follows: "Please be advised that your officials have long confused the junction between the Abubed and Shishay rivers with the junction between the Abubed and the Daro, another watercourse entirely, notwithstanding the many testimonies of nomads and local farmers. The true focal point lies fifty kilometres directly north of the Ram's Head outcrop. Hence, your militiamen were trespassing on the Negus's land when they attempted to arrest his troops."

'As you can see, Tekle has attached a detailed sketch of the area, illustrating his point.' The map was now on the screen, hand-drawn but somehow all the more compelling for that fact. Ink squiggles for rivers and roads, ice-cream cones for mountains, a square with a cross on it marking the Ram's Head outcrop. As Watts teased out the water-courses with his laser pointer, I caught a whiff of restrained excitement on his side of the room, the kind of suppressed tension you feel when a group of adolescents is watching porn together. This was intended to obliterate us.

'Our argument is this, Mr Chairman, esteemed commissioners,' said Watts. 'As this letter makes clear, there has been a fundamental confusion, dating back at least a century, over the name and location of two key rivers. This unfortunate mistake, on which the other side's belligerent action was premised, has ended up costing both countries dear. The letter sent by the Negus's secretary – one can only sympathise with his dismay – makes clear that every single map,' Watts hammered on the desk with his forefinger, 'submitted by the other side is incorrect. The hundred and twenty maps, of which the other side seem so proud, are a hundred and twenty worthless bits of paper.'

'Steady on,' muttered Winston.

I could see Kennedy's hand open and close spasmodically in a frustrated fist. As an ex-fighter, he probably knew how to handle himself in a brawl.

'By our measure,' continued Watts, 'there is no fifteen-degree angle. There has never been a fifteen-degree angle. The angle is a much sharper forty degrees. Not so much a gentle green slope as a double black diamond.'

'That's going to be the single solitary joke of their entire presentation,' predicted Winston, *sotto voce*.

Then Watts called up the 1998 Michelin map, and showed us what it meant on the ground. I shook my head in disbelief as he ran his pen over the contours of Darrar's claim. At its base at the Tolandino monastery, the difference in angles was barely discernible. But the long sliver kept widening, swallowing hundreds of square kilometres before hitting the new river, which meandered down to the sea north-west of Sanasa. The port sat marooned on their side of the border and landlocked Darrar had miraculously acquired a generous stretch of coastline. It was a very, very greedy land grab.

The second day of their presentation was devoted, as ours had been, to subsequent conduct. At Henry Alexander's bidding, a small, dark man in his mid-fifties walked to the front of the room and positioned himself in front of a lectern. He placed his hand on a leather-bound copy of the Koran and took the oath.

'Please state your name for the benefit of the commission.'

'My name is Suleiman Jama.'

'Did you live in Sanasa until the seventh of June 2001?'

'Sanasa is my home, yes.'

'And how long did you live there?'

'Since December 2000, when I was transferred there by Darrar government.'

'And what role did you play there, Mr Suleiman?'

The witness gave a big smile, revealing a large gold incisor. 'I am the mayor.'

I scribbled a note and passed it to Winston. 'WASN'T MAYOR KILLED IN FIRST BOMBARDMENT?' He inclined his head ever so slightly and wrote on my note. 'LET HIM TALK.'

'Do you have any official document confirming that, Mr Suleiman?' asked Alexander, with a sideways glance at us. 'A letter of appointment from Darrar's Ministry for Local Administration, for example?'

The witness gave an apologetic smile and shrugged his shoulders helplessly. 'I have nothing, nothing! When the shooting and shelling began, we all run. We leave everything. But everyone in Sanasa know Suleiman.'

'So please tell us what your official duties involved. What does the mayor of Sanasa actually *do*?'

The witness puffed his chest, stretching out his arms to encompass the globe. He was clearly a man who enjoyed being centre stage.

'Mayor does everything! *Everything*.' He ticked off the items on his fingers. 'He run local court, he pay militia. If someone beat you on the road, you come to Suleiman. You have sick child for hospital, Suleiman, he arrange.'

'And are you also responsible for making sure residents vote when there are elections?'

Judge Mautner leaned forward to interrupt. 'Please do not lead your witness, Mr Alexander.'

'My apologies, Mr Chairman. Let me rephrase.'

But the witness was talking already, defending himself from some accusation no one had voiced. 'My country is a modern democracy. Voting is good.'

'And who is responsible for distributing seeds, fertilisers and credits to local farmers?'

'In Sanasa, no farming. Just fishing.'

'Well, what about handing out food aid on the Darrar government's behalf?'

'I told you. Suleiman do everything.'

'Exactly,' said Alexander, gazing meaningfully at the commissioners.

'Exactly,' muttered Winston, under his breath.

I looked at him uneasily. However scratchy, Suleiman Jama's

testimony was doing us no good at all, challenging our attempt to prove a track record of administration by North Darrar. As Henry Alexander went on to talk the commissioners through a stack of bureaucratic records, a hint of a smile appeared on Winston's face and he closed his eyes. The books of supposed tax collections, the piles of utilities bills, the seed-distribution certificates failed to trigger a response. A couple of gratuitous references to how our side had initiated hostilities sailed past without disturbing his serenity. Hands clasped over his belly, Winston resembled a fuzzy, honey-coloured Buddha who had achieved Nirvana.

'You're looking very pleased with yourself,' I said, as Judge Mautner brought the morning's proceedings to a close.

Winston opened his eyes, heaved a sigh and looked at me with an expression of delighted wonder. '"And the Lord shall deliver thee into mine hand, and I will smite thee and take thine head from thee." First Book of Samuel, chapter seventeen. I think we've got them.' He shook his head, marvelling. 'It's a truly lovely, lovely thing when one feels that, Paula. Triumph hovering somewhere in the ether, so close that all you have to do is reach up and pluck it.'

We reconvened after lunch.

'Mr Peabody, do you wish to cross-examine the witness?' asked Judge Mautner.

'I certainly do.'

'Please ask the witness to come in.'

Suleiman Jama walked to the front of the room. The joviality of the morning had evaporated. Perhaps he had not expected a cross-examination. He took out some orange plastic prayer beads and began to thumb them across his palm.

Winston peered at him over his bifocals, the epitome of avuncular interest. 'No need to be nervous, Mr Suleiman. I'm just going to ask you a few questions about your time as a mayor. You have told us quite a lot about your professional duties. But perhaps you can tell us a little about your personal circumstances. For example, your house in Sanasa. How big was it?'

'Just a house. Nice house.'

'And where was it located?'

'Near the sea.'

'Sanasa is a port. Everything is near the sea. Were you, perhaps, near the oil tanks? The shipping yard? The container depot?'

'Yes.' He was looking rattled.

'Which one?' Winston was hunting now. You could hear a relentless, driving quality in his voice. 'The oil tanks, the container depot, the shipping yard?'

'The shipping yard,' hazarded Suleiman.

'I'm afraid Sanasa has neither oil tanks, shipping yard, nor a container depot,' said Winston. 'It is a very small place.'

He tried to recover. 'My English is not so good. Your question ... I did not understand it.'

Judge Mautner leaned forward. 'Would you like an interpreter? We can provide one.' The witness shot him a brooding, peeved look, but nodded. I controlled a spasm of irritation: Judge Mautner had granted him a precious breathing space.

There was a delay as a clerk clucked around, plugging in headphones and testing the sound before fitting them on Suleiman Jama's head. Across the Small Hall of Justice, there was a rustle of movement and a chorus of coughs as everyone donned headsets and fiddled with volume control. An interpreter in the booth behind us cleared his throat in anticipation.

'So, Mr Suleiman,' continued Winston, 'you were saying that you lived near the shipping yard, but we know there is none in Sanasa. How do you explain that?'

You could almost hear Suleiman's brain whirring as he made the most of the time it took to translate the question. The interpreter's voice finally came over the headphones, higher than the mayor's: I guessed he was a younger man. 'My neighbour mends boats. For me, that is a shipping yard.'

'You told us a lot about your work. You said,' Winston read from his notes, 'that you were responsible for the local court, paid the militia, dealt with local disputes and distributed food aid.'

'Yes.'

'And when you were not working, what did you do with yourself?'

'Suleiman work all the time.' He was beginning to sound petulant.

'Well, when it was a public holiday, for example, what did you do?'

'I have a vegetable patch where I grow beans, chickpeas, marrows, sometimes tomatoes. They grow well. I keep chickens and use the droppings as fertiliser. Vegetables like it.'

'And did you have any friends in Sanasa? People you played cards with, perhaps, or met at the mosque, drank tea with?'

'Yes, many friends.'

'Could you name a few of them, please?'

Suleiman paused. His eyes flickered towards the other side. It was clear he was reluctant to go ahead, but Alexander and Watts sat expressionless, offering no guidance.

'Mr Suleiman? You must know the names of your friends,' Winston said, with a small chuckle.

'I play cards with Ahmed Jibril and Hebron Getze. With Mama Katy I sometimes read the Koran. And with Abdul Farah I watch football.'

Then Winston did something that took my breath away. 'Ah … Ahmed Jibril and Hebron Getze … Abdul Farah … Now, if I remember correctly, those names are on the witness list presented by the other side, are they not?'

'Is that correct?' Judge Mautner directed his question to Alexander.

'We would need to check, Mr Chairman. It may well be.'

Wow, I thought. Winston knows their witness list better than they do.

'That would certainly be helpful, Mr Chairman, as I seem to remember that Ahmed Jibril is listed as a Sanasa tax collector and Hebron Getze as a council employee. I will come back to these names later. At this point I would draw the tribunal's attention to a letter. It was submitted by Darrar as part of their counter-Memorial. For reasons that remain unclear, it was never translated. Perhaps that explains why my colleagues missed its relevance to Mr Suleiman's supposed tenure as mayor of Sanasa.'

With a tap from Yohannes's index finger two pages appeared side by side on the screen. 'Do you recognise this, Mr Suleiman?'

It was the thin blue letter Winston had fished out during the long days spent reading in his Lira courtyard, the air thick with the scent of jasmine. Next to it sat Dr Berhane's English translation.

The witness squinted at the screen, making a show of being unable to read the words. Then he seemed to withdraw into himself. Any ebullience had drained away. He looked at Winston with obvious dislike, but said nothing.

'No? Well, let me compare the signature at the bottom with the signature at the bottom of your original witness statement.' At Yohannes's bidding, the last page of that statement, with its final scrawl, appeared on the screen.

'Would you agree that the two signatures are identical?'

Suleiman Jama nodded reluctantly.

'For the record, the witness has indicated his assent, so his authorship of this letter is not in dispute. As you can see *here*' – Winston used the laser to point to a postal address at the top of the page – 'it is addressed to the district police commissioner in Achamew, in the Federal Republic of Darrar. What is your connection with Achamew's police commissioner, Mr Suleiman?'

'We went to school together. I worked in Golpik, thirty miles away from Achamew in the 1990s, as deputy mayor. We had problems with lawlessness at the time, so I often was writing to him.'

'So that would explain the letter's chatty nature. Would you now oblige us, Mr Suleiman, by reading aloud the original, so we get it on the record?'

Haltingly, Suleiman Jama read aloud, the interpreter translating as he went. The letter began with official business. Then, at the foot of the second page, came a handwritten paragraph of family gossip, the kind of personal PS that busy people scribble on Christmas cards. At this point, he stopped.

'Please go on.'

'"The girls are doing well. The eldest has married now and is expecting her first child. With the second, we shall see, she is still young. I see you got the promotion you were after. As for me, my ambition to work on the coast has finally been satisfied. I am being posted to the village of Sebrahtu. You know how I love the coastal heat. It dries out my ageing bones. The job starts in March. I will send you my new address. In the meantime, please pass on my best wishes to the family."'

'And please read out the most important detail, just here, alongside your signature.'

'The thirteenth of December 2000.' His voice was dull and flat; the interpreter did his best to mimic the pitch.

Winston gazed around the room in insincere wonder.

'The thirteenth of December 2000. So this key witness, by his own admission, was nowhere near Sanasa when the conflict blew up six months later. Let me tell you exactly where Sebrahtu is, Mr Chairman.'

Yohannes's next image was a detailed map of the coast.

'Sebrahtu lies thirty-seven kilometres east of Sanasa, in the Federal Republic of Darrar,' said Winston. 'It shares many characteristics with Sanasa. It lies on the sea, it has a little pier, a mosque, a few old Ottoman buildings, and most of the residents are fishermen. I don't doubt that you were a mayor, Mr Suleiman, who played the vital roles you described, kept chickens and grew vegetables, but could you clarify whether you did these things in Sanasa, or in Sebrahtu?'

All eyes shifted to Suleiman Jama. The pause seemed to last a long time, but could only have been a few seconds. He stared at Winston for a moment, his lips working, then looked at Alexander and Watts. What was he seeking? Absolution? Sympathy? I held my breath. Running through my head were the explanations I'd invent in his shoes, none of them convincing. He gave a low curse, tore off his headset and stalked out of the Small Hall of Justice. From the heave of his shoulders, it was clear he tried to slam the giant door in a final fuck-you gesture to us all, but its heft defeated him.

'The witness … has left the room,' commented the interpreter. His voice was uneven; there came the sound of a suppressed squeak. Turning in my seat, I caught a flurry of movement in one of the booths. The interpreter had either succumbed to a fit of the giggles or fallen off his chair.

Judge Mautner finally broke the silence. He turned to Alexander and his deputy, who bore the stunned expressions of the recently bereaved. 'Does counsel have anything further or shall we break?'

Alexander shook his head

'Then,' said Judge Mautner, 'I think we are done for the day.' He brought the gavel down.

'Do you think they knew?' I whispered to Winston, as we collected our papers.

He shook his head. 'Couldn't have. You would never open yourself up to that kind of potential damage. No, as I said, witnesses are like landmines. They can win a war for you or blow up in your face.'

'And Suleiman Jama? Why invent it all?'

'Who knows? A craving for the limelight? I suspect he started with a small lie, and it spiralled out of control. But much of human behaviour is a mystery to me.'

* * *

232

The dogs knew before I did. Laurel and Hardy always served as the friendliest of doorbells, bouncing excitedly around any vehicle that drew up on the grass outside, thrusting snouts into crotches and licking palms. Not this time. Their ruffs rose along their backs and they barked at the car with its unfamiliar markings, keeping their distance, warning me to watch my step.

It turns out that police officers really do come to your home in twos and, yes, you do briefly consider not opening the door as you register that, once you do, nothing will ever be the same again. And one of them – the woman, if there is one – really will lead you gently into the kitchen and set about making you a nice cup of instant coffee as her colleague, having respectfully removed his cap, does the hard bit – just as they agreed on the way over.

'Sorry to bother you, ma'am. You are Paula Shackleton?'

'Yes, that's me.'

'And this is the residence of Jake Wentworth?'

'Yes, it is.'

'You live here with Mr Wentworth?'

'Yes.'

Both of them looked at me for a moment, waiting for me to fill in a near-visible blank. When I failed to oblige, the male cop shot a brief I-told-you-so glance at the woman.

'Are you a ... close friend of Mr Wentworth?'

'Yes.'

He cleared his throat. 'We're very sorry to inform you, ma'am, that Mr and Mrs Wentworth died yesterday evening in a motor-vehicle incident. It was raining heavily, as you know. We believe there was an issue with visibility. Mr Wentworth appears to have lost control of his BMW and it went off the side of Bear Mountain Bridge. The bodies have been recovered by a team of divers and are at the county morgue.'

I suppose mine was an unconventional reaction. I snorted with incredulous laughter. 'Oh, this is just ridiculous.' The timing of our make-or-break conversation followed, with such ruthless immediacy, by death? No, it was simply too much.

Another silence. I felt the two officers were struggling, as a point of professionalism, not to exchange glances again.

The woman took over. 'Ma'am. Is there anyone you would like us to contact to be with you at this time? A friend? A relative? It's good to have company.'

'No, there's no one.'

They gazed through the kitchen window. Then at the floor. The male officer fidgeted fitfully with his belt. The woman officer shot him a disapproving look, then looked pointedly at the cup of coffee, which I had not touched. She clearly wanted to get on. 'Do you have any questions, ma'am? Is there anything you want to know?'

Oh, so many, many things.

'Do you know if they had their seatbelts on?' Why ask that?

'Couldn't say, I'm afraid,' said the male officer. 'My understanding, though, is that it wouldn't have made much difference. The vehicle flipped after it hit the guardrail.' And he made a gesture with one hand, demonstrating how a car somersaults and lands upside down, that would stay with me for a long time, the most obscene gesture a man had ever made to me.

'Will there be a post-mortem? An inquest?' I suppressed a hysterical giggle as I heard the words from a million cop shows coming out of my mouth.

'Inquest?' The female police officer cocked her head to one side. 'Is that what they do in your country, ma'am? There's no suspicion of foul play, so, no. Cause of death just goes on the death certificate.'

'And ...' I found my voice was finally quavering '... you're absolutely sure Mrs Wentworth was in the car?'

'Yes, ma'am. The eldest daughter identified both of them.'

So Charlotte, Eric and Sophie already knew. But of course. After a few minutes of looking at their feet, staring out at the lake and commenting on the weather – during which I stood silently, trying to absorb the news – they put their caps back on and walked to the door. At that moment, one last question burst out of me. 'I'm not next of kin.' Didn't I know it. 'Why did you come here today?'

The male officer nodded in the vague direction of Griffin House. 'Julia Wentworth is an upstanding member of this community. She's got a lot of friends in the police department. When she asks a favour, we're only too happy to oblige.'

So this was Julia's work, a delegated, arm's-length errand designed to save her picking up the phone and sharing a moment of unbearable intimacy with me: the loss of the man we both loved.

'Well, that's one tough cookie,' I heard the male officer exclaim, as they walked out to their patrol car. There was relief in his voice and he gave his head and shoulders a little shake, like a setter after a rainstorm. 'Not a tear.'

25

I wandered the hotel room, stacking dirty plates, as Winston and Yohannes formed a huddle in one corner. Kennedy drew up a chair, straddled it cowboy-style, and forced Winston to make eye contact.

'I have just one thing to ask, Mr Peabody, before I leave you and your colleagues to your work. Tomorrow is a big day so I know you will want to focus. Are you or are you not intending to put our side of the argument over the original outbreak of hostilities?'

'My position is unchanged. I will certainly remind the commission that their jurisdiction does not extend that far, but anything more would constitute an insult to their intelligence.'

Kennedy gazed down at the crumb-strewn carpet, muttered something that sounded too long and complex to be a swearword, then looked at Winston. 'So be it. I will tell Him.' He disentangled himself from the chair and showed himself out.

Catching my reproachful glance, Winston held up his hands to Heaven. 'Look, he's known as Kennedy for a reason, and it's not because he declared himself a Berliner. That man enjoys the sound of his own rhetoric. Now please, Paula, Yohannes and I have a lot to do. Your Rome document is going to be the star of tomorrow's presentation, you'll be pleased to hear.'

* * *

Rebuttal day had arrived. The morning would be ours – our last chance to discredit their arguments and trumpet our own – the afternoon, theirs. There was an uneasy pause as we waited for Winston, who was sitting motionless at the table, staring at his hands, girding his intellectual loins. Then he rose with the grace of an opera diva about to deliver her last aria to a packed house.

'Mr Chairman, we are gathering here on this final day to examine, discuss and in many cases refute the arguments and evidence that my honourable colleagues on the other side of the room have presented.

'The other side has taken what I can only describe as a generous approach, and the result, if I can use a metaphor from the world of cuisine, has been an over-rich bouillabaisse of a case. Their casserole has included many juicy morsels, but also a great many ingredients' – he shot a meaningful look at opposing counsel – 'that should have been saved for another meal. I am referring, of course, to the constant attempts to persuade this tribunal that it is here not only to decide the course of the border but also to allot responsibility for the conflict. We were tempted at times to respond in kind. But to do so would be to show a profound disrespect not only for the agreement reached in Tunis by the two governments, but for this commission, which is well aware of the limits of its jurisdiction. I have refrained from entering into the argument over the origins of the war because I am confident that inter-national legal professionals of the integrity, experience and sophistication we see here need no guidance when it comes to resisting pressure, however bullying.'

This shameless bit of ego-stroking prompted a few smug smiles among the commissioners. Judge Mautner, however, was impassive.

Then Winston launched himself into the void. 'I have only a few points to make. You will see that much of my rebuttal shares a common characteristic. In many instances, we were supplied with the evidence required to expose the flaws in our respected colleagues' version of events by ... our respected colleagues themselves. Buried in the vast volume of paperwork they submitted – a quantity so huge I did wonder if their own team had found time to read it – was evidence that proves our case and undermines their own. I would therefore like to thank my esteemed colleagues for being so obliging.' He executed a little bow.

The other side stared at him. Alexander, I could see, believed this was all just bravado. Chin out, his body posture signalled 'Wanna fight? Any time.' Below his sandy hairline, however, Watts had gone a mottled pink. Perhaps he was the one responsible for vetting the cache of supporting documents and was now trying to work out what he had missed.

Winston's voice hardened. 'I am grateful to them for their unfailing generosity, but am also concerned as to some of the methodology this evidence appears to expose. This is not a court case, as we all keep reminding ourselves, and that is a mercy, in its way. For there have been times when the methods adopted by our esteemed counterparts, had they been attempted in a court of law, would have led to a harsh rebuke from a presiding magistrate and permanent damage to professional reputations. I can only assume that we are dealing with a series of accidental oversights for surely no lawyer, before a commission of this standing, would ever attempt deliberately to mislead.'

He had their attention now. François Rainier was frowning; Eddie Connors was furiously scribbling a note to himself.

'These are serious and troubling allegations, Mr Peabody,' said Judge Mautner.

'Indeed, Mr Chairman. I believe the other side's strategy has been both serious and troubling.'

'Well, let us be the judge of that. Please proceed.'

First Winston tackled subsequent conduct. Reminding the commission of the débâcle of Suleiman Jama's testimony, he suggested that every item of evidence associated with the would-be mayor – from Darrar election records to tax receipts – was equally tainted. Suleiman Jama's boasts about the extent of his administrative duties ensured the damage was satisfyingly wide. The same went for the witnesses he had helpfully identified as personal friends, and the evidence connected to them. It was like watching a Serbian sniper on his off-day, lazily shooting targets at a funfair. Through it all, Alexander and Watts sat staring straight ahead.

Then Winston addressed opposing counsel's mother-of-all-maps.

'First, allow me to turn to the 1899 letter and attached map sent to Rome on the Negus's behalf by secretary Heriu Tekle. This, if you will remember, formed the basis of the other side's contention that our hundred and twenty maps are mistaken and misleading, due to an alleged confusion over the rivers whose junctions serve as cartographical points. Hence, we supposedly ended up with a forty-degree double black instead of a gentler fifteen-degree green run.

'Yohannes, please show us the letter as submitted to the commission.'

A page appeared on the screen. Winston could have used his laser pointer but instead, squeezing every drop of drama from the situation, he rose from his seat and approached the screen brandishing a Mont Blanc. 'You will notice, if you look closely, that there is something a little peculiar about this document.'

'Is there, Mr Peabody?' asked Judge Mautner.

'You will notice how pristine it is, how suspiciously clean. No smudges, no notation marks, no marginalia. The only visible marking – very easy to miss the first time around – is a row of little ink dots on the letter's margin. I hope you can see them running down the right-hand side of the page? We have provided a helpful close-up.'

'We can, Mr Peabody,' said Judge Mautner. 'But they do not seem particularly significant.'

'Ah, but they are, Mr Chairman. I gazed at these ink dots for a long time wondering what they could be. It was only thanks to the efforts of my deputy, Paula Shackleton, and Francesca de Mello, researching on our behalf in the Italian Foreign Ministry archives, that we worked it out. They located this letter's original, which made everything clear. We have prepared a little video. Yohannes, if you please.'

Yohannes tapped on his keyboard and an enlarged version of the letter appeared on the left side of the screen, a human hand – Winston's – holding a piece of white card, its edges outlined in red, over the letter's right-hand margin. 'Here are the ink dots. If we pull the card a centimetre to the right we finally understand what they are. The dots are the tips of handwritten *letters*, gentlemen.' On the screen, Winston's hand moved the card a few centimetres more. '*Letters* that once made up *phrases*. And this, *this*' – Winston's voice was quivering with excitement now – 'is what the original looked like before it was doctored. Compare and contrast!' The pristine version now lay next to the document we had discovered in Rome. The copperplate text on both was identical, but our document's right-hand margin was scrawled with comments and exclamation marks.

'So let us look closely at these marginalia. First, who made them? We can see here the initials "GF". Giuseppe Franco was permanent secretary at Italy's Ministry of the Colonies at the time of this correspondence. Here are his initials and signature, on a letter sent the same year, concerning events in Cyrenaica. The calligraphy is identical.

'When confronted by the suggestion that the Italians don't know their Shishay from their Daro, Franco writes, "*Uno scherzo*" – "What a joke!" – "*Il Negus si prende gioco di noi*" – "The Negus is making fun of us!!" Note the exclamation marks. And then this coda: "*Risposta immediata richiesta.*" – "Immediate reply required." Here is the date, which Mr Franco, being a good civil servant, helpfully provided, and here, too, the words "*Risposta mandata*" – "Reply sent." So it is clear that the Italians never accepted the Negus's version of events and wrote to him to say exactly that. I wonder why,' Winston said archly, 'my respected colleagues chose to submit the letter in this dramatically truncated form.'

Judge Mautner looked at the team pointedly, but they said nothing. Watts's blush had deepened, and his mouth was slightly open. Alexander was studiously ignoring Judge Mautner. Lips pursed, he was using one thumbnail to extract a white rind from below the other.

Winston powered ahead: 'The commission may be wondering how it was that these key annotations could be eliminated from the version it was shown. Yohannes?' Up on the screen appeared the original letter. Then a pair of scissors materialised and, accompanied by an audible snipping noise, methodically trimmed the letter of its marginalia. It was another pizza-box moment: a melodramatic flourish designed to sear itself into the commission's collective memory.

Yohannes sat back with an audible sigh of satisfaction. The PowerPoint mini-drama might have been directed by Winston, but he was the one who had made it possible. The foreign minister turned to him and bestowed a quiet nod of approval, Yohannes bowed his head in sudden pleased embarrassment. On such moments, it suddenly occurred to me, civil-service careers were built.

Winston had prepared his dish, now he merely had to garnish it. He surveyed the commissioners, the diplomats, the UN personnel sitting at the back of the room, leaning slightly into his own brief as he did so, one hand splayed masterfully on his papers. 'Any suggestion on our part of sleight of hand, of course, would be inappropriate, given counsel's long years of legal experience. We are confident the other side will be able to offer some explanation for what was clearly a partial presentation. We look forward to hearing their account.'

242

He gazed in silence at the other side. 'You lied and cheated and you were found out,' said his eyes.

'Lunch!' decreed Judge Mautner, bringing down his gavel with a flourish. He seemed to be enjoying himself.

When it came to their rebuttal, opposing counsel did what they could. They claimed Suleiman Jama was just one of many witnesses they could have called; his departure in no way affected a host of other testimonies. The 'incomplete nature' of the Heriu Tekle letter had been a surprise to them, they said, but did marginalia really matter? Their voices, though, were pitched apologetically low, and they had the lethargic gait of men wading through treacle. As Judge Mautner closed the proceedings, I thought I detected a new expression on the commissioners' faces when their eyes darted to counsel for the Federal Republic of Darrar: embarrassed compassion.

26

The team flew back to Lira within hours of the hearing's end, while I stayed on. I needed a haircut and wanted to buy a few sweaters for Lira's chilly evenings. But, waving Winston, Abraham and Yohannes off at Reception, I regretted my decision, feeling strangely bereft.

That night Sharmila called. 'Your friend came to the office,' she said, 'asking if you could get him some stuff in The Hague. I told him you were there to work. The power has been on and off, so I've had my hands full.'

'Friend?'

'You know, Gollum. The one with those awful shirts. He wants the latest Bollywood DVDs. He seemed to think The Hague would stock them.'

I groaned. 'I'll make a token effort, but no more.'

'Fine by me, sweetie. He's your friend. Oh, just one small question. Is it OK if Steve uses that empty cupboard in your bedroom to stow some things?'

'Is he moving in?' My heart sank.

'Oh, don't be silly!' Her voice was fluty and flirtatious. 'He just wants a bit of space for overnight stuff. Toothbrush, shaving tackle, a few T-shirts. All my drawers are full. You know me!' she chirruped.

'I'd rather he didn't, to be honest, Sharmila. I've got some confidential work-related stuff in there.' That was a lie. But I'd be damned if super-size Steve, having already carelessly occupied Sharmila and the bathroom, would now claim my bedroom.

Her voice went flat. 'Fine. Well, safe trip.'

Hanging up, I knew that she would immediately pass on this exchange to Steve. Over the next few days, just to show who was boss, the two of them would probably have sex on my bed, commenting as they did so on Paula Shackleton's lesbian proclivities and speculating, giggling, on how desperately I needed to buy myself a vibrator in Schiphol airport.

I slept deep into the following morning, eventually staggering, befuddled, out of my room. The hairdresser was a short stroll away, down a street lined with funeral parlours and wedding-dress hire shops. I felt a pang as I passed a couple of career women in patent leather heels and silk shirts, Prada bags brushing against one another as they gossiped, versions of the woman I used to be.

By dinner time I felt perky enough to ask the Royal Delft receptionist to book the best restaurant in the area. Chez Bertrand turned out to boast two Michelin stars, and when I walked in, taking in the huge vases of lilies and snooty-looking waiters gliding through the tables like eels, I was glad I had bothered to smarten up. I sat at my table reading a John Grisham novel between courses, and it was as I was walking out, tipsy after a half-bottle of St Émilion and two grappa chasers, that it happened.

I had collected my coat and was turning to place a coin in the cloakroom attendant's plate when I spotted – it prompted the instinctive recoil of a slap to the face – Judge Mautner and Eddie Connors at a table on the other side of the dining room. Opposite them sat the US ambassador to Lira, Brett's boss. For a moment, I thought it was just the three of them. Then

I realised that there was a fourth diner. His back was to me but his face was clear in the mirrored wall. Henry Alexander. My sudden stillness must have been as attention-grabbing as a gasp because Connors looked up and his eyes met mine. We gazed at one another for what seemed like a long time, and then he coolly resumed his conversation.

'What you saw doesn't, strictly speaking, break the rules,' said Winston.

I'd taken a taxi straight to the office from Lira airport, and Winston and I were sharing a morning coffee brewed in the kitchenette. The balcony on which we leaned overlooked the jumble of rotting tables and rusting machinery that decorated the back yard. Perhaps my ears were still humming from the overnight flight, but the old colonial apartment felt strangely muted, as if the staff were moving around on tiptoe.

'I know. "Arbitration is not a court case", as you keep saying. But I can't believe it's so different that *ex parte* communication is considered acceptable. What the hell were they talking about? And why wasn't Rainier included?'

'I'll raise this with Him. Maybe He can pursue it high up. But it's difficult to object furiously to something that doesn't violate the agreed rules of engagement.'

Winston looked recovered from the ordeal of the hearing, fuller in the face, the fatigue of a habitual over-worker once again held at bay.

'So, what's our next move, Winston? How long till the award? And what do we do while we wait for our suddenly slippery commissioners to make up their minds?'

'It could take six months, though I'm hoping it'll be quicker than that. In the meantime we prepare the case the other side was so desperate to foist on us, the who-started-it argument. Which allows us, finally, to use the material you gathered about Yala, showing a pattern of encroachment, so we can put the whole trigger incident in context. We're also going to need to prepare for demarcation of the border by the UN mission once the award's announced.'

'What are we talking about? Barbed wire? A fence? Not a wall, I assume – too much territory to cover.' How strange, I thought, that none of us had focused on this detail before: how the border that so preoccupied us would actually be marked.

'Concrete posts, I believe. Which will require a fair amount of logistics. Digging equipment, concrete mixers and the like. The UN will have to liaise with the two governments on how many peacekeepers they can deploy in the border area and which roads they can travel. Kennedy has asked me to draw up a Status of Forces agreement clarifying the relationship between the UN and the North Darrar government. And, Paula, I'm afraid there's bad news.'

'What?'

'We're going to be doing all this one man down. When we got back there was an envelope sitting on Yohannes's desk. He's to report for military service. His assignment with us is at an end.'

'You're kidding! After all he did in The Hague? Can't they see we need him?'

He looked at his feet. 'I suspect it's a case of the left hand not knowing what the right's doing.'

'I thought office staff were off the hook. How can the government expect us to win their case if they don't give us the personnel?'

'I'll talk to Buster and Kennedy, but I don't expect to win. The military-service issue is more than a national obsession. Doing it is regarded as virtually a quasi-religious duty. When you try to discuss it with people in government you hit a wall. It seems the rules are tightening because, yes, I, too, thought our staff were exempt. Yohannes is very upset.'

I'm upset too, I thought. Yohannes had been a stranger to

248

me until the hearing. I had just begun to like him. The office's muted atmosphere was suddenly explained.

'And you, what's your schedule?'

'You know me. I'll stay as long as I can.'

My memories of the days that followed the police visit are blurry. I do remember being granted a strange kind of reprieve, although I couldn't say when it descended or how long it lasted. Three days? An afternoon? All I know was that I felt befuddled, lost in the fog, but very happy. Jake was with me there, in Lake Cottage. He had heard my summons and I hugged him close. We had drifted apart in the previous months but now he was back. Reassuring, funny, warm.

But then the phone began to ring. I ignored the first calls, but it wouldn't stop. It rang and rang, each call an ugly interruption, breaking the harmony. They sucked me back into the world, kicking and struggling, and writhe as I might, I could not stop Jake slipping like egg white through my clenched fingers as I woke to this new, terrible world.

When I finally picked up, it was Sarah, her voice wobbly and excited. 'I only just heard. Why didn't you tell me? Are you OK?' At that moment, I hated my best friend, with a pure intensity, for ending my reprieve.

Fall in the Hudson River Valley was magnificent that year, and I was grateful, because it seemed only right and proper that Jake's departure from this world should be marked by that general, county-wide shedding of colour, vibrancy and light, as though Nature was joining me in stunned mourning. The bride has rose petals scattered before her as she walks down the aisle; Jake's passing into darkness was marked instead by a carpet of apple-red maple leaves, yellow oak and coppery beech. I walked through the drifts, kicking leaves into the air as Laurel and Hardy gambolled, barking in excitement. To my half-mad ears, the susurration of dry leaves around my boots sounded like a whisper of loss from the Earth itself.

Anxious and uncertain, the dogs had taken to joining me on the bed – I no longer bothered to banish them. As we sprawled in a rank jumble of heaving fur and dog breath each morning, scraps of consciousness swirled in search of an anchor. Half asleep, eyes squeezed tight, I would will the chaos to continue. I knew there was a reason to dread becoming compos mentis. But the fragments gyrated, found their niches in the jigsaw, awareness building bit by bit until – oh, hell – I was awake, all present and correct, Paula Shackleton, a woman with an unacceptable past and unimaginable future, who knew now that Jake was dead.

My mind churned every day through the facts of the case, travelling the same way-stations of shock, disbelief, guilt, anger and blame, only to find itself back at the circuit's start each morning. Doomed to trudge through the grey tedium of a grieving present, I longed to fast-forward my life and resurface six months later. 'It's all so tedious,' I told my mother one day on the phone, prompting a disapproving, prudish silence.

I needed to get away, but could not. I had to be there for the postman's morning delivery. What was I waiting for? Why, a letter from Jake, obviously, posted just before he died, a serene, philosophical, typically ironic letter in which he told me not to mind too much, that he would love me for ever, giving me a precious formula of words I would learn by heart to take me through the rest of my pathetic life. A letter Jake could never have written because he had not expected to drive off the bridge that day. But I nursed the fond fantasy until even I had to admit the deadline for an envelope working its way through the US postal system had passed. Nothing would be arriving. There were never going to be any answers: that would be my punishment for having taken Jake for granted. I could already see the years of merciless self-examination that lay ahead. And they bored me rigid.

Over my new excuse for breakfast – a cup of black coffee – I would stare at the calendar above the kitchen table, a glossy Japanese production showing the rolling hill towns of Umbria, which Jake and I had planned to visit. The calendar had undergone a strange metamorphosis, acquiring a new set of significant dates: 3 October, Last Supper; 5 October, Jake dies; 6 October, police come round; 1 November, Jake's funeral. They had been hiding there all this time, masquerading as days like any other. I had breezed heedlessly through those perverse anniversaries year after year, never feeling so much as a twinge of premonition. Now they would be etched on my brain for ever, to be lived through each year with a wince.

There were other dates hidden in the structure of that calendar, I realised, which I could not make out yet but which would one day become apparent. My parents' deaths. My own. Which day was that, then? If I concentrated hard enough, would I be able to guess?

The geography of my life was similarly strewn with booby traps. On my few trips to the village where Jake and I had done our shopping, I'd weave my way carefully from one side of the street to the other. No, not that bakery: that was where we always bought our wholegrain bread. The owner would be bound to ask after my 'husband'. I'd virtually sprint past the entrance to the fruit and vegetable store, where the old codger behind the till had always talked French cinéma noir with Jake. No condolences, please. Anonymous Walmart: that was good – in the morning when the aisles were quiet and the likelihood of a chance encounter almost zero.

I waited for the memories of Jake to start to flow, the memories that would bring me solace, little mental recordings of good times I could replay in my mind's eye, like a wedding video. But there were none. They had made their excuses and left.

'I don't understand it. I can't seem to remember Jake,' I confessed, sobbing one night over the phone to Sarah, a large

Scotch in front of me, scrunched-up tissues scattered around me like shrapnel.

'You're probably in shock.'

'I can't seem to remember his voice or the detail of any of our conversations. Is that possible? Can I have lived with this man for four years and not remember anything about him? He's always been the voice in my head, but now? Nothing.'

'Your mind is trying to help you by forgetting for the moment. Those things will come back.'

But they didn't. Or, rather, the only conversations that played back to me in high fidelity were the bad ones. My recall of the verbal ping-pong of our last argument was pitch perfect. But the touch of his fingers? The smell of his skin? The warmth of his body in bed? Even just one joke? How he kissed? That was all gone.

I watched television obsessively, the schlockier the better. The only other thing that seemed to work was retail therapy. When I finally returned to the city I found I could rarely bear to spend more than five minutes at my desk. I walked for hours. The girls in the kind of SoHo designer outlets where clothes lie individually wrapped in tissue paper learned not to bother chatting to the gaunt-faced woman trying on the new collection. I instinctively bought and dressed as though preparing for a funeral. When I finally came to empty the cottage's cupboards, I was confronted by a sea of black cashmere and silk. Only the best for Jake. He had always said I looked my sexiest when most severe.

27

On the morning after my return from The Hague I came downstairs to find Steve, enormous in his unyielding peace-keeper's uniform, with his head in the fridge. He straightened when he heard me and turned in mid-yawn, snapping his mouth shut like a tortoise.

'Looking for breakfast? I don't think there's much in there.'

'Yeah, I figured that out,' he said grumpily. 'Don't you guys ever eat? Vodka and cranberry juice seem to be as far as it goes. Get hammered, get laid, treat your urinary infections. Gotta love the new breed of woman.'

He extracted a Tetrapak and poured himself a large glass of juice, shook the carton against his ear and threw it casually into the dustbin. Then he stood, juice in one huge, freckled hand, gazing out at the back yard. The household's failure to provide him with a morning meal had clearly riled him: the set of his bull neck and shoulders radiated resentment. He watched in silence as Abraham drew up outside. I called a warning up the stairs, where I could hear Sharmila in the shower.

'So, another busy day at the office, eh?' Steve said, with heavy sarcasm.

'Yup.'

'Tell me. What I never really get about you lawyers is,' he

spun round with a pretend-curious smile on his face – goodness, I did not like this man – 'when you look at yourselves in the mirror in the morning, how do you justify what you do? I mean, you guys get to represent the government in The Hague, right? You collect all this evidence and stand up on your hind legs and somehow argue a case on behalf of North Diarrhoea, a shitty little police state that, when it's not too busy fighting Diarrhoea, gets a kick out of arresting its own citizens. A government that started a war, made sure it went on twice as long as necessary, then jailed anyone who pointed that out. And they sign your pay cheques. Ever bother you?'

I blinked. 'It's a bit early for this, isn't it?' Why was he arguing with me when he could have it out with his girlfriend?

'Just wondering.' His eyes were wide with fake innocence.

'You're on the UN's payroll. That might keep some people awake at night.'

He scoffed. 'Not quite the same thing, though, is it? You can accuse the UN of incompetence, most people do, but it doesn't make life so unbearable the locals will do literally anything to get away. You guys should see the reports that come across my desk. We just got another – a hundred and sixty refugees drowned in a boat that sank in the Mediterranean, most of 'em from here. I guess ignorance is bliss. Don't ask, don't tell, eh?'

Sharmila was taking her time upstairs. I was stuck till she emerged. I debated going outside for a cigarette, then thought, No, I'll take him on.

'OK, let me run you through this, Steve. It's not that hard. Think of the most heinous criminal in recent US history. Timothy McVeigh, perhaps? And as he's walking out of the courtroom, where he's just confessed to making the bomb that killed all those toddlers, someone steps out of the crowd and shoots him. He's rushed to the emergency room where the surgeon fights like a demon to save his life. It would never occur to you to tell that surgeon what you just said to me.

Because if you did, he'd say, "What are you talking about? This is what I spent years training to do. I do it very well, and this is what our society has decided is a fundamental human right." So why is McVeigh's lawyer any different? Why despise the lawyer and admire the surgeon?'

'It's not a valid analogy.'

'Why not?'

'Because the surgeon values human life, which is an absolute good, and you guys ... Well, God knows what you guys value. Winning for the sake of winning, even when you're representing a bunch of assholes. Your own salaries. You tell me. There's a reason for all the jokes about lawyers at the bottom of the sea.'

'How about the principle of a fair trial? If you believe in an adversarial system of justice, in thrashing out arguments in public, then you accept the principle that McVeigh should get the best representation the legal system can offer. I'd be perfectly happy to work for someone like that,' I claimed. Even as the words left my mouth I wondered if they were true.

'I must see you. Come to Zombie's NOW,' read the note on my desk.

The peremptory tone immediately put my hackles up. Sharmila and I had just emerged from Winston's office, where the three of us had agreed to focus our attentions on the guards killed during the original border incident in Sanasa. 'We need to know if they had children, wives, dependents, where they prayed, what card games they preferred. We need to turn them into fully rounded human beings who were slaughtered and left grieving relatives behind, not statistics. And photographs, I need photographs,' said Winston. But, reasoning that I might as well get it over with, I made my excuses and set off. I found Dawit on the large chocolate-coloured sofa, scowling at the barman, who scowled back with equal malevolence. He gestured for me to join him at a table in the tiny courtyard at the back, away from prying eyes.

'What's up, Dawit?'

'I have to leave. You must help.'

I felt a sour twinge of disappointment. I had been half anticipating this request from the day we'd met. 'Just you wait. All they want from a Westerner is a visa,' had run the line in my mother's email: she had picked up on a mention of 'a possible new friend' in Lira. Dawit's steady failure to live down to her expectations had been a quiet source of satisfaction to me. Not any more.

'You and a million others. You know there's nothing I can do on that front, Dawit, so why ask?'

He stared at the wall and tightened his jaw. I gradually registered how dreadful he looked. The hollows around his eyes were the colour of ripe plums. He had not shaved for days, and the uneven patches of black stubble gave his face a mottled appearance. He was sporting the full Afro, in which I could spot specks of lint. His eyes were more watery than I'd ever seen them, and it occurred to me that he might have been crying. 'This is the only favour I will ever ask you, Paula. Just this once. To save my life. You must know people.'

I placed a hand gently on his skinny wrist. 'What on earth has happened? You always said you wanted to stay. Why this change of heart?'

He took a deep breath, nearly a gulp, grimaced over the dregs of his cold cappuccino, and began. 'You know my idea for the cybernet café? Last week I finally received the satellite-dish equipment I ordered from Dubai. So I told the builder to pour the cement for the foundation. A great day. If you hadn't been in The Hague I would have invited you to watch.'

'I would have liked that.'

'We were about to start on the walls. These buildings don't take long to put up. So yesterday I went to the Ministry of Trade to get a licence. You need a licence for everything here, to run a café, to own a car, to fart, to sleep, to fuck. So I take my number and I queue for two hours and I hand in my ever-so-carefully filled-in form, all in my best handwriting. And the official, you know what he does?' He looked at me with huge spaniel eyes, his cigarette trembling in his hand.

'What?'

'He laughs in my face. Yes, he laughs. He asks me if I would like to tear up the application right now, or whether I prefer him to do it after I have left. He tells me I should read the newspaper more carefully. And then he shows me a very teeny article reporting that the government has withdrawn the licences of the cybernet cafés in Lira and advising the owners that they must either remove the satellite dishes or turn the premises over to the government. The article quotes the minister of trade as saying these cafés have become "hotbeds of political intrigue" – hotbeds! – and are being used by enemy spies. The internet is the new front line and the government must control it, for the sake of the nation, blah-blah-blah.'

Oh, God. 'Is there any chance this is just a temporary thing, while the crisis lasts?'

He laughed bitterly. 'What makes you think this crisis is temporary, Paula? You haven't read your Orwell. Dictators make sure their countries are in permanent crisis so they always have an excuse.' It was the first time I'd heard him describe the president in that way. 'At the moment we are in an unde-clared state of war with A, next year it will be B, the year after that C, and then we can go back to A, maybe. We have six neighbours. There are plenty of variations available.'

I tried desperately to think of some solution. 'What if you open a café without the cyber bit?'

He shook his head. 'Oh, I asked that, too. There was no level of begging I would not stoop to. And this bastard laughed again. He was having his funniest morning for the year. And he said that in future any new cafés in Lira would be opened by the government. Apparently His Supreme Greatness has finally understood that the private sector cannot be trusted, so in future the government will run the economy.'

'Jesus.'

'But you know the real reason, Paula?' He pointed a trembling finger at me. 'This guy says to me, "Did you really think we fought the revolution, my brother, in order for a bunch of teenagers with their arses falling out of their jeans to watch porn?" As though a man like that ever carried a gun.' He snorted. 'It's envy. "We suffered, so now you must, too." I hate that mentality.'

'I'm so sorry.'

'So, that is the end of my dream,' he said dully. 'I went out to the site and I told the builder to go home. He will take the bricks and the bags of cement and sell them. That bit is easy. The satellite dish will be harder. I'll try to sell it on the black market, but who will want it? Maybe some cabinet minister who fancies watching Manchester United at home. There's probably a law against that, too.

'There is nothing left for me in this place. Living in a police state is a habit, like everything else, and if I stay I will get the habit, coming to Zombie's, going home, coming here, going home, backwards and forwards, backwards and forwards, backwards and forwards ...' his voice rose in a strained falsetto, reaching a near scream, and then he pounded the table, our cups bouncing on its metal surface, bellowing '... UNTIL I FUCKING DIE.'

The barman came over, threw Dawit a meaningful glance, then walked away. I waited for his rage to subside. Finally, he said quietly, 'This place is only good for people who have already died inside. You can see that for yourself. So you must help me leave.'

I kneaded my forehead in my hands. 'Oh, Dawit, Dawit, I wish I could. I could help you get a US visa – I can act as guarantor – but that's not the point. You need the exit permit from the Ministry of Immigration. And I have no sway there.

In fact, if I intervene, it could make things worse. Winston tried it a while back with an intern, and that intern is still stuck in Lira. "No special favours," we're always told.'

There was a long pause while he digested my refusal. So that's the end of the friendship, I thought. It was nice while it lasted. I felt numb.

Finally, he nodded. 'OK, I understand. Forget.' His tone was surprisingly gentle. 'I had to ask.'

'I know.'

He was silent for a long while.

'Can you do me a smaller favour, then? If I cannot leave, then I need a proper job in Lira, or I will go crazy. The UN peacekeeping force is advertising. Support-staff jobs. Would you provide me with a character reference? Lie and say how much you like my driving and how punctual I am.'

Something I could do. 'Of course. Just give me the form.'

He was kneading his forehead as he thought. 'Once I have my toe in the UN crack, I will work my way. You have never seen that side of me, Paula. I have been a layabout all these months because I was working on the cybernet café, but I know how to make myself indispensable. It was how I survived at the front. The commanders needed me too much to send me off to die.'

The moment of desperation had passed. He had recovered. He was already working out possibilities, making plans. But I noticed, as we talked, that he was no longer meeting my eyes.

Sarah came to stay for a few days, stopping off on her way back from a conference in Mexico. 'I'll have you know that I've never been involved in anything like this before, but I'm going to do my best,' she announced, when I opened Lake Cottage's door.

She was good at inventing obligatory little tasks – 'We have to go shopping now, Paula, there's nothing in the fridge'; 'We have to walk the dogs – they're going crazy'; 'We have to clear the gutters or those leaves will block the drains.' We worked ourselves into a sweat raking the lawn and burning leaves and, as the mundane routine took over, I found myself joshing with her, greedily soaking up her stories of office gossip and sexual peccadilloes, anything as long as it wasn't Jake.

But in the evenings, over suppers I could only pick at, the horrors re-established their dominion. The first few nights, I kept them to myself. Noticing my tight mouth and hunched shoulders, she switched on the television and thrust a glass of wine into my hand. 'I brought a couple of mindlessly cheerful 1950s rom-coms, the ones you like.' We pretended to watch them. On the third night, my defences crumbled, and I gave her a blow-by-blow account of what had happened in the days leading up to Jake's death.

Sarah gazed at me uncertainly. 'I don't really get this, to be honest. I've never understood why people get so fixated with the precise circumstances in which people die. If you and I had a row right now, I stormed out and got flattened just outside the gates by a truck, you'd obsess about the fact that we were on bad terms at the precise moment that the tyres ran over my chest. But why pick that split-second? Why is it representative? Why does it matter more than a split-second two hours earlier when we were giggling over a coffee, or all those evenings when we did homework together as kids, or played rounders in your back garden? Why does one atypical moment – certainly not a moment that held the key to our relationship – cancel out a lifetime's friendship?

'OK, so you had a period of estrangement from Jake. Do those months really "count"' – she crooked her fingers in aerial quotation marks – 'for more than the four years you spent with him? You two were good together, Paula, good enough for me to envy you, truth be told. I'm willing to bet you would have got back together again. Don't overdo the self-flagellation.

What did the workers trapped in the Twin Towers do when they realised they weren't going to survive? They called their girlfriends, husbands and mums to tell them they loved them. Dying gives you a sense of perspective. Do you really think as the BMW flew off the bridge that Jake was going through a Paula-said-this-and-then-I-said-that-and-God-she's-being-such-a-bitch routine in his head? Give him a bit of credit. If he thought about anything at all, he was thinking, I'm about to die and I really love her.'

We were both weeping now. 'But I'm never going to know that for certain.' My voice came out as a croak. 'For all I know, he looked across the seat at his wife and thought, I'm glad she and I are here, dying together. I may have strayed but this is the one who really matters. And you have to admit, Sarah, that that rather pulls the rug from under my feet. I don't know whether I even have the right to mourn Jake. Maybe I'm the fool of the piece.'

She sighed and wiped her cheekbones, smearing mascara across her face. She pottered around the kitchen for a bit, hunting for teabags, then turned to look at me. 'You have a point. But even if that happened – and I doubt it – it doesn't wipe out your time together. Nothing can. Perhaps it might help – I know you're a joy-defying puritan at heart – if you tell yourself that that question is your life sentence, the price you have to pay for being a bit of a bitch at the end. Call it God having His ironic belly laugh.'

'It's a fuck of a heavy price.'

She thought for a moment. 'You know that Rolling Stones song, "You can't always get what you want, but you might get what you need"? It's not quite right, I've worked out. You get what you can stand. If you couldn't stand it, you'd check out before you got there. In your case, I think you can stand a lot. You're pretty tough, Paula.'

28

Abraham was standing in front of my desk, wearing an unfathomable expression. 'Paula, I just got a call. The man did not identify himself. It was a bad connection, a mobile phone. He mentioned you. He said there had been some problem and that the doctor we met at the IDP camp – you remember him? The one who was arrested?'

'George?'

'Yes, George. The man said he is at Victory Hospital and we should go and find him there. *Right away*, he said.'

I looked around the office. Winston had closed his door and was in murmured conversation inside with Sharmila. No point disturbing that. Two interns were on the balcony, sharing a coffee. 'You got the car keys?'

'Yes.' We clattered down the marble stairs and I watched as he reversed the Toyota from its tight parking space in the courtyard with urgent precision. I hopped up into the passenger seat and we hit the main road, Abraham somehow managing to lock the doors, light a cigarette and switch on the air-conditioning as he roared through the gear changes.

'But who was it?'

'I don't know. When I asked him, he said, "Just you go," and then we either lost the connection or he hung up. But I think ...' He frowned.

'Yes?'

'I think it may have been Sammy.'

Victory Hospital, a white two-storey building on a scrubby stretch on the outskirts of town, had been a gift from the People's Republic of China. A symbol of co-operation, it replaced Lira's colonial-era hospital, where settlers and Africans had once been treated in separate tin-roofed wings and family dependants camped on the lawns, draping drying laundry over the decorative flowerbeds. I had heard that the new facility was clean, modern and had a range of scanners the envy of the Horn of Africa. But it had the feel of a laptop computer that has yet to be extracted from its polystyrene packaging. Its glass front doors were smeared with the dusty handprints of the labourers who had installed them. I could see a couple of stainless-steel trolleys, still wrapped in plastic, parked down a corridor, and a stack of painted signs leaning against a wall.

Abraham and I paced the lobby, waiting for a member of staff to materialise. I was beginning to feel uneasy. If George was still in detention, he might be there under armed guard. We might not be allowed to speak to him. That would be even likelier if we asked permission of a receptionist with no real authority. I looked at Abraham and could see he was thinking along similar lines.

'Let's find him ourselves.'

We pushed on the nearest swinging doors and walked quietly through Accident & Emergency, pretending to know where we were going. Only two beds were occupied: a grandfather attached to an IV, mouth agape, wizened hands curled like crow's feet on a bony chest; and a bored-looking young man with a bandaged leg, running a rosary through his hands. The rest of the beds were unmade; their red plastic mattresses had never been used.

Swinging through the doors on the other side, we paused. 'OK, we need to be systematic,' said Abraham. 'Military-style operation.' We cased what was clearly Paediatrics next. A boy

264

with an arm in plaster stared at us from his bed with soulful eyes as his mother stroked his brow. On another bed, a four-year-old was being rocked in the arms of a young woman. There was no one else. And so it went on: we sidestepped Surgery, Maternity, X-ray and Diagnostics and then – after exchanging apprehensive glances – ventured carefully into ICU. A young man, his face sallow with pain, lay sprawled behind a blue curtain, an oxygen mask over his face. It was not George. We took the stairs at a run and checked out Oncology, Geriatric, Male, and Geriatric, Female. Nothing.

'I don't understand it,' I whispered. 'We've been in just about every ward and haven't met a single member of staff. This is the *Mary Celeste* of hospitals. Where is everyone?'

'At lunch?'

'All of them? At the same time?'

We returned to the lobby. We looked up hopefully when we heard a woman's heels, running, but they were not heading our way and the sound faded. A snatch of conversation exploded and was abruptly cut off, perhaps by one of those swinging doors. Abraham shrugged and went outside to light a cigarette, gazing into the near distance. I hiked myself up on the main desk, bottom in the air, craning to see if I could spot a register, files of any kind. I whipped around at a sharp tapping noise, fearing I'd been caught in the act. It was Abraham, rapping his knuckles on the dirty glass wall and gesturing for me to join him.

'There's one place we have not looked,' he said sombrely, inclining his head. 'There.'

I followed his line of sight and felt a wrench to my stomach. 'HOSPITAL MORGUE,' read the sign. 'STAFF ONLY'.

I think we both saw it at the same time. A trail of dark blotches running from a bristle of weeds over the gravel to the concrete ramp that disappeared under the morgue's metal doors. There the trail became a scarlet smear, the sort left when a leaking package is dragged rather than carried. Abraham walked over slowly, inspecting the ground, then crouched and touched the smear with one long, elegant finger. He looked at me, straightened and pushed at the doors with two hands.

Noise, fear and panic hit us in the face.

The staff were all inside, of course: that was why we hadn't bumped into any of them. They were working frantically over the multi-limbed heap that covered most of the floor. Some of the bodies were wrapped, Lazarus-style, in white winding sheets, but most were clothed, dusted in blue-grey powder. There had not been time for cosmetic preparation or discreet concealment. Looking around, I took in a snarling grimace of teeth, curled fingers, an exposed buttock, bare feet that had lost their shoes in some final, scrabbling panic. A splinter of bone poked untethered from a thigh; a curl of yellow entrails trickled, obscenely suggestive, from a stomach gash. I found myself, surreally, thinking of the offal that hangs in the windows of Chinese restaurants. They did not smell. Or, rather, they did not smell as I expected – the sweet stink of putrefaction you so often read about. No, they smelt of ... fresh meat. Which was disgusting in its own way. Human beings are supposed to smell of sweat and sex, hormones and vomit. They should not bring to mind fresh sawdust and a butcher's chopping block.

As the light streamed in, everyone froze and looked up, like murderers caught in some terrible act. Then the paused video returned to 'play'. A middle-aged doctor was shouting instructions to two morgue attendants, one of whom shouted back. His voice had slipped into a higher register, near hysterical with – what? Anger? Fear? The veins stood out in his neck. His colleague, hovering over that jumbled pile of human meat as though uncertain where to start, turned from time to time to join in, his gesticulations of frustration unmistakable. A stocky matron pulled on the arms of a shoeless corpse, aiming a flood of high-pitched recrimination at a young nurse, whose uniform was smeared with some livid paste too thick to be blood. Sobbing quietly, the girl obediently bent, picked up the feet, and the two transferred the jack-knifed body to a trestle table.

'Yes? What is it?' A woman in a beige suit, her face made up with incongruous care, was at our elbows: our missing receptionist.

I stared at her, my mind blank.

'We were called here.' said Abraham. His voice was impressively steady. He had given nothing away, while careful not to tell an actual lie.

He turned to me. 'Paula. Have a look and see if you can find him.' *I can keep her occupied*, said his eyes. *But not for long.*

I turned back to the pile. How to tell him, this battle-hardened colleague, that I had managed to reach my mid-thirties without ever seeing a dead body, that in my pampered culture this was not a moment to be quietly risen to, as he clearly expected, but would be regarded as providing meaty – ah, meaty, very witty – fodder for the therapist's couch? I took two steps towards the weeping nurse, who was now bending over a second trousered body, wrapping her arms around its knees to get a better grip.

And then I recoiled, so suddenly that the nurse looked up in shock, the black kohl smudged around her wet eyes. Behind her, I had spotted George. Stacked on a shelf on his back, sandwiched by two other bodies in a grotesque version of Sardines. A purplish bruise disfigured the side of his face, one eye was half open – I could see the iris, clouded like that of a fish on a slab – and he had lost a tooth. But the neat, clipped beard was unmistakable and so was his aquiline profile. He was wearing the same blue-and-white-checked shirt he'd had on when we'd first met at the IDP camp.

I took a deep breath. 'He's over there,' I said, jerking my head to where George lay. My voice was shaking.

Abraham continued murmuring to the receptionist, nodding

sympathetically. She was talking in a low, urgent voice, interspersing her comments with sharp little intakes of breath. She lifted one nail-varnished hand to wipe away a tear. 'If you want to find out what his wounds are, Paula, this is the only chance you will have,' he commented quietly.

'I'm not ... I'm not sure ...' I looked at the white daylight framing the exit. 'I have to get out of here, Abraham.'

'OK. Wait outside.'

I stumbled to the exit, sending the doors swinging like a drunk cowboy. Outside, I sat on the ground and put my head between my knees, shutting my eyes. I opened them as a white Toyota pickup drew up, braking hard. Two middle-aged men in anonymous beige windcheaters got out. They did not waste any time with the main doors or Reception, heading straight towards the morgue, men on a mission. The clean-up squad? They stopped when they saw me, momentarily nonplussed.

'Who are you?' said the older one, who sported a thin moustache. Both his eyebrows were notched.

No point lying. There were so few foreigners in Lira that anonymity was never an option: you left a trail of sightings like fox scent wherever you went. 'A British lawyer. I work for the government.'

'What are you doing here?'

'Following up an enquiry,' I said, mimicking Abraham. Vague but accurate.

Now his colleague spoke. He had a coarse, broad face and two gold teeth. His English was nothing like as good as the first man's, so he dispensed with politeness. 'You leave.'

'I am waiting for a colleague.'

'Leave.' He jerked his head back to the gate.

I couldn't leave. Not without Abraham. My voice shook as I attempted a show of courage. 'And who are you, may I ask?'

The smoother colleague interrupted: 'Ministry of the Interior. We have come to help the people at the hospital. There has been an accident. Some of our boys have died.'

I know. I saw them. And then, finally, Abraham emerged. The three men stared at each other for a moment, some form of exchange taking place, a silent assessment. It occurred to me that they had probably seen action together.

'Let's go,' I said, and the next moment we were in the Land Cruiser, heading back to the office.

Abraham took a right off the main road, turned into a quiet suburban street, took a left and parked under a fig tree, so sharply my head nearly hit the windscreen. He switched off the engine. 'The office can wait a bit,' he said quietly, avoiding eye contact. It was easier, that way, for both of us to pretend not to notice that I was weeping, not like a grown adult but a thwarted toddler, a hand clamped over my mouth, tears streaming down my nose and dribbling over my fingers.

As I gulped and gasped, he took two paper tissues from a pocket and handed me one, then used the other to dab fastidiously at a bloodstain on the sleeve of his soft suede jacket.

'What ... what did you see?' I managed at last.

'He was shot. Twice in the chest. Here and here,' he said, picking out the wounds on his own body with precision.

'From behind or in front?'

'I don't know. I am not a pathologist, Paula.'

'No, I'm sorry. Stupid question. But what the fuck happened? All those bodies ... all those young men. How many were there?' I had failed in every respect. Failed to establish the circumstances of George's death, failed to check genders, failed even to count the bodies, the most basic piece of information. Shame swept over me like a rash.

'The receptionist said seventeen.'

'Only seventeen? It looked more, many more.'

'Dead bodies always look more,' he said quietly. 'Because one is already too many.'

'So what happened? Was this an execution? Oh, God, poor George.'

He stared at me with reproof. 'We are not in Congo. The

269

receptionist said those youngsters all came from the central prison, the old Italian one near the shoe factory.'

Prison? George? But of course. We had failed to spring him, after all.

'I think I recognised a few of them, boys from decent families, jailed for refusing to do military service. They were all placed in the same cell, along with some thieves and murderers. The receptionist says it is not clear what happened. Maybe there was a protest, maybe just too many people in a small space. I've seen those cells. Sometimes they squeeze so many people in that everyone must sleep upright. She said some of the dead were crushed, others shot by the guards.'

'But why?'

'Who knows what happened?' he said. 'She was not there. And neither were we. We can guess, that is all.'

We sat in silence for a while.

'Do you think Sammy – if it was Sammy – already knew that George was dead when he sent us to the hospital?'

'Oh, yes, I think so. He just wanted us to see it.' The need to bear witness, I thought. The instinct of the investigative journalist and human-rights activist. George's passing had, at least, been acknowledged.

Abraham ran a hand down his face, as if wiping away the vision of the morgue. He opened the door a crack and spat onto the cement verge. Then he yanked the door closed, leaned over the steering-wheel and reached for the ignition. His voice was stubbornly matter-of-fact. 'It is a big shame. A big shame. This country needs qualified doctors. Now we have one less.'

The following day, Winston summoned me into his office and gestured at me to sit. 'I saw Him today, to discuss the AU inquiry. The incident at the prison came up.'

'Aha,' I said, noncommittally.

'It's going to be on the television news tomorrow. They're

270

waiting to contact each of the seventeen families first, just as we would in the US. It's the considerate course of action.'

A memory jolt: of baying Laurel and Hardy and that awkward police duo, doing their reluctant duty. 'The considerate course of action might have involved not shooting them, I'd have thought. Did the president go into what happened?'

'At greater length than I'd expected. It appears to have been a tragic combination of inexperience, incompetence and panic. Apparently there'd been growing unhappiness among a group of the conscientious objectors, if we can call them that. Your friend George, I was told, was part of that more vocal group … In fact, I gather he was its ringleader.'

'Good for him,' I said defiantly.

'Over the weekend, the more experienced prison guards went home, handing over the keys to a bunch of conscripts. Usually guards empty the cells in shifts so that everyone takes a turn in the yard. Because these guards were new to the job they emptied everyone out at the same time, which seems to have created a volatile situation. The conscientious objectors got chatting to the guards, asking to be set free. Some of the young men were sympathetic to their arguments and showed signs of weakening. Others held firm. At this stage George and his friends began kicking at the main wall. The building dates back to the Italian era and it's been crumbling for years. When the other prisoners saw that the wall was collapsing, they piled in. Then the conscripts, realising they had a prison break on their hands, lost their nerve and opened fire. He said that if the older, permanent, members of staff had been on duty that weekend probably nothing would have happened.'

'Whatever happened to shooting in the air? Or at people's legs? George was hit in the chest. Twice.'

'That's what happens when young men with guns, who are afraid of looking stupid in the eyes of their superiors, panic.'

'And the crushed bodies?'

271

'Flattened by the falling wall. Or trodden on by inmates scrambling for the exit.'

'So let me get this right. George is actually responsible for his own shooting. If he hadn't behaved like a firebrand and whipped up the mob, he'd be alive today. Is that what we're supposed to think?'

'It was a horrible, avoidable tragedy, Paula, and everyone regrets it bitterly. I've rarely heard Him sound more sombre. He made no excuses, just recounted the sorry chain of events.'

'But none of this addresses the central question, does it, Winston? Which is that George shouldn't have been in an overcrowded cell in the first place. He hadn't committed any crime, unless being a bit of a loudmouth counts. He hadn't been charged, as far as we know, and he certainly hadn't been allowed to see a lawyer – I'd have been the first one there. There's no way of getting round that. And while others may not get too excited about the total disregard for due process and denial of basic human rights, I can't help feeling that, as lawyers, we should.'

Winston bowed his head and shut his eyes for a moment, his hands resting flat on the desk's surface, like a yoga practitioner's. Then he gave me a long look.

'Paula, I'm only going to say this once. George's death was repugnant and clearly unnecessary. But the administration of justice in developing countries that have just come through a war is often an imperfect, rough-and-ready affair. I'm taken aback when I see the old man at the school gates near my villa caning pupils who arrive a few minutes late. Back home, he'd be arrested for child abuse. The husband in the villa next to mine, a sophisticated man with whom I've discussed local birdlife, beats his wife regularly: I hear her screams. This is a society that has soaked up violence for centuries, and violence will take a long time to drain away and be replaced by something as dull and colourless as the process you and I believe in. That is, actually, why we do what we do here. I consider our efforts part of a long-term campaign to implant the rule of law. But none of that will happen overnight. And in the meantime, we must practise a little selective blindness, if you wish, in a greater cause. Don't fall into the classic American trap, Paula, of reducing everything to the individual – you're too intelligent for that. George was one man, just *one man*, and what we're doing here is going to affect the lives of millions. Whatever your young man felt about the government, I bet he loved his country enough to want us to secure its borders, and that's what I'm focusing on right now. One step at a time, sweet Jesus, one step at a time.'

I never got to see Jake's body. I wasn't invited to the funeral or the reception, attended, according to the local newspaper, by more than four hundred relatives, friends and dignitaries. That day I was walking Laurel and Hardy. I pressed my back into the wet bushes as the chauffeur-driven limousines swept by on the way to the wake at Griffin House, laden with well-dressed, subdued families in black, navy and grey. Cream silk scarves, a glint of pearls around withered necks, a hat. I suspect they mistook me, in my muddy wellingtons and faded jeans, with my frizz of uncombed hair, for a gardener.

The day after, Sophie called. Her voice was tight, higher-pitched than usual. 'Look, this really isn't a conversation I want to have but I'm calling on behalf of all of us because there are some things we have to figure out and everyone is hoping we can be adult about it because that's what my dad would have wanted,' she gabbled. 'Charlotte, Eric … Aunt Julia, well, everyone agrees the time has come,' she spoke as though Jake had been dead several years, 'for you to move out.'

'How long do I have?'

She ignored the question. 'We're thinking of renting out Lake Cottage. We're going to sell the Jetta. And the paintings.

Charlotte asked me specifically to mention the Klimt litho-graphs. She wants them valued.'

'They're not worth much, actually.'

'Well, that's not for you to judge, is it?' She ran through the other items Jake's children 'expected to find' in the cottage once I had cleared out: a long list of my anticipated larceny. I kept hoping her tone would change. This was plump, bosomy Sophie, with whom I had sat at the kitchen table to discuss boyfriends; Sophie, to whom I had recommended Clearasil, who used to run up and hug me ostentatiously to her bulky breasts at family reunions, hoping to shame Charlotte and Eric out of their stiff handshakes. In her grief, she had returned to the fold. She had seen the error of her ways and would not serve as my Trojan horse again, the hard little voice was telling me.

I tried softening my own, because there was a piece of information I craved that only someone in the family could provide. Who but Sophie would relent long enough to let me have it? And this, I knew, was going to be my last opportunity. Once this conversation was over I would never hear from her again.

'Sophie, there's something I don't understand. How come your mother was in the car that day?'

She made a strangled noise and half sobbed, half shrieked her answer. 'I would have thought that was obvious!'

'What do you mean?'

'They were going to give it another try!'

I felt myself flushing, my hand on the receiver juddering with adrenalin. 'Do you know that for a fact, or is it just speculation?'

'Why else would they have both been in the car? If you had only agreed to bow out, Paula, if you hadn't always been so selfish, they'd probably have got back together ages ago. Charlotte and I have always been convinced of that.'

I clenched the receiver. As crumpled tissues were honked

into, hot-water bottles clutched, vodka bottles gradually emptied, an Orwellian rewriting of history had clearly taken place in the Wentworth household. And, as always happens when I am confronted with a claim so wild it seems to come from a parallel universe, my brilliant legal brain couldn't conjure up a single argument in my own defence. Only a limp 'That's just not true, Sophie. The problems between your parents predated me by years.'

She had recovered her poise. 'Look, I just said, I don't want to talk about this stuff. Could you just drop the keys off at the lawyers' office? Or leave them in the cottage when you go. Charlotte and Eric don't want to see you. They blame you for the separation.'

A morsel of charity there because what she actually meant, I knew, was 'We blame you for their deaths.' Grief is a cluster bomb. It scythes down anything in its path.

'Oh, and, Paula, one last thing. You can keep Laurel and Hardy. I know Dad really loved them and all that, but Charlotte's allergic to dog hair and Eric doesn't have room in his apartment.'

'Couldn't Aunt Julia take them? I don't know my plans.'

'She's got cruises booked and says Miguel won't have time to exercise them while she's away.' And taking custody of the dogs might conceivably mean meeting me face to face, of course, a scenario she was determined to avoid.

So I was homeless, car-less, Klimt-less, but I had two pedigree dogs worth around three thousand dollars a head to my name. Maybe, I thought, I could eat them.

29

'Why are you so upset? Unless I missed something, you hardly knew the guy.' Dawit was looking at me with curiosity.

'It's the waste of it all. I can't bear it. I feel guilty, too. We're lawyers, we should have got George out. Instead, I made a token effort and left it at that. And then ...'

'What?'

'Sometimes I have a superstitious feeling' – a big bubble of air was rising up my throat, suddenly making speaking difficult – 'that if I take a liking to a man, I've signed his death warrant.'

In all our drinking sessions, it was an area we had never explored: my life before Lira. So I finally told him the story of Jake, the Last Supper, the accident and my recruitment in the lobby of a Boston hotel.

Dawit stared at me. Then he looked at what remained of his beer, swilled it around in the bottle, downed it, studied the floor for a long while and raised his eyes to stare at me again. It was not a friendly look.

A split-second ago we had been sharing intimacies but now he seemed utterly distant, a spindly stranger sporting a velveteen trouser suit that bordered on the ridiculous, the kind of nicotine-stained bar regular I'd normally have moved discreetly across the room to avoid.

'So,' he finally pronounced. 'So, after all. After all there has been between us, it turns out you are one of them.'

'One of who? What are you talking about, Dawit?'

He put the beer bottle down, gestured to the barman and started, with some difficulty, teasing coins from the pocket of his hip-hugging trousers. 'There's a film showing at the Cinema Gloria I want to see,' he muttered. 'It involves a great number of dancing girls. A friend told me the hip-grinding is so explicit he almost embarrassed himself.'

'You're off? Right now?' I was baffled. 'What's going on, for fuck's sake?'

He paid for the beer, not looking at me. Then he took out and lit a cigarette, and deigned finally to meet my eyes.

'What I always liked about you, Paula, was your honesty. Your cynicism. You were straight. You told me you came here to do your job and earn a nice fat salary. It was such a relief. I cannot tell you how bored I get – we all get – of you Westerners and your perverted motives.'

'"Perverted"? Isn't that a bit strong?'

'I wonder, was the African continent created just to provide poor little whiteys with somewhere to hide? You are like children running away from those strange schools English novelists write about, the ones full of homosexualists. But none of you are honest enough to admit it. No, you have to dress it all up and suddenly, a miracle, it turns out that you're actually doing us Africans a favour. Putting your careers on hold. Risking your lives. Spending years on Lariam – terrible side-effects, you know. All just to rescue us – God save us from your fucking salvation – to feed us, cure us, train us, train us to train others, teach a fish to catch a fish to eat a fish and all that bullshit' – *boulesheeet* – 'to make us care about democracy and human rights and then scold us when we don't care enough.'

He was in full rant now, middle finger jabbing at me, cigarette ash scattering like dandruff.

'What's the slogan on the statue, Paula?'

'Which statue?'

'Statue of Liberty, that one, yes! "Give me your tired, your poor, your huddled masses." Africa's slogan, what is it? "Give me your preachers, your fucked-up journalists, your secret racists and all the wankers' – *wunkers* – 'who wouldn't get a job with a villa, pool and driver anywhere else.'

'You're being obnoxious, Dawit.'

'You know, I thought, with you, I had met the first foreigner with pure motives, which means, for me, normal human motives. The profit motive, that's something a former Communist like me can respect. Not some personal neurosis twisted like one of those American pretzels' – his hands and arms were snaking around one another now, his face contorted with simulated discomfort – 'till you turn it into something noble. And then it turns out that lovely Paula is one of our continent's many damaged Western imports. I suppose you thought since your life was ruined, your Jake dead, you might as well donate what was left to Africa. Are we supposed to be grateful for the crumbs?'

My face was ablaze. I had given my only friend in Lira custody of this, the black hole of my life, and he had doused me with mockery.

'This is just revenge, because I couldn't get you an exit visa.'

Now he was unbuttoning the top of his shirt, a psychedelic monstrosity of swirling 1970s design. 'You people ...' Dawit's fingers were shaking '... you people are so scarred. Well, you know what? I can beat you for scars.' I could see it now. A shiny yellow snake that extended from his collar-bone, missing the nipple, to a strange puckered valley above his stomach. His navel winked at me, two inches to the left of the standard position.

'For God's sake, button up, Dawit.' I could see the barman glowering at us. Maybe he'd seen this performance before.

'I remember now who you remind me of. It's the nun in

that old movie, the one played by Katharine Hepburn, who cuts off her hair and goes to the Congo.'

'Audrey, not Katharine. Audrey Hepburn.' My throat felt so clotted I could barely get the words out.

'Audrey, Katharine … I don't give a shit,' He put his hands together, cigarette still burning, in mock prayer. 'The doe eyes, the Little Miss behaviour, that constant expression of smug self-righteousness … Yup, that's you, Paula. You once told me this country's appeal was that it was a blank place on the map. This isn't the Middle Ages. Did you expect two-headed monsters, men with eyes in the middle of their stomachs? We have a history, we have dates.'

I was gathering up my things. 'I should have listened to what everyone said. You're just a malevolent little prick, Dawit.'

His last lines were shouted at my back as I plunged through the bead curtain.

'We're not a blank place on the map, Paula. Maybe you should have done that reading after all.'

30

The weather changed. I had grown accustomed to being perched above the clouds like a modern-day Zeus, but the blue horizons vanished, growling storms swept up from the south and we were reduced to mere mortals, trapped under a slate-coloured sky. The rains came early and proved as brutally sudden as a car wash. Trapped in a doorway one lunchtime, I watched pedestrians being chased down the street by a frothy river of brown water. Gutters silted up with debris, pavements were littered with broken roof tiles and snapped tree branches, and large stains formed on the office ceiling from leaks whose origin no one could identify.

The change seemed appropriate because everything felt different now. When I first moved to New York I had noticed the psychological shift a traveller makes from outsider to local. On first arrival, everything is picturesque. You have walked into a large, fascinating postcard, a Hollywood movie being shot entirely for your benefit. You lap up new impressions, but somehow they don't touch you. Sunlight creeps over your duvet in the morning and you relish the warmth, but it is *their* sun, not yours. A scandal breaks in local government: you read about it with interest but feel no sense of grievance. A madman shouts gibberish outside a supermarket, and you watch him with equanimity: he is not your problem. Then one day it ends. The famous New York skyline stops taking your breath away – in fact, you barely notice it: it is *your* skyline now. The sunshine is *your* sunshine, that abrasive taxi driver *your* problem, and that scandal a disgusting waste of *your* tax dollars. You have lost your distance; you notice less but understand more. You have become invested.

George's death had pushed me across that line in Lira. I put in my usual long hours at the office, helping Winston with his work on the Status of Forces agreement. We had expected it to be signed weeks earlier, but a row had broken out, with Kennedy insisting co-operation would depend on a pull-back of enemy troops to pre-2001 positions. It had been a long-standing gripe, with the Lira government arguing that the situation put demarcation at risk and the international community shrinking from confrontation with Darrar. But as I bustled about, my thoughts kept returning to the scene in the morgue. The fresh-meat smell clung so insistently to my nostril hairs that I decided – after retching on a ham sandwich – to go vegetarian for a while. I'd sit at my computer and find myself gazing into space twenty minutes later, my mind turning over images of stacked bodies, shattered bones, George's milky fish-eye. Lira no longer seemed picturesque. It was *my* city now, and with familiarity had come not contempt but a gritty reckoning.

Winston left for Washington, to put in time with one of his corporate clients. I dutifully accompanied him to the airport. The commission had just emailed to announce the date of the award – 15 November. We agreed to meet at the Royal Delft. 'I might fly in a few days early … There are things to be hammered out with the ambassador. Perhaps you could send Abraham then. I'll need a chauffeur and all-round flunkey to do the boring stuff before you turn up.'

As I watched the lemon suit cross the tarmac to the waiting aircraft, I was aware that something had shifted in my attitude to him, too. When we'd met in Boston, despite my sneering at his groupie entourage, I'd been ready to play the role of acolyte, the impressionable youngster imbibing wisdom from the fount. There was a matter-of-fact pragmatism about our dealings now. I asked fewer questions, wary of his likely answers. My admiration had given way to grudging affection, which allows for the admission of a host of faults. He was just a man, after all, a man moulded and warped by personal circumstance, a race's bitter understanding of prejudice and a superpower's irrepressible chutzpah. Increasingly, I kept my counsel. With Dawit estranged, Sharmila and Steve freezing me out and Winston gone, life in Lira was going to be a grimmer experience.

'Halt.' On automatic, I nearly careered into him, a soldier barring the road. The sun was still high but I could see a sliver of moon in the sky, no more than the shaving of a baby's fingernail. My evening jog was behind schedule.

'Yes?' I said testily, prancing up and down, keeping the momentum going. I really needed this. My joints felt drained of lubrication, my legs stiff sticks that might snap under my own weight.

'No.' He was young – barely old enough to shave – skinny, determined.

'No, what? What do you mean?' This was the first time I'd ever had any problems on this route. The urchins who usually ran alongside me had also halted and were gathered in a curious cluster, watching.

'No walk.'

'I'm not walking, I'm running.'

'No run. No pass.' It was getting late. Behind him, the freedom of the plains beckoned. I made to trot round him. He thrust out one clenched fist and arm. 'It is the law.'

'What? What do you mean "It is the law"? I do this every day. Are you mad?'

'Today, no. New law.' He gestured at our feet, and I noticed a knotted brown length of string, thinner than you would use to tie a parcel, trailing across the tarmac. I had clearly pulled it off the posts erected on either side. I finally spotted the tin-roofed shack, just large enough to hold a man, inside which I could see a chair, a blanket, a folded newspaper. This was a new checkpoint where none had existed before.

I had never shouted in Lira. But now I did, hands on hips, breaking all the rules, aware of a wonderful, marrow-melting sense of release. 'WHAT LAW? WHAT FUCKING LAW? GET OUT OF MY FUCKING WAY, YOU FUCKING ARSEHOLE.' My voice, I noticed with abstract interest, was getting higher and higher, heading towards some plateau of hysteria where it had never ventured before. Would I be able to coax it back down?

He clutched his rifle and hollered back at me, an incomprehensible jabber in which the only thing I could make out were the words 'foreigner' and 'border'. Then I suddenly became aware of a quiet, apologetic voice in my ear.

'Can I help, please? Are you having some problem?'

The frightened face of a rotund man in his fifties, a local resident, whose face was vaguely familiar from the many times I had passed it on this road. His familiarity helped me claw back some of my sanity. 'I'm trying –' I was so choked with rage that it was hard to speak '– to go on my daily run and this man won't let me through.'

An urgent exchange between the two of them. The soldier gesticulating, expostulating, eyes wide, pointing first to me and then to his little hut.

The resident turned to me, nervous, stumbling over his words. 'Well, the way it is, it is this. The government has issued a new law for foreigners. I think you call it tit-for-tit? Because the West is not putting pressure on our neighbour to withdraw troops from occupied territory, the government has decided not to let Westerners go outside the city limits. He says he has

284

written orders. This is where the border goes now,' he said, pointing to the piece of string.

'So I can't run?'

'You can run over there,' he nodded back to the maze of narrow streets behind me, 'but not here.'

'How long is this going to last?'

'Oh, I think for ever.' He didn't even bother to translate the question.

'So Lira is just a big prison, then, for us Westerners, is that right? But then,' I sneered, 'I suppose it's nothing but a big prison for all the locals, too, eh?' He gazed at me in silence, anxious to help if he could.

I looked down the road, saying my goodbye to the landscape. A memory came to me, so fresh it was almost tactile: the sensation of lightness, freedom I had experienced the first time I had landed in Lira, of soaring giddily above my own personal tragedy. I could not recapture, now, what had prompted that feeling, making it feel urgent and true. Without bothering to thank my self-appointed interpreter, I turned on my heel and stalked back towards the city centre.

When I got to the villa, I kept walking, aware that I needed to work off my adrenalin. It was dark now, and my feet stumbled against loose bricks, grassy tufts. I nearly barrelled into Amanuel, the night-watchman, swerved and jumped just in time over an open drain. I headed for the main streets where the well-swept pavements and streetlights would keep me safe. Local housewives, wraithlike in white shawls, materialised from the gloom, then disappeared into darkness. I turned a street corner and found myself on Liberation Avenue. Lit from the inside, the barber shops, pizzerias and cafés were transformed into stage sets laying on performances for my benefit. Here, an elderly gentleman in a three-piece suit sat reading a newspaper, while an equally aged barber snipped the back of his neck, brow furrowed in concentration, tongue tip peeping from lips. Two friends sat behind them, hands loosely clasped in casual affection, their jokes bouncing harmlessly off the victim. I was only inches away, I could see their lips moving, but I might as well have been on Mars. There, a courting couple at a café table laughed over a shared ice-cream – pistachio and strawberry? – dribbling down the side of a giant frosted glass. My eyes flitted past them and stopped. I had spotted the bulbous, slightly obscene outline of a shaved white head. Steve. Steve locked in conversation with … a dark, ferrety outline. Dawit? There, at the back. Seated at the bar. Dawit and Steve. I stared in baffled wonder. When had they got to know one another?

I watched them for a while, aware that I was virtually invisible in the street darkness. I noted how protectively Dawit sat hunched over his beer. Even if our recent argument hadn't jinxed a friendship that had once seemed so natural, his body language would have warned me not to make my presence known. I turned and made my way home.

31

Dr Berhane looked uncharacteristically unkempt. His beard, usually carefully trimmed, had formed wispy little grey-yellow corkscrews and there were dried crusts around his eye sockets. As we talked, he pulled spasmodically at one earlobe: the fidgeting of a man ill-at-ease.

'I do not like to abuse our professional relationship, Paula, but it seems I am about to do exactly that.'

'What is it?'

'I cannot tell you how it distresses me to have to do this. To turn into one of those feckless Africans who expect white people miraculously to solve all their problems, like a child running to Mummy.' He gave a bitter laugh. 'Oh, no, I had really not expected to become that person. But I'm afraid I have to ask you a massive favour.'

Not another. I gazed at him in silence, dreading what was coming next. If he thought this favour was a lot to ask, then clearly it would involve something unpleasant on my part.

He stopped fidgeting and looked me in the eye. 'You are familiar with the problem people face in this country when they try to leave? The bureaucratic hurdles the new government puts in their way?'

'Yes.'

'They jump over them, one by one, and then, just when the

tired little lab rat thinks he is about to exit the maze, he enters the last in a long line of offices, offices he has taken months to work his way through, and some under-secretary pulls out his file, looks at it and says, "What, you? You are never going to leave, my brother. Your country needs you. Aren't you a patriot?" And the under-secretary brings down his official stamp and –' Berhane clicked his fingers '– that's it. "Request denied, but feel free to start the whole process again next year. And if you do that it will, of course, be recorded in our files and held against you in future."'

'Yes, I've heard.'

'I have two friends … We were naughty boys at school together. An ophthalmologist and an accountant. They have both lost their faith, if I can put it that way. We argue. I point out that new governments need time to learn the pitfalls of power, that nothing happens overnight. But they feel there is less and less to choose between the current administration and the one we overturned at such a cost.' He paused to run his fingers across his brow, wiping away, perhaps, the faces of dead friends. 'For them, living here means accepting a permanent state of personal disrespect. They feel they are choking to death. They cannot breathe.'

'I know the feeling.'

He sighed heavily. 'I must rely on your discretion, Paula.'

'Lawyers are good at discretion. Like priests and doctors. It's part of the job description.'

'The point is that both my friends have decided to run for it. They fantasise about new lives in Sweden and Norway. They have tried the official route and been refused. After all the years of contributions to the Movement – it was not always easy, you know, for us to find that money when we were frizzy-haired, despised migrant workers cleaning tables and driving taxis in the West – this is their reward. Next month my friends will take the bus that gets them closest to the border, wait for darkness and walk. It seems everyone knows how to do this now.'

His lips curled. 'There are established routes through the rocks that take you round the landmines, established rates for bribes to persuade our soldiers to turn a blind eye, and refugee camps on the other side where everyone can repent their folly at leisure. I have tried to dissuade them, but have not succeeded.'

'That's very sad, Dr Berhane. But you don't need me to tell you I have no influence at the Immigration Ministry.'

'I know that. No, the problem is that when our nationals cross over, the Darrar soldiers immediately take their ID and money. They do that to contain them in the camps, prevent refugees wandering around and peeping at their military installations. As far as they are concerned we are all potential spies. My friends will lose not only their passports but their professional certificates, which they studied so hard to win. They cannot enter Scandinavia without the passports and they cannot become accountants or opticians – or, more likely, underpaid assistants to Scandinavian opticians – without those certificates. They are desperately worried about this.'

'And?'

'They need a courier. This, too, is an established strategy, I'm told. Someone who will not be searched at the airport and can carry their papers and savings out of the country, then DHL it all to them. They will do whatever is necessary to make their way to Europe. They are resourceful men so that bit will be easy. You would be an ideal courier. You work for the Legal Office of the President. No one will ever search you.'

'I see.' Despite his careful priming, I was slightly shocked by the brazenness of the appeal. There was nothing half-hearted about the violation of professional ethics he was requesting: this was an offence that warranted a jail sentence.

'OK. I'll do it.'

My reply came so quickly that he was taken aback. He had been braced to cajole and persuade, to assure me of his friends' trustworthiness and reliability.

'You ... will? Are you ... are you sure about this?'

'Yes. Look, you're right. I'm the perfect courier. No one touches me. I work for the government. I'm always carrying files full of confidential information.'

My heart was pounding, my face flushing. I had a sudden sense of vertigo. For a moment I had a vivid memory of Jake staring at me through the lift's metal grille on our first date, a man almost afraid of what was to come, then pulling me into his life. Someone else had just given my destiny a yank, and I had agreed without hesitation.

'It'll be fine,' I told Berhane. 'It doesn't bother me in the slightest.'

But I was lying. His request had exposed something treacly and dark inside me, flicked a provocative forefinger at a cara-melising bubble of fury. It wasn't panic I felt, but a surge of vindictive euphoria. I was going to enjoy sticking it to the fuckers.

On my desk the following morning I found a sealed package. Inside it was a chunky, leather-bound book – Gibbon's *Roman Empire*, the volume Dr Berhane had weighed in his hands when I had admired his library. There was a Post-it note inside the fly leaf. 'Tank Graveyard at 7 p.m., Wednesday. Corner of Giolitti and Vincent St. Mussie will be there.'

I guessed why Mussie had chosen seven o'clock when I got there. It was the moment just before the sun goes down, when what was harsh becomes soft, eyes no longer scrunch protec-tively against the light, and faces whose lines were drawn with the sharpness of a rotary pen mellow and blur. Whoever I met at this forgiving, shifting hour, I realised, I would struggle to identify again.

The evening's cool was bringing out fragrances numbed by the sun. There was a waft of piercing jasmine, the smell of domestic cooking, and a deeper, earthier note of wet mud, tinged with decay – maybe rotting loam, maybe excrement. I took a breath and savoured it. A skinny black cat set off on its nocturnal adventures; a tethered dog whelped in a courtyard nearby. The valley below was a jumble of twisted metal hulks. I was early, so I strolled along the path that ran alongside the wreckage, tilting my head from side to side as I tried to decipher constituent parts. It seemed to be mostly made up of army trucks, first squashed and then stacked, like the bodies in the morgue. But I could also see armoured personnel carriers, jeeps and tanks, train compartments and shipping containers, machine-gun stands and multiple rocket launchers. Someone stepped from the shadows, moving more quietly than I'd thought physically possible.

'Are you interested in geology?' He was small and white-haired. In his fraying shawl and sandals cut from old tyres, I might have taken him for a goatherd, but his English was good enough to suggest a middle-class upbringing and education abroad. It made sense. Any contact of Dr Berhane's would be a man of some sophistication.

'Geology?' I stammered, caught off guard.

He smiled, showing tobacco-stained teeth. 'A geologist would love this place. It's like a quarry. Our warmongering history caught in the sedimentary layers. Start at the bottom,' he said, pointing at a pile of metalwork with one horny finger, 'and go up. Every episode of foolishness is there. First the days of the Darrar empire. Lee Enfields, Schneiders and Winchesters. Above that, the Italian conquest: the Camionetta AS 42, with its Breda submachine-gun. The British occupation: howitzers, Matildas and Bishops. Courtesy of the Americans, we get the M24 Chaffee and the Walker Bulldog. And then, at the very top, thanks to our Soviet love affair, the BRDM, the T-34, T-54 and the ultimate in tanks, the T-55. There are even some downed MiGs in there, you know. And I suppose soon we will be adding the weapons Libya and Qatar have sent to the latest bunch of idiots running this country. I'm Mussie.'

'I thought you might be. I see you are a historian rather than a geologist.'

'Just an amateur. But I grew up fascinated by mechanical things, like all boys. And if you like weapons,' he said, with a wry laugh, 'this is a place of endless delight. But, here, I have something for you.'

He beckoned me forwards, twitching his scarf so it covered half of his face. Darkness had fallen while we were talking. He could simply have passed me the envelope, but instead he drew me under one of Lira's few functioning streetlamps and riffled clumsily in it. He handed me two passports, some papers I guessed to be certificates, and a receipt. Then he extracted a thick wad of hundred-dollar bills, wrapped in a red elastic band, and started counting them with one shaking Parkinsonian hand. 'One hundred, two hundred ...'

'It's OK, I can count them later.'

'No, no, you must be sure. I want everything clear.' He continued counting as we stood amid a whirl of midges in the cone of light, two actors in a spotlit performance. I felt a crawling unease. Why was he making such a song and dance of it? Why choose such a remote spot for the handover, only to then put on such a public display? The man was being about as discreet as a hooker in a red-light district.

'It's fine. I trust you,' I said brusquely. 'Just give it to me and I'll do what I can.' I thrust the passport and dollars back into their envelope, lifted my shirt, and tucked the package into my belt. 'Now, I have to go.' But Mussie had already disappeared, his work done, a white-shrouded ghost dissolving behind the metal tombstones and mausoleums of the twentieth century's armaments industry.

'Come home, darling,' my mother said between gulps over the phone. She had met Jake only once, but had decided to make this tragedy her own. Hogging all the weeping during our

exchanges, she left nothing for me. 'At times like this you need family. Come back to where you belong.'

I thought of her waterfront flat in Canary Wharf. The tatty souvenirs of my childhood, the well-sucked toys, scribbled drawings and photo albums, along with the relics of her unhappy marriage to my father, had been packed into plastic tubs and placed in storage after the divorce, stowed in one of those brightly coloured warehouses you speed past heading out of London. 'No space in my new digs,' she had explained, 'and I'm going for a more streamlined look.' So streamlined, I'd noticed on my last visit, that I might as well have been staying at a boutique hotel. The purple-tinted glass tumblers in the bathroom matched the towels; the linen curtains went perfectly with the cream rugs. It was impeccably tasteful, stripped of all past associations and devoid of individual quirks. 'No offence, Mum, but that doesn't actually feel like home to me. I'll stay here.'

Instead, I handed in my notice at Hitchens and asked my colleagues to relay news of any jobs available for someone with my experience. The looks they shot me were sympathetic, but I also detected a hint of relief. I had become a memento mori. 'Where are you looking?' a secretary asked over lunch.

'Anywhere, as long as it's not here. Short-term contracts would be fine.' The forwarded adverts came flooding into my email inbox and I used the simplest of selection techniques, involving a map of the US, a stretched piece of string and a fingertip pressed hard on New York, to decide which ones to apply for. The longer the piece of string, the better.

All my life I'd been the queen of the radical departure. I wanted to go where the Wentworth name possessed no resonance, to work such long hours my skin would turn eggshell white in an office, any office, where my co-workers would be so frantically busy I would never have an intimate water-cooler conversation again. A three-month job at a commercial law *firm in Chicago, doing due diligence on a major merger, fitted the bill perfectly.*

There is a grim kind of relief that descends when the worst possible thing you could have imagined actually happens. Hope is such a strain on the nerves. The burden of anticipated happiness – a burden I had clearly never handled with the requisite care and attention – had now been lifted from my shoulders. Whatever happened in the rest of my life, I would never now count as normal. There was nothing left to plan. I was officially allowed to give up.

I packed anything I could not see myself using on a daily basis. As Laurel and Hardy nuzzled the cardboard boxes with tail-thumping curiosity, I wrapped up the Piazza Navona cartoon sketch of Jake, the silver bracelets and necklaces he had bought me one birthday in Istanbul, my books and CDs. I hesitated over the photos of the two of us together, then shovelled them into a brown envelope and slipped it into the side pocket of the bag I was keeping. When the storage van pulled away from the cottage, I controlled the childish urge to scrunch up the business card the driver had handed me and throw it away. It was just possible, I supposed, that I might one day want to reclaim my possessions. Possible, but unlikely.

I hoovered the rooms, poured bleach down the toilets, scrubbed the bath, mowed the lawn and went into the village to carry out all the myriad duties that effectively topped and tailed my life with Jake. On the last morning, I left the keys to the cottage and the Jetta in a drawer of the Welsh dresser for Sophie. I closed the cottage door softly on the latch, put my luggage on the front seat of the hire-car and coaxed Laurel and Hardy into the back – they always hated driving.

I suppose it's a tribute to just how busy I'd been that I only registered my route would take me over Bear Mountain Bridge when I was already on it, and the buckled gap where Jake's BMW had burst through the railings zipped by so quickly I almost missed it. There was a flash of flapping yellow police ribbon and curved metal flanges, grey tongues twisted as easily as strips of chewing gum. An image to be mulled over later, later, later. There would be plenty of time for that.

I headed south towards Peekskill, turning off the highway into the forecourt where Dr Fickling, the vet Jake liked to use, ran his clinic. I remember that an elderly customer, her mewling cat box on the counter, stroked and fussed over Laurel and Hardy at the desk, complimenting me on their beauty, as though the glossiness of their coats, the softness of their muzzles and the trust in their eyes were a credit to my care. They nuzzled her hands and kneaded the carpet with their paws, soaking up the attention. Dr Fickling gave me a discount on the lethal injections, just as his receptionist had said he would, because there were two.

32

So that was the answer to Dawit's Frank Zappa question. That was how I came to be sitting in a Lira taxi, driving back from my airport encounter with Green Eyes at a time when most law-abiding citizens – I no longer came into that category, of course – were just beginning to stir.

I had a load I was in a hurry to shed, and I was starting to fathom how tricky this was likely to prove in a city where the head of state saw fit to comment on your choice of watering-hole and everyone knew your business before you did.

I trundled my bag as quietly as I could past Amanuel, a Michelin Man flexing gloved hands and stamping his feet as dawn took the bitter edge off his night shift. I slipped into the villa and immediately froze in the entrance. Making the most of my presumed absence, Steve and Sharmila were having a rambunctious bout of morning sex. To my jaundiced ears, his baritone grunts and her wails sounded a tad theatrical. I went into the sitting room, swivelled one of the armchairs so that its high back blocked the view from the front yard, hunkered down in it so that I was virtually invisible and wept: a release of self-loathing and fear.

By the time Sharmila descended the stairs, I had composed myself, the only give-away a raspberry blotching beneath the eyes. Her wrap flapped open, offering a glimpse of smooth stomach as she headed towards the kitchen, her hair dishevelled, expression languorous. She saw me, flinched, and pulled her wrap tight. 'Jesus Christ! What the fuck are you doing here? Aren't you supposed to be in The Hague?'

'Long story. I'll explain later. Right now, I have to make some calls.'

Winston first. I knew exactly where he'd be. At his usual table in the Royal Delft's restaurant, where he'd be sipping a cappuccino and expecting me to walk in off the street at any moment to join him for breakfast.

'What happened?' It was the first time I'd heard him sound genuinely disconcerted.

'They wouldn't let me get on the plane. I was detained overnight at the airport, then put in a taxi back to town. My passport's been seized, too.'

'The reason?'

'None given.' I would tell him the truth, but not on this phone line, not in front of Sharmila, and not until I was safely out.

'Do you still have all your paperwork?'

Unfortunately, yes, rather more than I wanted. 'It's safe and well.'

'OK, I'll call Buster and try to sort this out. Don't unpack. Let's count on you being on tonight's flight. Keep in close contact.'

So I waited, making myself as inconspicuous as possible while Sharmila and Steve, exchanging silent, eye-rolling glances, grumpily fixed themselves breakfast and finally left for work. Then I telephoned Barnabas, gave him an edited version of the night's events, and asked him to go to the Ministry of Immigration, Room 805, to pick up my passport.

He called me back twenty minutes later, and he was talking so quietly, I could hardly make the words out. 'Miss Paula. They have your passport here. But they are not letting me have it. They won't say what the problem is. It is very strange.'

'Sorry, Barnabas, but could you please stay there as long as it takes. Winston has asked Buster to sort this out. Any moment now, he'll call them.'

'OK, no problem.'

The confidence was entirely simulated. Could Winston actually sort this one out, especially when he wasn't in possession of the full facts? For all I knew, my detention had been ordered by Buster himself.

The morning ticked by. The turquoise case sat in the middle of the sitting room like an interrogation mark. I still had no idea how to rid myself of its incriminating evidence. I wandered from room to room looking for an answer. Staring out of the kitchen window at the messy back yard, I spotted the rusting grill Steve had wrestled with at our Christmas party, the can of accelerant propped helpfully nearby. I unlocked the back door, shook the can to see how much fluid was left and inspected the grill, crouching to check sight lines to the surrounding villas. If I couldn't see them, they couldn't see me. But a fire in the middle of the day would undoubtedly draw the day-watchman's attention. He'd smell it, even if he couldn't see it. Did he clock off at lunchtime, abandon his perch to find a sandwich? I just didn't know. I had never been at the villa in the middle of the day. I didn't even know the guy's name.

So, repeating Winston's words to myself like a mantra – 'Let's count on your being on tonight's flight' – I pulled a spare holdall from underneath my bed and packed the few items I didn't want to leave behind. Mostly photos: the sacred brown envelope containing the snaps of Jake I never looked at but couldn't bear to throw away. And a more recent stack: Lira at sunset, Abraham in front of the IDP camp, the team on the last day of the hearing. A mini chessboard Dawit had given me on my birthday. Ah, yes, Dawit. I knew without bothering to dwell on the thought that I would leave without saying goodbye.

From my bedroom window, I studied the day-watchman. It was midday now, he must be starting to feel hungry. With a sinking heart, I saw him reach into one of the pockets of his huge overcoat and extract a small package wrapped in grease-proof paper. A packed lunch. *Shit*. Then the answer came to me. I ran out.

'What's your name?'

'Yonathan.'

I thrust a banknote into his hand and mimed a puffing nicotine addict. 'Would you mind buying me some cigarettes, Yonathan? I desperately need a smoke. I'd be so grateful. I've got so much work to do that I can't go myself.'

Who would have thought my addiction would prove so useful? Yonathan gave me a complicit smile, shouldered his AK-47 and set off, perhaps grateful for the brief distraction. As soon as he disappeared around the corner, I ran into the villa and through into the back yard. How long did I have? It would take him fifteen minutes to get to the corner shop, I calculated. Five to ten minutes chatting to the shopkeeper, if I was lucky, fifteen to walk back. Forty minutes maximum.

I scrunched up a few newspaper pages and dropped them into the grill, dousing the crumpled paper in lighter fluid. My hands were shaking as I struggled with the box of cheap Chinese matches. The first match exploded like a sub-standard firework, the second broke at the stem. On the fourth attempt, the flames took. I waited impatiently for embers to form, then cracked open the passports and fed them, one by one, into the fire. It was surprising how long it took for the stamped pages to curl slowly into charred onion rings and turn a lustreless sorcerer's black. The certificates were a lot quicker, their ornate calligraphy buckling and withering in seconds.

Burning the money was more painful. As I peeled off each creased, hundred-dollar bill I thought of the long chain of sacrifice, hope and good intentions that had placed these well-thumbed notes, with their faintly gamy aura, in my hands. The taxi drivers, telephone operators, cleaners and nurses out in the diaspora who had worked double shifts, slept fifteen to a room, collected supermarket loyalty points, all to be able to send this money home. And how it had been smuggled into the country tucked into cleavages above pounding hearts, slipped into underwear and hidden inside sweaty shoes, treasured by each grateful recipient, counted and recounted for the eventual contribution it would make to the planned Great Escape. 'I'm sorry, I'm sorry, I'm sorry,' I mumbled as I stirred the notes to ashes. There was an assignment for me, should I ever succeed in leaving this country: paying off this moral debt.

It was done, just in time. Yonathan had reappeared in front of the house, brandishing my cigarettes. As I thanked him effusively, pressing a large tip into his hand, his nostrils crinkled, picking up, perhaps, a whiff of charred paper on my clothes. He shot me a curious glance but said nothing.

Fifteen minutes later, I was in a taxi heading to the office. When we reached the junction between Giolitti Street and Liberation Avenue, I asked the taxi to pull up. Across the road, behind the ugly cement bollards designed to thwart suicide bombers, its walls fringed with barbed wire, sat the US Embassy. I could walk across there now and ask for protection. It would be the easiest thing in the world. The terms of the necessary deal would not have to be spelled out between consenting adults: top-level intervention and a flight home in return for a privileged view from inside the President's Legal Office. The officials would be discreet and sympathetic and would try not to say anything censorious, but we'd all know. Snooty Miss I-Can-Manage-On-My-Own would have been taught a timely lesson in who her real friends were. I looked up at the mirror, where a plastic-beaded crucifix swung from side to side, and met the driver's eyes. I would not give them the satisfaction. 'OK, no, let's go.'

Ignoring the buzz of comments and exclamations – 'Yes, yes, it's me, bit of a cock-up at the airport' – I took up my customary position at my desk. A pile of witness statements sat waiting to be appraised. I shuffled through them, trying to convey an impression of routine activity to Sharmila and the interns. I leafed through tallies of raided livestock, looted corrugated-iron roofs, trashed clinics. The micro-costing of war, so petty to the outsider ('Four goats, including ram. One camel'), yet so vital to those concerned. But nothing connected.

When Barnabas finally returned from the ministry, he was carrying my passport. The page with my visa, a pretty affair of curlicues, flowers and tropical birds, none of which I'd ever spotted during my time in Lira, was now scarred by a large, angry felt-tip cross. A covering note from the Ministry of Immigration read: 'As of 14/11/05, the entry visa and work permit of Ms Paula Shackleton are cancelled. A government protocol will ensure her safe boarding of the Alitalia flight at 2315 hrs tonight.' I felt my face flush, although I could not tell whether it was from anger, humiliation or relief. In the politest possible way, I was being deported.

I was right to burn it all. I've been searched, scanned and patted down at many frontiers, but all those were desultory inspections compared to what I underwent on my final passage through Lira airport, overseen by Green Eyes and my silent government minder.

I was still braced for an 'Excuse me', a hand on my shoulder and a request to come this way as I queued at the bottom of the aircraft steps. Even when the Airbus doors closed with a sealing *whumpf* and we were trundling down the runway, I refused to let myself believe I had escaped. I waited till I felt the weight of the aircraft float off the ground and heard the wheels clunk into place in the undercarriage. Then I turned my face to the window, where the city lights were already being swallowed by the vast darkness of that great plateau. As the aircraft banked and shrugged off the contours of the familiar landscape, I closed my eyes. I was done with Lira, I knew, and it was done with me.

33

DECISION
Regarding delimitation of the Border
between
The State of North Darrar
and
The Federal Democratic Republic of Darrar

By the Commission, composed of:
His Excellency Judge Ulrich Mautner, chairman
Professor François Rainier
Eddie Connors

VENUE: Small Hall of Justice, Peace Palace, The Hague

The State of North Darrar represented by:
His Excellency Mr Simon Gebreyesus, Foreign Minister of State
of North Darrar, Agent
His Excellency Mr Hailu Gebremedhin, Ambassador to the
Netherlands
Winston Peabody, Legal Adviser to the Office of the President,
Melville & Bart, Co-agent

Paula Shackleton, Oxford University, London School of Economics

Ismael Aregai, University of Lira

The Federal Democratic Republic of Darrar, represented by:

His Excellency, Minister of Foreign Affairs Mikael Senai, Agent

His Excellency Mr Gebre Selassie, Ambassador to the Netherlands

Henry Alexander, Newton & Maud, Boston, Member of the Bar of the District of Columbia, Co-agent

Reginald Watts, Newton & Maud, Boston

Spencer Greene, Newton & Maud, Boston

Katherine Hughes, Newton & Maud, Boston

Joel Winter, Yale University

Tracey Mulligan, Brown University

With onlooker status:

Michelle Winthrop, US State Department, Washington

Alan Middleton, US Ambassador to the State of North Darrar

Brett Harris, economics officer, US Embassy to the State of North Darrar

Johan Svenstrum, Ambassador of the Republic of Sweden to the Federal Republic of Darrar

Alistair Ruddock, Ambassador of the United Kingdom to the Federal Republic of Darrar, holding rotating EU presidency

Shu Wan Jing, Ambassador of the People's Republic of China to the Federal Republic of Darrar

Bosire wa Bosire, head of UN Mission to the Horn of Africa (UNMHA)

General Jaime Sanchez, commander-in-chief of UNMHA

Members of the international media

JUDGE ULRICH MAUTNER: Let me welcome you all to the Peace Palace on this foggy winter's day.

Given the importance of what is about to be announced, I

took the decision to invite not only the parties directly concerned, but those members of the international community whose role will be to facilitate and monitor subsequent developments. The inclusion of these weighty witnesses will, I hope, focus everyone's minds on the work that is to come. In the coming months and years, the very principle of international justice – this commission's *raison d'être* – will be put to the test in your two nations. Your legal teams have shown commendable dedication in preparing your respective cases and I thank all the witnesses and experts for their contributions. But this, in itself, will not suffice. Arbitration's purpose is to produce an award, and for today's award to have any value, it must be respected politically, diplomatically and militarily.

Your governments' duties will be to anticipate, direct and weather domestic response to what happens here today. We do not underestimate the challenges or complexity of that task, but as an institution created to administer international law, such factors have not been allowed to influence our decision-making. Our concern is that you remain cognisant of the undertakings your governments made on signing up to this arbitration process. To underline this point, and at the risk of being accused of melodrama, I would like, before I read out the award, to put a simple question to both parties to the dispute. Foreign Minister Simon Gebreyesus, does your government stand by the commitment it made under the 2003 Tunis Agreement that this commission's ruling will be final and binding?

FOREIGN MINISTER SIMON GEBREYESUS: We do, Mr Chairman.

JUDGE MAUTNER: And you, Foreign Minister Mikael Senai?

FOREIGN MINISTER MIKAEL SENAI: Hand on heart, we do.

JUDGE MAUTNER: Thank you. I will now read the award. I appeal to all those present to remain silent until this procedure is complete. We anticipate that feelings are bound to run high, but this is not the appropriate forum for comment or criticism. My officers have been instructed to eject anyone who fails to respect these rules.

Given the well-informed nature of this audience and the limited time available to us, I intend to omit a read-through of the procedural and substantive introductions that open our report, along with the definition of the commission's task and exploration of applicable law. Let me proceed to the nub of the matter on page ninety-five and present the detail of our findings, moving geographically from western through central to eastern sector. I must ask Mr van Straaten to oblige us with illustrations as I do so.

After a couple of minutes, the ambassador had leaned forward to whisper in my ear, 'Why are they doing it like this? Why don't they just give us the place names?'

Winston whipped round. 'Silence,' he hissed, then turned back. It was the first time I'd seen him lash out at a Lira official.

Judge Mautner was picking his way along the spine of the border with the fastidiousness of a diner dismembering a sole on a plate. His delivery was generously sprinkled with grid co-ordinates for latitude and longitude, degrees of divergence, numbered terminal points, tributaries and mountain ranges. But towns and villages were barely mentioned, and the focus of each segment of the map displayed on the screen was so close and tight it was hard to grasp where the agreed overall border lay, which side had won and which had lost.

Strictly speaking, Judge Mautner was doing exactly what he had been hired to do: experts on international law rarely go in for broad-brush assessments. But as I looked at the row of expectant journalists – BBC, Reuters, Associated Press, AFP, Xinhua, CNN, NPR and five international newspapers – I thought: That's why. Stripped as far as was possible of its human content, this bone-dry map reading was the commission's attempt to slow down news delivery. Several reporters had maps of the Horn of Africa unfolded in front of them but their expressions were as baffled as the ambassador's. Deliver a dense enough judgment, the commissioners must have thought, and it will force the parties to count to ten before declaring themselves vindicated or wronged. I could just imagine them congratulating themselves on a wheeze that would prevent any reporter sprinting out halfway through Judge Mautner's reading to shout a headline into his mobile. I hoped they were right. Maybe all they had actually come up with was a formula for future misrepresentation.

I sat with the report open before me, struggling and failing to find my bearings. It had been a manic journey, fuelled by guilt, fear and a hunger for absolution. I knew my days as an employee of North Darrar were over, but I also knew that I needed to hear Judge Mautner's gavel come down that one last time. I had landed at Schiphol, immediately boarded the train to The Hague, hailed a taxi at the station and walked into the Royal Delft, giving the 'Never Less Than Welcome' logo over the main desk a wry grimace as I took the stairs in twos. 'I'm here. I'll explain later,' was all I'd said to Winston, suppressing the instinct to unburden myself. A curt nod from him, and I'd just had time for a three-minute shower before the team assembled in the lobby. I was simultaneously aware of a huge fatigue, to be paid for at some later date, and a driving restlessness.

I craned my neck to look at Winston and Kennedy, huddled together like doctors over a patient. Brows welded, Winston was staring at Judge Mautner with absolute concentration. Before him on the table was a list of place names, collated under three headlines: WESTERN, CENTRAL, EASTERN. As Judge Mautner read, Winston's pencil ran down the villages and towns: a tick if we'd won our argument, a cross if it had gone to their side. The marks, I knew, were entirely for

Kennedy's benefit: Winston had long ago internalised North Darrar's geography. Taking it for granted that the award would be incomprehensible to a politician, he had come prepared. Mimicking Kennedy, I was reduced to taking notes of Winston's notes.

In the western sector, we had essentially won the argument. With the exception of the villages of Achamew and Golpik, the commissioners had taken our side. The west was secure. But no one gave a fig about the west.

Judge Mautner began on the central sector. Tick, tick, tick, went Winston's pencil. Then, opposite the name 'Shanti', he placed a cross.

'No, not Shanti,' blurted Kennedy, 'Not there.' I had a sudden vision of our three wise men, their expectant, laughing faces and gleaming eyes. We had failed them. Judge Mautner continued reading, ignoring the interruption. Collateral damage, I told myself. Sanasa is what matters. Sanasa represents overall vindication or guilt.

Judge Mautner paused, took a slow drink of water and surveyed the room. He was ratcheting up the tension with all the subtlety of a pantomime artist.

'And now we turn to the all-important eastern sector. Given the confusing existence of two versions of the 1899 correspondence between the Negus's secretary and the Italian Foreign Ministry, the commission decided to rule both inadmissible. Evidence of subsequent conduct submitted by the Federal Republic of Darrar's counsel also proved problematical' – Winston's lips twitched at this – 'and the commission accordingly agreed it did nothing to undermine clear evidence of an uninterrupted pattern of unchallenged administration dating back to the Italian colonial period.'

This time I didn't need Winston's list or the foreign minister's excited, triumphant bark. Sanasa was ours. We had pulled it off. A temazepam calm flooded my limbs. I bowed my head, overcome by a feeling of loosening, the unravelling of some tight internal knot. When I opened my eyes, Winston was looking straight at me, honey-coloured eyes alight. The way a lover might look at the woman he is about to marry. When I remember that moment I see a man afire, all blazing eyes and golden mane.

Things seemed to shift into slow motion then. I watched with curiosity as Kennedy slowly pulled an Orthodox crucifix from inside his shirt, kissed it, clenched both fists and buried his head in the crook of his elbows. Hey, drawled a voice in my head, I thought these guys in the Movement were atheists. I looked across the room, dreamily noticing Henry Alexander's strange grey colour and that Reginald Watts was trying not to cry. Languidly I took in the fact that the other side's ambassador and foreign minister, in defiance of instructions, were engaged in febrile *sotto voce* conversation. Sloth-like, I turned in my seat to survey the room. Some of the journalists, I could tell, thought they knew what had happened; the others were still lost. My languorous gaze moved to our VIP observers: UNMHA's Bosire wa Bosire and his general, the bevy of Western ambassadors, the woman from the State Department, Brett and his boss, then stopped. Something was wrong, I thought, but I couldn't immediately place it. They looked so … unsurprised. Yet so tense. Like a bar crowd watching a football match as it goes into extra time, knowing everything is still up for grabs.

And then Judge Mautner rapped his gavel on the desk, and I snapped out of my reverie. 'Please, everyone, if I can beg your attention, we are not quite done,' he said. There was an edge to his voice. 'Not done at all.'

Silence descended. He adjusted his glasses and began to read.

'The commission has so far confined itself to the crucial task of eliminating historical and political ambiguities over the trajectory and course of the border that have blighted relations between two Red Sea nations.

'However, we are well aware that such ambiguities do not,

in every instance, lead to war. A poorly defined frontier does not ineluctably imply conflict. Alternative methodologies for resolving disputes exist. It is in this context that the stance and behaviour of parties to a conflict becomes of pressing relevance.

'The Tunis Agreement, as you know, catered for an "independent and impartial body" to be appointed by the secretary general of the African Union, in consultation with the secretary general of the United Nations, to address the issue of whether either side violated the rules of international law on the use of force, or *jus ad bellum*. The commission understands that this independent body has never been constituted, despite the pressing importance of this issue. One of the respondents,' he looked pointedly over his glasses at Winston, 'has asserted that this commission enjoys no jurisdiction over this issue. We find this argument unpersuasive.'

And then he proceeded to weave his intricate grey web. He compared and contrasted sub-clauses of the Tunis Agreement, carving out vast territories of jurisdictional possibility from gaps in the language; he cross-referenced it to rulings in the cases of *Argentina v. United Kingdom* (1982), *Cameroon v. Nigeria (2001)* and *Democratic Republic of Congo v. Uganda* (2002); he reflected on the contrasting and complementary roles of claims tribunals, border commissions and the overall philosophies guiding the Permanent Court of Arbitration and the International Court of Justice. Softly, insistently, he pulled at these wisps of gossamer, rolling them into a thread of argumentation, then followed that thin string down the narrow, dank corridors of international law, weaving his way through the labyrinth until he reached a dripping Minotaur's cell, where his prey lay waiting.

'Consequently,' Judge Mautner seemed to be enunciating with special care, his mind on the final transcript that would record his words for posterity, 'the commission finds it has jurisdiction over the government of Darrar's *jus ad bellum* claim, pursuant to Article Six of the Tunis Agreement.' I heard the rasp of heavy breathing next to me and looked at Winston. His chin was almost resting on his collar-bone, his mouth was slightly open and the bags beneath his eyes, which were fixed upon Judge Mautner, had formed aubergine portmanteaux of fatigue.

'Having dealt with the question of mandate, let me address the merits of the respective cases,' continued Judge Mautner. We hadn't put our case, but there was no stopping him. Like a builder who smears dollops of mortar into the gaps in a wall after running short of bricks, he simply used the explanatory statements our side had made to the UN back when initial peace negotiations were under way to build a case on our behalf, then went on to demolish that wobbly structure with the pounding blows provided by Henry Alexander's relentless complaints.

'This commission accordingly finds that North Darrar violated Article Two, paragraph four, of the Charter of the United Nations. This article requires that all members refrain in their international relations from the threat or use of force against the territorial integrity or political independence of any state.'

Jurisdiction, merit, findings. Judge Mautner looked up with the air of someone expecting applause for executing some remarkable counter-intuitive manoeuvre. As, indeed, he had.

Winston lurched to his feet. 'I'd like it on record, Mr Chairman, that my client rejects this interpretation and that this ruling, by short-cutting agreed procedure, denies North Darrar a key opportunity to present the facts of the matter.'

Judge Mautner simply ignored him. 'That winds up this commission. I understand that the two governments have arranged a press conference this afternoon. The commission itself does not plan to make any comment, but copies of the award will be made available. May I take this opportunity to thank the two delegations and their legal representatives for their diligence and professionalism. Working with you has been a pleasure and an honour. With that, I declare these proceedings formally adjourned.'

The crack of the gavel, the scream of scraping chairs, the shuffling of papers, a low murmur of excited voices. Kennedy and the ambassador had disappeared, gone, presumably, to consult their master. Winston and I sat immobile in our chairs, staring straight ahead. Only a few pages. It had taken Judge Mautner less than ten minutes to read out the commissioners' last, idiosyncratic, finding but it had changed everything. With one hand the tribunal had given, with the other they had slapped us across the face. A smart-alec line ran through my mind, best not uttered: 'So much for the red socks, eh, Winston?' Judge Mautner had turned out to be more closet reactionary than secret revolutionary.

I felt Abraham leaning over us, seeking guidance, worried by this sudden uncharacteristic passivity. 'So, we take all the equipment back to the hotel, yes? I pack up and load the car?'

Winston cleared his throat. 'Yes. That's right, Abraham. Please excuse me for just one moment.' He jerked back his chair and marched briskly out of the room, his exit followed by thirty pairs of eyes.

Raising myself to my feet seemed to involve a superhuman effort. I made a half-hearted attempt to help Abraham, as he quietly unplugged the laptops and started stacking documents, but my hands were shaking so violently he caught them in two calming palms. 'I will do this, Paula. You are putting these in the wrong order. Go, go and have a cigarette. I will see you in the parking lot. Twenty minutes.'

I punched the door leading onto the fire escape, like a boxer. And there, in the winter chill, stood the man I wanted to see at that moment more than anyone else: Brett Harris. He whirled around, surveying me with an expression of wary speculation.

'So what the fuck just happened?' I spat at him.

He looked down, turning his two polished brogues the better to admire them. 'Well … The commission delivered its award, and everyone won a bit and lost a bit. Seems pretty even-handed to me.'

'Lost *a bit*? *A bit*? We've just been labelled mindless war-mongers by a supposedly neutral commission.'

'You got Sanasa, which I seem to recall mattered rather a lot to your side. Treat it as a fair trade.' His jaw, mottled with the blue-black sheen of rising stubble, seemed suddenly very square. His voice was high and nasal, his face devoid of sympathy. So this was the real Brett Harris.

'I'm not sure it was worth it, if it meant being anointed the Antichrist in the eyes of the world.'

'If your side doesn't like it, try to appeal. But you don't need me to tell you that you'd better have some pretty hefty technical justification. And it won't win your employers any friends. "Final and binding", remember?' His lips curled into something very much like a sneer. 'No one likes a sore loser.'

'The commissioners' decision to appoint themselves judge and jury on an issue totally outside their jurisdiction strikes me as a pretty hefty justification. Talk about straying off the reservation. They set up their own fucking independent republic.'

He shrugged. 'Well, it's your call. In your shoes, I'd be feeling content today. Not happy, but content. You got a lot more territory than I expected, to be frank. It could have been much worse.'

He was anxious to go back inside. But the fire escape was too narrow to allow two people to pass without touching and the last thing he wanted was physical contact. I wasn't about to make things easier for him by flattening myself against the wall. I registered his gathering irritation with sadistic satisfaction.

'So, was this the neat little formula your boss, Judge Mautner,

Eddie Connors and Henry Alexander cooked up in Chez Bertrand over that dinner I stumbled on six months ago? It was, wasn't it?'

'I don't know what you're talking about.'

'Why was it all so furtive, if there was nothing underhand going on?'

Even as I spoke I realised his expression of surprise wasn't fake. He hadn't been briefed about that particular meeting.

'You're getting paranoid in your old age, Paula. Are you honestly suggesting my country leaned on an independent commission to produce an award that suits our strategic interests?'

I cocked my head and looked at him. It was something about his use of the words 'my country' and 'strategic interests'. We stared at one another as a silent acknowledgement took tangible shape between us, almost as visible as his breath, caught in the damp air. I knew, with absolute certainty, that he had just inadvertently spelled out exactly what had happened. He flushed.

'Yes. Yes, I am ... And why *did* you, actually, Brett? I'd really love to know. You're the one who delivered the lecture about the delights of international arbitration. How neat and tidy everything was going to be once the law was allowed to take its course. Does that apply only when the outcome goes the way Washington wants?'

Turning his back on me, he took hold of the iron banister with both hands, hunching his shoulders for a moment, relieving some tightness. Then he straightened, gazed meditatively out over the gardens and spoke from the heart. Perhaps, I thought, for the last time in what would no doubt be a stellar career at the Agency.

'I don't expect your sympathy, Paula, but as it happens, this hasn't been that easy for me, either. I guess when we had lunch in Lira that day I was still a rather inexperienced diplomat. What I told you was certainly US policy. It still is US policy.

316

But there are nuances. You can't blindly apply abstract principles to complex, shifting scenarios. Compromises have to be made.'

'Is that what your bosses tell you?'

'If we suspend for a moment the tactful euphemisms, your guys lost the war, right? It was a rout. You weren't here. I was. Soldiers were commandeering civilian buses to get as far from the border as they could, ministers were packing their bags, aides were shredding documents, the presidential jet was revving its engines on the tarmac, ready to whisk the first lady off to Qatar. So you take that set-up, and then you say to a government whose army could have walked into Lira unopposed, looted, raped and burned at will, but which magnanimously decided to hold back – in part, if I may say so, at Washington's urging – and you say, "Hey, funny thing, it turns out you got it wrong on the border all along. Sanasa doesn't belong to you. Terrible shame about the hundred thousand dead soldiers, but you'll have to withdraw." You think that's going to hold? They desperately wanted control of that port, you know, and they didn't get it.'

'Well, maybe they shouldn't have put a congenital liar on the stand.'

He rolled his eyes as though he was dealing with a tiresome child. 'Look, the grim truth is that peace deals that don't match up with realities on the ground never stick. History shows that time and time again. OK, so the other side fucked up in their choice of lawyers and they came a cropper with a Walter Mitty fantasist. But they had to leave the table with *something*. A sweetener to help the medicine go down.'

I smacked my hand to my forehead. 'But this isn't a peace treaty, it's a border commission! That's what they signed up for! If "Anything to keep you happy" is the only acceptable answer from the get-go, then it's not a "neutral and independent" arbitration process, is it?'

He stared at me. 'These guys simply won't accept public humiliation, Paula. They can't. Our ambassador over there has told us the government believes it would be swept from power if the award went entirely against them. They're already being torn to shreds by the opposition for having agreed to arbitration in the first place, rather than simply taking what the hardliners see as territory won in battle, rightfully theirs. They had to have something to throw to the jackals.'

'Oh, come on. They would tell the ambassador that, wouldn't they? Has it ever occurred to any of you that they might be playing you?'

He wasn't listening. 'Look at it from Washington's perspective. Is that what we want? To help topple one of the most progressive governments in the region? Not perfect, sure, not democratic in the sense you and I understand, but investment-friendly, pro-Western, and our closest ally when it comes to fighting Islamic extremism. You have no idea how worried the State Department and the Pentagon are about what's happening on that front. Let's not kid ourselves what life is going to be like in the Horn if the Islamists ever come to power. Women stoned for adultery, amputations, public floggings, and Al Qaeda firmly entrenched on the African continent. Would that be a good outcome for all concerned?'

'But that's not the point.' I slammed my hand down on the iron banister. 'You sound like a Congressman justifying support for the Shah of Iran. We're supposed to have moved on from the Cold War. This wasn't supposed to be about realpolitik, remember? It was supposed to be about justice, pure and simple. About the law.'

He gave me a pitying smile. 'Don't be naïve, Paula. You're all grown-up now.'

A wave of fury washed over me, setting my face aglow. 'Why bother with any of this charade if that was the plan all along? All these extraordinary minds brought into one room, all that knowledge and expertise,' my voice was beginning to wobble, my hands were tracing cartwheels in the air, taking in the whole of the Peace Palace and everyone in it, 'the commissioners, the legal best and brightest, the translators and drivers and fixers and witnesses and all those poor IDPs ...' *All that fucking goodwill.* The trust Winston and I had whipped up with our clearly ludicrous claim that there was order in the universe, a Right and a Wrong, and we would guide North Darrar and its citizens steadily towards the Ultimate Truth. How had Brett and his bosses dared, how could they bear, to turn it into one big joke?

He shrugged again. 'You got paid your salary, didn't you? I gather it's a fairly generous one, too. At the end of the day, don't forget you're just a hired gun.'

So I was the one who turned on my heel and flounced off the fire escape.

34

Abraham was stowing boxes in the back of the hire car.

'Where's Winston?'

'He said he preferred to walk. He wanted the fresh air. Don't worry, I made him take his coat.'

I got in, and we drove the long route back to the Royal Delft dictated by the one-way system, silent together until the first set of traffic lights, where we sat and waited. As the early darkness of the European winter closed around us, the rain began.

'So, we got Sanasa.' Abraham's voice was tentative. He knew this was not the whole story. 'But …'

'But. They said we started the war. We are morally responsible for all the deaths.'

Both his eyebrows shot up. 'That is absurd. Everyone knows we were attacked first. Any Lira resident who was listening to his radio on the seventh of June can tell you.'

'Unfortunately that doesn't count as evidence.'

A long pause. 'Can we appeal?'

'I'm not sure. My guess is it's all over bar the shouting.'

Fat drops of rain splattered noisily against the windscreen. A few degrees colder and the drops would have been snow-flakes. I leaned my head on the window and savoured the pane's cool moisture on my hot brow. A few cyclists cruised by us, model citizens heading back to orderly Dutch homes. I caught a potent, feral tang from my groin and armpits and wondered if I was stinking up the car. I felt as though I had been awake for weeks, for months.

There was a silence as Abraham mulled things over. He stroked a sideburn meditatively. 'So, perhaps it will be war again,' he mused softly.

'Christ, I hope not.'

He gave a long, slow sigh. 'Foreigners never understand this, but sometimes there are worse things. Humiliation is worse, most of my countrymen would say.'

The lights changed, and we set off again, Abraham smoothly manoeuvring through the heavy traffic.

'You're always so calm, Abraham, I wish I could find your serenity.'

He gave a light laugh. 'Maybe it's my time at the front. It used to get a bit crazy with all the bombing. There was nothing we could do. We just had to sit there, waiting to die. It was important to find some peace inside you at those times. I tell myself that if someone doesn't actually get killed in front of me, then it's not so bad.'

Another set of traffic lights. He switched on the fan heater, then adjusted it to its quietest setting. 'And also ...' He paused.

'What?'

'Well, please do not misunderstand, Paula, but your kind has different expectations. I've learned this over the years, working alongside you. Americans, Westerners, the human-rights people, the NGOs, you all have this quality. You really believe you can change things.' There was incredulity in his voice. 'It is the great strength of your culture. This is why we need you. But sometimes you remind me of big, noisy children who want to have everything. And children are often disappointed.'

'Hey, you and your comrades fought for decades for what looked like a doomed cause. Surely you only did that because you thought you could make a difference.'

322

'It wasn't the same.' He shook his head, thinking aloud: 'We fought because ... because the Struggle was who we were. It was our father, it was our mother. All my friends were fighters, my brothers, my cousins. But I don't know how many of us ever thought we would live to see Liberation. The Struggle was the thing, to be there together. It was a terrible time, but also a very happy time. The result was not so important, in a way.' He shrugged. 'No, your kind are different. Sometimes I feel very sorry for you. Hope is a terrible thing.'

He had not meant it to come out that way, I knew, but I winced. I wasn't used to being patronised.

I found Winston back at the hotel. For a moment, scanning the frenzied mess of files and documents, laptops and extension cables, uncollected mugs and mustard-smeared plates, I assumed the room was empty. Then I realised that what I had taken to be a crumpled blanket thrown into an armchair was my boss. He sat with his eyes closed, head resting on his chest, hands limp in his lap. It wasn't clear whether he was sleeping or gathering his wits. He had taken off his tie, which streaked across the floor, and the top of his shirt was unbuttoned. It was shocking to see a man so rigidly self-contained in a state of virtual undress. I noted the sunken chest, the folds around his collar-bone, the way his sallow skin sagged around his cheekbones. Then I felt a spasm of guilt at witnessing this moment of nakedness.

I started moving around the room, installing a modicum of order. The clink of cups stirred him. After a moment, he opened his eyes, yellow and rheumy. He saw me, but for a brief moment I could tell that he had absolutely no idea who I was. He gestured vaguely towards the bathroom and I fetched his pills, handing them over silently with a glass of water. I watched, fascinated, as he returned to himself, a scrunched-up sponge soaking up substance. He straightened in his armchair, rolled his shoulders and reached in one fluid motion for the TV remote.

We always kept the screen permanently tuned to BBC World. Together, we watched the ribbon of headlines unspooling below a soccer match … 'BLAIR HINTS BRITISH TROOPS COULD PULL OUT OF IRAQ' … 'BIRD FLU RESISTANT TO ANTI-VIRAL DRUG' and then, finally, there we were: 'NORTH DARRAR STARTED WAR, HAGUE COMMISSION RULES'. No mention of Sanasa. The focus of every news story since the war, the port had been related to fourth-paragraph status, a virtual irrelevance.

'Well,' said Winston, 'that's one decision the international community is going to live to regret.'

'Are they? I bumped into Brett at the Peace Palace and he seemed to think it meant peace in our time. Darrar gets moral vindication, our side keeps Sanasa, regional stability assured. It may not be legal, was the message, but it keeps everyone happy.'

Winston looked at me in astonishment. 'Is that what they really think? Good God, I wouldn't have thought such naïvety possible. That award's a perfect recipe for a new war. The other side is never going to withdraw its troops from occupied areas now that it's been anointed innocent victim. Their troops will remain *in situ*, harassing and bullying the population, and in two years' time or ten, there'll be another trigger incident and the fighting will break out again. And when that bust-up ends, you can rest assured that no one will call in the lawyers. They'll have learned their lesson. The only advice someone like me will be able to offer a government will be "Fight to the death. Throw your sons and daughters into the fray. Shed as much blood as you want, because if you don't win on the battlefield you'll see your fate being decided in cynical deals struck by white men who can barely locate your country on a map."'

'That is what happened, isn't it?' I wanted my instincts confirmed.

He snorted contemptuously. 'This award comes trailing clouds of stale cigar smoke. I'd be surprised if the documents don't have circles of dried brandy on them. The gentlemen's club that thinks it runs the world and knows what's best for the rest of us met late one night and came up with a bullies' charter. I guess it's a habit they just can't break.'

'Abraham asked if we were going to appeal.'

'Well, officially we can't, of course. Binding arbitration, and all that. But one way or another, we'll have to throw a spanner in the works.'

He rose and began to pace the room, weaving a nimble path around a discarded sock, a laptop and a pile of plates, occasionally twitching the curtains to stare at the street below. 'We can't let an award of this legal incoherence stand. Tribunals, commissions, can't unilaterally decide what falls within their jurisdiction: that way madness lies. And, besides, I've got a hell of a lot of evidence now establishing a pattern of steady territorial encroachment over the years that needs to see the light of day. So … let me think,' he muttered. 'You and I will go through that ruling with a fine-tooth comb, identifying every legal inconsistency and contradiction, however minute. There won't be any shortage, believe me. We'll need to have our killer response ready before we fly back to Lira.'

This conversation could not be avoided any longer.

'I can't go back to Lira, Winston. I have to resign.'

He swirled round from where he stood at the window. I think it was the first time I'd ever surprised him. For a moment, it felt like an achievement, to have succeeded in nonplussing the great Winston Peabody III.

'Perhaps it's time you told me what exactly happened on your way over.'

I sat on the office bed, taking it slowly. 'There's no point going into the details. But I was asked by someone in Lira for a favour that involved breaking the law, and I agreed.'

'Why?'

A childishly simple question. And, as with all children's questions, the hardest to answer.

'I don't really know. I was angry. I find I still care desperately about the case but I don't care for my clients. In fact, they repel me. Is that a contradiction? Or just an irrelevant emotion I'm supposed to brush aside? I don't know any more. I didn't expect this to happen. In any case, I violated all sorts of professional codes of conduct, risked discrediting you and the office, and I'm really sorry for all of that. Really sorry. But I *have* to resign. My detention at the airport was just a warning, a rap across the knuckles. They're on to me. Someone ratted on me, and now I can't go back.'

'Is Dawit behind this?'

I must have looked astonished. 'I really don't want to talk about it,' I stammered. The possibility had never occurred to me. There was a much more obvious candidate, by my reckoning, for the role of informer. The man who had arranged the original exchange.

His face had gone as tight as a nut. 'Since you're hugging so much to your chest, my dear Paula, maybe you could tell me whether what you've done also makes it impossible for the rest of us to keep operating as a legal team. Do we, too, risk detention at the airport when we return? It would be helpful to know. I'm not too bothered about us expatriates, but Abraham, Ismael, Ribqa and the others have families to support.'

I bowed my head, accepting his reproof as my due. 'I've thought about this, but I think it's very personal, very specific. There's been no raid on the office. I think they knew exactly who they were going for.'

'I'm very angry with you. Very angry.' His voice was as thick as tar and his face so pale it had taken on a ghoulish, greenish tinge. In the penumbra, his eyes had the dark gleam of obsidian. 'I've never needed your help more than now. So far there's been no talk of claims for war damages, but we can expect that now, and the other side will go for the jugular. Razed villages, flattened factories, stripped businesses, gang-raped virgins, stolen goats, barbecued cattle, lost sandals – there won't be a claim that won't be quintupled, exaggerated and hyped, with the Americans, the UN and the Scandies playing a plaintive violin serenade from the sidelines. And the world's press won't have any trouble deciding who to believe now that they've been so helpfully served up with a B-movie villain. And this, *this*,' he boomed, as he bounced his fist so hard against the window I feared the glass would shatter, 'is the moment you choose to go rogue?'

He was panting, his thin chest rising and falling. In the offices across the street, I could see workers looking up from their desks, alerted by the pounding, gazing at us in alarm.

'I'm really sorry, Winston. I didn't anticipate any of this. Until two hours ago I was convinced we would win it all. And then you wouldn't have needed me in any case.'

He jerked his head away from me and stared into the middle distance. 'I was always afraid of this,' he muttered. 'I feared something like this from the start. You were close to tears that morning we met in Boston. Too emotional, too passionate. I needed your brain, your crunchy, rigorous, muscular brain, not your passion. But I suppose at the end of the day you were looking for a cause, just like all my puppy-dog students. Something to cling to, because you can't forgive yourself for not clinging harder to your boyfriend when you had the chance.'

I glared at him with hatred. During all our intimate working sessions, our overnight flights and eccentric, married-couple meals, Jake's name had never once passed my lips. Knowing that Dan had provided the bare bones of the story, I had never burdened Winston with it further, more out of pride than modesty. How dare he now fling it in my face?

'And, what, I'm the only romantic in the room? Have you looked at yourself recently, Winston? Don't you realise how

327

deep you're in? Don't you ever stop to wonder what it must be like to be a citizen of the country whose case you're fighting with such determination? Have you read what Amnesty said in its last report about your adopted country? Seen how the government performs on the Press Freedom Index? Yes, it's at the bottom, last out of a hundred and seventy-eight countries.'

'You think any of that's new to me?' His look was one of total contempt.

'Is that why you became a lawyer? Does this summon up the ghost of Martin Luther King? Don't you ever feel a teensy bit uneasy at the thought that you've become the attack dog for a president regarded as an international pariah?'

'That's just a lazy label applied by diplomats who can't be bothered to think. There's never been a time when He couldn't explain his actions in a way that morally satisfied me. He just doesn't wrap it up in the hypocritical protestations required by the West. Maybe that's where you and I simply part ideological company, Paula. Your skin colour means you can't even see the hegemonic status quo, let alone challenge it. As a black man, I know what it's like to operate in a system that's stacked against you.'

I slapped my hand to my forehead in exasperation. 'Jesus fucking Christ, Winston, do you realise that in all this time I've never once heard you say his name? I don't think I've ever heard anyone in Lira say it, and you're just as bad as the rest of them. It's always "He", "Him", with a capital H. You all tiptoe around it like it's sacred ground. Are you afraid of turning into a pillar of salt or something? What exactly is he, in your eyes? Rather more than just an employer, I'd say, more like Lord of Lords, God of Gods.'

There was a sudden rap on the door. We both stood in silence, then Winston went to open it and muttered something quietly reassuring to the hotel employee on the other side. Then he put his back against it, heaved a long sigh and turned to me. 'You were shouting quite loud, Paula.'

The interruption had calmed us both. My rage was drying up. But I could not resist one last jab. 'You may not care about the morality of it, Winston, but I'm surprised, quite honestly, that your instinct for professional self-survival doesn't kick in. I get the odd email whisper of what your colleagues back in Washington say about you, you know, and it isn't pretty. Defending He Who Must Be Obeyed isn't going to do your career much good, long-term.'

He guffawed. 'Long-term? I don't have a long term, Paula. I'm seventy-five years old. I've got a minor amphetamine habit and I'm in the early stages of prostate cancer – not something that will kill me but which whittles relentlessly away at my energy levels. This is my last hurrah.'

I gaped. Winston had always seemed somehow ageless, a man I struggled to imagine dark-haired and smooth-skinned, someone born mature. I had always assumed him to have years to go before official retirement. And how had I missed the implications of all those pill bottles on his bathroom shelf? 'Seventy-five? I don't seem to recall that on your official bio.'

He shrugged. 'Some details are best glossed over. You reach a point in our culture where no advantage accrues with the advancing years. Consultancies dry up – you get passed over in favour of former interns. I've been somewhere in my sixties for at least ten years now,' he said, with a bitter laugh.

I had never heard him speak like that before. The imperturbable, unassailable Winston Peabody III, faking his age and popping uppers like an anxious soap star.

And as though it was determined to confirm his words, my mind immediately started racing back to key episodes of the case, reinterpreting them in the light of this new information. His reluctance to leave his desk. The reliance on me to do his running. The time he fell asleep in court. What had turned out to be the catastrophic error in deciding not to contest the issue of who had started the war. Maybe he *was* losing his edge, an ageing legal warrior who'd become fatally slow on the draw.

There was a long silence between us. Then he smoothed his hair and began buttoning his shirt. 'Well, I need to prepare for this press conference. Kennedy will want back-up. In the circumstances, it's probably best you don't attend. I have no wish to be vindictive, but we need to establish as much clear water between you and the team as possible.'

I had been dismissed. Nodding – what else had I expected? – I crossed to the door connecting our two rooms and closed it behind me, then put my ear to the wood and listened as, with utter inevitability, he quietly locked it behind me. He would be going through the same intellectual and emotional procedure as he withdrew his trust, walling off areas of intimacy, roping off the avenues of thought in which, until now, I had been welcome to stroll.

For a moment I sat perched on the corner of my bed, trying to think it all through. Not just my time in Lira, but the events that had led me there. No doubt, as the months passed, I'd formulate some glib stock response explaining, to anyone who bothered to ask, why my stint at the Legal Office of the President had been cut a trifle short. Eventually, I might half believe it myself. But what I *felt* at that moment was simple: traitor's guilt – towards Jake, Winston, George, Dawit and every citizen of North Darrar.

It took me half an hour to pack. On my way out of the Royal Delft, I knocked on Abraham's door, but he was long gone, ferrying Winston to his excruciating encounter with the international media. I scribbled a note, put it into an envelope with a packet of Red Marlboro cigarettes, and checked out.

35

The doorbell rang and my mother's voice wafted up the stairs. 'Paula, the man from the storage company is here.'

He was short, sturdy and very dark. I initially took him for a Spaniard but as we talked I realised he was probably a Bosnian or a Croat. His company had opted for deep purple as its brand colour, not the most becoming colour on a heterosexual male, but he looked stolidly resigned to the lurid shade of his blazer and cap. He eyed my possessions sceptically, computerised tracker in hand. 'Only five boxes?'

'Only five.' Too little, almost, to bother with, I knew, but my mother had made it clear that every inch of storage space in her Canary Wharf flat was already accounted for.

'Destination?'

I gave him the address of my new employers in Toronto. Another year, another city. Winston had once called me 'unrooted', but you have to have a reason to stay in one place, a pretext for permanence.

'So, one of these human-rights types, eh?'

'Not really, no.'

'None of my business, but why don't you just take the stuff with you? There's not much here.'

Because I want to start again. 'Oh, I don't know how much room I'll have at the other end,' I lied.

Shrugging, he stickered the boxes, then stowed them in the back of his purple minivan, where they looked silly and forlorn. Then he consulted his notes. 'The boss wants to know if you ever used the company Sure Options, which we bought up a few years back. Because we have some boxes belonging to a Ms Shackleton, which date back ten years. She keeps paying the fees, but we can't seem to track her down.'

'Ten years?'

He checked his clipboard. '1996, a Miss Shackleton, moving from Balham, London, to New York, left her stuff with Sure Options. Fifteen boxes.'

'Not me. I think Shackleton's a fairly common name, actually. Why?'

'There was a small flood and some of it has water damage. We like to let customers know.' He typed a few co-ordinates into his handheld device and waited for it to make some mysterious connection, chatting the while. 'You know, people are crazy. Me, if I buy something, I use it. If it's old stuff that belonged to my grandparents – photographs, furniture, painting – I want it in my house. Either that, or I sell it on eBay. Our customers, they pay us to take stuff away and they never come back for it. They don't want it, they don't use it, but they won't dump it and they keep paying and paying. Great business for us, but I don't get it.'

That's because it's not 'stuff', I thought. It's memories. And no one knows where to stow those. I gave a fake-cheerful laugh. 'Well, not me, anyway.'

'No, not you,' he said, giving me a steady, disbelieving look. His device had found a signal, so I signed on the screen. He printed out a receipt, closed the back of the van, checked two fingers to his purple cap and drove off.

My last physical encounter with anyone connected to Lira came about by chance. I was on a short stopover in London and I decided to spend the afternoon in the British Museum.

I ordered a cappuccino in one of the cafés in the Great Court and stood for a moment, cup and saucer in my hand, craning my neck to appreciate the curve of Norman Foster's glass-vaulted ceiling. In Rome, or Madrid, the place would have been flooded with sun, but this was London on a dull winter's day. Muffled by the sky's soft white blankness, the quadrangle felt like the inside of a space pod, a giant goldfish bowl. Voices were muted, distant figures blurred. I suddenly found myself focusing on a profile, just five feet away, heading towards the main doors. A shiny brown nut of a head. Goatee beard. Unmistakable.

'Dr Berhane!'

He stopped and turned, flustered. 'Miss Shackleton. My, my. Good to see you. Yes. Indeed.'

He darted a sideways glance towards the exit, yearning for escape. To my own surprise, I found I desperately wanted him to stay.

'This is unexpected. What are you doing here?' I had already forgotten the first rule of Lira: don't pin people down. No names, no locators, keep it vague.

'Oh, research, research,' he said, with an airy wave of the hand. 'Some documents the museum authorities want advice on. They opened an old box – it's incredible how much material lies in the vaults – and found more than they anticipated.' He turned to face me, cocking his head. 'You might have found them interesting, in fact.'

'Why's that?'

'Oh, I came across some correspondence from the British consul in Darrar, a wonderful, malicious gossip. He tells London about a meeting in 1893 between Count Lorenzo Fittipaldi, the Italian explorer, and the Negus's secretary, Heriu Tekle, to agree the border. The two men hit it off, he says, and drank so much of Fittipaldi's Chianti they had to be carried to their quarters. The following day, neither of them could decipher their notes or remember what was said but didn't like to admit as much, so they just guessed where the line was.'

'Don't tell me an entire war was fought over a drunken agreement struck by two nineteenth-century louts?'

'Maybe. But, then, do we trust the British consul? That's what your Mr Peabody would no doubt ask.'

'I think I'm glad I didn't know any of that when we were in The Hague. Are you in London long? When do you go back?'

He gave a grim little smile. 'Oh, yes, quite long, as it happens. I am part of our rich diaspora now, Paula. I have even been granted political asylum here. I doubt I will ever return to Lira.'

I must have looked as surprised as I felt. Nursing my suspicions, I had taken it for granted I had fallen into a trap laid, at the very least, by a man at peace with a system.

'Political asylum? You? I didn't think ...'

'Yes?' he asked, raising a quizzical eyebrow. 'You didn't think?'

'Well, I thought you were on good terms with the Movement.'

'Oh, these days, only sycophants and praise-singers are considered supportive enough,' he said. 'There was always destined to be a falling-out.'

'But what about your wonderful library?' I blurted. 'What will happen to it? Your encyclopaedias, your dictionaries?'

He shrugged. 'I left the keys with the cleaning ladies, who are good, decent women. My gift to the nation. Although I suspect the nation will not appreciate the gesture.'

His new cynicism dismayed me. I wanted to put down my cappuccino – froth had slopped into the saucer – but I was afraid that if I turned to deposit it on the table behind me I would turn back to find him vaporised, a figment of my imagination.

'But what about your history book? Are you still writing that? All the material you collected.'

'Oh ...' He gazed off into the distance. 'When I left I was forced to make some radical decisions. I have a wife and two children. Officially, the family was only leaving on a two-week holiday. Carrying too much luggage would have raised suspicions. The documents had to be sacrificed, for expediency's sake.'

I had a clear mental image of the shelves in his study, stacked with coloured floppy disks. The carefully labelled cassette tapes. The dog-eared notebooks. Without meaning to, I expelled a slow sigh, trying to dull the vicarious pain of the loss of the book that would never be. 'I'm so very sorry, Dr Berhane.'

He grimaced. 'I think, perhaps, I was over-optimistic. Ahead of my time, or rather, ahead of the times. You know, the problem with my country is that it is still waiting for an ending. We need to have a happy ending, before anyone can sit down to write our history. We cannot bear, after all that we suffered, to admit things went wrong. So if the ending is not the right one, maybe it cannot be written at all. I should have understood that.'

'But only fairy tales ever have completely happy endings,' I said softly.

He shrugged. 'Intellectuals like me are out of tune with our era. We sound like bad violin-players to many ears. Revolutionary regimes have no interest in examining the past. No,' he gave a sardonic bark of laughter, 'they are looking ahead, still building that shining Utopia! You know what happened when I submitted my passport for my exit permit? It was delayed for a few months and no one would tell me why. I began to worry – you can imagine. Finally, at a party someone from the Interior Ministry confessed. He was almost giggling. It was a bit embarrassing, he said. The ministry had been burning a huge cache of old files and somehow a bunch of passports had been incinerated alongside the old Italian paperwork. I went pale when he told me that. I felt a little giddy. He thought I was angry at their carelessness in burning passports. It did not even occur to him that, to a historian, there could be no greater outrage than what he had just revealed. That even an ordinary citizen of Lira, even a lowly peasant who could barely write, might have the intelligence, the vision, to object to this obliteration of our past. Those are the men who run the Horn of Africa today, brutes who burn files because they clutter up the place.'

'That's appalling.'

'Yes, but the damage has been done, too late to stop it. And you?' he asked, happy to change the subject. 'Are you content?'

I chose my words with care. 'It's good not to feel angry all the time.'

'You have a new job?'

'Yes, with a rather earnest think tank. Nothing very exciting. I felt after Lira some boredom was in order.'

He frowned. 'I heard about your driver. What was his name again?'

'Abraham.' It was how Winston and I had started talking again. Sharmila had tracked me down to Toronto. The line was fuzzy with interference and it had taken me a few moments to recognise her voice. I'd been confused, at first, by the unfamiliar friendliness of her tone, then understood the reason. She'd got what she wanted: Winston had promoted her. She'd put me through to Winston, who'd explained the reason for the call: a landmine, laid on a road in the western sector, apparently with no particular target in mind. Abraham had driven over it as he'd headed to an IDP camp with a new researcher, first week on the job. 'It could have been a local jihadist guerrilla group,' Winston had said, 'or it could have been the other side, we just don't know. They must have died very quickly, Paula. I saw photos of the car. It flew about fifty feet – it looked like a scrunched-up piece of tin foil.' I had put down the phone with an image in my mind of a pair of male hands on a steering-wheel, Abraham's elegant ones this time, not Jake's. 'It's a ghost driving you,' he had joked on our trip to the IDP camp.

'I am very sorry,' said Dr Berhane. 'He was a decent man. I heard he was a brave fighter, too, in his day.'

'Yes.' Two tears were slowly creeping down the sides of my face, salt water brackets framing a mouth that was struggling to remain level.

He spoke softly, embarrassed by my emotion. 'Do you have much contact with Mr Peabody?'

'No, I'm no longer involved with any of the cases. I had some ... problems, you know. With the authorities. You heard?'

I tried to search his eyes – now was surely the moment for any guilty quiver. But he looked at his feet. 'Yes, and I am ashamed to have played a part in that. I hope you do not resent me too much for exposing you to such danger. I was desperate, so upset for my friends, and I'm afraid I made some misjudgements.'

What was he apologising for? Selling me out to the authorities, or merely for having involved me in the first place?

'Thank God you are safe, and away from that place. My friends and I often talk about the bravery of a white woman who owed us nothing. You have not asked about them – you always were very discreet – but they are doing well, still sorting out their papers, but very glad to be out. And you must not return, no matter what pressure Peabody brings to bear on you. Do not consider it.'

'I won't. To be honest, I think he's happier working on his own. He didn't really need me. I was just there for psychological support. A cross between a mother and a nurse.'

'And what does he say about the border situation? I heard on the BBC a few days ago that the African Union has warned a new war might break out. It was calling on both governments to cool their rhetoric.'

'Apparently there's been a build-up of troops on both sides. New trenches being dug. I hope it's just grandstanding, but I gather the diplomats are worried. So much for our "final and binding" ruling, eh?'

He gazed towards the entrance, where a gaggle of Japanese tourists was mustering around a dowdy guide in a brown corduroy smock and John Lennon spectacles, pink umbrella held aloft like a medieval coat of arms.

'I did not like to say so at the time, Paula, because I truly believed in the importance of what you were doing. But it has occurred to me, not once but many times, that perhaps the international justice system is built on a misapprehension. It is possible that history and progress require bloodletting, that societies only learn wisdom and self-restraint through the scarring pain of a high death toll. Perhaps some wars have to be fought to the very end. If anyone is to accept the result, you need clear winners and losers, and nothing is as clear as defeat on the battlefront. If I can be a bit *risqué*, *bellum interruptus* can be as unsatisfying as *coitus interruptus*. And it may be that, long-term, frustrating that human drive will mean more lives are ultimately lost.'

'I have to hope you're wrong.'

He laughed. 'I hope so too! It was good to see you again, Paula. You are still young enough to start again, and you really must do that. When it comes down to it, this isn't your story or your fight. As for me, I long ago disappeared into the maw.' He spread one palm over his stomach. 'I'm here, caught in the entrails of the beast. There are thousands like me, embittered, grey-haired veterans, still dreaming the dreams of little boys. When I think of our younger selves, I am amazed how impressive we were. I often wish that was less true. If we had been less idealistic, less inclined to self-sacrifice, it would be so much easier, now, to allot that episode its rightful place. We are all doomed romantics, hopelessly in love with what we were.'

He tapped me on the shoulder with his rolled-up newspaper, said goodbye, and strode across the foyer. A moment later, I lost sight of him in the milling throng.

* * *

A week later, in my apartment in Toronto, I set about the long-delayed task of cleaning up my virus-infected laptop. There were email accounts to close down, PDF files to be returned to Winston, intense exchanges with Francesca and transcripts of Captain Peter Lewisham's diary to delete. And there, quite suddenly, it was. An email from Dawit. Months old and tagged 'A GIRL LIKE YOU'. My Dell had turned up its nose at the unfamiliar sender's address and dumped it unceremoniously into 'Spam' where I had been within a hair's breadth of deleting it. What struck me most, as I began to read, was how clumsy this articulate master of the impassioned tirade was when it came to the written word.

Dear Paula

I am sorry it is so long since I contact you – I hope you are well and enjoying your new life in London.

Did you hear that I am in Australia now, land of the kangaroo? I meant to go to America but, as you do know, beggars are Africans and do not choose – and it begins with the same letter of the alphabet! So I hop, hop, hop, just like a kangaroo from the UN in Lira – thanks for that – to UN in Cyprus to the regional office in Canberra and then, bye-byeee, UN. Also all thank to Steve, your very good friend, hah hah hah.

You will really luagh to here yours truly is working as all-round dogbody and driver for the Indian Embassy. I remember your opinion on my driving. All those Hindi films, turns out they were good preparation for my new life. I meet Deepak at an Indian Film Club night, he was impressed by my knowlege. He is third secretary at embassy and has a big pile of Bollywood CDs. I go to his flat to watch the new releases and drink his beer.

The Australians are a big delusion to me, they are not cultured at all. They do not even know where Africa is so I think it is good that mostly now I meet Indians – they know about oppression and colonialism and fighting, my favourite subjects.

Anyways Paula there is something I must say because it is lying heavy on my heart. I heard on the network – you know we diaspora are nosy baggers and all keep in touch – you had trouble with THEM. You know I would never want to hurt you. An ex-Fighter who talks in my culture that is worse than a whore. But after our argument, when you told me about your dead rich husband in America I was so angry I drank all night at Zombie's. I complained about these stupid foreigners who come and fuck us with their good intentions (sorry but that was you). You did not know I knew about Berhane and his friends but I knew everything in Lira it all came out with the beer at the bar. As my Indian teacher used to say, you're a quick learner, Dawit, sometimes to quick. That's how I know Steve organise the sex orge with those girls which I discuss with him and he said Hey, maybe I get you a job at the UN in Cyprus and an exit permit, if you shut the fuck up about the orge, my friend. Hah hah. Anyway after we qarrel an old friend was at Zombie that time, we were together in Reconnaissance Patrols 1981-3 and for a moment I forgot to be careful. Later I remember he had links with intelligence. A good man with the gun but he is different now he is civilian. So I don't know for sure what happen but still I am very, very sorry for my big blabbery bullshit mouth. I am a shame, so a shame. But if you were a local you would be in jail for sure by now. So nothing really harmed, eh? You Westerns always do OK.

Your drinking buddee for ever,
Dawit

PS Please come see me in Canberra

I choked for a moment, my breath tangled between a laugh and a gasp.

Throughout my stay in Lira, people had warned me against Dawit. I had always blithely ignored them. Just why I had been so certain I knew best, I wasn't entirely sure. Gut instinct, I'd told myself at the time, carelessly claiming searing insights into human behaviour. Perhaps it had seemed too obvious, the notion that the unreliable maverick should prove to be exactly that. Or perhaps my insouciance had boiled down to something a lot simpler: Dawit amused me, so it had to be all right.

You got me in the end, Bingo. You got me.

I paced the room for a while, marvelling at my own stupidity, swearing at the freshly painted, innocent walls. Then I closed the laptop, put on my trainers and went for a long, purging run. Pounding the unfamiliar pavements, I realised I felt no anger towards Dawit. There was, instead, a sense of settlement. A satisfaction at seeing a mess of straggling threads neatly tied up.

On the way back I passed a neighbourhood convenience store, turned on my heel and went inside. Back in the apartment, I wiped the sweat from my face, washed my hands, and carefully extracted the slim envelope of photos of Jake from my luggage. I used the Blu Tack I'd bought at the store to stick the pictures in a neat line above my bed, starting with the Piazza Navona caricature. In between each I carefully positioned a gold star, the kind used to mark a child's homework. I stepped back and surveyed the result.

It would do, for now.

A while back, Sarah emailed me an internet link. It called up a video advertising the delights of Griffin House, 'Orange County's most exclusive conference venue'. I couldn't help wondering which family member had come up with that idea and what had persuaded Julia to agree. Had she decided that, with Jake gone, running the estate was simply too much for her? Had she retired to one of the wings, or checked herself into a deluxe care home? A Google search threw up no answers.

The firm that produced the video had clearly not stinted on costs. It had hired a helicopter to capture the footage. It opens with a distant landscape shot: bottle-green woodland, rolling hills, a highway running along the valley below, city suburbs just discernible in the distance. It looks like early spring. We pan closer, and we see a glittering lake – our lake – dotted with dark tussocks of islands, and then the woods suddenly open up and there, in a bright green glade, sits the house: Jake's Manderley, the Wentworth family's Hearst Castle, my Thornfield Hall. As ever, I'm struck by its uncanny resemblance to the Peace Palace.

It's uglier than I remember, more solid, more domineering. Why build anything so big? Who had that rifle manufacturer thought would ever live there? No family, not even a multi-generational Irish-Catholic one with hangers-on and servants galore, would ever have been able to fill that space with noise and warmth. 'Ideal for team-building seminars and weekend-long motivational courses,' claims the video, as we zoom over the tennis courts and stables, the terraces and pretentious dovecote. There is not a roof tile out of place, not a speck of rubbish on the lawn. It's only on the third viewing that I realise the image must have been doctored, cleaned up. We swirl a couple of times over the battlements, then zoom away over the valley, heading back to the world of uncollected garbage, peeling walls and sudden car accidents.

I find myself playing that video again and again, looking for some sign of life, a hand shaking a cloth out of a window, perhaps, Miguel walking across the gravel, a cat prowling those perfectly maintained gutters. I never find it.

Acknowledgements

This is a work of fiction, but it contains elements of reality, which ensure that those who helped most would appreciate least being publicly thanked. They and I know how many months of discussion were involved, how repetitive my questions about law firms and legal procedure became, and how many emails and phone calls were exchanged. Thank you for your forbearance and for tolerating a storyline that was a constant reminder of personal grief.

The less camera-shy include my literary agents, Charles Buchan and Sarah Chalfant, whose delicate counselling and rock-steady support were invaluable. Andrew Hill, Susan Linnee, Dawit Mesfin, Dusan Lazarevic, Clive Priddle and Daniel Bekele were patient and insightful readers. Judith Flanders and Gillian Stern helped me whip the manuscript into shape in its closing stages.

Last, but not least, I owe huge thanks to James Flannery, who is as masterly a subeditor today as he was when I first met him in the Reuters newsroom thirty years ago. I benefited hugely from his skills and encouragement.